THE AURELIAN ARCHIVES VOL. I

PALATINE FIRST

by
COURTNEY GRACE POWERS

PUBLISHED BY
Courtney Grace Powers

ISBN-13: 978-0615650227
ISBN-10: 0615650228

For Sharayah
big sister, faithful reader, and
geek extraordinaire

Table of Contents

I

That's One Way to Make Friends

The planet Honora had three moons: two small ones, green and red, and one bulbous white one, called Atlas. They hovered like balloons against the pink dawn sky. Silhouettes of ships in route for Atlas and its esteemed Aurelian Academy were like odd, far-away birds flying without wings. Oldest to youngest, the students of the academy were being shipped off to another year of study, another year of Airship Architecture and Alien Linguistics and Industrial Maintenance, all the sorts of things a bright young citizen of the Epimetheus Galaxy ought to know.

Reece just wanted to be a pilot. Most ten-year-olds waiting with their parents to board their bus-ship for the first time stood on the docks and stared up at Atlas as if trying to make out The Owl—what all the older kids called the Aurelian Academy. Reece watched the ships.

Now and again he looked at other things too, when he could sneak a glance and get away with it. His mum and stepbrother were standing on either side of him, and, being Easterners, neither liked the west end of the capital city very much. The three had physical similarities— ashy-brown hair, dark eyes, straight-nosed faces. The difference was in their expressions. Abigail and Liem sneered. Reece grinned.

"Bogrosh," Abigail muttered. "Absolute bogrosh."

"I think it's great," Reece announced, and started to say more, but stopped to stare at a Dryad-class ship whistling by overhead, sleek and pointed like a hornet.

Without looking at him, Abigail sniffed. "Bad taste, child."

That's how it was with Reece's mum. "Child" this, "Child" that. Sometimes, when Mum was feeling particularly stern, he got, "You Incorrigible Child."

Craning his neck, Reece watched till the Dryad turned into a fleck in the eastern sky. It was with his head turned that way that he saw them—a knot of people, pale with black hair and standing as far back from the hubbub of milling parents and students as possible. He'd never seen more than one or two Honorans with hair that color. And he'd never seen Honorans that looked so dangerous, so hard-faced and tense. Even the child with them had a posture like a cat faced with a whole world of dogs.

"Who are those people, Mum?"

Abigail glanced sideways at the huddle of strangers and pursed her lips. "Those aren't *people*, child, they're Pans. And if they or those filthy Westerners give you any trouble at all you are to go straight to the headmaster, understand? You are the Palatine Second. Remember your place. Honor, superiority."

Nodding absently, Reece stared at the Pans in their funny clothing, all dark woolens and leather waistcoats. He should've guessed. He'd heard loads about them, or at least enough to know that they weren't actually called Pans. They were Pantedans, refugees from the planet Panteda. People said Panteda was all green fog now, all acid that would choke you quicker than you could swallow, and that the thousands of Pantedans that hadn't escaped the war there were ghosts that climbed up and grabbed ships right out of the thermosphere.

No one liked the Pans. From what Reece understood, Honora had been rooting for the other guys in that war—the Glaucans. The only reason Honora had taken the Pantedan survivors was because Glaucus had used forbidden chemical weapons. They'd ruined a whole planet. That kind of thing was frowned upon.

Suddenly, the young Pan looked over at Reece, face blank, eyes dark. Reece waved without thinking.

"Plumb-headed child." Abigail slapped his hand down. "You would, wouldn't you? Liem, you will keep him out of trouble? As much as is possible?"

Liem was polishing his bronze class ring on his jacket. He was a Fifteen now, and that made him an upperclassman. "If I have time. With all my new courses, I—" He cut off, noticing Abigail's glare, and nodded. "As much as is possible." As soon as Abigail turned away, he made a face at Reece. Reece ignored him.

"Honestly," Abigail muttered as she knelt before Reece and began pressing wrinkles from his overcoat that weren't there. "You'd think they were letting any sort of dimridge into The Academy these days. I should put in a word with Thaddy."

By Thaddy, she meant Thaddeus X. Sheppard, Grand Duke over Honora, her husband and the boys' father. She only called him Thaddy when she wanted something very badly, or else did not want it at all.

"The Pans are dimridge for sure." Liem began digging through his shoulder bag, double-checking his supplies as if this wasn't his fifth year returning to The Owl. He shot the Pans a baleful glare and shrugged. "But Headmaster Eldritch wouldn't let them in if they weren't exceptional. He screens the students very closely."

Abigail sniffed again. "I believe Bus-ship Fifteen is boarding now, Liem. Have a productive term." Liem was only her stepson, after all.

Liem swaggered off to join a handful of older students, boys and girls already in their crisp black uniforms with the patch of Atlas on their sleeves. One or two of them saluted, then laughed at themselves, though Liem didn't laugh at all. He liked it when people remembered he was the Palatine First, heir to Honora's dukeship.

Reece snorted. "Liem's such a sisquick."

"I clearly remember forbidding you to use that filthy term, Reece Benjamin. Look at me." Abigail used two fingers to jerk Reece's face so that his brown eyes locked with hers. "The duke has high hopes for you. Silly though it may seem, you are inexplicably dear to him. Your stepbrother understands. Honor. Superiority. Hold these in high regard, and you just might grow out of being a walking catastrophe." She almost smiled. "We can only hope as much."

"Transit-ship Ten, now boarding," a voice echoed through the large brass windpipe that was the megaphone of the Boarding Director, a paunchy fellow wearing a golden sash across his peculiar olive suit.

"That's you," Abigail said without warmth. "I'll see you come holiday. Go."

Scooping up his things—a small trunk and a lumpy leather satchel—Reece nodded goodbye, pushed back his shoulders, and marched toward the rectangular bus-ship marked with the numeral ten on its aft motor frame. Circular windows lined her sides like the portholes on a sea ship, and the air around her aft rippled and wavered with steam. Her engines whined loudly. She was not a young ship.

There were already twenty, maybe thirty Tens in line to board, hefting their luggage and fidgeting as the Boarding Director's student assistants walked up and down the line and pinned identification tags to their sleeves. A pretty blonde assistant who looked about Liem's age stooped beside Reece, punched a few keys on a handheld datascope that spat out a line of serial numbers, and then stuck those numbers to a badge. Without ever once looking Reece in the eyes—though likely, if she'd known he was Liem's half-brother she would've been fluttering to get in his good graces, because girls did that for some reason—the assistant stamped the badge onto his sleeve and ducked on to the next Ten in line.

"I'm gonna be an Airship Mechanic," the Ten, a little girl with her hair in blonde braids, said proudly. She had the Westerners' twang in her voice. "Do ya need to put that on there?"

The older girl rolled her eyes. "No."

"Why not? It's important, ain't it?"

"No, it *isn't*." The assistant forcefully tacked the little girl's number to her arm and moved on. She reminded Reece of Abigail.

The line slowly, *so* slowly, inched forward, till Reece's toes brushed over the threshold of Bus-ship Ten. It had three aisles of leather-padded seats draped with straps to hold students safely in their arms. Though, out of the dozen Tens who had already been seated, only three actually paid any attention to the safety gear, two of them because they were seated by the portholes where their parents could see them, and one because he seemed the type to actually worry about an old lugger like this crashing. His face was a little green behind his overlarge bifocals.

Reece was jostled to a seat near the back by the other Tens crowding in. He shot a look at the filled window seats, envious. This was his first time off-planet, and he had wanted to watch the sky as they broke atmosphere.

It was very loud in the bus-ship. There was tittering and shouting and obnoxious jokes being made in those drawling Westerner accents, not to mention the constant squeal of the ship's engines underlying everything, comforting and somehow warm. So when the coach suddenly went as quiet as a classroom, Reece craned his neck to see why.

It was the Pan boy, stepping on-board with just one bag strapped over his back. He was tall for a Ten—taller than Reece, and Reece liked to think of himself as kind-of tall. And frightening, though not in a bullying kind of way. Intimidating…that was the word that came to mind.

There were three seats left: two snuggled up near the exit hatch and the line of hanging canvas bags containing compressed life rafts, and one next to Reece.

"Hey!" Reece hailed. He felt the girl on his left jump. The little one that didn't look old enough to be a Ten. "Back here!"

The Pan looked up in interest, frowned, and turned to sit by the hatch with his thumbs hooked in his trouser pockets. He had disconcerting blue eyes that were the light color of the sky, the same eye-color of the royal wolfdogs, and black hair that was close-cropped but messy. There was a small green ribbon pinned to his jacket, not so different from all the ribbons and honors the duke wore on his.

"Well, you tried," said the little pig-tailed girl, patting Reece's arm. "It was a nice thing to do, anyhow."

The bus-ship took off in a tumble of noisy cheers from the students and screaming steam from the engines. As the coach rattled into a blur, the little girl on Reece's left began muttering to herself ("Betchya I could make it rattle less with a couple'a rotational rings and an undulator! These downtown mechanics sure do botchy work, huh?"), and the boy with the bifocals vomited into a pail. It wasn't the best first take-off.

The noise died down after an hour of flight, once the windows had all grown dark with that inky blackness that was the void between stars, The Voice of Space. The boy up front stopped being sick, though he almost had a relapse when he had to carry his pail to the head to dump it.

For five or so minutes during the second hour, Reece, leaning around the chirpy blonde girl, could actually see The Euclid Stream glittering out in The Voice. A real Stream. A current in space, like a throughway for captains and their ships. A ship caught in a Stream jetted forward at up to twenty times its normal velocity; that's how captains could explore the galaxy without being gone for years and years. You had to have a special liscence to pilot in the Streams, but that was alright. If Reece worked hard enough, he didn't see why he shouldn't have one by the time he was twelve, maybe thirteen.

By the third hour, the Tens were all bouncing in their seats again, chattering about housing assignments and aptitude tests, about who was most likely to become a law enforcer as opposed to a botanist and what handcraft elective was the best, sculpting, carpentry, or painting. Atlas loomed beyond the starboard windows, its landscape milky with the fog that gave it its white glow. Barely discernable through the fog was a great grey ocean, and a smallish continent hiding in its forests the sprawling brick city that was The Aurelian Academy. Aesthetic pride of Honora. Or something like that.

The bus-ship suddenly shivered hard enough to rattle Reece's teeth. Everyone else felt it too; a few hands flew to the safety contraptions on their seats, buckling them as the photon dome lighting the cabin flickered as if a pair of great clumsy hands was trying to cover it. Someone in the cockpit gave a muffled shout, and the ship shivered again, this time to a few startled screams from the students. Then everything went silent.

Even the engines.

"What's going on?"

"Are we crashing?"

Reece could hear the engines sputtering in attempt to kick back on. The backup levelers hummed in exertion as they struggled to maintain the gravity barrier on their own. A man in an olive jumpsuit broke out of the captain's cabin and came running down the aisle, barking orders to remain seated as he lowered himself through a hatch that he pulled open on the floor.

"Wonder if I should go help," the little girl next to Reece muttered.

Blinking over at her—the photon dome had just winked out for good, and it was now too dark to see much more than outlines—Reece shook his head. "Probably not. I'm sure it's just a hiccup."

Even though he couldn't see her face, Reece was sure the girl was giving him a look. "Let's just hope it ain't the right galving link....elsewise we'll prolly burn up in the atmosphere."

Bus-ship Ten gave its biggest tremble yet, so that Reece lifted out of his seat and then slammed back into it. It felt like a giant wolfdog had grabbed the bus-ship up in its jaws and started shaking it like a toy.

He wasn't sure why, but right then, it occurred to him. Bifocal Boy and his pail were still in the head. Twisting in his seat, Reece squinted against the dark and was sure he heard even over the frightened cries of the other Tens a tiny voice calling for help.

He fiddled with his safety gear, hesitating. This was exactly the sort of behavior Mum wasn't likely to forgive. Luckily, with no Liem on board, there was little chance she'd ever hear tell of it.

"What are you doin'?" gasped the little girl as the ship popped Reece up out of his seat and pitched him down the aisle. He tipped left and right, went down to his knees once, and nearly had a disastrous collision with the open hatch before he reached the sliding screen door hiding the ship's facilities. The tiny voice was that much louder back here, chanting, "It's just turbulence, it's just turbulence…"

Planting his legs firmly apart, Reece grabbed the handle to the sliding door with both hands and waited for the ship to shudder. When it did, he used its momentum to throw the door to the left.

Bifocal Boy flew out at him with a garbled shout, and together, they smashed to the floor.

An alarm went off, shrill and wailing, just as a red auxiliary light came on and painted the cabin with eerie color. Bifocal Boy jerked on the floor next to Reece, covering his ears with his hands.

"Come on!" Reece shouted. "We've got to get to our seats!"

"We can't!" the boy shouted back and made a grab for his spectacles as they flew from his face. "We're…we're starting to turn!" Craning his neck, Reece saw with a pinched stomach that he was right.

It almost looked as if the moon Atlas was circling the ship…when really, he knew that the ship was going into a slow, flat spin. "If we tried to get back to our seats, the centrifugal force—"

Reece could already feel it. In his balance as he started leaning backwards, in his knees as they began to slide over the polished wooden floors. He threw out a hand and tried to catch the leg of the nearest seat and missed it by a hair as his body rebelliously rolled back into the wall, where he felt pinned by an invisible weight. In a second, the other Ten joined him with a yelp.

Even shutting his eyes required effort—not because of the pressure, but because the white, cycling blur of Atlas was hypnotizing even while it was dizzying. He wished he wasn't pinned quite so close to the airsick kid.

Then there came a scream even louder than the students'—the engines! With a *pop*, the white dome light came back on, and cool, fresh air erupted out of the air vents under the students' seats, replenishing the oxygen supply. As the horrible shaking stopped, the ship's spin slowed, slowed till Reece and his companion slid down the wall and landed in a dazed heap.

"At…at least you didn't get sick…" Reece panted, wiping his forehead with the back of his sleeve.

"I don't get airsick," the other boy gasped. "I have…food poisoning."

A snort burst out of Reece before he could stop it. "Right. And I'm—"

It was instantaneous. If the bus-ship were a push bike, Reece would have said that the captain had back-pedaled, throwing the whole thing into a midair halt. The other Tens flew forward into their safety gear while Reece and the boy sailed down the aisle with strangled cries.

The landing was, if not quite comfortable, still softer than Reece could've hoped for. And it had some bounce to it, as if the wall actually had give. Rolling down onto the floor for the third time in just a few short minutes, Reece groaningly looked over his shoulder. They had landed on, of all things, a grey inflatable life raft which was quickly deflating, melting down over their shaking bodies.

"Bleeding bogrosh," Reece muttered, lying down on his stomach with his arms spread at his sides. He glared at the nearest porthole window. Going by the fine blue sky outside, the ship had made it through Atlas's atmosphere.

"Hey." Someone kicked the raft away from Reece. "You okay?"

Reece pushed up onto his knees and returned the Pan's strange blue stare without really registering the warmth sliding down his forearm. "Yeah...did you do that?"

"What, save your life?" The Pan gave a wolfish grin and leaned back in his seat, satisfied.

"Ladies and gentlemen," a warbling voice came over the intercom, "a medic will be circling the cabin shortly. Please remain stationary and raise your hand if you require attention. We will be making a smooth landing presently. Thank you."

With a small whimper, Bifocal Boy wriggled his way out from under the raft, clutching his broken lenses in a white fist and looking ready to heave. But what he did was look at Reece, look at the Pan, look at his bifocals, and then lay the side of his face flat against the cabin's floor and raise his hand to wait on help.

"I'm Reece Sheppard. What's your name?" He couldn't very well call him Bifocal Boy for forever, even if it did have a kind of ring to it.

The boy opened one blue-grey eye and attempted a feeble smile. "Hayden. Hayden Rice." Surprising Reece, Hayden rolled his eye up toward the Pan and said, "And you?"

The Pan looked a little taken aback, and slouched deeper in his seat. "Gideon Creed. From Panteda," he emphasized.

"That was...good of you," said Hayden matter-of-factly, but not unkindly.

Gideon studied both Hayden and Reece with a kind of suspicious curiosity, his eyes narrowed, and said nothing.

The medical assistant came, looking shaken and a little sick herself, and tended to Hayden, who had rolled his ankle. Reece waited patiently for his turn as he pushed up his sleeve and whistled at the impressive gash on his elbow. It didn't really hurt, but it was messy, and everyone was staring at him, Hayden, and Gideon with eyes the size of cricket balls.

"Is it true?" Reece asked Gideon suddenly. "What they say about Panteda?" He was referring to the war and the acid fog, but as soon as he'd spoken, he wondered if there were other, less nice things people said about Panteda that he'd never heard.

Gideon straightened, his icy eyes measuring for an uncomfortably long moment. Then he suddenly grinned, and it was the kind of smile that made a person feel like they'd just made an ally.

"Every bit'a it."

II

(Almost) Plummeting to a Fiery Death

Reece turned about in front of the four-paneled mirror for the third time, scanning and double-checking. Military-issued boots, laced and tied off tightly. The black uniform of The Owl, steamed and pressed and by some miracle, actually clean. The white patch of Atlas on his left sleeve, balanced by the pair of flight wings pinned to his right—what real pilots called a captain's first feathers. Tonight, he'd take off those tiny gold wings and replace them with a bigger silver pair. If he didn't completely botch up his test, that is.

The student dormitories were as quiet as they always were on a testing day. For Eighteens, this day determined their level of success in their field. For the rest of the students, it just determined what marks they would be taking home to show their parents over the midyear holiday, but that was still reason enough to be studying rabidly.

Swinging around, Reece put his fists on his hips and blew out a long breath. His and Hayden's shared suite had been in chaos last night, its hardwood floors covered in books and flight graphs, its sofa turned into a bed for Gideon, who had stayed late claiming to help his friends study when really, he'd been reveling in the fact that testing day held no power over him. He already had his future figured. At this point, bad marks were more of a joke to him than anything.

Hayden must have been up cleaning before dawn. The suite was back to looking like a handsome lounge. Both beds had been retracted into the walls, leaving a wide open space around Hayden's crammed bookshelf and their pair of wardrobes. It was a standard suite, identical to every other on this floor, but it was more of a home to Reece than any place else. He'd be sad to leave it in another six months, when he and the rest of the Eighteens graduated.

The handle on the bedroom door suddenly jiggled, and the door swung inward, revealing a frazzled-looking Hayden struggling with an armload of books. In eight years, he hadn't changed much. He still wore secondhand spectacles and clothes that smelled like musty books and hung loosely over a very lean frame. He'd let his dirty gold hair grow out so that it brushed the back of his neck.

"What are you doing?" Hayden exclaimed when he saw Reece. He dropped his books onto the sofa and dusted off the front of his wrinkled uniform. "You're going to be late!"

"I'll be fine." Reece carefully avoided the cloud of dust swirling around the sofa. "Where have you been?"

Hayden hesitated, then fixed Reece with a level stare. "I took my test."

Reece scowled, scratching his jaw. It was important to be clean shaven on testing day. The judges were persnickety about these sorts of things. "Gid and I were supposed to be there to watch."

"I thought it'd be better to get it out of the way so I didn't have to rush off after your test. Father and Sophie will want to congratulate you and visit, not hurry away to hear me recite theorems."

Chances were that was at least halfway true. Hayden's twelve year old sister, Sophie, had had a liking for Reece since before she could walk.

"Well, yeah, but—"

"Reece." Hayden pulled a book out from his jacket and added it to the pile on the couch, his voice stern. "Today is important. We all know it. There's not a chance of you getting liscenced to captain in the Streams as an Eighteen unless you fly loops around the judges, Palatine Second or not. Besides," he suddenly looked embarrassed, and lowered his eyes to the floor, "I… that is, I finished my test kind of...quickly. I think I might have studied too hard."

"Of course you did." Hayden probably could have taken his vocational test when he was a Fifteen and passed it with flying colors. Come to think of it, he probably could have taken someone *else's* test and passed it with flying colors, and no matter that the test wasn't even in his field. "I know what this is really about. You're nervous because you know you'll be out of a job if I don't pass today. After all, I can't give you a spot on my ship if I'm not promoted."

Hayden's embarrassment grew till his face resembled a bright red beet. He busied himself with clapping more dust from his uniform. "Reece, you know I won't really be joining your crew if you qualify for one, right? Not if I get offered a spot on Doctor William's research team."

"Relax, I'm kidding. I know you get airsick."

"I don't get airsick!" Hayden looked affronted, even more so when Reece raised his eyebrows disbelievingly. "I don't!"

"Right." Scooping up his satchel, Reece gave the suite a final eyeball to make sure he hadn't forgotten anything and started for the door. "I don't know what I'd do with you anyways. I suppose there might be a place for a physicist or a chemist or a doctor on an airship…but all three? One of your hobbies is going to have to go."

Hayden only smiled as he followed Reece into the corridor and shut the door behind him. The hallway, lit by photon globe chandeliers at intervals, was quiet enough for the clapping of their boots to sound awkward and loud.

The brisk walk from their dormitory to the aerodome where Reece's test would begin was nearly silent. Somehow, the silence made The Owl that much more beautiful, that much more serene. The tall oaks lining all the brick-paved paths, the black iron fences trapping off patches of meadow where students were sprawled, immersed in their studies…even the architecture had an elegance to it, a sort of dark, brooding design. On every road were columns wrapped in ivy, pointed rooftops and cornices, and windows trimmed in deep purples and greens. At night, when the fog over Atlas lowered onto the streets and the black lampposts were all lit, The Owl's beauty became nothing short of eerie.

Reece and Hayden had to circle the weedy grey lake in the middle of campus to get to the aerodome. The day was golden and fresh; if it weren't testing day, the lake would have been full of punters. If it weren't testing day, Reece would have jumped in without a thought for his nice clean uniform. If it weren't testing day…

Drawing up short, Reece stared, sure he was seeing wrong.

"Who are *they*?" he coughed out, blinking hard into the sunlight.

There were dozens of people crammed into the meadow next to the Airship Command Center, some in The Owl's black uniform, but most not. He knew Hayden's father was out there, and Sophie too, but Abigail had only made a halfhearted attempt at booking a flight off-planet, and the duke…well, Reece hadn't seen the duke in going on two years. An imminent reunion seemed unlikely.

"Fans, I suppose," Hayden said, suppressing a smile. "It's not every day the Palatine Second becomes a captain. They're probably all here to apply for your crew."

Reece gave a shudder and swerved toward the AC's side entrance. "Paperwork, lovely. See, Hayden, *that's* why I need you."

"To do all the hard work," Hayden said, hitching his bifocals up on his nose with a finger. There was nothing sharp at all about how he said it. But then, even if there was, Hayden had too honest a face for anyone to think he'd purposefully say anything hurtful.

The AC, while having every appearance of being just another brick school building from the outside, was a labyrinth of desks on the inside. Most people didn't know it, but it took a lot of work to keep track of who flew where, in what craft, and for what reason. Parliament had a ridiculously meticulous system for registering captains and their ships because there was always the chance of stolen cargo flying under the radar, and no Honoran lord was keen on unapproved goods getting to another planet. But it still happened. In fact, Reece knew things about Gideon's Pantedan family that could've had the lot of them incarcerated. His grandfather, Mordecai Creed, had just recently traded stolen medicine for a whole crate of spicy Freherian tobacco.

As Reece and Hayden maneuvered between desks and air officers talking into headsets and making notations on maps of the disc-shaped Epimetheus Galaxy, a deep, feminine voice declared, "Reece Sheppard. There you are."

Cringing before he could help himself, Reece looked up. Scarlet Ashdown was a nice enough girl. And not exactly an eyesore either, with her slender height, golden hair, and probing hazel eyes. But the fact of the matter remained: if the duke's grandfather hadn't abolished arranged marriages a century ago, Abigail would have tied Reece up in a ribbon and handed him over to the Ashdowns as soon as he came of age. Sooner, likely.

Dressed not in uniform, but in a high-necked brown dress that made her olive skin glow, Scarlet glided across the foyer, twirling a white parasol over her shoulder with hands gloved in lace. Hayden slid behind Reece and was instantly engrossed in the buttons of his jacket. Girls could make him sweat where Yules's Theory of Unstable Molecular Conjunction could not.

"Tutor Clauson is looking for you," Scarlet said, looking up at him from under long yellow eyelashes. "Everyone was wondering whether or not you would show. I told them you had probably overslept again. No one seemed surprised."

"Thanks for that. Where's Clauson?"

"In the flight tower, about to tell the engineers to power down your Nyad."

"They have me flying a Nyad?" Reece exclaimed. That part of the test had so far been kept a secret; he hadn't known if he would be flying a heliocraft or an outmoded bus-ship. A Nyad was better than he could have hoped for. Small cockpit, sharp wings that could pull tight turns, and an Axil 59-Eight engine with a purr to put a baby to sleep. Nyads were all from the Aurelius line, which meant that each one had inherited some small clockwork piece of *The Aurelius*, one of the two original airships. The other was *The Aurelia*. She sat in The Owl's museum, one of Honora's most venerated historical artifacts.

Scarlet smiled. Her parents had both been wealthy ambassadors before her father had passed away, so she'd grown up having her future in Intraplanetary Politics picked out in advance, but she was sharp all on her own. She probably even knew about the Axil 59-Eight.

"I'll go tell Tutor Clauson you've arrived," she offered smoothly, then leaned in to kiss him on either cheek. When she was near enough, she whispered so only he and Hayden could hear, "There's been some trouble with your Pantedan friend. I'll do my best to keep Clauson busy for a few minutes, but you'd better hurry, Reece."

It was hard not to consider Scarlet a friend when she did things like this, and she did them often. Reece was inclined to believe it was because they'd practically grown up together, but then, who knew? He gave her a grateful grin before hurrying for the open archway leading to the observation platform. Gid now, Scarlet later.

"Good morning, Scarlet," he heard Hayden stammer behind him.

"Good morning, Harold," Scarlet replied politely.

It turned out the crowd in the meadow was actually overflow from the observation platform, which was jammed with chattering students and tutors, most of them unfamiliar faces. Beyond the white platform with its columned rail stretched a strip of smooth grey land framed by blinking towers. Usually there were bus-ships parked on the airstrip, but today it was empty except for Reece's Nyad, a sleek rust-colored ship with propellers on the undersides of its wings.

Hugh and Sophie Rice stood out like geese in a flock of swans. They had the same habitually-haggard look as Hayden. Mr. Rice's grey suit looked like it'd been pulled out of the dusty recesses of his closet while his bow tie drooped tiredly. The red lion head pin he wore on the breast of his jacket clashed wildly with the rest of him, so colorless. Hayden said Sophie looked just like their mother had before she'd died in the Five Year Pandemic. Straight, faded yellow hair and eyes that shone like a pair of polished blue marbles.

"Reece!" Sophie half laughed, half screamed when she saw him, throwing her arms around his waist. "I knew Hayden could get you out of bed!"

Reece ruffled her hair and threw Hayden a look. "Everyone has such faith in me. It's moving, really."

"What's this about Gideon?" Hayden asked worriedly as he took his turn hugging Sophie, whose sparkling smile wilted a little.

"They wouldn't let him in," she explained, shaking her head. Attending a planetside school as she did, she got to witness the prejudice against the Pans every single day. Reece was sure she'd been hoping to outrun it, here.

Reece and Hugh locked eyes, and Reece tried to keep his voice light as he joked, "He didn't try to bring in a gun, did he?" It had happened before. In fact, it happened all the time.

The joke was for Sophie's sake, so Reece wasn't bothered when Hugh didn't smile. "He tried to bring Mordecai. There were some remarks made by the aerodome sentries, and…well. That's not important. Miss Ashdown was of some help, but—"

"Gid has to be here," Reece said firmly. He hadn't been nervous up till the moment he'd heard Gideon was in trouble. That in itself was nothing new, but trying to fly while worrying whether or not one of his best friends was going to be spending the night in The Owl's detention facility with his madcap pirate grandfather was going to take effort.

Hugh nodded. "We'll try to get him in. But you'd better hurry. Rumor has it Headmaster Eldritch has come to personally observe the test, and it's a sorry soul that makes that man wait for anything."

Reece made a face, not disagreeing. Headmaster Eldritch made the duke look cute and cuddly, and Hugh probably knew as well as Reece how troubling *that* thought was, being the duke's chief librarian.

As Hugh and Sophie melted into the crowd with a round of good lucks, Hayden grabbed Reece's elbow and pressed something small and metallic into his palm. "Here. Keep in touch."

Unrolling his fingers, Reece arched an eyebrow. The bit of brass was shaped like a flattened U, with one of its tails holding a microscopic speaker mouth. "Isn't that cheating?" he whispered even as he reached up and slid the com link over his ear so that it hugged his temple.

It was hard to tell in the sunlight, but Hayden might have actually paled a bit. "Of course not. I mean, not if I don't tell you anything helpful. And I won't."

"Why, that's completely unhelpful."

"It's for moral support."

"Thanks." Reece paused, deliberating, and then added quietly, "You know if anyone finds out about Mordecai's…pastimes…"

Hayden had already started nodding. "I know. We'll take care of it. Oh, and Reece…" He looked around, wary of who in the crowd could be listening. "Liem's here."

"What?"

"I saw him climbing the flight tower with Headmaster Eldritch."

This, of all things, turned Reece's nervousness into a ball of hard anger sitting in the pit of his stomach. Reece's association with Pans and bottom-class librarian's sons had been a black spot on the thin imitation of friendship the stepbrothers had had since Reece had been a Thirteen. Five years later, Liem wouldn't touch Reece with a stick if he needed pulling out of a Freherian marshbed.

"Probably hoping my engines catch fire and I plummet to a fiery death," Reece muttered dryly as he nodded a last goodbye to Hayden and started for the airstrip.

At last, the crowd was realizing that he was the captain-to-be they had come to watch, marching out in his black uniform, his shoulders hunched. His mood had been spoiled. He couldn't help thinking as he passed beneath the shadow of the spidery tin flight tower that the crowd was probably hoping he'd crash too, because that would be more exciting for the lot of them, wouldn't it? They were all a bunch of stuffed, morbid pigeons.

The engineers rushed out from under the wings of the Nyad, branded *Felicity* on her right flank, and started shoving his gear at him. A headset that he'd wear on his free ear, a pair of black leather gloves, breathing apparatus to be kept under his seat in case of emergency. He nodded and grunted at their rambled instructions. He knew how to fly a Nyad. He'd known since he was a Fourteen. If the crowd and the headmaster and Liem wanted to see some flying, then they would see some flying. Let them get a good look at his aft burners.

He entered *Felicity* through a squat door under her left wing and then locked the sealants on the hatch. With a *hiss*, he was closed in. Just him and the helm. He breathed a sigh of relief and tossed the apparatus and the gloves carelessly aside.

He ran through the standard checklist, reading it off over his headset for the judges in the tower to hear. He took care to use the formal names of all the parts, rather than the slang he'd picked up from outside of class. Applicators, not greasers, joint coils, not springs.

Taking off was a simple matter of pumping the pedal that determined the level of intensity the gravitational levelers would work at, then taking hold of the yoke, a wide, two-handed wheel, and pulling it up toward himself. Liftoff was immediate and smooth, and with the levelers doing their job, his ears didn't even pop.

Felicity climbed up and up, her engines humming their low melody, till a voice came over the headset asking Reece to hold his altitude and perform a standard series of maneuvers. Reece flipped a collection of switches, and the Nyad trembled as her propellers shifted position to his specifications.

The test couldn't have been easier if Reece had written it himself. And *Felicity* handled like a well-oiled dream. Gradually, Reece's anger ebbed away to nothing, till he was grinning as he wound Felicity down in an impressive corkscrew, then rolling her up to starboard without ever losing speed. Not quite what the judges had asked for, but better. He saw high marks in his very near future, celebrated with Gideon, Hayden, Sophie, and Hugh over a dinner of clam chowder and rice.

"Felicity, you are cleared to return to Airstrip 12 for landing. You've performed wonderfully," the calm voice on the other end of the headset, quite familiar at this point, announced.

"Yes, she has." Reece patted the console in front of him. "We'll be there in a wink." In response, there was only a pause, then static. He tapped the headset with a finger. "Hello? Friendly intercom person?"

Nothing. But Felicity was high enough that the sky was a deep blue, so it was hard not to notice when the photon globe over his head flickered and then went out. Only the green radar panel on the console lit the cockpit, and that light was dull and ghostly.

Frowning, Reece switched the radar to a heat-sense view of the engines. They looked to be in good order, though there was a strange flickering in the connectors, which was troubling. Maybe a loose wire? Could the engineers really have missed that? Maybe it was sabotage. For a second, Liem's face flashed through his head, but he pushed the thought away. For the most part, he'd been kidding about the plummeting to a fiery death thing.

Touching the brass com link over his left ear, Reece cleared his throat and said, "Hayden?"

"Reece...*tsshhht*...broadcasting your communication over the sonic transducer...*tsshhht*...you cut out!" Static interrupted whatever it was Hayden was trying to say, but at least he was there.

"I'm getting some kind of interference. Hold on." Reece leaned forward in his seat, straining against his safety harness, and switched the radar to standard view, which showed the wide open space around the ship. A pulse passed over the radar, reading for foreign objects. Reece felt his chest constrict as the radar gave a little *bleep*, showed a glowing dot growing closer and closer to *Felicity*, approaching from space. There was something disturbingly familiar about the readings.

"Hayden, you there?"

"...*tsshht*...Go ahead..."

"You remember our first day at The Owl, on the bus-ship? What they told us about how we nearly crashed?"

"...tsshhhhh..."

"They said it was caused by a meteorite breaking atmosphere close to our ship and jamming the controls with an electromagnetic wave."

"What?"

"I think it's happening again! I'm losing my controls, and I'm picking up—"

Felicity jerked, shivered, and then went silent. Her controls darkened, and both com links whispered static into Reece's ears. For a horrible second, she didn't move at all. Then she started to fall.

III

Gideon Makes Guns, Reece Makes Trouble

The Owl's medical facilities were some of Honora's finest. To Reece, that just meant they were twice as uncomfortable as a normal hospital's would have been. Everything was white and sterile, his crisp bed sheets were about as comfortable as newspapers, and then there was the horrible robe he must have been slid into when he'd been brought in from the crash…because if he had been any kind of conscious, he would have fought hard against that.

His bed was alone in a wide chamber with wooden floors that bounced light in every direction. A grandfather clock in the corner tick, tick, ticked, its gears in constant rotation, like the sun arching beyond the windows behind Reece's headboard. Reece started counting ticks. To keep himself sane.

Finally, after nearly fifteen hundred ticks, one of the double doors opened soundlessly. Hayden peeked his head in, and seeing Reece, heaved a sigh of relief.

Reece sat up—his head swam for a minute, making him all the more irritable—grabbed a pillow, and hurled it at him. "Where the bleeding bogrosh have you been?"

Hayden pulled the door shut behind him and skipped to dodge the pillow. He was out of uniform, wearing trousers with their suspenders caught up on the shoulders of his white shirt. That's right. For everyone else at The Owl, school holiday had started this morning, when Reece woke to find himself with a plasma bag hanging at his bedside, his only friend.

"Trying to find out what happened," Hayden said, resting his hip on the windowsill. "I knew you would want answers when you woke up."

"And?"

"What do you remember?"

"Before or after I received a very nice log telling me I'd failed my test?"

Hayden almost slipped off the windowsill in his surprise. Reece felt a pang of guilt. So Hayden *hadn't* known. He had almost worked himself up to believing that everyone knew and hadn't come to visit him because they didn't know how to deal with the subject of his humiliating failure.

"They *failed* you? On what grounds?"

Reece slouched against his headboard. "I didn't communicate with the tower when I experienced the power flux. I crashed my Nyad into the lake. And then I didn't have my breathing apparatus handy, so I nearly drowned. Pretty good grounds, I'd say."

"But they'd announced the test over *before* the power flux!" Hayden looking so horrified made Reece feel a hair better. Hayden didn't question judges, tests, and rules, not without good reason. "And what happened—Reece, that wasn't your fault. You're right. I looked at the datagraph they were able to salvage from *Felicity's* console. The readings were identical to the ones Bus-ship Ten took eight years ago."

"A meteorite." Reece pinched the bridge of his nose with two fingers, sighing. "I failed because of a bleeding...Hayden?" Hayden was staring out the window thoughtfully, his forehead scrunched into a mass of wrinkles. "What's wrong?"

"It wasn't a meteorite, Reece. It couldn't have been. Everyone saw it. For a second, we thought it was your ship crashing. But it wasn't. It was too small, almost like an escape capsule. I know what a meteorite looks like coming through the atmosphere, and this was nothing like it. It was generating some serious heat, but it was stable. It didn't leave a tail. It just...landed." As Hayden spoke, he tapped his fingertips together and started pacing. "Some of the others in the crowd might not have recognized the signs, but surely those in the flight tower...but why would they fail you, if they knew?"

To keep his poor concussioned head from combusting, Reece held up a hand to stop Hayden's tirade. "Wait, wait, wait. You think they knew it wasn't my fault, and *still* failed me?"

Hayden waved a hand as if that was trivial and kept pacing, clicking his fingers and muttering.

"Why?" Reece persisted. He could feel his hands forming into fists around handfuls of his sheets. "Why would they do that?"

"Maybe so they wouldn't have to provide proof of why it wasn't your fault. Maybe they don't want attention drawn to the supposed meteorite." As if annoyed, though he rarely got annoyed except with Gideon, Hayden threw out his hands and made a growling noise. "This is going to drive me insane. What could it be?"

"Maybe it *is* an escape capsule. It's not the first time aliens have come to Honora. Look at the Pantedans."

"But don't you see the connection? If *this* isn't a meteorite, and its readings are identical to the supposed meteorite of eight years ago…then *that* wasn't a meteorite either. And it couldn't have been an escape capsule either time or they would've had a broadcast about it. We would have heard about the survivor, I'm sure of it. So it stands to reason that cover stories were fabricated for both events. Maybe—"

"Here's a thought," said Reece, sitting up slowly to keep his headache in check. "Will getting that answer for you get me proof that the crash wasn't my fault?"

Thereby getting him his promotion. That was all he wanted, all he had ever wanted; a ship, a crew, and the right to fly them. It was just a pair of wings. What right did a panel of judges who probably hadn't flown in thirty years have to tell him he couldn't have that much?

Looking suddenly uncomfortable, Hayden plunged his hands into his trouser pockets and ducked his head. Reece could tell he likened the mystery to an equation in his mind, something to be solved. Just not at the risk of…risk.

Before either of them could say more, the doors opened inward, and a stream of visitors trickled into the hospital chamber. Tutor Clauson was at the head of the line, a small man that hunched like a vulture and had the nose to match. He gave Reece a limp handshake, offered his regrets at the outcome of the test, and said in his dry, wheezy voice, "There's as much important work to be done on the ground as in the air, my boy. You'll get the sky out of your system in time. I did."

A few of Reece's fellow aspiring pilots came and had the decency to not mention the test. Then there was Scarlet, in her peacock blue dress and silvery hairnet, bending over to whisper that she was seeing if there was anything to be done about rescheduling the test under fairer conditions. Sophie and Hugh were the most welcome of all, dear Sophie with a tin full of his favorite biscuits. Liem, Abigail, and the duke didn't show. His accident likely would've merited a visit from them only if it had been fatal.

Reece polished off his third biscuit, and as he reached for a fourth under Sophie's delighted eye, asked carefully, "No Gideon?" The other visitors were all gone, but there was a male nurse standing at the door in a white jumpsuit.

Leaning back into one of the mechanical spring chairs the nurse had helpfully cranked up out of the floor, Hugh shook his head. "He and Mordecai are back at the shop. They came to see you this morning, but you weren't awake yet, and Mordecai was…Mordecai."

That sentence made perfect sense to anyone who'd ever carried on a three-minute conversation with the man. Among his numerous quirks, Mordecai had an acute case of paranoia when it came to Parliament-run facilities. He had once faked leperhives just to get out of renewing his citizenship in The Guild House.

Chewing on his fourth biscuit and deciding against a fifth even though Sophie was holding the tin practically under his nose, Reece had a thought. Smiling slyly at Hayden, he asked Hugh, "Did you see the…meteorite?"

Hayden choked on his biscuit, and behind his father's back, shook his head pleadingly. Sophie saw it all, but she was Reece's through and through, no need to worry about her allegiance. She gave the tin a little shake so that the biscuits rattled.

"I did, if that's what it was," Hugh sighed. "It's a bad bit of timing. I truly am sorry, Reece. But they'll test you again after the standard year is over. I'm sure you'll have no trouble finding employment until then."

Reece opened his mouth very slowly, making Hayden first roll his eyes, then hesitantly nod his consent. He was in, so long as Reece didn't mention his sleuthing to his father. Triumphant, Reece grinned.

"No, no trouble," he said, and indulged himself with another biscuit.

There was one small town on Atlas, a half hour's drive by bimobile from The Owl. It wasn't much as far as towns went, not after you'd lived on Honora, but it had plenty of storefronts to peruse, huge glass windows with advertisements projected onto them, black and white moving pictures of ladies modeling dresses or gentlemen examining their shiny new pocket watches. And for those unfortunate students who were still riding the public locomotive to get to and from Praxis, there were even bimobiles (bims for short) for rent, though the models the shops carried were not nearly as nice as the ones Reece and Hayden rode.

Technically, both bims were Reece's, since Hayden had humbly refused to accept one for a birthday present (Gideon had had no such qualms accepting his). They were motorized pushbikes, really, chunky two-wheeled mobiles with low, flat handles. Huge funnels coughed steam from either side of the rear tires. The oily steam was a smell Reece had come to love.

After rolling his bim up to the pedestrian walkway and propping its hulk against a lamppost, Reece tipped his goggles onto the back of his head and squinted into the sunlight. Praxis was as busy as an anthill. The brick-laid Main Street was split down the middle by tracks for The Iron Horse, the public locomotive, but people crossed it freely, lugging brown paper shopping bags or licking cones of frozen dairy. Main Street's buildings were all double stacked and identical, with colorful fronts, bright, coordinating shutters, and spinning glass doors in constant rotation. Well, nearly identical. The one Reece and Hayden had come to find was the exception.

It had a bland olive paintjob and a congested window display filled with springs, cables, shockgun shells, ammunition trays, macro-plasma candles, and little curving pieces that Reece knew by now to be triggers. It was dark beyond the window, but that didn't mean anything. Someone looking to buy spare parts could get them at any old junker's on the next lane over. No, if you came to this shop, you wanted the second floor.

Reece and Hayden exchanged a look—Reece thought Hayden might be steeling himself—and went in through the dilapidated door, which groaned on its rotator. The shelves on the walls were nearly bare. Chances were, anything laid out didn't work anyways and was just sitting there to keep up the appearance of this being a shop at all.

There was a mechanical whine coming from the swinging door behind the counter where an old cash register sat gathering cobwebs. Reece hopped over the counter, making a path through the dust for Hayden, who was having a sneezing fit into his handkerchief, and hurried through the door and up the winding staircase it concealed.

At the top of the stairs they came to the real shop, where there were no shelves, just countless pegs on the walls holding guns of every kind by their trigger guards, shockguns, revolvers, hobs, repeaters, ALPs and all the rest. Hayden gulped loudly behind Reece, as if scared the guns might spring to life and open up fire on each other.

Thud, thud, thud. The footsteps preceded the shirtless bear of a man that had to duck to get through the curtained door to the left of the staircase. He was as carved as a statue, as white as one too, with long black hair stuck to his back by sweat and grease. He lifted the visor of his welder's helmet and glared at Reece and Hayden, hard faced and solemn.

"Peh," he rumbled. "Couple'a clean ones."

Hayden abruptly stopped trying to wipe his hands clean on the lap of his pants.

"Gideon here?" Reece asked Varque.

With most of the Gideon's Pan friends, even the ones Reece liked, it was best to just stick to the point and avoid any chance of there being a misunderstanding. Reece had never met a Pan who wasn't a Handler. They made art out of gunplay, Handlers did, trained with guns like the ancient Honorans had trained with swords—except guns killed a lot faster than swords, usually, and every Handler forged his own. There were forms, stances, styles... according to Gid, you could tell a person was a Handler just by looking at how they stood, the way they held their shoulders, where they kept their hands. He could pick Handlers out of a crowd like they were waving banners.

Varque turned his big square back to Reece and Hayden and disappeared through the door. He had a hob stuck through the back of his belt.

"What happens if it accidently goes off?" Hayden wondered in a whisper, and Reece glanced sideways at him, trying not to smile.

Varque returned not with Gideon, but with Kayl, a least favorite among Reece's least favorites. Kayl was twice again as thin as Varque and a head shorter, but he had a presence of character that made him somehow loom. His black hair was shorn to a bristle except for the skinny braid behind his left ear.

Kayl rubbed his thin nose with a thumb. Like Varque, his torso glimmered with sweat and oil, and there were fresh burns on his hands. "You really crash into a lake, Sheppard?"

Like the gauze wrapped around Reece's forehead wasn't answer enough. "Good and truly. You should've seen it."

"Wish I had. What brings you here? In the market for something you can throw your royal money at?" Kayl studied the wall before reaching for a stocky black-bodied hob. "Hobs make good sidearms. Discreet. Hide well."

"Not today. Just looking for Gideon."

"Now, that's a shame," Kayl said as he pulled a few metallic slivers out of his pockets and slipped them into the hob's chamber. Bullets. "Because you know if you ever actually carried, I wouldn't feel bad in the least about killin' you."

"Seems a good enough reason to avoid carrying a little while longer. I kind of like life."

Kayl thought on that as he swaggered forward with the gun twirling on his finger. He drew chest to chest with Reece and prodded him in the shoulder with the barrel of the hob. "Don't forget who you are here, Sheppard. Not Palatine Second. Not nobody. You lose your rights the second you walk in that door. I'm startin' to think you're doin' it to test me. Don't. I'll kill you. Take off your shiny clothes, and you bleed just the same as—"

With a view over Kayl's shoulder, Reece could see when Varque slipped out of the room, lowering his mask to return to his gunsmithing, and Gideon, tugging on a pale green shirt, stepped in. Gideon, a runt among Pans, a contender among Honorans. Years of gunsmithing had made him broad of chest and shoulder so that he was built like a solid V. He looked neither surprised nor impressed to see his friends standing at gunpoint.

"Kayl," he said in his low, drawling voice, "you wanna be leavin' this room right about now."

Without turning, Kayl grimaced. Gideon might be the runt of the litter, but if anything, that had just given him sharper teeth than all the rest. "Yeah? And if I don't?"

Gid shrugged. "I'll just shoot you, I guess."

For a second, Kayl hesitated, but only a second. Muttering and glaring, the Pan pumped the unused bullets out into his palm, replaced the hob on the wall, and shouldered his way past Gideon.

When the three friends were completely alone, Hayden blew out a long breath and leaned his weight on the stair railing. "Did he really think you would shoot him?"

Pulling a grubby rag out of the back pocket of his trousers, Gideon began wiping oil from his hands. His blue eyes twinkled. "Why wouldn't he?" It was clear Hayden didn't know quite what to say—or think—about that, so Gideon turned to Reece. "What's goin' on?"

"We're going hunting for the fake meteorite that wrecked my Nyad to prove I passed my test," Reece said simply, and left it at that. Things didn't have to be polished with Gid; words didn't need to be fancy. Not because he was slow, but because fancy words wasted breath. That's how he would've put it.

For example. There was a pause after Reece's statement, and then Gideon carelessly tossed his rag away and said, "Sounds fun. I'll get my guns."

IV

All Manner of Creepy

It was early evening when the three friends drove their bims out of Praxis. Honora consumed the horizon, but Nix and Telesto, her green and red moons, stood out brightly against the pink and purple-swirled sky. The colors made Reece feel like he was a small customer in a giant candy emporium.

After driving north for a good hour, they turned off the road, pulled their bims into the trees flanking it, and gathered around Hayden's handheld datascope. Even though the sun hadn't quite set, their breath swirled in white clouds about their heads.

"My readings put the landing site about a half hour east. On foot." Hayden cringed. "We have to cut through the forest, and I don't think the bims will fit."

"And they'll be too loud," Reece added.

Gid looked up from the belt holster he was strapping above his hips, interested. "You think there's someone else out here?"

It was hard to imagine anyone but themselves tramping through the Atlasian Wilds after dark, especially with it getting colder every minute. But if Hayden was right…and this wasn't a meteorite…

In answer to Gideon's question, Reece reached under the rucksack on the back of his bim and dug out his coppery hob. He knew better than to carry it in plain sight. He was no Handler, and he didn't want some Pan like Kayl thinking he was claiming to be. But, call him old fashioned, he liked to feel safe when wandering through dark forests and encroaching on alien objects' landing sites.

Gideon smiled without showing teeth and glanced at Hayden, who was whispering to himself and punching calculations into his datascope with a shivering finger. "Hey, you want—"

"No thank you," Hayden said without looking up. "I'm not carrying a gun. I'd probably end up shooting one of you in the foot like last time."

"I'd nearly forgotten about the old foot shooting incident," Reece said quietly as he loaded his hob. Feet bled a lot more than you'd think.

The Pan snorted. "I *was* gonna offer you a spare pair'a gloves."

Eyes still on his datascope, Hayden smiled. "No, thank you. It'll be more—"

"Alright then." Gideon reached into his holster, pulled out his double-barreled revolver, and loaded it with a few swift clicks.

"Reece," Hayden cut in, finally looking up. He was frowning fretfully, eying Gideon sideways. "Do you think the guns are really...necessary?"

"Yup," said Gideon. His forefinger moved deftly over the three triggers of the revolver, and he gave his wrist a small, practiced jerk that sent the barrels of the gun sliding at an angle, till they aimed off to one side. With another jerk, the barrels slid frontward again. It took a Handler to use a revolver and its ball-in-socket design to its full functionality. Come to think of it, it might have been with a revolver that Hayden had almost shot off Gideon's toes.

"There are animals in the Wilds, Hayden. Non-friendly ones that occasionally like to chew on human appendages. The guns are for self defense only," Reece said with a pointed glance at Gideon.

Gideon grunted and slid the revolver home in its cradle. Hayden let down his shoulders with a sigh. And Reece, Reece just tried hard not to smile.

Dark blue bled out into the colorful sky as the friends hiked into the forest. By Reece's pocket watch, it was about twenty minutes before they saw signs of the crash. Heard, rather. Everywhere else in the dense Atlasian Wilds, owls would be hooting and nightcats would be screaming, trying to frighten field mice out of their holes. Here, now, there wasn't the tiniest hoot to be heard. The animals had all cleared out.

Gideon, who was leading the march with his thumbs looped comfortably through his gun belt, suddenly stopped and moved a hand toward his revolver. "Lights up ahead," he said quietly.

Reece saw them. White flood lights, probably from some sort of photon generator judging by their flickering quality, were turning several of the pine trees into hazy silhouettes. It was nearly fog hour. Back at The Owl and in Praxis, the streets would all be rivers of white mist.

Stepping up beside Reece, using one hand to shade the lit screen of his datascope, Hayden whispered, "It's thirty yards west." He was breathing hard; his bifocals were fogging up. "Maybe we should—"

"Shoulda brought a gun," Gideon said without looking back at them.

Drawing himself up, Hayden whirled on him, voice hoarse. "I brought a *real* weapon." He held up his datascope, and, exasperated, Reece lifted a hand to block the light of its blinking screen.

With a glance over his shoulder, Gideon snorted. "Don't be so bleedin' superior."

"That's enough," Reece said sharply, grabbing Hayden by the sleeve and towing him past Gideon. Truth be told, he was feeling a little high-strung what with being only—what was it?—thirty yards from a crash site that was probably quarantined and off-limits to boot.

They crept the last ten or fifteen yards, squeezing around trees one at a time and keeping well away from where shafts of foggy light broke up the branches. Ahead, voices shouted back and forth, and there was a whining engine sound, and a shuffling noise. Chains rattled. Someone yelled at someone else for being a clumsy fool.

Reece dropped to his hands and knees, then dragged himself forward on his belly till he had a narrow view of the site from under a low-hanging branch. He stayed back in the shadows and took it all in, stumped.

There had definitely been a crash of some kind. There was a shallow crater about ten yards across cut out of the forest, framed by rubble and trees that had surged up around it. But what the men in olive jumpsuits were drawing up out of it with a chain as thick as Reece's arm…it could have been an escape capsule, he supposed. But it wasn't like any he'd ever seen. The Pantedans' had been boxy, a mass of wires and airpumps to provide life support. This capsule, if that's what it was, was a sleek patinaed oval with a glass top. And the emblem on its side…an A inside a circle, inside a pair of wings…that emblem was famous. It was on *The Aurelia* and *The Aurelius*, the first of all airships. It was on Reece's bleeding uniform!

Hayden slithered up on Reece's left, Gideon on his right, to watch as the jumpsuited men swung the capsule away from the crater with their crank-crane and then clustered around it, making observations and taking notes or pinching dirt from its window with tiny metal prongs. Others walked around the site with huge dark chambers and paused now and again to pull the curtain over their head, frame their picture, and set off their flash to capture it. There were still others hanging back from the glare of the photon globes suspended on portable tin towers, faceless observers who made Reece's skin crawl.

"Thoughts?" Reece muttered.

"It's empty?" Hayden offered.

Shifting to get a better view of the capsule, Gideon grunted. "Dirt if it don't look like a hunk'a metal broke right off Aurelia."

He was right. The vintage gold design, the way the glass looked more fine than functional. If Aurelia had ever had escape capsules, this could have been one. But she hadn't. And she hadn't moved her belly from the floor of The Owl's museum in centuries.

Hayden started to say something, but choked and gave a noise of despair instead. Reece glanced up sharply. A lean man with a black crop of hair and long sideburns had stepped into the light. The Aurelian Academy's very own headmaster, Charles Eldritch. This was bad, worse than judges, worse than sentries. Eldritch—

"I think it's time to go, Reece," Hayden said, and it sounded close to a plea.

—Eldritch had the power to crush the future of any student in an iron fist. He reveled in this. He used this. And if he found Reece, Hayden, and Gideon out here, there would be more than expulsion to fear. Eldritch ruined lives.

So Reece was inclined to agree with Hayden.

"Findings?" Eldritch called in his breathy manner of speaking as he stalked the circumference of the crater. His wore black everything—suit, ascot, tight leather gloves—and it made his skin look sallow. His nose was very sharp, his eyebrows thin and manicured, his chin a little too long. He looked too young to have been the headmaster for thirty-five years, even with the wings of white at his temples.

"Strange, sir," one of the jumpsuits reported, scratching his head. "We got boot prints comin' in, and boot prints goin' out, but no sign'a what was in the capsule."

Eldritch stopped walking to stare at the man for a long moment, not blinking. "And?"

The man fidgeted, unsure. "My guess? Someone came and carried the cargo out. Threw it over his shoulder, put it on a bim, somethin'. And the emblem on the capsule—"

The man stopped as Eldritch dismissively turned and started walking back the way he had come, circling the crater again. Hayden gave Reece's arm a pinch, but Reece shook him off.

Halfway around the crater, not ten feet from where the friends lay concealed, a squat little man spinning a bowler cap in his hands came and met Eldritch, his pencil thin mustache quivering. Reece thought he recognized him: Robert Gustley, Secretary to the Headmaster.

Eldritch held up a finger to keep Gustley from speaking and said quietly, "It's sad, isn't it, Gustley?"

"What's sad, sir?" Gustley stammered, crumpling the rim of his hat.

"That none of these men survive the crash."

"C-crash, sir?"

"Yes. The one that will happen later this evening, when the engine of their transit-ship inexplicably fails."

Reece grit his teeth against wanting very badly to mutter an invective. Gideon didn't bother gritting; he muttered away.

"I—that's tragic, sir. Tragic."

"Indeed," Eldritch mumbled thoughtfully, then stooped, throwing out the tails of his black jacket as he knelt to examine something on the ground. A boot print. "Do you know how a fox steals eggs? She waits till the goose leaves its nest, then wades upstream to hide her scent. She takes the eggs one at a time in her mouth, careful not to hurt them. So careful." He dragged a leather-clothed finger through the dirt, outlining the print. "So how does the fox steal the eggs, Gustley?"

Gustley opened and closed his mouth stupidly.

Standing, Eldritch turned to stare at the capsule twirling on its chain. He held up a gloved hand, pretended to be the one orchestrating the twirling, turning the capsule around and around. "One at a time. She steals them one at a time."

"That fellow is all manner'a creepy," Gideon mumbled. "Thinkin' we best get us outta here, Cap'n."

Reece nodded and started to slide backward, not caring if he was streaking the front of his clothes with dirt. His head was swimming, and it wasn't from his concussion. Something in the capsule had been worth stealing, to somebody. Eldritch seemed to think so too. He was going to have his workers killed just to keep them quiet. And that emblem—

Crunch. Jumping, Reece glanced sideways at Hayden, who stood frozen. The branch under his foot was cleanly snapped in two.

"Keep moving," Reece mouthed. "Watch your feet."

Despite his size, Gideon moved easily through the trees, one hand on his revolver, the other gesturing sharply at sticks he spotted before they did, or branches that could snag. Reece followed without breaking a sweat, but Hayden...*crack, crunch, thwack.* Finally, Reece stopped and traded him for his place at the rear. At least he had a gun. If someone jumped Hayden, all he could really do was throw his datascope at them—though he'd probably hesitate before even letting go of the bleeding thing.

A gunshot echoed through the night, a sharp crack. Reece instinctively ducked his head and brought up his hob in both hands. There was a spell of silence.

"Was that…at us?" Hayden breathed.

Gideon peered about, eyes narrowed. "More than likely a warnin' shot. Wouldn't waste coin bettin' they're on our trail, though."

With a much louder crack, another gunshot rang out, this one a good deal closer. Reece thought he might have heard the bullet rough up some nearby branches.

He used the guiding hand he had on Hayden's shoulder to shove him forward. "Run!"

Another gunshot. Bark-turned-powder exploded out of a trunk to their right.

The bullets followed them through the forest, smacking trees, rustling branches, occasionally whistling near their heads. Gideon shot off a few rounds of his own, aiming at nothing, hoping to make their trackers hesitate. Reece had never run so hard. His boots were cutting into his heels; his hair was sticking to his forehead. Each breath he drew of the cold evening air stung his lungs, made the stitch under his ribs burn.

They had crashed into their bims, kicked the engines to life, and peeled out onto the road to the sound of one last gunshot before Reece realized. He'd dropped his gun.

V

Scandal!

For three days, Reece waited for the sentries to come. He looked over his shoulder, checked around corners, and laughed too loudly at himself when he jumped at a small, innocuous sounds.

And if that was bad, what was worse was poor Hayden's state. Reece should never have told him about losing the gun. The purple rings under his bifocals made Reece think he hadn't been sleeping, and he knew he hadn't been eating, because he never left the suite, and the food Reece brought him back from the dormitory kitchenette kept ending up in the garbage. Gideon was scarce, busily working on the gun commission that would pay for his next few months at The Owl, but Reece doubted he was any kind of worried. Which must be nice.

When the duke's personal Dryad arrived on Atlas the morning of the fourth day to retrieve Reece for his three week holiday, it marked the first time the friends had all been together since that night.

"I don't see what all the bleedin' fuss is about," Gideon muttered as he pushed his bim up a ramp and into the Dryad's cargo hold. "I can make you another gun in a matter'a hours. A better one too, likely."

"It's not about the gun." Hayden grunted and tried a third time to push his bim up the ramp only to have it roll its weight back down and nearly run him over. He'd been at this for a while. His suspenders had been let off his shoulders, and his sleeves were rolled up past his elbows. "It's about someone *finding* the gun."

Seated cross-legged on a travelling chest in the hold, Reece made a shushing noise, reminding them to keep their voices down. He didn't want the captain or any of his crew hearing something they might report to Abigail for a pat on the head. He was already paying them off to keep their mouths shut about giving Gideon and Hayden a ride planetside. For all their fine clothes, Easterners were a shifty lot.

"So what if they do?" Gideon grabbed Hayden's bim by its handlebar and dragged it up the ramp toward himself. Hayden tripped after it.

"Guns bought *legally*," Hayden emphasized the word, "are all registered, identifiable by a numeric code on their…grip thing."

With a snort, Gideon drawled, "That's why you don't buy them *legally*."

Hopping up, Reece crossed the hold and pulled a lever that raised the ramp and closed the airlock hatch behind it. "Gid, have you heard anything particularly telling?"

Gideon sat, leaning his back against the pile of their luggage, and then readjusted to pull a gun out from behind his belt. "Not since the crash. The second crash."

Reece frowned. The one of the transit-ship that had been carrying all those workers. The first thing he had done upon returning from the Wilds was send a log to Caldonia's Sentry Center, tipping them off about the forthcoming crash, but the warning had been dismissed out of hand. He blessed Hayden's foresight; it had been his idea to send the warning anonymously. The reports on the wireless all said too little remained of the ship to determine what had caused the engine failure.

"Hayden, what are the chances your father might be able to find something on Eldritch in the archives? He should have access to the duke's personnel files, shouldn't he?"

Hayden abruptly stopped digging through his travel sack to cast Reece a look. "Maybe. But the headmaster isn't technically employed by the duke, he's employed by Parliament."

"That doesn't mean he might not have something on Eldritch. Those two have been chummy my whole life."

"That's a bit of an exaggeration. They're...business partners, Reece. Besides," Hayden added, "couldn't we just...*ask* your father about the headmaster? I mean—"

"Oh, certainly," Reece said curtly. "I'll have to make an appointment with his secretary. I'm sure the duke will slide us straight onto his schedule, right between the Mead Moon Parade and my fortieth birthday."

Hayden said nothing for a moment, lowering his eyes to his bag and gently pulling out his auto-encrypting journal. He looked so guilty, so tired and thin and pathetic, that Reece found himself opening his mouth to apologize. But what came out was, "He hasn't been my father in a long time now."

Something stirred deep in his chest, and he thrust the feeling away harshly, scowling. He didn't allow that to bother him anymore; he couldn't. The duke and Abigail both preferred Liem, the shining prodigy, the intragalactic politician, the Palatine First. The duke's partiality, Reece could understand. The two of them had had an abysmal falling out two years ago, when the duke had tried to send Reece to the other side of the galaxy to pursue politics, of all things.

And Liem was the son of his first wife, Genevieve, who had died from a virus she had contracted shortly after childbirth. That merited some favoritism.

But Abigail? Was Reece's friendship with Gideon and Hayden really that appalling?

No, that was only half of it. As for the other half, Reece didn't care that she considered a captain's chair a "substandard aspiration". It seemed a perfectly good chair to fill to him.

"Well." Hayden flipped the copper-plated cover of his journal open and drew out the finger-sized metal wand needed to type figures into it. "In any case, Father and Sophie both are ready to have you back to the house. You too, Gideon, so long as…" He hesitated, ticking the wand between his fingers.

Gideon looked up with interest from the hunk of gear-laden machinery he'd dislodged from the belly of his bim. "So long as what?"

Despite how immersed Gid often got in his work, Reece got the feeling he'd been listening, and wondered how it had all struck him—him, whose parents had both been killed in Panteda's war.

"Well, last time you came to stay, you taught Sophie about throwing knives, and Father's been a little concerned about our eating utensils all gone missing…"

It wasn't home, but The Estate at Emathia was something to look at, that was for sure.

Reece draped his elbows over his bim's handles and drew a deep breath. The Honoran country air was sweet, full of autumn smells, dying leaves, ripe vineyards, busy chimneys. The brick-laid drive before him stretched a straight half mile, edged by towering oaks bearing bouquets of red, gold, and brown leaves.

Set against those colors, the mansion at the end of the drive jarred the eye. A deep teal, it had red and white shingles patterned in swirls, red roof crestings, and white banisters along all three of its elaborate balconies. Its two chimneys stretched like fingers into the sky; its bay windows, huge and trimmed in deep purple, were made of stained glass. Excess was the key to being royalty, apparently.

Starting his engine up again, Reece glanced sideways at Gideon on his bim. The Pan wouldn't be getting a warm reception no matter what, but it might help that he had changed out of his grungy gunshop dunnage and into a brown leather waistcoat that fit too snugly to hide any guns. A small green military ribbon was pinned to his chest pocket. On the other side of him, Hayden was wearing his ratty brown jacket, a riding cap, and his oversized goggles. Reece sighed.

They rolled up the drive together in a noisy line, the shadows of the oaks flickering over them like moving pictures in a kinema. Two of the royal wolfdogs, Midas and Hera, loped along through the grass, barking and howling. The breeze was cool, pushing Reece's muddy brown hair out of his eyes.

At the foot of the mansion, three servants in matching white jumpsuits hurried forward to park the bims in the motorvehicle stables. Reece briefly hesitated beneath the stairs winding down from either side of the front doors, then charged them, taking the steps two at a time with Hayden and Gideon close on his heels. Sometimes it was best to just get this part over with. He threw one of the doors open, stepped into the parlor, and stared.

His eyes normally would've gone to the chandelier overhead made of black and red stained glass, or to the swanky throw rugs cast over the hardwood floors, or the grand piano. Paintings that cost as much as a decent education, antique paperbound books confined to glass cases, tall love seats upholstered in fine jacquard and velvet.

All he saw was Liem, chatting with Abigail near the tall fireplace, a saucer and a cup of tea in his hands. And the girl standing with them.

Abigail looked as stately as ever in a purple dress and bustle, her cold eyes mostly hidden behind the black veil on her feathered monstrosity of a hat. Liem's fine grey suit with its banded collar and ivory gloves was, as Gid would say, "dirt near princely". As for the girl standing with them…

…she could have been a Pan. Lank black hair fell down her back, and her skin was pale white. She was dressed like a Westerner, with her skirt hitched up to her knees, showing off scuffed workboots. She was running her thumb along the edge of the necklace she wore close against her neck, like a black ribbon.

"Reece Benjamin." Abigail surveyed him from behind her veil, pursing her lips. Liem jumped as if she'd shouted and sloshed his tea. "What have I told you about bringing the dogs in the front door?"

Realizing he was gaping like a numpty, Reece pulled himself together and glanced back at Gid and Hayden. He scowled as the jibe sank in. Abigail had as much tact as a teapot.

"Reece," Liem greeted dryly, recovered from his start. For only being stepbrothers, they shared a remarkable amount of genes, but today Liem's eyes looked darker even while the rest of him seemed strangely paler. Reece thought he looked feverish.

"We were just discussing your test." Abigail's eyes flickered to the fading bruise on Reece's forehead. She raised the fan she'd been holding by her side, spread it artfully, and fluttered it before her face. "It's just as well. Perhaps now you'll consider a worthier vocation."

"You're absolutely right, of course, Mother," Liem said smoothly. "If I've said it once, I've said it a hundred times…there's nothing worse than a man who has to put his head in the clouds to find a stable job." He raised his cup to smell his tea—and hide his smirk, if Reece wasn't mistaken.

Trying though it killed him to keep his face neutral, Reece shrugged. "Gideon might be able to teach me some guncraft. That's a pretty stable market."

The strange girl hadn't turned to face the conversation—she was still staring off into space, motionless save for the hand on her necklace.

Liem must have followed Reece's eyes, because he put down his tea and cleared his throat loudly. "Nivy," he said, and clicked his fingers at her.

Slowly, the girl turned, and Reece was struck by her. Not just by how pretty she was, but by how lean and scrawny, like someone who hadn't seen bread in a while, and especially by her eyes. They weren't the Pantedan blue, but they were bright, clever. And a little cold.

Reece could only stare as Liem shuffled forward, raised his arm, and settled it stiffly around the girl's shoulders. "Reece," his voice cracked, "this is Nivy. She has been my guest here at Emathia these last few days while we've been waiting for Mother to return from her stay in Olbia. We've just told her the good news. Nivy…has agreed to marry me. We're engaged."

Silence, except for the gentle swishing of Abigail's fan, moving faster than ever now.

"Congratulations," Hayden said timidly, reminding the lot of them he was there, a small shadow next to the frowning Gideon.

Reece just kept staring. It had to be a farce. Liem was the Palatine First, heir to Honora's dukeship. This girl was…

"Well. Nivy." Abigail's tone was nothing short of patronizing. She had to be a tempest inside. This ordeal (if it wasn't a hoax) was probably giving Reece an edge over Liem for the first time in years. "You'll have to introduce me to your parents so we can arrange a proper date."

Something in Nivy's eyes flickered, but her face remained blank, perfectly controlled. When she said nothing, Abigail pressed testily, "What are their names? I may recognize them."

Reece's mouth opened in surprise when Liem pulled Nivy a little closer into his side. His darker-than-usual eyes shot Reece an unreadable glance.

"Nivy doesn't speak," he explained.

Abigail looked as if she'd been slapped. "She's a mute?"

"She doesn't speak," he repeated, voice tighter than before.

And then Abigail's dam broke. In a huff, she threw down her fan, actually showing teeth as she growled, "How *dare* you, Liem Cage Sheppard! How dare you bring this upon your father and me! I would never have expected this of you! Marching her in here in those rags, presuming to call her your fiancé, just moments after I've arrived! When I speak with Thaddy—"

It was enough to make anyone want to plug their ears with local vibration dampeners. Reece glanced over his shoulder at Gideon and Hayden and nodded for them to follow him out of the parlor, carefully creeping around the wailing Abigail, whose tantrum had evolved to include foot-stomping.

Just before he passed from the parlor into the dining hall, Reece looked back. Nivy's blue eyes, calm and steady, were on him.

VI

Do You Prefer Water, or Engine Grease?

Reece tilted his head and let the sunlight soak through the backs of his eyelids, washing out the black. He tried to make sense of a number of things and wished not for the first time he had Hayden's mind. Hayden could compartmentalize, put order to his thoughts and connect the lines between them. Reece felt like his thoughts were a bunch of blocks, rattling around untethered in his cargo hold of a skull.

The crash of the capsule, the theft of its cargo, Eldritch's murder of his workers, and now Liem and Nivy.

The hovering dock under Reece's legs shuddered as Gideon thundered down its length, tucked in his feet, and leaped into Emathia's pond. Hayden made a tsking sound and used his sleeve to wipe droplets from the screens of his journal. Gid was the only one who cared to swim this late into the solar cycle. In fact, Hayden couldn't swim at all.

"But the thing of it is," Hayden continued, "if that capsule *was* from Honora, why wasn't its cargo just sent by ship?"

Reece thought for a moment, dangling his legs over the edge of the dock. "I don't know. Maybe whoever sent it didn't have one." Reaching out, he grabbed the dock's vertical adjustment crank and tweaked it a few degrees till his feet brushed the startlingly cold water.

Gideon stroked over to them and wildly shook out his black hair, spraying Hayden's journal all over again. "Mighta done it so the cargo would fly under the radar." When his friends stared at him blankly, he hoisted himself onto the dock, dripping wet and shirtless. "Capsules are too small to be picked up by any'a that fancy equipment at the AC. If they ain't carryin' weapons or magnetizers or any foreign bells and whistles, they glide right over sensors. Chances are, those ginghoos in your flight tower really did think it was just another meteorite."

"But Eldritch definitely knew differently. He must've had the judges fail me to distract me from looking into the readings I picked up on my console." The blocks were settling into place one at a time. "Only I did it anyways."

"Hold on!" Hayden exclaimed, glaring up into the sunlight and at Gideon. "How do you know…wait, on second thought, don't tell me.

Then I won't be guilty by association when you and Mordecai get found with a load of—of smuggled tobacco, for example."

Gideon grinned, did an about face, and dove off the dock again with a boisterous whoop.

Reece was still stuck on the fact that Eldritch had known all along. Known, and failed the Palatine Second to cover up his own lousy tracks. That cargo must be bleeding valuable. Had he been expecting it? Was that the whole reason he had come to Reece's test, to watch for it from the flight tower? Maybe—

"Son of a toffer!" Reece shouted. "Hayden!"

Jumping, Hayden stared aghast at Reece. "Good gracious, what?"

"I just remembered...*Liem* was in the flight tower with Eldritch!"

Hayden continued to stare. "You don't think he knows something?"

"He might." Troubled, Reece shook his head. He'd never really liked Liem, but he hated to think of him knotted up in this tangled conspiracy. "He always was the celebrity pupil. Followed Eldritch around like a lost puppy at The Owl, remember? The capsule, the cargo...even my dropped gun...he could know about all of it."

"That's...you don't know that."

"That's why I said he *could*. But I bet he does. It would explain why he was so jumpy to see me."

"There's no proof, Reece." Hayden folded his legs beneath him and pressed his face into his hands, like he did when he was tired. "No factual evidence."

Reece looked at his wet rag of a friend. "Why are you defending him? He doesn't exactly delight in your existence."

"Because you can't blame someone for something out of mere gut instinct...it isn't right. Besides, you're naturally inclined to blame things on Liem. You always have been."

"True, but that's only because he's such a sisquick."

"Reece?" a voice crackled over the interestate com speaker built into one of the four posts of the hovering dock. A small red button lit up beside it with a bleep.

Liem.

Hayden scrambled to hold Reece back, but Reece dodged him easily, punching the red button beside the speaker hard enough to hurt his knuckles.

"Fancy that! We were just talking about you, Liem, and Eldritch, too."

The speaker was silent for a moment, and then Liem's voice came again, a little edgier, "Can we meet? In private?"

Reece gave Hayden an "I told you so" look. As he reached to push the button again and tell Liem to go lie down on an airstrip, Hayden caught his wrist and held it at bay.

"Reece. Meet with him, but please don't bully him. A whole ship of people are dead. You might be able to find out why. Remember that."

Dropping his arm, Reece blew out a hard breath and closed his eyes. The blocks were tumbling in his head; he needed order, focus. A captain picked the farthest point on the horizon and watched it as he steered the ship. To see everything, rather than just the stars underfoot.

He pushed the button. "Meet me in the west library tower."

"You'll come alone?"

"I'll leave my Pan behind, if that's what you mean."

The round library tower was narrow, lined with books accessible only by the vertical translocator running up and down its middle. Liem was waiting on the translocator platform with his dinner jacket folded over his elbow. He frowned impatiently as Reece took his time joining him on the platform and closing the gold carriage door behind him. At the push of a bright blue button on the panel inside the door, the translocator started grinding its way upward, hissing and occasionally spitting steam. Reece had always loved the tower. It was as close to the sky he could get without being in a ship.

"I never liked the tower," Liem said, hanging his jacket over the carriage rail. "I never came here."

Reece stared at the books sliding by just inches beyond the edges of the platform. "Why?"

Gesturing idly, Liem said, "They're all fiction."

It was time to gamble. "No. Why did Eldritch fail me?"

Liem's eyes searched Reece's face, and Reece noticed again how dark they were, almost black. "Eldritch didn't fail you. The judges failed you because of your lack of professionalism in dealing with the meteorite and the failure of your Nyad's systems."

"Right. The meteorite. You really think that's what it was?"

"What else would it be?"

"You were in the flight tower, you tell me." After a pause, Reece ventured, only half-joking, "An alien escape pod?"

Liem's eyes shot open wide, then narrowed dangerously. "Don't say things like that."

"We're in a bleeding tower! Who's going to hear?" Leaning his back against the carriage railing, Reece looped his arms over his chest. This must be really good. Liem was acting as skittish as Uncle Uriah on a bad day. "Liem…you know it's not a meteorite, don't you? Oh, quit acting like a ninny, no one's listening."

"You never can be too careful," Liem whispered hoarsely as he thoughtlessly plucked at the silver cufflinks on his folded jacket.

The translocator shuddered to a stop at the top of the tower, where one solitary window looked out over the grounds. There was the pond, a wide grey rug on a floor of green, and there were Gideon and Hayden, two miniscule dots standing on its dock. The domed ceiling of the tower was painted with a depiction of the Streams that roped around the planet Honora and her neighbors, here portrayed as glittery oil slicks in space.

Liem slid a finger under his collar and pulled it away from his neck as it expanded with the deep breath he pulled in. It must have calmed him to some degree, because he was composed enough to sound almost like his usual uppity self again when he said, "What makes you think it isn't a meteorite?"

"Are you kidding me? You—"

"Humor me." Liem tugged again at the cufflinks. "What makes you think that?"

After giving it a moment's thought, Reece hesitantly explained. He couldn't say why—this was Liem, after all. Maybe his want for answers was making him reckless. A captain couldn't be reckless, not when he had a crew to watch out for.

"You should have left it alone," Liem said, dabbing his face, which Reece suddenly noticed was as white as a sheet, with a handkerchief. "Eldritch could expel you for a whole number of things, now."

"He could, but he won't. Because then he'd have to explain why, and that would direct everyone's attention back to the crash site."

"Eldritch doesn't have to explain anything to anybody. Even Father."

"What do you mean?"

"He's a very powerful man, that's all."

"He still answers to Parliament."

Liem's pause was deliberate, left open long enough for Reece to know that when he said, "Of course", he didn't really mean it.

"The capsule was the strangest part," Reece said, almost as an afterthought. He watched Liem closely. "It had Aurelia's crest on it, and it looked like it could have been one of hers. But that doesn't make any sense."

Liem frowningly rubbed his chin, immersed in thought.

Reece pried a little more. "I've never seen the like before."

"I have."

"You have? Where?"

"It's...not important."

"Dirt yes it's important!" Sometimes, it took Gideon-speak to get a point across. Reece slapped his hands together, fist into palm. "Eldritch had a whole crew of men killed to cover up his tracks. He used my failure to distract everyone from the meteorite's crash. He needs to be bagged! If you have some kind of evidence—"

"I don't have any evidence," Liem hastened to say, holding up his hands, which Reece noticed were trembling. Liem noticed too. He lowered them again with a scowl. "I'm strictly uninvolved in this. You shouldn't have told me anything at all."

"Why for the love of engine trappings did you even want to meet with me? All you've done is give me more holes to fill in." Pausing, Reece studied his brother, sighed, and shook his head. "I'm going to fill them in, Liem. I just hope for your sake that when I do, you've picked the right side. Because I won't withhold any evidence. Even if it implicates you."

Liem set his jaw stubbornly. "This is just like you—setting up some idiotic plan to make you the hero and me the villain. It's not going to change how they see you, you know! Mother and Father will never forget that you chose your second-rate Westerner friends over the future they built for you!"

Reece stepped forward to let brown eyes sear into brown eyes. To Liem's credit, he didn't flinch, just stuck his nose up higher in the air. As if putting it up there would keep Reece from knocking it into his skull.

"You have no idea what you're up against."

"Then give me an idea," Reece said through his teeth.

"I have nothing more to say on the matter. Other than that I have laid the groundwork for you. Just look closely at what I've said. It's there." Reece made an unimpressed face, and Liem added with a disdainful sniff, "You want to know what I asked you to meet me for? Alright. I need a favor."

Reece blinked and in his surprise, accidentally let his anger go. Liem didn't need favors, and he would certainly never ask Reece for one if he did. Not on a normal day, anyways.

"It must be a real heliocraft of a favor. You did, after all, just call my friends *second-rate*."

"I wouldn't apologize if it wasn't. So…I'm sorry. I shouldn't have said that." His look added, "Even if it's true."

"Right. So what's the favor?"

Reclining against the railing, Liem closed his eyes in thought. "As you might guess, I know things, Reece. Things I'm not at liberty to discuss—so don't bother asking." Reece shut his mouth with a click. "For the last eight years, I've conducted research on a matter of explicit importance to the Honoran people…and, in short, turned out more than I perhaps should have. When I'm found out, you'll very likely never see me again. I suppose that might make you happy. I know I've never particularly enjoyed your company. Surely you feel the same about me." Reece didn't need to say yes aloud. "I need you to promise me you'll take care of Nivy."

Reece felt his eyebrows shoot up his forehead. "Nivy? The Westerner girl you're charading as your fiancé?"

His stepbrother's laugh sounded more than a little numptified. "Oh, she's no Westerner."

Reece waited to feel the sensation of surprise that had been pouncing on him all day. Nothing. Part of him had suspected Nivy was something…else.

"You know, I'd be more prone to agree to your terms if you were a little less vague and a lot more likable."

"Nevertheless, I need your word, unreliable though it may be. You can't let her out of your sight. She has no one else. *I* have no one else. In fact, the only reason I'm involving you at all is because you're already involved."

Thinking of the dropped gun, Reece stepped forward so he and Liem were only a hand apart and asked in a low voice, "How involved, exactly?"

Liem hesitated. "More involved than you know. And if you promise me this, I doubt there'll be any turning back. It only gets deeper from here. I learned that the hard way."

"And that's supposed to make me want to say yes?" Well, if he was going to be wading in something, he might as well know if it was water or engine grease. "Alright. You have my word. I'll keep your *fiancé* out of trouble."

The tension slid off Liem's face, and he relaxed, slumping as if he'd been held up by marionette strings. Reece glimpsed a liquor flask stuck through the back of his belt. He thought that tea had smelled a little off, earlier.

"I don't know if you'll be able to do that much. Nivy's very—" Liem broke off to glare at something out the window with an expression of disgust.

Reece sidled along the carriage's edge till he was before the window. They had been in the tower longer than he'd thought; Nix, Telesto and Atlas were high on the horizon while the sun was sitting low, wreathed in smudges of warm color. Hayden and Gideon were still waiting on the dock—Gideon was pacing up and down it, and by his steps, Reece could tell he was uptight—and Nivy was with them, a slight figure sitting with her back to a post.

"One more thing," Liem began as he pressed the button that started the translocator rasping back down the tower shaft. Reece could already tell that this thing was not going to bode well for their tenuous truce. "Keep your Westerner friends away from her."

Teeth grit, eyes determinedly locked on the bookshelves, Reece made himself ease up his stony grip on the carriage railing. Because he knew Hayden wouldn't approve of him nobbling Liem, he pretended he hadn't heard that. With effort.

It was a long, slow ride down the tower.

Reece knew he was glowing—not a happy glowing, but a burning embers glowing, as he stomped toward the pond with his hands in his pockets, Liem a few carefully-measured paces behind him. The rim of the sun was sinking into the western hills, and Emathia would have been under heavy blue shadow if not for the servants bustling about, lighting the oil lamps lining the estate grounds. Everything flickered under their light.

"Reece," Hayden sighed, clearly relieved to see him, but just as clearly stunned to see a harried-looking Liem hurrying up behind him. "Is everything…okay?"

Reece made a noncommittal noise and scanned the dock. Gideon was towering behind Hayden, watching Liem. In the far corner, Nivy had something cupped in her hands and held at eye level so she could stare at it intently.

"Nivy," Liem said sharply, and clucked his tongue. "Come. It's time for tea."

"Haven't you had enough 'tea'?" Reece muttered. Liem's jaw tightened.

Nivy looked at Liem sideways, impassive, before unfolding her hands. A glowbug crept over her palm, and she blew it away, sending it into the air like a tiny shooting star. Taking her time, she stood, dusted her hands, and then strode past the lot of them as if they were invisible. Liem made an indignant noise and stalked after her without another word.

"What did she want?" Reece wondered aloud.

"Nothin' I can figure." Gideon shrugged. "Just came and sat there. Think she was spyin'?"

"For Liem? Unlikely. She's not his fiancé."

Hayden looked surprised. He didn't like to think of people as liars, as they generally were. "No?"

"No. She's his..." Reece began slowly, trying to make sense of all he had learned in the tower. It was like looking under a Dryad's communication board and trying to pick out the one snaking red thread in the tangle of panel feed wires. "Actually, I don't know quite *what* she is."

He started walking away from the dock, down a path that would circle up to the front of the mansion after it meandered through a plot of forest perfect for muffling what he had to say. Gideon and Hayden followed and listened.

Neither said much, but it wasn't for lack of thought, because at the end of the path and the end of the story, when the friends stood waiting for the servants to retrieve Hayden and Gideon's bims, Gideon said, "Here," and held out an Automatic Laser Projector that could've fit in Reece's palm. Count on Gid to find a way to pack at least one gun, even if it was the smallest in his arsenal.

"Might want to be keepin' that close. I got a feelin'."

Hiding the ALP in his waistcoat, Reece raised an eyebrow. Gideon's telltale feelings rarely missed their mark.

"Be careful, Reece," Hayden added, pointedly avoiding looking where he had slipped the ALP. "If it looks like—" He nearly leaped right out of his clothes as a terrible crack of thunder cut him short.

Looking skyward, Gideon frowned. "Don't recall hearin' any storm warnin's."

A raindrop, fat and cold, caught Reece on the cheek. "Me neither."

Even this far into the countryside, the foul weather foghorns in the city of Caldonia blared at unnecessary decibels. Maybe they'd been too immersed in their conversation to hear. Or maybe the foghorns were just one more thing that wasn't quite right about these days.

VII

Glances

After Gideon and Hayden's taillights had disappeared into the heavily dark night, Reece jogged around the mansion till he came to the private iron staircase climbing to meet the door of his personal chambers. He'd have to have a death wish before dragging his soaking wet self through Emathia with Abigail on the prowl, looking for something to bite after her spat with Liem.

His suite was sprawling and luxurious, neat bordering on the absurd. Its green-quilted canopy bed (three times the size of his bunk at The Owl) was made perfectly, no wrinkles, no crooked pillows. The rest of its furniture, nightstands and bookshelves, a wardrobe, desk, and leather armchair, had probably never seen a mote of dust. There was nothing of *Reece* to the room at all. He didn't dare keep out the drawings Sophie had made him, or his borrowed book on Handling, or even his lucky riding gloves, because he's made that mistake before, and it seemed the servants all had orders from Abigail to sequester anything that suggested he had any more personality than the rest of the Sheppards. Sighing, Reece pulled out Gid's ALP and slid it between his two mattresses.

In the suite's head, he dropped his clothes on the floor and closed himself in the water closet, letting the warm water from the spigot wash down over him. He nearly fell asleep right there, and would have if the thunder hadn't kept rumbling the closet walls.

When he finally sank into bed and pulled a blanket over his still-wet head, his dreams were of playing Pantedan foxtail with Liem, who wouldn't stop drinking his tea long enough to make a return pass with tail. Reece tried yanking the teacup out of Liem's hands, and was disgusted when he slopped some on himself and saw that it wasn't tea at all, but black, bubbly tar, like—

Disoriented, Reece leaned up out of his sleep to the sound of a scream, tangled in his blankets. He panted, listening with his heart in his throat. Another scream. Abigail! He rolled off the bed and thrust his hand between its mattresses, gripping the ALP in a hand slick with cold sweat. He'd never heard his mother scream like that before.

Abigail screamed a third time, a horrified wail, and Reece hurled open his bedroom door, sprinted down the hallway, and launched himself down the southern stairwell. On the landing of the second floor, he broke off into the dimly lit corridor he usually tried to avoid. Portraits of the duke's ancestors lined the walls in identical golden frames, all with the duke's probing chocolate eyes, painted with unsettling realism. Those eyes seemed to spring off the canvases, to Reece. They had always been another good reason to avoid visiting Liem's rooms.

Liem's rooms.

And suddenly, the rest of the hallway came into focus. A photon stand was tipped up against the wall, its shade sitting on it like a crooked hat. There was a smell in the air—like sulfur, like hot, smoky metal. Burstpowder? Had there been a gun fight?

Reece felt…asleep. Like he couldn't make his mind catch up to what his eyes were taking in, and his thoughts were all shorting like a bad connection. Earlier today, Liem had said a time would come when the two of them might never see each other again. Reece hadn't thought that would really happen, let alone happen so soon. And he would never have thought it would feel like…this.

In a daze, he walked down the corridor and turned into Liem's open doorway.

Abigail stood in the middle of the suite in her nightdress, clutching her arms around herself. All around her lay the debris of Liem's life. His clothes, torn out of his dresser, his books, ripped from his shelves, his desk drawers, dumped and left upside down. But there was no Liem.

Servants were digging through the mess or waiting on the weeping Abigail, bringing her tea and then a bottle of bourbon when the tea wasn't strong enough. The world moved around Reece. He stood in the doorway and watched.

The soundproof shutters on this floor were all closed; that was the first thing to warn him that the growing rumbling he heard wasn't thunder. The noise swelled for two or three seconds, and then like the crack of a giant bullwhip, broke over the mansion. Abigail dropped her glass of bourbon with a shriek and clutched her ears while the servants dove to their stomachs as if to hide from the terrible sound, but Reece ran for one of the windows and pushed back its shutters, sure he would see the aft burners of a ship disappearing into the hills. That deafening boom had come from an aircraft breaking the sound barrier. Whoever had taken Liem had had a ship close by, maybe even on the roof of the house. A small ship then, Nyad or Furies class.

"Reece," Abigail's tremulous voice called him away from the window. He turned. She looked like a specter, willowy and pale. "W-we must hail the duke. We must tell him. Liem. Oh, Liem."

After a hesitant pause, Reece stepped over the refuse littering the floor and put a hand on her arm. Abigail sniffled and nodded as if this was a good thing for him to do, then, dabbing her eyes with a handkerchief, mumbled, "Who could have done this? The Palatine First. What are we going to do without a Palatine First? If Liem is dead…" As her eyes grew round, she lowered her handkerchief and looked at Reece thoughtfully. "…if Liem is dead, *you* are the Palatine First."

Reece flinchingly drew back his hand. "If Liem was dead, they'd have left the body. That boom? That meant they were running, and fast."

"Then hail Thaddy," Abigail said. "Send him a log and tell him to come home."

"Where is he?"

"Cronus Twelve. He's speaking at the inauguration of their new prime minister. Nine days out, by Stream."

"I—maybe you'd better do it." Reece wasn't scared, not of the duke. It just seemed a shame to break their spell of silence with this kind of news.

Abigail scowled at Reece as she snatched the bottle of bourbon from one of the cowering servants. She pointed a finger at him with the hand clutching the neck of the bottle, for all her superiority, looking more like a drunk than a duchess. "I don't care about your petty feud and your…your big, stupid head! You will hail him, and you will do it now, or so help me, the box-dwelling, bottom-feeding Westerners in Caldonia's filthiest brig will be your envy! Now stop staring and MOVE!"

The gulp was just to wet his throat. Not because he was nervous.

There was a log interface just down the hallway, in the guest room that had been Liem's study for as long as Reece could remember. The room had suffered as many casualties as the last by way of gutted shelves and trampled books. Reece tiptoed around the chaos. It felt wrong to disturb it, disrespectful.

The log interface was a wooden box on the wall with a bulbous lens protruding from its top and a speaker mouth from its bottom. Easing himself into Liem's desk chair, Reece flipped the switch on the side of the box that turned the dull blue light behind the lens on with a soft buzz. At the same time, part of the wall behind the desk folded aside like a stiff curtain to reveal a blinking screen.

He didn't bother recording the moving pictures of himself that usually supplemented the audio half of the log. The first time he saw the duke again, he wanted to be in uniform so as to have something to present of himself, not in his nightclothes with his hair as messy as a jumble of underengine coil wires. And if that was a selfish thing to think at a time like this…it could be chalked up to the fact that Reece was still having difficulty believing any of this was real.

"Sir, this is Reece. There's been an accident."

His message was brief. Every word of it burned in his throat like a shot of Pantedan burnthroat.

After a few minutes, the log interface gave a startlingly loud *beet*, and the sound of the duke's voice rolled out from the speaker, low and smooth and as cold as deep space. Reece involuntarily jumped when the screen winked on, facing him with a head-and-shoulders view of his father. At a glance, he was an older man who had come into his prime past his middle years, getting handsomer with age. He was taller than Reece, fit and square-shouldered, and his head was neatly shaved.

At a glance.

"I'm leaving Cronus now," the duke rumbled. He couldn't see Reece, not with Reece's lens turned off, but he seemed to stare him straight in the eyes. "How is your mother?"

"She's shaken. But she'll be fine."

"Take care of her until I get there."

"I will."

The duke paused, not blinking, his curveless lips pulling tighter at their corners. *Beet*. The interface turned off with a lingering crackle, and the screen went dark.

Slowly, Reece leaned forward and flipped the switch to hide the screen, but he didn't leave. Instead, he slouched in his chair, idly pulled the book sitting on the desk into his lap, and tapped his fingers on its leather cover. He sat like that for some time, tapping and thinking until suddenly, it hit him. *Nivy!* Bleeding bogrosh, he'd completely forgotten!

He stood so quickly that his knees struck the desk on their way up, rattling it and sending pens rolling noisily. Grumbling, he tried to gather them back together before they skittered off the precipice of the desk. With his back bent, and his head level with the shelf over the desk, he stared at one of Liem's antique candlesticks, the stout kind with a flat top and aged yellow wick. Four silver cufflinks sat perfectly balanced atop the candle, one on top of the other. They were the cufflinks carved into the Aurelia's winged emblem, the very ones Liem had worn earlier that day. An odd place to put them, but then, Liem was an odd fellow.

Something nagged at Reece as he replaced the pens, making him hesitate. Scooping up the cufflinks, he held them under his nose and squinted at them. Thread and tattered fabric clung to the posts of the small pins. Liem had either been in a hurry to undress, or his kidnappers had been rough with his jacket and popped the cufflinks loose....and then balanced them on a candlestick? Strange kidnappers.

Or clever Liem.

Bouncing the miniature emblems on his palm and then dropping them in the chest pocket of his nightshirt, Reece crossed the study and turned into the corridor, which was busy with servants and now also sentries that had been called up from the capital to investigate. Abigail was in the middle of it all, fanning herself with her handkerchief and allowing herself to be comforted by several of her maids and a man whose grey uniform's badges named him the Sentry Captain. Reece made sure the ALP was carefully secured under his shirt in the band of his trousers.

"Mum!" he called. Abigail froze in the act of dabbing her eyes and gawked at him. He hadn't called her that since he was an Eleven, but desperate times, desperate measures. He had her attention. "Have you seen Nivy?"

"Nivy?" Abigail repeated vaguely. "Oh, you mean that horrid little ragdoll. No. I imagine she fled the scene when…" Her eyes widened, and she lowered her handkerchief thoughtfully. "Of course! The dollymop must have let some of her dimridge Westerner friends into the mansion and—Sentry Garth, you must have her found immediately—"

Reece was already off and running, leaving behind the crowded hallway. Nivy couldn't be involved like Abigail thought, because Liem had known Nivy would be left alone if he was taken. Why had she run?

It wasn't till Reece had reached the mansion's ground floor that he realized he was still clutching the book that had been on Liem's desk. Crossing the parlor, where a sentry with a voice transcriber was recording the testimony of a maid with her hair in a net, Reece flipped it open. He paused. It was antique-bound with real parchment and fabric, and its pages were so thin, they were nearly translucent. But that's not what held his attention. Every one of the pages was crammed to the edges with writing in a strange language made up of blocks and strange squiggles. What was this? He didn't have time to wonder.

Nivy couldn't have gone far, and she couldn't outrun a bim.

VIII

The Merits of Minding Your Own Business

…laryngotracheal groove in the caudoventral wall of the primitive pharynx…

Hayden was studying. Every other student home from The Owl was probably enjoying the brisk yet sunny weather, but he wanted to make sure he entered his final clinicals especially ready for Tutor Macintosh's infamous exams. Besides, he liked studying. And he *was* enjoying the nice weather.

The Rice home was number nine on Chippenham Way, a road of identical brick row houses all squeezed for space. It had a flat face with green and red ivy curling about its white shutters, an iron picket fence in bad need of repainting, and a single rocking chair on its front step. Hayden was sitting cross-legged on his patch of a yard, letting the sun light up the pages of his books, *The Neurosciences* by G.H. Smith and *Qualifying for Physics* by Rudolf Ayre.

He moved his hand back and forth over the pages of his journal, filling out an equation with fervor. Numbers spoke their own carefully articulated language. That language made sense to him, while a lot of other things, things that Reece or Gideon excelled in, confounded him. Girls. Guns. Those were the two biggest, but there were more.

Speaking of Gideon. Tapping his writing wand thoughtfully against his chin, Hayden looked up just as the Pan vaulted over the picket fence. He was supposed to be staying with the Rices for the holiday, since Mordecai's house was back on Atlas, but since leaving The Estate at Emathia, he hadn't been to Chippenham Way once.

Hayden wearily set down his journal and looked him up and down. He hadn't changed his clothes, he hadn't shaved, and he looked decidedly smug. The first two weren't all that surprising, but the smugness was something to be uneasy about.

"Do I even want to know where you've been?" He'd probably been catching up with some of his more unruly Pantedan comrades or visiting with Ariel, his stop-and-go Pantedan flame (who Hayden thought was a bit of a nightmare, to be honest).

With a wolfish grin, Gideon crouched down on the grass, letting the canvas bag he'd been lugging over his shoulder flop down beside him. "I would."

"You and I aren't exactly similar. But fine. Where—"

"Pullin' a job for Mordecai. Paid pretty good too, considerin'—"

"Stop, just stop." Hayden waved his hands with a grimace. "Forget I asked."

Gideon shrugged, eying Hayden's books with a twinkling eye. Hayden's study habits had always been a joke to him. Him, who never scored higher than a .3 in any of his classes except his GR's (Generally Required courses, meaning his handcraft elective, which was Artisan Carpentry, and his physical application class, which was…was it Ship Repelling or Gentleman's Combat?). Thinking this, Hayden colored and busied himself with piling his books in a neat and alphabetized stack. It hadn't been a very nice thing to think.

"We have a bed made up for you on the sofa, and there's celery soup in the coolant pantry."

"Sophie home?"

"She's at the postal office," Hayden answered, lifting his books with a strained grunt. Gideon swept them out of his hands with one arm and started for the house. "She's been working a lot recently."

"Huh," Gideon humphed, kicking open the front door. He marched in through the kitchen, narrowly avoiding a run-in with a tower of Father's books, leaning in a precarious stack on the yellow-tiled floor. "Those ginghoos in her department still botherin' her?"

Gently closing the door, pulling off his scuffed-up clogs, and then lining them up evenly against the wall, Hayden laughed. Sophie worked sorting mail for pneumatic tube delivery with other children her age, including some rough-around-the-edges Westerners. There had been a few times she had come home from work in tears because of a hurtful word from one or another. One of those times, Gideon and Reece had been visiting. The way Hayden understood it, their next visit had been to the postal office.

"Not since you spoke with them, no."

Gideon snorted as he dropped Hayden's books onto the wooden countertop. "You mean not since we mussed them up."

"You didn't do that."

"Dirt straight we did."

"They were just a couple twelve-year-olds."

"Big 'uns, though. Almost had to shoot them."

Hayden opened his mouth, cross, but paused when he heard heavy footfall on the drive. He turned around just as his father came rushing in, nearly tripping over the doorstep. He only had one arm in his jacket; the other was struggling with an overstuffed briefcase.

"Boys, there you are," Hugh gasped, panting. Hayden hurried forward to take his jacket and fold it over a kitchen chair. "I only just heard."

"Heard what?" Gideon asked as he opened the tin coolant pantry built into the wall, rummaging around to find the celery soup. He made a noise of triumph and reemerged with a small pot and ladle.

Sitting down with a heavy sigh, Hugh pulled off his spectacles to rub the bridge of his nose. "The duke is coming home."

"But you said it would be weeks yet before he was done on Cronus Twelve," Hayden said, surprised, as he pulled a chair out from the table for himself.

Hugh altogether folded his spectacles and placed them to the side, then laid his palms flat on the table. "There's been…an accident. At Emathia."

CLANG, Gideon heavily set down the pot of soup. "What kind'a accident?"

"Reece?" Hayden added anxiously.

"No. Liem. It's all over the log casts and wireless waves. He was abducted from the mansion last night."

The room was silent for a moment as Gideon and Hayden took this in, each in his own way. For Hayden, that meant putting his face in his hands and absorbing his father's words in thoughtful silence. For Gideon, it entailed slamming himself down into a chair with a grumbled curse that made Hugh frown disapprovingly.

"Abducted?" Gideon repeated.

Hayden said quietly, "Kidnapped."

"I ain't stupid, I know what it means!"

Hayden let him stew, his mind hard at work on something else. The timing. Reece was right—this was all too coincidental to be coincidence at all.

"Would…" Hayden chewed his lower lip as he lifted his eyes to his father's. "Would you happen to have access to the duke's personnel files?"

Hugh considered for a moment, staring steadily at his son though without his bifocals, he probably couldn't see much beyond his nose. After a moment, he let out a breath, felt around till his hand found the spectacles, and stood to start gathering the accoutrements needed for tea, a red tin kettle, a strainer, and a leather sheaf of herbs.

"I do, but that's the last you'll ever hear about them from me. Every last one of them is confidential. Put it out of your mind, boys. The duke will have sentries and Vees on the case. If there was any reason for him to doubt someone in Parliament—"

"Not Parliament," Hayden interjected as he reached into the cupboard behind him to ready three stout mugs for his father. He paused to shudder as the word *Vees* caught up to his ears, tinkering the mugs, giving away that he sometimes still had nightmares about The Veritas, about what Parliament allowed them to do. "Eldritch."

Realization dawned on Hugh's face, followed by horror. He noisily dropped the kettle on the thermal burners. "You are *not* to get involved in this, Hayden! Headmaster Eldritch is not a man to be trifled with! What do you think he would do to you if he thought you were being a busybody? Expel you, at the very least. Promise me you'll leave it alone. If the headmaster has anything to do with this— perish the thought—The Veritas will smell it out."

Ashamed, Hayden made himself small in his chair and avoided looking at Gideon, who he heard snort dismissively. But he didn't know. He'd never met a Vee, like Hayden had when Parliament had sent one to appropriate Mum's body for medical research after The Five Year Pandemic. That's when the nightmares had started.

The kitchen door swung open so unexpectedly that Gideon and Hayden both leaped to their feet, Gideon brandishing his revolver quicker than Hayden could have brought up his fists—not that he did, of course.

Reece stared at them, looking amused, but first and foremost tired, with red, bleary eyes.

"Tea, Reece?" Hugh asked politely, as if nothing were out of the ordinary about the lot of them behaving like a bunch of jumpy first-time-flyers.

"No, thank you." Reece reached into his black flight jacket and pulled out a floppy leather book, which he dropped on the table in front of Hayden with a thud. He pulled his riding goggles out of his wind-tousled hair and pocketed them. "Do you recognize this language?"

Hayden took one glance at the book's strangely shaped letters, like different-sized squares and little decorative spirals, and shook his head. Peering down over his shoulder, his father made a fascinated noise and asked, "Where did you get this? I've never seen such a script...and the book itself...it's in pristine condition, despite its obvious age. Beautiful."

"So you have no idea where the language is from?"

"No," Hayden and Hugh said together.

Frowning, Reece swung a chair about and straddled it. "It was Liem's." He pulled a handful of tiny metal fragments out of his coat pocket and rolled them in the flat of his hand. Cufflinks, Hayden saw in bewilderment. "It's the only thing I got out of his study before the Veritas swept in and confiscated everything down to his dirty socks. That and these cufflinks."

"We just heard, I'm so sorry—"

"Think it's important?" Gideon broke in, grabbing the book out of Hayden's hand and squinting down at it.

"Wishful thinking, I'm sure." Wrapping his fist around the cufflinks, Reece rested his head on his arms and closed his eyes. "But look at the last page."

Licking his thumb, Gideon turned to the last page. His dark eyebrows pinched together. "I don't get it."

"What?" Hayden asked, craning his neck to see.

Reece raised his head and gratefully accepted a cup of tea from Hugh even though he hadn't wanted one. "It's on a few other pages, too. I found it early this morning when I was flipping through there. It struck me as odd after these." He rattled Liem's cufflinks in a fist.

"What?" Hayden repeated.

Gideon brought the book around to Hayden and Reece's side of the table and laid it open on its back. He jabbed a finger at the emblem messily scribbled in the margin of the righthand page—an A inside a circle, inside a pair of wings.

"Aurelia's emblem. It keeps turning up. Like I wish Nivy would." Reece sighed. Aware of the confused looks passing over his head, he explained, "She's gone. She bleeding disappeared with all my answers the same time Liem did. I searched for her all night on my bim, but it's like she just vanished. I couldn't have picked up a trail if I had a Triton-class ship to level the whole forest."

Thumbing the barrel of his revolver, Gideon raised his eyebrows, impressed. "You want I should go look for her?"

Before Reece could say either way, Hugh cleared his throat pointedly, cupping his mug of tea in long, bony fingers. "Reece, Gideon, you know you both are like sons to me. And while I know that doesn't guarantee me any sort of authority…maybe you'll hear me out as a friend." Gideon and Reece both looked up curiously. "Don't do this. The deeper you delve into this—"

"Hey!" Sophie's delighted voice broke in. She was so light and quiet when she walked, they hadn't even heard her come in the back door. Standing in the doorway in a faded yellow dress and bloomers, she looked like a flower, like a bright posy. "Golly, it's crowded in here. I didn't know you were coming over, Reece."

Reece smiled and straightened up in his chair, smart enough to know not to let Sophie think anything was wrong. If she was a posy, she was a posy with the most curious disposition a flower ever had. There was also her knack of remembering things she heard almost to-the-word to consider; it made her a quick learner, a valuable employee at The Postal Office, and a very adequate little spy.

"Does that mean you didn't make me any biscuits?" Reece teased.

Glowing, Sophie stepped up to her father, who stooped to let her plant a kiss on his pale cheek. "I'll make a batch quicker than you can say chimera."

As Reece started teasingly, "Ccchhh....", and Sophie laughed, rushing about to gather her ingredients, Hayden thoughtfully fiddled with the red pin on his father's jacket, a lion's head in the shape of a heart. It had been Mother's. Juliet Rice had had such a strong personality, warm, selfless, brave—lionhearted—sometimes he felt the echo of her here in this house, like she'd left an imprint of herself behind for them. He tried to wrap up himself in that now, to ward off the sudden cold he didn't know if anyone else felt.

Another week passed, the first uneventful one in what felt like ages. Hayden didn't see much of Gideon and Reece, Reece because he was being forced to help Abigail in her preparations for the duke's return, Gideon because he kept slinking off in the middle of the night to work jobs probably of the illegal sort, but he was busy enough on his own. He watched six projector books cover-to-cover, practiced his physician skills on elderly Mr. Muggets next door (who had the hissing sniffles), dug the house out of the dust and disrepair that Hugh never had time to tend to, and tried not to think about what his return to The Owl would entail.

Being friends with someone like Reece sometimes occasioned the kind of adventure Hayden would rather read about. This time, Reece had it in his head they should sneak aboard *The Aurelia*...with her sitting square in the middle of The Aurelian Academy's Museum of Antiquities! It wasn't that Hayden didn't think they might find something of value aboard the ship—there was no denying that her emblem did seem to be showing itself in conspicuous places—but the fact remained. In real life, villains were smart enough not to leave a trail, and protagonists were smart enough not to follow them if they did.

The end of holiday came too quickly. Hayden had only gotten through half of his library when he'd wanted to review all of it, and it wasn't till his second to last day on Honora that he realized he'd been badly neglecting Sophie.

His little sister tapped on his open bedroom door as he pinched a test tube between his gloved thumb and forefinger and lowered it into a tarnished stand already holding three seemingly empty tubes. One of them actually held a gas, if a gas that was a fairly common household commodity. Coal gas.

"Hmm?" he said idly. "What is it Soph?"

"Do you want to go for frozen dairy in the city? I've saved up, I could buy us a trolley ride in, wouldn't that be fun? Hayden? Wouldn't that be fun?"

"Just a minute. I'm almost…blast!" Hayden leaned up off his rusted old desk and glowered at the tube filled partway with dark metallic flecks. "I must have miscalculated. I've done this a thousand times!"

Walking in her birdlike way around the room, her hands behind her back, Sophie said, "Maybe you need a break. Did you hear what I said? Do you want to go for frozen dairy?"

But Hayden was still staring at the tube, the thought of frozen dairy not breeching the buildup of numbers he had bubbling in his head. What had he done wrong? The triphospherine should have started to take on a telling blue tint…but it looked rather green.

Making an exasperated noise, Sophie moved in on the desk, bent over to examine Hayden's array of beakers, and carelessly snatched up the triphospherine in her bare fist, studying it. Hayden yelped and gently prized apart her fingers to take it back.

"Sophie!"

"What?"

After the tube was returned to its safe and proper place, Hayden scolded, "Never do that! Ever! Do you realize what that is?"

Sophie gave him a wry look as she dusted the lap of her blue skirts. "Triphospherine?"

"I…yes, but do you know what it is is? Triphospherine is the base component in burstpowder!"

"Maybe you shouldn't be playing with it, then."

"I'm not *playing* with it, Soph. I'm doing homework, and—look, that's not the point. See this?" Hayden pointed carefully at the clear but not empty beaker. "That's coal gas. Very flammable. If you'd spilled one…if there had been a leak in either…if—"

Sophie suddenly snorted. "If *I* know both those things are mostly harmless on their own, then you certainly should."

Drawing a shaky breath, Hayden lowered his face into his hand and rubbed his forehead. "I wouldn't say *harmless...*"

"Burstpowder doesn't just explode randomly, Hayden. That's why guns that use burstpowder have a flint, and burstpowder shells have a trigger."

"Remind me not to let you alone with Gideon anymore," Hayden chuckled despite himself.

Shrugging, Sophie perched herself on his windowsill and cocked her head to the side. "What's your homework?"

"It's actually quite interesting. You and Gideon would both enjoy it," he said dryly. "It has to do with how triphospherine can cause explosions in The Voice of Space where most projectile bombs fail to because of the oxidant it contains. It doesn't require outside oxygen to create fire."

Sophie looked at him for a minute, computing what he said, and then laughed and kicked her feet. "Oh, Hayden, you're such a brain. Can we please go for frozen dairy now? I don't have to work today, and it's so sunny out." She rolled down her bottom lip in a pathetic pout.

Hayden couldn't help but laugh, though it felt rather weak. Frozen dairy. Something cold to jam up all the worries in his brain.

They did ride the trolley into the city, but Hayden paid for it and told Sophie to keep her savings for the Mead Moon Festival. They left behind the identical row houses with their chipped paintjobs and chugged in the steam-powered boxcar into the eastern end of the Honoran capital, Caldonia. The houses here were still packed together, leaving only narrow alleys between them, but they were wealthy, huge, with steepled roofs and elaborate trimmings often painted in a spectrum of clashing colors.

It was a half hour ride into the heart of Caldonia, where the buildings all loomed, dark and uniform in brick and black glass. The birds perched on their ledges wouldn't have looked real if it weren't for the twitching of their heads that gave them away as they watched the traffic below for signs of littered food. Screaming black owls pressed wing to wing with spotted owls and tiny yapping owlets, snowy owls with their draping wings, and the terrible king grey owls, with their flat black faces and perpetually surprised eyes, all used to the tumult of the city and the ships whizzing by over the buildings' peaks.

And there were *so* many ships, ships Hayden couldn't name but Reece could've recited the engine type and model number for without looking twice. They were mostly small, zippy vessels, but there were a few that had to be Kraken class because of their size. They looked like huge wooden sea ships floating on the clouds, with house-sized hot air balloons suspended above them. Those were the heliocrafts, luxury cruisers, another indulgence of the rich.

There were also automobiles bumbling along the roads, boxy and much less graceful than their cousins in the sky. Bims growled as their drivers tried to maneuver them through the holiday traffic, but there were horse-drawn buggies to be managed as well, and horses never took kindly to the loud rumbling of a bim.

All along the streets, people milled in their fine or else not-so-fine city wear. Milling among the downtown folk, the Westerners in their grungy work clothes and sleeveless undershirts all looked as if they'd been coated in ash, because the downtowners' clothes were as colorful as their houses. The ladies carried parasols and wore pillbox hats with little veils, and a lot of the men had handlebar mustaches or overly wide sideburns that came all the way down to their chins.

"Can we walk by Victoria's Hat Menagerie?" Sophie begged Hayden as he deposited a copper cog into the automated expense till on the side of the trolley. The coin clanked to the bottom of the till.

"Must we?" Hayden pretended to moan as he led her away from the trolley, which started to scoot along again after spraying them with the cold mist of its pipes.

"Please? It's just beside the dairy stand."

"I suppose we could walk *by* it," Hayden teased, "so long as you don't make me walk *through* it..." He trailed off, pausing on the busy pedestrian walkway, as he saw her.

His first glimpse was so brief, he wasn't sure it was really her, but when he pushed up onto his toes and looked out over the shoppers jostling about him, there couldn't be any doubt. Nivy was barreling toward him, wearing the same clothes she had when they'd met, though she didn't fill them out nearly at all now, she'd gotten so thin. Her hair was in a tail on the back of her head that kept whipping her hardened face as she sprinted right through the middle of the crowd, determined to outrun her pursuers.

"Nivy?" Hayden choked, and barely yanked a confused and startled Sophie out of the charging girl's way. Nivy hurtled past, ignoring or not seeing him. The three sentries doggedly tailing her with their ALPs drawn were huffing and puffing when they passed Hayden a second later.

Sophie tugged on Hayden's sleeve. "Do you know her?"

Hayden gaped down the street, watching Nivy disappear around an alley corner, little more than a blur of black clothing.

"I…Soph, do you feel like running? Just a little? To see where she goes?"

With a grin, Sophie plucked up her skirt in two handfuls and started the pursuit, Hayden jumping to follow and probably having a harder time breathing besides.

Sophie led the chase hard down East Capitol Street, then turned into the mouth of the alleyway where Nivy and the sentries had disappeared. It was empty save for disposal bins and a few stray dogs that were yapping at each other's heels, but it broke off at a sharp right angle, and Hayden could hear the echo of the sentries shouting, "Halt! You are bound by law to halt!"

"Come on!" Sophie panted and veered around the bend in the alley despite Hayden's breathless, "Soph, wait!"

Hayden turned the corner and skidded to a gasping stop, heart flying into his throat. The alley was a dead-end. Nivy was gone, but the sentries, hard-faced men in grey uniforms, remained, and Sophie had run right into their midst before she'd pulled herself to a stop.

"What's this now?" one of the sentries growled, frowning at Sophie. "You spying on us, girl?"

"I…no…just…that lady…" Opening and closing her mouth, Sophie took a step back and helplessly looked over her shoulder at Hayden, who hurried forward.

"No, she's not," he insisted quickly, still breathing hard. He put his arms around Sophie from behind, pulling her into him. "We were just playing a game. We didn't mean to disrupt…er, whatever it is you're doing."

"Conducting a chase is what," the sentry said gruffly. He glared out from under the black visor of his hat at Hayden. "You following that 'lady' too, boy? Care to tell me what for? Seen her before, have you?"

Lie! Hayden felt himself going white in the face, and he gripped his hands together in front of Sophie to hide their fidgeting. "No, never. It was just…just a game."

The sentry suspiciously pulled off his cap to reveal a receding yellow hairline and tucked it under his arm. He held out a flat palm to one of his companions, who dug into a pouch on his black utility belt and pulled out a tiny—and so all the more terrible—syringe. Sophie trembled under Hayden's hands, and he tucked her behind him.

"Then you won't mind if we administer a quick compulsor, do you?" Seeing Hayden's expression, the sentry said sternly, "It's perfectly legal, son, The Veritas use them all the time. It won't hurt in the least. Just a prick in the arm. Of course, if you're lying," he flicked the liquid capsule with his forefinger, "we might have to change our methods."

"I—" Hayden gulped. "I might have been—that is, if you'll just let my sister go back and tell my parents, I'm sure they—"

"Alright," the leader sentry allowed, waving a hand. Hayden felt his knees rattle together. He hadn't expected that to be alright at all. "Have her go on then. Like I said," another flick, "perfectly legal."

Thinking frantically, Hayden turned and put his hands on Sophie's shoulders. "Soph, go wait for me at the dairy stand. Everything will be alright."

"Hayden," she whispered, white-faced, "remember what Father always says about not crossing the city sentries? What if…what if they…"

Hayden forced a laugh and was afraid it sounded rather…hysterical. "Don't be silly, Soph. I'm just going to speak with them. Go on, here, take some cogs and order for us, I'll be there in no time."

"Promise?"

"Sure. Absolutely. Just go."

Hayden felt lightheaded as Sophie ran away, throwing uncertain glances over her shoulder as she went. He could feel the sentries moving in behind him, their hulking forms crowding him against the wall. What would they do to him when they found out he had lied?

"Go ahead and roll up your sleeve, son," the head sentry said, smiling a hardly friendly smile.

He had mentioned The Veritas. When it came out out Hayden had lied, would he be given to a Vee for questioning? One of the sentries caught him under the arm as his knees buckled and held him in place as the head sentry aimed the serum over his forearm and then slid it into his largest vein. It was a second before the strange compulsion to talk struck him.

"Now," the blond sentry leaned in close to Hayden, handing the empty syringe to one of his cohorts. Still smiling, he grabbed Hayden's jaw and squeezed till Hayden could feel his teeth cutting into his cheeks. "Were you following us?"

"Yesh." Hayden shook his head, tried to free his mouth.

"Why?"

"Nivy."

"The girl?"

Hayden nodded, sighing with relief when the sentry released his face. Then the man grabbed a fistful of his shirt and slid him up the wall till his toes swayed over the ground, kicking but not touching. One of the other sentries looked on with amusement while the third stood at the bottom of the alley. Keeping watch, Hayden realized as he coughed. Because the compulsor might be legal, but this was something else entirely.

The sentry began, "Where did she—", but stopped and dropped Hayden in a gagging heap when the man standing guard let out a strangled cry.

Hayden massaged his throat and pushed his eyes open even though they wanted to stay closed. Even that took him so long that by the time he'd managed it, two of the sentries were already sprawled on their stomachs, and the third, the leader, was fighting not to be shoved stomach-first up against the brick wall by a very put-out looking Gideon.

"Total breech of conduct! Interference with the law! Assaulting a sentry!" the man roared and then grunted when Gideon flattened his face against the wall.

"Don't rightly care," Gideon growled and drew back a fist.

"I'll have you incarcerated in the deepest brigs in the city, Pan! On the planet!"

Managing to get to his feet, however unsteady, Hayden stumbled across the alley. "Wait, you can't!"

Gideon looked over his shoulder, fist still pulled up to his ear. "Ain't a time to be forgivin', Aitch. These dimridge got no right to be pummelin' anybody, and dirt if I'm gonna let them pummel on you. Now get goin'. Sophie's waitin' for you on the road."

Hayden froze, examining Gideon's grim face. "What…what are you going to do?"

Gideon smirked, but the smirk turned into a snarl when the sentry squirmed and called him a filthy name. "I'm gonna make them forget."

A zap of a gunshot echoed through the alley, and Hayden ducked what would have been a second too late to cover his head with a shout. Even Gideon jumped, shoving his hand behind his belt for his revolver. As for the sentry…he was slumping down the brick wall, leaving a paint stroke of blood behind him. Dead.

"What the—" Gideon started, swinging around with his revolver lifted.

Zap, zap, two more shots burrowed into the bodies of the downed sentries. Hayden dove for them, turning them over, but they were already dead, shot through the heart.

Gideon's revolver clicked as he found the shooter and set his sights on her. Hayden watched the exchange in a daze, unknowingly clutching the bloody front of one of the dead men's uniforms, perhaps trying to wring some life out of it. Gideon with his revolver and Nivy with her stolen ALP stared at one another, Nivy looking down at him from the roof of the building at the head of the alley. She looked resigned. Gideon looked thoughtful.

"Don't shoot! Please don't shoot!" Hayden pleaded. "No one else should die here!"

Not even a murderer. Nivy had *killed* these men. Shot them when they couldn't defend themselves!

Gideon's gun stayed level. "I wasn't goin' to," he said in a low voice.

Nivy must have heard him, because in one swift motion, she let the gun swing down on her finger and then dropped it into the alley, where it shattered. Then she was gone. Just a blur of black clothing.

IX

Babysitter for Hire, Must be Good with Guns

Reece sat stiffly across from Scarlet Ashdown, who stared at him with a smile that would've frightened a Freherian boar. This was the price he paid for leaving Honora before the duke arrived. He couldn't use the family's Dryad to get back to Atlas, not if he wasn't willing to wait around to greet his father when he landed. But even in her fury at his "gall" (her word, not his), Abigail still didn't want Reece riding the bus-ship back to The Owl, not after Liem's disappearance. So here he was. Hitching a ride with the graceful, breathtaking, totally unattainable ship of the Ashdown's, Pegasus class.

"Why am I not surprised at this, Reece? You running away before you have to face the duke," Scarlet said, crossing her legs. Her golden hair was bright against her red dress.

Reece frowned and looked out *Galatia's* window and into the soft blackness of space. His fingers toyed restlessly with the cufflinks in the bottom of his coat pocket. Liem's. "It's not running away. It's avoiding."

"He's not all that bad, you know. He has quite the sense of humor."

"Thank you. I love hearing about how other people know him better than I do."

"And yet you run from him."

"*Avoid*, Scarlet, avoid him."

Reece kept his gaze strained on the window and the streaking stars in the very far distance. If Gideon hadn't been able to pick up Nivy's trail from the alley in Caldonia, he certainly wouldn't be able to, but he still felt like he should be there, trying to keep his promise to Liem. Trying to get some answers. Nivy had killed sentries to keep her secrets. Doing so had confirmed her deep involvement in Reece's budding conspiracy theory.

At this rate, he'd be as numpty as paranoid old Mordecai before long.

"Something is going on, isn't it?"

Reece looked up. Scarlet had removed her sequined hat so that her hazel eyes could probe without obstruction. Her face was solemn.

"What makes you think that?"

Pausing, Scarlet stood, crossed the aisle, and sat next to Reece on the long leather seat so that their elbows brushed. Reece pushed himself closer to the window, but there was no escaping the smell of her, like roses.

"I'm a politician," Scarlet reminded him, playful but grave at the same time. "I feel the waves that humans make on the order of Parliament very distinctly. And there *are* waves."

"With who?"

"Everyone. Something is going to happen."

"You're sounding a smidgen superstitious, Ms. Ashdown." Finally looking away from the window, Reece faced Scarlet in the seat. "What do you know about Eldritch?"

"The headmaster? Well, he's very involved in Parliament."

"Well, he's employed by them, right? So—"

"This is different. He has…a presence. I've seen it in my clinicals in The Guild House. He is a powerful man, there can be no doubt there. Why?"

Shaking his head, Reece looked back out the window. The white fog of Atlas was parting over the Pegasus, lighting their tiny cabin with misty light. Scarlet made a displeased noise and returned to her seat to replace her hat on her head.

"Reece, you know you can trust me, don't you?" she said softly as she rearranged the delicate netting on the front of her hat. "I hope eight years have given our relationship some semblance of a friendship."

Arching an eyebrow, Reece took his turn studying Scarlet—in a completely platonic way, of course. She seemed sincere enough, holding her golden clutch in both hands and frowning worriedly at him. It made him smile, because if there was one thing that could be said about Scarlet Ashdown, it was that she didn't beg anyone's approval that wasn't a superior. So he guessed he was that. Very satisfying.

"I trust you," he reassured her, and she smiled back, thankfully not in that feminine wiles kind of way. "Do you trust me?"

"Yes."

"Then if I asked you to keep an eye on Eldritch?"

"You would have to tell me what for, of course," Scarlet reasoned, gesturing, and paused as the captain of *Galatia* announced their forthcoming landing on The Owl's aerodome. They had passed from the black of space through the atmospheric fog and were now drifting down through fair blue skies. "In a show of good faith."

Reece took his time stretching, standing, and gathering his bags and Scarlet's from the compartment nets overhead. He felt her condition hanging in the air between them, and her growing curiosity, helped on by his hesitance.

"The less you know, the safer you'll be." His answer seemed to amuse her, because she laughed and drew out her tassled fan, sweeping it before her face in full renewal of her flirtatious ways. Reece dropped her suitcase with a scowl. "I'm serious, Scarlet!"

"Oh, I know. It's just so dear, how protective you are of your friends. I'm quite flattered."

Reece stared after her as she glided from the cabin. The girl was totally numptified. With a sigh, he caught up the handle of her suitcase and trundled along after her.

"This is a terrible idea," Hayden moaned, sitting with his elbows on his knees on the pedestrian walkway in front of the Handcraft Center. Reece looked up from lacing his boots. "We're going to get expelled. I can't get expelled, I just can't!"

"Get a grip, Hayden. You're our resident genius; we need you to get us into the museum without setting off any pesky alarms."

Hayden didn't reply, but kept up a steady stream of anxious mutters.

The campus was otherwise quiet. Classes resumed tomorrow, which meant students were either tucking in early or spending their last night of freedom carousing in Praxis. Not that it could be called exactly early anymore, Reece thought as he flipped open his pocket watch and counted the numerals on its pearly face. It was almost fog hour, so the lampposts and their orange halos of light were muted and misty. The perfect night for a caper.

Across the brick road from them was The Aurelian Academy's Museum of Antiquities, a massive dome made entirely of glass except for where rods of thick brown steel separated panes. All that glass was going to be tricky. Reece could see the exhibits, shelves, and displays of books, guns, automata, and antiques from here.

"I can't believe you told Scarlet to watch Eldritch," Hayden said suddenly. Under his knit grey cap, he was frowning deeply.

Reece leaned back on his palms, stretching his legs out over the brick road. "She'll be fine. She's a politician. She's good at slinking around and being a double agent."

"Liem was a politician too. And Scarlet isn't *that* kind of politician. She's a diplomat."

"Oh, buck up. Aren't you the least bit excited about this?"

"Can one be excited about one's professional demise?"

Laughing, Reece tousled Hayden's hair, unseating his hat, and spotted Gideon jogging up the street toward them. He was wearing a black jacket like Reece's and Hayden's, only the sleeves of his were rolled up to his elbows, showing skin as pale as the fog rolling into town.

"Ready to earn your stripes?" Gideon said to Hayden, grinning as he wrapped an arm around his head and mussed up the hair that had already been made a sight by Reece.

Hayden unhappily squirmed out of the headlock. "No."

"Sure you are," Reece tried telling him, putting a hand on one of his shoulders and leading him across the road, toward the museum. "You've got the makings of a great delinquent."

Gideon grabbed Hayden's other shoulder so they could drive him on together. "You're a regular ole' hoodlum."

Hayden groaned.

As they walked across the museum's lawn, Gideon outlined his inspection of the building. Glass all the way around, but one of the maintenance doors was steel. Locked with a robust iron padlock, which he could take care of, and sealed with a seven digit security code for Hayden to crack. They could belly crawl to *The Aurelia* to keep out of sight and stand under the shadow of her left wing while Reece did his part jimmying their way into her cargo hold.

A few moments later Reece was sliding on his belly across the cold marble of the museum floor, looking up at *The Aurelia*, his stomach leaping. He used to visit the museum every day and sit on the bench over by the refreshment dispenser bar just to watch her *be*. She was the first Honoran airship, the mother ship that all others had been crafted after. After generations of aviation advancement, most ships had lost the look of her and her brother Aurelius. They'd gained curve and color, had steel and iron incorporated into their bodies, acquired propellers or lost their wings. Aurelia was a *real* airship, a classic. Her name (the first A of which had the circle and wings around it) was actually hand painted on her wooden hull.

"You gonna sit there droolin', Lover Boy, or are we gonna work this job?" Gideon whispered as he pulled himself soundlessly over the floor. Hayden slipped after him, his clothes squeaking comically against the marble.

Smirking in spite of himself, Reece followed, scanning the lobby of the museum. There was a circular guest desk off to one side of

Aurelia, festooned with banners advertising two tours, one by a live guide, one by a projected actor who would pretend to lead the tour from a cockpit so guests would feel as if they were being flown around the museum. Reece's second favorite exhibit was on the level underground. It was called Food from Epimetheus, and offered sample delicacies from all over the galaxy. The people on planet Oceanus had a kind of edible rock that was surprisingly delectable when smothered in tartar sauce.

Gideon and Hayden stopped beneath Aurelia's wing, taking care to hold close to her side even though they could see that outside, fog hour had struck. Everything was white beyond the glass walls, as if they were sinking in an ocean of milk.

"Alright, girl, talk to me," Reece said quietly as he stood and pressed his hands to the warm belly of the wooden hull. He knew from studying Aurelia in his History of Aviation class that she had a round hatch on her underside that lowered down on hydraulic legs for easy cargo pickup, but exterior cargo bay controls hadn't been incorporated into ships until the last two hundred years, so that was a no go. Her cockpit would have a ladder tray, but that would require climbing on top of the ship. The back exit hatch had probably been locked down tight at her decommissioning. That left…

Groping under the ship, Reece slid his hands along the lip of a panel, found a handhold, and curled his fingers around it.

"Mind your feet," he warned his friends, and pulled back on the handle. With a gasp of compressed air, a hatch dropped open. A mechanic or pirate's best friend—the gut engine nook.

Reece dropped to his knees, crawling. There were rungs in the dropped hatch, a good two dozen leading up into Aurelia's mighty engine, The Afterquin. The only one of its kind. From down below, it looked like a series of fans strung together by hollow tubes and chunks of misshapen metal. But up at that twenty-fifth rung, the Afterquin was a steel jungle.

Reece stepped off the ladder at the tenth rung, into a squeezed aisle leading into what he believed would be the cargo bay, the hub that all the other corridors of the ship joined onto. He hoped Hayden was ready for a long night on his feet. Aurelia wasn't a quarter as big as her brother Aurelius—he had had the capacity to carry over a thousand passengers—but she still had a lot of nooks and crannies to comb through.

The cargo bay looked like the drawings he'd seen in his schoolbooks, if dustier. It had been more than two hundred years since Aurelia had been flight-worthy, and she'd never been opened to public tour, for fear some fanatic might try to break off a part of her to take back to his ship. That's what *The Aurelius* had been for, to gut and dissemble and incorporate into thousands of other ships. Aurelia had been preserved for all of history, and was missing only six or seven of her key components.

"It's so dark," Hayden whispered, standing next to Reece and looking worriedly around the cargo bay. Bridges of mesh steel, wood, and chains crisscrossed overhead, pathways connecting halls on one side of the ship to halls on the other. "Can we turn on some of her auxiliary lighting?"

Reece held up his photon wand, waving its bright yellow beam around. "That's what these are for. Besides, I doubt we could even get her auxiliary systems online. It'd take a dump load of power to wake this baby up." He tossed the wand to Hayden, who fumbled to catch it. "You can stick with me. We'll search the starboard halls. Gid, you take port."

"What're we lookin' for, again?"

"Signs of someone being here recently. Anything related to Liem or Eldritch. Just keep your eyes peeled."

Gideon split off from Reece and Hayden, sauntering down a black hallway, twirling his photon wand around his wrist. Reece thought they should start at the top corridors and work their way down. Get those old steel bridges out of the way while Hayden still had some resolve left.

There were no decorations left on the corridors' walls, though Reece had seen drawings of a time when paintings and tapestries had made the brass and wooden halls almost homey. Now they felt like dark tunnels, narrow, constricting. Reece loved it. He could see crewmembers running up and down the halls to get to their posts, could imagine feeling the soft vibrations of the Afterquin running through the floor beneath his boots.

"The dust on the floor," Hayden said suddenly. "It's undisturbed. Nobody's been this way, not recently."

"Mmhm."

"So shouldn't we try another hall?"

"This one leads to the bridge."

"But if no one's been here—"

"There are multiple corridors connecting to the bridge. They could've come another way." Reece quickened his step, swinging his photon wand. The bridge. How many times had he wondered what it would be like to stand at *The Aurelia's* helm?

Hayden kept pace with him, frowning. "I thought we came here to look for clues."

"What? We are! I just figure, as long as we're here, why not enjoy the experience?" When that made Hayden frown deeper still, Reece sighed. "Oh, come on, Hayden. It's *The Aurelia*. When will we ever get the chance to see her like this again?"

Hayden slowly nodded, but he didn't look best pleased.

The bridge was a step down from their corridor, alone on the level between the upper and lower halls. The narrow stairway leading down to it felt isolated despite its arched ceiling being a clear heavy glass looking out into what should have been open space. Reece descended the stairs with a knot of excitement in his stomach and a pinch of guilt in his chest because of it. Hayden was right. He should be looking for something to help Liem. Not fantasizing about piloting Aurelia into dangerous, unexplored Streams.

Stepping onto the bridge, they paused and looked around. It was spacious enough in whole for a working crew of four or five, but there was only room for two at the helm, for the captain and his first mate. Two ancient leather chairs, some of their padding tufting through their fabric, faced the canopy window crossing the front of the bridge like a visor. Before the chairs was the flightpanel and its levers, buttons, gauges, pedals, and pumps; separating them was the extension of panel displaying the green graph radar. An old-fashioned speaker com dangled from its curly wire over the helm.

Footsteps sounded in the corridor behind them, shaking Reece out of a kind of blissful trance.

Hayden patted his shoulder. "That'll be Gideon. I'll get him." He turned and left Reece staring sheepishly at the flightpanel.

Clearing his throat, Reece spun one of the leather chairs about to face him, sat down, and let it swing back into position. Sighing contently, he let his hands wander from the yoke to the flightpanel, feeling the raised edges of worn buttons, the cool metal grooves of levers. There was a smallish hole behind the yoke he wasn't sure the purpose of—unless it had once held some non-essential part that had gotten auctioned off, a pressure-ometer or a gauge.

Suddenly, Hayden shouted, "*Reece!*" and then cut off with a grunt. Something crashed against a wall with a thud, and it sounded suspiciously like a body. Reece regretfully stood and grabbed the ALP hidden under his jacket. Hayden had probably just tripped, but a little extra caution never hurt.

"What's—" Reece started, jogging up the stairs. He was interrupted by a flash of shadow swinging down from the ceiling, and the hard sole of a boot smacking his hand, knocking his aim askew. He made a noise of surprise as the shadow kicked again and this time sent the ALP flying down the corridor, past where Hayden was trying to stand, holding his broken bifocals in one hand and his photon wand in another.

When the shadow swung again, this time with an arm, Reece ducked and brought up his fists, ready. Hayden switched the photon wand on; a beam of light lit up the shadow from behind. Reece gaped. At Nivy, and at her gun, a strange foreign model that was currently held level with his forehead.

"See, Hayden?" he said quietly, and turned his fists into hands raised in surrender. "I knew we'd find something if we came here."

Nivy looked starved, the hollows of her cheeks deep, her lips chapped, her dark hair a matted mess in a tail on the back of her head. She stiffly gestured with her gun for Hayden to join Reece at the stairwell, which he did blinking and tripping without his bifocals. If she felt sorry for him, that didn't stop her from cocking the hammer of her gun with a menacing click and nodding for them to step down onto the bridge. Guiding Hayden by the elbow, Reece obeyed.

"Where did you go?" he asked as they stopped with their backs to the flightpanel. "Why did you run?"

Nivy raised her eyebrows and wagged the gun a little, and somehow Reece knew what she meant. She had the gun. He shouldn't be asking questions.

"So you're going to shoot us like you shot those sentries in Caldonia."

"Reece," Hayden whispered, "maybe you shouldn't—"

"What?" Reece glanced at him out of the corner of his eye. "She won't shoot. Gid would hear, and then she'd have nowhere to run." He looked back at Nivy, hardening his gaze so there'd be no question as to his not backing down. "What do you know about Liem?"

Nivy tightened her jaw, gun unwavering.

"He wanted me to protect you, you know, if he was taken. He said neither of you had anywhere else to go."

Though Nivy didn't seem at all surprised by this, it made her look at Reece anew, with a gaze almost...sympathetic? Fine. He could use that.

"Do you know if my brother's alive? Is there any getting him back?"

Finally, Nivy responded. A small, stiff shrug. Reece swallowed, finding his mouth dry, and lowered his hands slightly, testing the waters. She eyed him warily.

"Does this have to do with the capsule that landed here three weeks ago?"

Nivy smiled a grim smile and shook her head, but Reece didn't think it was in answer. It was more the kind of gesture a person made when they couldn't believe you weren't seeing the obvious.

"Do you know what was in that capsule?"

She looked right at him then, and lowered the gun to her side. Her blue eyes burned upon his face, and he felt a sort of gravity come over him, as if she was forcing something heavy on him with that gaze, something he should understand but couldn't quite see. He opened and then closed his mouth. He wanted to shout, "*What?*"

"We…we thought the capsule might be some kind of escape pod," Hayden bravely ventured. "Is it?" Something danced in Nivy's hard eyes. Affirmation. "So it carried a person?" He suddenly gasped, and Reece looked at him sharply. "Wait…were *you* in the capsule?"

Reece's stupefied choking noise sounded like a stepped-on crow.

Just then, Gideon lunged out of the stairwell behind Nivy, his revolver held in two hands and aimed at the back of her head. "Drop it!" he growled, standing in the deep stance of a Handler, legs spread, body facing sideways. "Drop it now!"

Reece opened his mouth to tell Gideon to stand down and swallowed his words as Nivy sprang into action, spinning and lifting her gun in the space of a blink. She and Gideon stared one another down like a pair of wolfdogs fighting for territory, each sizing the other up, neither blinking.

"Wait! Gid, lower your gun."

"Not likely, Cap'n."

"Just do it. She's not going to hurt you."

Nivy rolled her eyes back to look at Reece, amused, and Gideon used the chance to strike. Flashing out, he grabbed her arm and rolled it till her fingers uncurled and released her gun. Clearly he hadn't planned on her spinning right on under the arm to come up beside him, pull back her fist, and hit him hard on the side of the face. He took the punch with a grunt and stared at her like she was a creature from the Freherian marshes.

"*Hey!*" Reece snapped again. "I said hold it! Both of you!"

"Please," Hayden added while trying to piece his bifocals back together. "We're on your side, Nivy. Really. Whatever you're running from, we can help you. You can trust us."

Nivy looked doubtful, but she lowered her fists.

For a moment, the four of them stood apart and waited for one of the others to speak. Reece knew he should be taking charge, but his head was dammed up with images, images brought on by Hayden's realization...

They slowly fell into order in his head. Nivy came in the capsule, noticed only by a few—Eldritch and Liem included. Liem made it to the crash site first, took Nivy, chose to protect her. Eldritch found out and had him abducted, and then Nivy came here, to Aurelia, whose emblem had been on her escape capsule. But why?

"Hmph," Gideon suddenly grumbled, turning Nivy's gun sideways and running his eyes from its curving, elongated grip down to the end of its the barrel. The two bits of metal standing up on the end of the barrel—the front sight—gave it the look of a peculiar skeleton key.

Reece didn't know guns, and he couldn't say what made this one different apart from its outward design. But he knew ships; he knew Aurelia. The colors of the gun...half dark red wood, a cherry or rhubarb, and half tarnished gold...they made it as much a mystery as the capsule. Because they made it look like it belonged to this ship. It belonged to *The Aurelia*.

"She couldn't'a shot you," Gideon decided. "This ain't loaded, and anyway, I think it's broke. Never seen one like it, but I'm pretty sure it takes burstpowder, and the frizzen's missin'."

"Where did you get that?" Reece asked Nivy. "Did you find that on the ship? Wait, never mind that for now...Nivy, *were* you on that capsule?"

Nivy shut her eyes for just a second, then, when she opened them, nodded. She held out her hand to Gideon and waggled her fingers, asking for her gun, but he swung it around on his finger and slid it into his belt.

"For safe keepin'," he told her. She dropped her hand, expressionless.

Reece drew a breath, ready to open the floodgates and let his questions pour out, but then paused to listen to a peculiar ticking sound coming from the museum lobby. He hushed the others with a gesture and strained an ear to the silence and the faint *tick, tick, tick*. Bleeding bogrosh. Those were footsteps on the marble.

"Sentries," he mouthed.

"If they're in, they'll be seein' Aurelia's hatch sittin' open any second," Gid added. He grabbed Hayden's sleeve and yanked him to the back of the bridge, away from the canopy window. A heartbeat later, beams of light from high-power photon wands swept across the heavyglass.

"That's our cue." Reece turned back to Nivy, whose face looked especially gaunt in the harsh contrast of the beams and shadows. "What Hayden said about trusting us is true. You can or you can't, but you're coming with us either way." Nivy raised an eyebrow. "Oh, we can make you, alright. Gideon knows a dozen ways to knock a person unconscious, and that's *without* the help of blunt objects."

A distant voice sounded, "Look! Under Aurelia!"

"Know a back way off this boat?" Gideon asked.

Reece considered, and then began feeling his way along the cabin wall till his hand found a padded lever. "We'll use the ladder tray to get on top of the ship. We can climb down her wing and end up by the door."

"Which will probably be guarded," Hayden pointed out as Reece forced the lever. There was a loud rush of decompression as the sealants released the overhead hatch.

Hanging back near the cabin door to make certain Nivy—whose slight frown was the only sign she was fazed at all by their dilemma—didn't bolt, Gideon said, "So long as there ain't more than seven or eight of them, I'll manage."

Enough milky light outlined the edges of the hatch for Reece to make out the ladder folded up against it. With a jump, he grabbed the lowest rung and drew it out. "Hayden after me, then Nivy, then Gideon. Keep to your stomachs." He clambered up the ancient rungs, hoping they could take the weight.

Aurelia was tall enough that the sentries wouldn't spot them unless they were searching the museum's upper levels, which spiraled like a continuous balcony up to the top of the dome. And by their voices, they were under the ship, checking out the gut engine nook. Reece began dragging himself along the smooth metal surface of *The Aurelia*, planting his palms to keep from sliding when the fuselage began to slope down.

He led the way to the tip of the wing, the head of a silent train. He felt Hayden let out a relieved breath down by his ankles when they reached the door and found only one sentry on post, blocking the way out with his considerable width and nervously trading his ALP from hand to hand. Reece waved with two fingers for Gideon to do his business.

Gid always assumed an air of reckless casualness when he was on the prowl. Like a cat balanced on the edge of a fence, daring to leap from post to post because he knew he couldn't possibly fall. In three quick steps, he had the sentry slumping unconsciously against the wall and was nodding for Reece, Hayden, and Nivy to hurry down.

"You didn't hurt him, did you?" Hayden whispered.

Gideon nudged the sentry's leg with his boot. "Nothin' more than a mornin' headache's worth." He grabbed Hayden by the back of his collar before he could inspect the sleeping man. "It's just a bump on the skull, he ain't gonna bleed to death!" He gave him a shove in the right direction, and Hayden, holding his twisted bifocals to his face with both hands, very nearly fell out the door.

Reece waited till Nivy dropped silently from the wing, then latched onto her arm. He wasn't about to risk her running off with his answers again, and if him being a little rough with her as he hauled her out the door for fear she'd disappear again was an overreaction, well, it was her fault for disappearing in the first place.

They ran in a cluster, their photon wands' beams cutting less than a foot into the dense fog. From the Musical Arts building, the bell tower sang its midnight melody, tolling the hour.

"Do you…" Hayden panted as they stopped in the square separating The Owl's motor vehicle stables from the largest of the male dormitories, Linus. "Do you think we were followed?"

"It doesn't matter. We'll have lost them by now." Reece glared into the fog over his shoulder. "We should get back to Taurus. They might search the dormitories if they think it was a student who broke in. We don't want to get caught out of our suites."

"What about her?" Gideon's blue eyes darted to Nivy, who, intent on ignoring him, casually peeled Reece's hand off her arm. "She stayin' with you?"

Hayden made a despairing noise in the back of his throat. "Girls aren't allowed in the male dormitories!" Blushing, he quickly added, "No offense, Nivy, but I've had enough rule-breaking for one night."

Reece said dryly, "Yeah, we don't want to push him too hard. One doesn't become a criminal mastermind overnight, after all."

When it came to hiding Nivy, he had two things to consider. First, her safety. Secondly, the safety of whomever he hid her with. That being said, he didn't have many choices.

"Gideon, take Nivy on your bim and go to Mordecai's. Tell him I have a job for him, and that it'll pay well."

"A job?"

Nivy looked up at Reece as if anticipating what he was going to say. He returned her unenthused look with a smirk.

"Babysitting."

X

N...I...V...Y

He wasn't gonna say he wasn't as mystified as Reece and Hayden were by the girl...he just thought he might understand her a little better. Not because he knew anythin' about where she'd been or what all she was hidin', but because he knew the look'a someone resigned to livin' on the run. Dirt hard not to, when you'd lived in the western slums'a Caldonia and seen folk that ain't ever had a meal that wasn't taken off'a someone else's plate. Most'a those folk hated havin' to steal, but they did what they had to to keep livin'. Nivy had that look about her.

She waited patiently while he rolled his bim outta the stables.

"Don't try anythin' funny," he warned her. Usin' his heel, he kicked the bim to life and settled himself on it. Nivy sat behind him and tentatively put her hands on his shoulders. "Grab around my middle if you don't wanna fly off."

After a pause, she roped her arms around him, weavin' her fingers together rather than actually touchin' him. Good enough.

It started rainin', turnin' the back roads to Mordecai's into a minefield'a muddy potholes. Couple'a times they started to twist in the mud and Gideon had to plant a foot, but Nivy still didn't grab hold'a him, just sat quiet and still like an owlet on its perch.

"You don't say much, even for someone who don't talk," he said, spittin' out the rain runnin' down his face. Another mile down the road, Praxis's lights showed blurry and blue through the rain. "But you're gonna have to learn to. The cap'n ain't gonna—bleedin'—" He jerked his handles sideways and saved them from tippin' over in the mud. Then he shifted down, puttin' the bim in a lower gear.

They put-putted into Praxis's abandoned downtown, in between shops with darkened storefronts and lampposts that flickered through the rainfall. Instead'a stoppin' in front'a the gun shop, Gideon drove his bim right onto the pedestrian walkway and rolled it around the corner'a the buildin' and into the three walled shed where the shop tools were stored. A tunnel ran from the shed into the basement'a the shop, which Mordecai had refurbished, made his home.

After Gideon had turned off his bim, he crossed the shed and pulled the tambour door to the ground, lockin' it in place. He turned. Nivy was against the wall, gazin' at the different mallets, tongs, and wedges.

"Hey," he barked. When she looked up, he knelt, grabbed hold'a the handle to the trapdoor, and held it open. "In."

The tunnel was lit with lamps that smelled like old oil, and it had floors'a gritty cement and bellyin' walls'a dirt and beams. It was long and straight; the round door at its end, an old escape hatch from a dissembled Nyad, had fire glow creepin' under its bottom.

Liftin' the hatch, Gideon jerked his chin at Nivy, and she ducked into the livin' area. Kinda looked like one'a them old sea ships, with its wooden beams and creakin' floors and the bulbous woodstove in its corner, blushin' red with flames. 'Course, most'a the house was just parts salvaged from junkyards, condemned buildin's and the like. Here a table that was actually a piano with its keys gutted, there a photon chandelier made outta an old sea ship helm. Mordecai could make somethin' functional outta any kind'a junk.

"What's this, now?" boomed a tenor voice from the kitchen. Mordecai stepped through the saloon-style swingin' doors and brought a cloud'a pipe smoke with him. He fanned it away from his white push broom mustache. "Well, heckles and hoots, you dirt brought a girl to see me, finally."

Gideon grimaced sideways at Nivy. "This here's a job from Reece. He wants you to keep an eye on Nivy, make sure she don't go nowhere."

Mordecai leveled a stare at him and smacked his lips around the stem'a his long black pipe. "Wish I had more jobs like that. Sittin' around and watchin' pretty girls." He waved with his pipe for Gideon to join him in the kitchen. "Nivy, is it? You just sit tight and make yourself comfortable in front'a the fire. I'm gonna have me a word with my grandson. When he comes back, I reckon he'll be a tad more polite."

In the kitchen, Mordecai sat in one'a the metal desk chairs The Owl had thrown out a few years back. Tappin' his pipe on his chin, he asked, "So who is she?"

Gideon leaned against the tin countertop holdin' a couple'a days worth'a dirty dishes. "Don't know. She came outta that capsule I told you about."

"Really? An alien. That's fascinatin'. What's Reece fixin' to do with her?"

"Not sure. Not your place to ask, though."

Blowin' out his mustache, Mordecai leaned back in his chair and kicked his feet up onto the kitchen table. He was still wearin' his work boots, all charred with burstpowder and scuffed. "I just wanna make certain he ain't gonna bring Parliament down on our lovely establishment. Sometimes that boy's gotta head like a goose."

Gideon snorted, not disagreein'. Suddenly aware'a the cold metal seepin' through his shirt, he reached behind his back and pulled out Nivy's strange gun. Mordecai lowered his pipe and squinted so that the lines about his bright blue eyes gathered.

"That's a pretty iron if I ever seen one."

"It's the girl's. It's busted; I'm gonna try to fix it up."

"For her?"

"For me. Trust me, I ain't ever puttin' a gun in that girl's hands."

"So you brought her to a gun shop. And folks say I'm the crazy one."

Examinin' the gun by holdin' it level with his eyes and glarin' down its barrel, Gideon muttered, "Reece's idea. Anyhow, where can I put her up to sleep?"

"We don't exactly got guestrooms. Put her on the cot or the couch, whichever one you don't want. Or whichever one you *do* want, if you wanna be all gentleman like."

Gideon blew out a long breath. He knew Nivy was just a job, but she *was* a girl, and girls had that thing about them where they generally liked to bathe more than once a week. She might fancy a stand in the water closet, not to mention a clean change'a clothes, though Gideon himself didn't have any that wouldn't fall right off her. He had a box'a his mum's old stuff, though. Leah'd been tiny. Maybe he'd find somethin' that wasn't eaten through by mothballs.

He found Nivy hunchin' by the woodstove, drippin' wet, her teeth chitterin'. She glanced over her shoulder at him without really liftin' her eyes.

"Come on," he said stiffly. "I'll show you where you can wash up."

The head was positioned off'a Mordecai's personal workshop so he could rinse down after work. Gideon stood at the door and waved Nivy in to show her what knobs to turn to make it so the water wasn't scaldin' hot, as it tended to be. Then he backed away from the spicket and waited for her to get started.

Nivy stared at him, foldin' her arms over her chest awkwardly. "What?"

She widened her eyes with meanin'.

"I ain't leavin'," he snapped. "I don't wanna have to shoot you, if you try runnin'."

Rollin' her eyes, Nivy held up a finger and twirled it around, askin' him to turn. He recoiled, felt his face goin' red like a beet.

"Listen, you ain't gettin' nekkid while I'm in here. Just—just wash with your clothes on."

Sighin' silently, Nivy started pullin' her hair outta its tail. It fell down past the middle'a her back. Hesitantly lookin' at him, she motioned as if brushin' her hair, then held out a hand. Gideon irritably pointed at his own hair, which never stopped lookin' like it had bed head.

"Does it look like I own a brush? Use your fingers."

Well, that ended up takin' about three times longer than it should've. He was dirt near positive she dillydallied on purpose, too.

He ended up sittin' on the floor by the door while she stood in the stream'a water and rung out her sticky clothes. He dug through his mum's old box and picked out the only thing fit to be seen, a short sleeved nightgown with funny little stichin's around its gathered neck. Nivy took it from him and then firmly pointed him out the door so she could change. He obliged. Still red as a beet.

She emerged in the gown, wet-haired and still wearin' that black ribbon necklace of hers. The gown funny on her because she was so skinny, which made him remember that she probably hadn't eaten. He wasn't really tryin' to be hospitable on purpose, but he was supposed to be helpin' keep her safe, and that kinda entailed makin' sure she didn't starve to death.

They silently returned to the sittin' room together, and Gideon pulled the retractable cot outta the wall under Mordecai's old oil paintin' of Panteda.

"You'll sleep here," he grunted at Nivy, who was waitin' by the wayside, her hands behind her back. "I'll be on the couch. I'm a light sleeper, in case you was wonderin'."

Since the kitchen was attached to the livin' area, he felt alright leavin' her on the cot and steppin' out to see if he couldn't find somethin' halfways edible to keep her alive with. He dug up some room-temperature butterscotch puddin' and a pear and some dried beef, and carried them out to her with a glass'a famous Pantedan burnthroat.

He found Nivy sittin' with her knees pulled to her chest, studyin' the paintin' over her. Gideon knew she was famished, so was surprised when she started in on the puddin' good and slow. As he made up his bed on the couch, she slowly polished off the lackluster meal and downed the burnthroat without coughin' even once.

When Gideon bent over to take away her dirty dishes and add them to the heap in the kitchen, she pointed at the paintin', curious. He glanced at it even though he knew it by heart. Crimson grasslands and lakes bluer than a summer sky, cliffs carpeted with moss, fields full'a wild antlered horses. He frowned and looked away again.

"Panteda. Where I'm from."

He stood to go, but with worrisome quickness, Nivy snapped out a hand and caught his wrist. She looked back up at the paintin', eyebrows pushed together in question.

"It ain't there no more. Got burned up in war."

It was odd, talkin' (in a manner, anyhow) with someone who didn't know about Panteda and the Eudoran Civil War. Sometimes that was all Gideon felt his life was about, the war. First half had been about survivin' it while it swallowed his family and left him and Mordecai alone. The second half was about livin' on Honora and tryin' to forget it had ever happened. Either way, it all came back to the war. Kinda felt like he'd never stop runnin' from it.

Risin' to her knees on the cot, Nivy pointed at the paintin', then spread her hands in a graceful kind'a way.

"Yeah. It was nice," Gideon said, watchin' her carefully as he stacked the dishes against the wall. He'd move them later.

For a long moment, they stared at each other, not talkin', and not just because Nivy couldn't. Then Gideon lamely nodded at the the paintin'.

"The place you're from. It anythin' like that?"

She was like a wild animal retreatin' into its cave when someone got too close. Shuttin' out his words, Nivy rolled up in the heavy quilt on the cot and turned away.

"Fine," Gideon growled in her direction as he pressed his back into the couch's uneven cushions. "Hope you like the cot. It's like sleepin' on plywood."

Gideon expected Reece first thing in the mornin'. Could hardly wait for him to come, actually, because Reece was good at makin' things unawkward, at sayin' all the right things at the right time and makin' people laugh. Gideon didn't care about bein' bad at that, but the quiet between him and Nivy was an uncomfortable sort.

"Sit here," Gideon instructed as he upended an empty barrel in the corner of a dim upstairs workshop, the smallish one away from the other gunsmiths'. It was past time to start the day, and Reece still hadn't shown up. "Don't talk, don't touch nothin', and don't get in the way."

Nivy lifted herself onto the barrel and folded her legs beneath her. He grabbed his weldin' helmet and sat it on his head, but before lowerin' its screen, put on a pair'a leather gloves with just the fingertips cut outta them, because his were all calluses anyways.

Mordecai strolled into the workshop, wearin' a leather tabard with a tool belt and smokin' a cigar. His wavy white hair was pulled in a tight tail away from his brass weldin' goggles. "Don't you let him talk to you like that, Nivy Girl. If he gets your goat, you clock him one, alright? Split his face clean open, if you like."

"This is a job, old man," Gideon told his grandfather as he opened one'a the many drawers built into the cave-like walls'a the workshop and pulled out the gun he'd left half finished before holiday. "Quit bein' so nice. I've gotta class tonight. I won't be here to make sure she doesn't kill you."

"Kill me?" Mordecai twirled his cigar between his lips as he picked up a thermal torch and spun its dial to adjust the heat settin's. "Wha'dya do to him, Nivy? He seems to think you've got some kind'a problem with shootin' folk."

She kept her face guarded, but Gideon thought he saw her wince a little before the shield went up.

Mordecai gazed at her through his goggles. "Well, now. That's interestin'. You ain't denyin' nothin'. I've gotta bit'a problem with it myself, truth be told. Once shot six men in one day. Over a llama. Not *physically* over a llama, you understand. Just *because'a* it. Anyhow—"

Forcin' Mordecai and Nivy outta his thoughts, Gideon turned his unfinished artwork over in his hands a few times, to refamiliarize himself with its weight. "I need a couple more grams'a scrap metal," he realized aloud. He frowned over at Mordecai and pointed a finger. "Watch her. No more flirtin'."

Downstairs, he grabbed a couple'a hard steel pegs picked up at the locomotive tracks, bounced them on his palm calculatingly, and then slipped them into the front pocket'a his lap apron. He couldn't'a been there more than five minutes when Reece and Hayden stumbled in the shop's front door, pantin' and lookin' like they'd run all the way from The Owl.

"Somethin' wrong?" Gideon asked, reachin' without thinkin' for his revolver. A habit from Handling since he was eight years old. Back then, he hadn't used a revolver—he couldn't've, not with little kid arms and hands. He'd forged this revolver when he was fourteen, and it'd taken every bit'a two years to work up the forearm strength and dexterity to wield it like he could now.

Reece glanced at Hayden, who had doubled over and put his hands on his knees. "We've been drafted."

Gideon dropped his hand. "What?"

"Battle drafted. Recruited into the Honoran military by lottery."

"But…there ain't no war goin' on…"

Interruptin' him with an impatient gesture, Reece started for the staircase, towin' the gaspin' Hayden along behind him. "Forget that. *Both* of us drafted, on the same day? Not only that, but on the day after we broke into Aurelia and kidnapped Nivy?"

Mouth twistin' around a grimace, Gideon grunted, "Guess that does seem a bit much. You think someone wants you outta their way?" His grip tightened on the steel pikes just thinkin' about it, and his steps fell heavy on the stairs he marched up behind his friends.

"Reece…" Hayden panted, "Reece i-isn't even s-supposed to get drafted. He's exempt. Palatine…Second."

"Which means someone inside Parliament set me up. I'm thinking Eldritch." Reece paused at the top'a the stairs, briefly listenin' to the metallic grindin' of Mordecai's tools. "Where's Nivy?"

Gideon started to answer when he felt a flicker'a somethin' inside'a him. "Hold up. Why didn't I get drafted?"

"You can't be," Hayden explained. He'd replaced last night's busted bifocals with another one'a his hand-me-down pairs. This one had thick, square red rims that were too wide for his face. "Aliens are prohibited from serving either voluntarily or involuntarily. No exceptions."

"So—"

"So Eldritch will find some other way of making sure you butt out of his business." Reece looked from doorway to doorway, eyes narrowed. "Nivy?"

Frownin', Gideon jabbed his thumb toward the workshop where by the sound'a it, Mordecai was still whettin' somethin' down. Reece pushed past him, rollin' up the sleeves'a his jacket as he went.

"Wait," Hayden held Gideon back with a hand. "Gideon, you've got to talk sense into him."

"Huh? What about?"

Hayden glanced over his shoulder to make sure Reece had gone and couldn't hear what he was sayin'. "Reece is glad he got drafted."

Gideon squinted after Reece. "Don't seem like it."

"Well, he's not happy about being set up, but he'd never be allowed in the military under other conditions. He can fly in the military. Pilot a ship without being captain."

"So why do I need to talk him outta it? You know how he feels about flyin'."

Sighin', Hayden rubbed his tired eyes, which were red-rimmed even without his bifocals. "It's my belief," he began in his textbook voice, "that Reece and I were drafted so that we will be out of the way *permanently*."

"You mean...dead?"

"What better way to get us killed and have no one to blame for it?"

Gideon thought for a moment. "Cattle stampede?"

"That was a hypothetical question."

"Just sayin'. There are other ways."

Raised voices from inside the workshop brought the two'a them back to attention. Gideon picked up his feet and jogged through the door, hand diggin' for his revolver and bringin' it up in a taut arm.

Reece and Mordecai were havin' a standoff, Mordecai separatin' a very displeased lookin' Reece from a calm-as-ever Nivy, who had risen from her barrel and was standin' with her hands in fists at her sides.

"I'm not going to hurt her!" Reece said in an exasperated voice a key short of a shout.

Mordecai puffed out his mustaches. "Then you shouldn't tell her you're gonna. I'll not abide empty threats in my house. If you're gonna make threats, they should at least hold some water."

Reece threw out his hands with a growl. "I don't have time for this. I hired you to protect Nivy for me, not *from* me."

"You didn't ever sign the contract."

"What contract?"

"Why, the one I'm gonna go write up right now. About not threatenin' pretty girls under my roof and raisin' your voice above polite decibels."

"Mordecai—"

"Bird-on-a-stick?"

"What?"

"It's what I'm callin' my new recipe. I'm gonna go make some." Mordecai chuckled at Reece's nonplussed expression, winked at Nivy, and waltzed outta the room to the tune'a his own whistle.

"Wow," Reece muttered. "I'd forgotten how *completely* crazy he is."

Gideon shrugged. Mordecai wasn't half as crazy as he made himself look—he just liked throwin' people, puttin' them off balance until he could get a handle on them.

"Nivy," Reece began, becomin' stern again as he scanned the girl up and down. She'd changed back into her old clothes this mornin', and if they still looked a little tatty after bein' washed, well, at least they were mostly clean. "No more games. No more running. I need to know what you know."

Unrollin' her fists, Nivy turned about and started idly lookin' over the messy tables framin' the room, now and again pausin' to pick up some spare part and turn it around in the light with a kinda offhand fascination. Gideon could hear Reece grindin' his teeth.

Hayden shot him an anxious look, but he waved it off with his gun. Reece had this under control. If he didn't, he would'a turned to Gideon and asked for assistance. Nothin' much. Just a little muscle flexin' to remind the girl he was there and had a gift with breakin' stuff.

"I said I wasn't going to hurt you, and I won't. But I *can* turn you in to Eldritch."

Nivy froze with a punch held between her thumb and finger. Her hair swayed against her back as she turned to face Reece and his frown with one'a her own.

"Liem was keeping you away from him. You give me some answers, and I'll do the same. I swear, whatever reason you want to stay out of the headmaster's hands, I'll protect you, even help you. All I want is to know what's going on. And how Liem is involved."

Sighin' silently, Nivy frowned down at her hands. Seemed to be gatherin' herself up to do somethin' she didn't want to do. Lookin' embarrassed, she touched her throat with her hand, tapped it, and shook her head.

"Well, you can write, can't you?" Reece said, already reachin' into his jacket to pull outta small journal, one'a the old fashioned kinds with real carbon paper. He stopped in the act'a retrievin' a pen when Nivy, blushin', shook her head. "You can't write?"

"But you *can* read?" Hayden ventured hopefully.

Nivy's mouth twisted sideways, and she shrugged one shoulder.

"Not really?" Hayden interpreted for her. "Well, that's problematic. Why can't you read? Didn't anyone ever teach you?" Not bein' able to read was to Hayden what not bein' able to breathe prolly was to a normal person. "*No?*"

"Hayden," Reece sneaked in smoothly. He and Gideon shared a smirk. "You should teach her."

"Well...maybe I will!" Hayden announced, nobly puffin' out his chest. "Nivy, I'm going to teach you to write, read, and—"

"That's all she needs to know. I just need information from her." The cap'n added with finality, "However she can give it to me."

And that was that.

Because their classes had been in the mornin', Hayden and Reece stayed through the afternoon. Gideon was able to finish up his commissioned gun while Hayden worked at gettin' Nivy to understand the Epimetheus alphabet, which she picked it up right quick after her first few fails at drawin' letters. Always, Gideon watched her closely, not entirely bought by her and Reece's deal. Aside from not bein' able to talk, she seemed close to normal. But Gideon was short'a forgettin' how quick she'd been to put bullets in those sentries in Caldonia.

Afternoon passed, and the rain from yesterday came again for dinner. Which was Mordecai's exotic bird-on-a-stick recipe, washed down with burnthroat. Mordecai regaled Reece and Hayden with stories from Panteda that they'd already heard ten times, and they humored him, laughin' in all the right places and askin' things like how he'd gotten away with what he'd gotten away with and how somebody had replied to somethin' witty he'd said. Nivy listened, but she didn't laugh, just quietly cleaned her plate and then practiced sketchin' letters on her napkin.

When the cuckoo clock on the wall let out a hoot, Gideon gratefully rose from the kitchen table and grabbed his ridin' coat from its peg on the wall. Time for his Advanced Artisan Weaponry class.

"We'll save you some dessert," Mordecai offered as he struck a match on the table and lit up his cigar. "I call it 'bird in a cake'. Or 'cake on a stick', whichever you like."

Gideon chuckled as he shoved his arms through his coat, mostly at Nivy's dismayed expression. "Don't bother. It's gonna be a late night. You stayin' here?" he asked Reece and Hayden, who looked at each other and shrugged.

Hayden helpfully started stackin' everyone's plates. "We might as well. Nivy and I are almost halfway through the alphabet. We're making good progress."

"Then we're staying," Reece announced. "How soon till she starts writing words?"

Nivy carefully scratched somethin' on her napkin, then less carefully wadded it up and chucked it at him. He caught it before it smacked his forehead and curiously opened it. Then he laughed.

"There are two L's in troll, and no E. I commend the endeavor, though."

Gideon left them like that, closin' the hatch door behind him, glad to shut out the voices for the calmer sound'a rain hissin' down outside.

The rain became a full-fledged storm in a matter'a minutes, drenchin' him as he rode in the murky light back to The Owl. He glared through his steamy goggles. Life had been more or less simple before the capsule and Nivy and Liem had fogged things up. He wanted to go back to makin' guns and goin' on heists with Mordecai. Least that kind'a danger was familiar. This kind just weren't right.

The headlights came outta nowhere, dull yellow photon bulbs fixed to the fronts'a bims like his. He made room on the road, but as the five riders passed him in a blur, they still nearly crowded him into the ditch. Growlin', he veered back into the middle'a the road before he could get whacked outta his seat by a branch.

His back tire suddenly started swervin', draggin' noisily. Deflatin'. Usin' his front brakes, he tried to slow the bim before it could hurl him off, but he'd been goin' fast, and the brakes screamed in protest, handlebars rumblin' under his gloved hands.

The bim jerked to the left, hard, and he flew off to the right, into the grassy ditch that helped break his fall. He rolled out his momentum, gruntin' when he slammed to a stop with his arms tangled up under his back. Groanin', he tested his legs. Nothin' was broke, but his forearms were skinned practically bare.

On the road above him, the five other motorists pulled up to a stop. At first he thought they were comin' to help. Then he saw one'a them climbin' off his bim, reachin' behind his back, and his Handler instincts sent a jolt through his muscles. He rolled outta the way'a the shockgun pellets that exploded in the damp soil beside him and deftly whipped out his revolver. He managed to pump out two rounds that dropped two'a the strangers like sacks'a coal before somethin' like a hot knife sliced open his eyebrow, sendin' him reelin'. A bullet, skimmin' his forehead.

Turnin' up outta his stagger into the second'a the four Handling stances, Gideon held down one'a the revolver's three triggers and twitched his wrist three times. The barrel swung up and over on its ball with a *click-bang, click-bang, click-bang*. With blood streamin' in his eyes, only one'a the shots was deadly; the other two were just cripplin'. But he was standin', and they weren't. That's all that mattered.

Except he was startin' to think the graze over his eyebrow wasn't just a graze, because he didn't get two steps before he started seein' white spots and hearin' his loud and raspy breathin' inside his head. His legs bowed inward, and he collapsed, joinin' the others on the ground.

XI

Round One, Eldritch Trumps Reece

"Is he going to be alright, Hayden?"

"I—"

"'Course he is. He's a Creed. We got skulls like bleedin' batterin' rams."

"Even so—"

"I mean bleedin' figuratively of course, not literally. Though he is still bleedin' a lot, ain't he?"

"Mordecai," Hayden said firmly, leaning up from over Gideon with a roll of gauze in one hand. "I'm going to have to ask you to leave so I can concentrate. Please. If you go down to the smoking lounge, my father and Sophie would be happy to make you some tea."

Reece speechlessly shook his head as Mordecai, grumbling to himself, turned from the suite, taking the musty aroma of tobacco along with him. With him no longer clogging the doorway, Nivy was able to slip in from the corridor. Her eyes fell on the makeshift work table that Gideon was sprawled limply across, as pale as the sheet beneath him.

"If Mr. Rice and Sophie hadn't spotted Gideon's bim on their way into Praxis, he could have died," Reece told her severely, tapping his fingertips on his folded arms. "Someone tried to kill him."

Without looking away from the table and Gideon, Nivy spread her hands as if at a loss.

"Yeah, yeah." Reece returned his attention to Hayden, who was stitching Gideon's torn eyebrow back together with swift and smooth precision. "Can you tell what happened?"

Sighing, Hayden paused to massage the small of his back. "Well, for starters, he crashed his bim and landed on his arms." He gently lifted Gideon's arm and studied the shredded skin stuck to it. "Father said the bim's back tire was blown out. Shot. He couldn't whether that was on purpose, or if they had been aiming for his back and missed. Can you help me roll him over? It shouldn't wake him, he's pretty sedated."

"They?" Reece repeated as he slid his hands under Gideon's back and tried painstakingly to flip him onto his stomach. "What makes you think there was—bogrosh, he's heavy!—more than one of them?"

Face reddening with the effort of moving Gideon's considerable mass, Hayden choked out, "His revolver was missing five rounds."

"Hayden, I'm inclined to believe—" Reece grunted as at last, Gideon settled on his stomach. "—you've been hiding a detective behind all your genius."

Blushing at the praise as he gingerly rearranged Gideon's tattered arms, Hayden mumbled, "It's just common sense. I checked his revolver while you all were bringing him in."

"Lucky your father and Sophie were in town."

"Yes. Lucky."

Suddenly, Gideon groaned in his sleep, quieting the both of them. Hayden set to work piecing his skin back together and sealing it with a solvable medical glue, and Reece entertained himself with thoughts of what he'd do to the person responsible for this. Thunder and lightning alternated strikes while rain tapped endlessly on the outside windows.

After a while, Sophie came to the door with a tray of steaming teacups, peering in before entering. Her face whitened when she saw the bloody gauze and smelled the disinfectants in the air.

"How is he?" she asked Reece in a peep of a voice as he took the tray from her and sat it on his unmade bed.

"He'll be juggling knives again in a couple of hours," he assured her. He pretended not to see the short glance Hayden threw him over his bifocals.

"Shouldn't we have taken him to a medical facility?"

"Hayden's a medical facility on legs; he's all we need." And they didn't need anyone asking questions about a Pan being brought in with a gunshot wound to the head. That was the last sort of attention they wanted.

Hands playing with the fabric of her bright pink skirt, Sophie quietly said, "I've never seen him looking like that before. It looks like someone could break him in two, if they wanted."

Smiling, Reece put an arm around her and pulled her into his side, so she could rest her blonde head on his chest. "Nah, they couldn't. You should have seen me and Hayden trying to roll him over."

Sophie started to giggle, but as her eyes glanced over his shoulder, she gasped instead. "You!" she yelped, very nearly stopping Reece's heart.

Nivy, perched with a knee bent to her chest on the windowsill in the corner, raised her head. Florescent lightning flooded the room and made her look for a second like a wild, roosting creature. Reece had all but forgotten about her, which made him shiver, because in that second she'd looked like the kind of thing you never wanted to forget was in the room with you.

"You're the girl from Caldonia!" Sophie squeaked, pointing.

"Good grief, Soph," Hayden scolded, straightening out the tin tray of tweezers and forceps he had bumped. "I almost stabbed myself with an ophthalmoscope." He paused, looking to them with an expectant look. His face fell a little. "That was a joke. You can't stab yourself with an ophthalmoscope. *This* is an ophthalmoscope." He held out a flat, blunt instrument with a miniature photon globe fixed to it.

After a beat, Reece laughed, and he felt Sophie melting under his arm, relaxing to the sound. "Sophie, this is Nivy. She's a…friend of ours. Visiting."

Sophie quirked her head to the side and considered Nivy. "From where?"

Reece was saved from having to lie by Gideon making an odd glubbing noise that, as it turned out, was supposed to be words.

"Waaa…goo….onnn?"

"I thought you said he'd be out till morning," Reece said, leaving Sophie to join Hayden by the table.

Hayden was too busy pushing open one of Gideon's eyes and looking into it with his opha-whatever to answer for a minute.

"Interesting," he mumbled to himself, thoughtfully tapping his tool in his palm. "I wonder if his adrenaline levels—well, never mind that. I'll put him under again."

"Don't bother," Gideon finally got out. He managed to open his eyes on his own to look first at Reece and Hayden, then at Sophie, who held his gaze. Clearing his throat roughly, he said, "Biscuits?"

Sophie's face split into a grin. "I'll go make some up in the kitchenette! I'm glad you're alright, Gid!"

As soon as she'd planted a kiss on top of his head and scampered out of the room, Gideon clenched his eyes shut and made a sound that Reece had never heard from him. One of bone-deep agony.

"Forget it." Hayden opened the leather satchel at his feet and started digging around, causing a cacophony of rattling glass. "You're going back to sleep."

"No, that ain't it." Before Hayden or Reece could stop him, Gid leaned up and swung his legs over the edge of his bed. He winced when he saw the backs of his arms, running with veins of glue. "If I'm here, that means they must'a got away, huh?"

"There was no one else around when Father and Sophie found you." Snapping on a fresh pair of medic's gloves, Hayden checked Gideon's pulse, eyes, and ears.

"Lay mushta mood bear bed," Gideon rumbled around the tongue depressor Hayden was forcing into his mouth.

Reece put a hand on the overeager doctor's shoulder to keep him from gagging Gid. "Come again?"

Gideon spat out the depressor with a sour face. "I said, they must'a moved their dead."

"Dead?" Hayden gasped. "You…you *killed* them?"

"A couple, anyhow." He eyed Hayden, all the more menacing for the new scar dividing his left eyebrow in two. "They was gonna kill me, Aitch. Did what I had to."

"But surely you could have, I don't know…shot out their kneecaps instead?"

Remembering not to forget Nivy again, Reece glanced back at her. She was peering out into the storm with her forehead pressed to the window, for all the world, seeming oblivious to their conversation. Sophie came in with biscuits for Gideon, and then her big brother, blinking in surprise at his pocket watch, sent her to the guestroom where their father and Mordecai were staying for the night.

"Girls in the dormitory," Hayden tsked under his breath, dividing his anxious look between Sophie's retreating back and Nivy. "What next?"

Reece didn't want to know the answer to that. They'd been through enough turbulence as it was; surely now that he and Hayden had been drafted, things would calm down until they were shipped out for off-world training, wherever that might be. He was going to guess on Castor or Leto, two of Honora's ally planets. Castor had tropical jungles and giant lizards, and Leto, well, he kind of hoped it wasn't on Leto. For a few reasons, but mostly, he didn't like the thought of it always being night there.

There was a heavy quiet hanging over the suite as Reece cleared off his desk and spread out the physical clues he had to study—just the ancient book and Liem's cufflinks. Nivy came and stood at his shoulder, her hands tucked into her armpits. He didn't think he was imagining her eyes widening ever-so-slightly as they found the book.

"I'm not crazy," he told her, laying one protective hand on the worn leather tome. She twitched. "Aurelia's emblem is here and here, on these things Liem left behind for me to find."

"That we *think* he left for you to find," Hayden interjected from where he was fluffing a pillow for the bed he was making Gideon on the couch.

"Okay, we *think*. But it was also on your capsule. And a little more than twenty-four hours ago, we had our run in on the Aurelia herself. You were there looking for something, weren't you?"

Her chest rising with a silent sigh, Nivy lifted a hand and tipped it from side to side. *More or less.*

"Don't forget about the gun," Gideon muttered through his teeth as he limped toward the couch.

Reece slapped his palm on the desk, energized by the reminder. "I'd forgotten about the gun. Can I see it?"

Gideon paused above the couch, looking on the verge of tipping over onto it. He touched his hip as if remembering something, then, scowling, spat, "They must'a taken it. I had it when I left Mordecai's."

Twisting around with sudden liveliness, Nivy threw out her hands, then propped them in fists on her hips. When Gideon, Reece and Hayden returned her angry look with blank shares, she rolled her eyes and made a gun with her hand that she shook vehemently in Gideon's direction.

Gideon went as red as a ripe cherry. "It ain't my fault! You don't gotta get all—all—prissy!"

Even though it was hard to concentrate with Gideon growling at Nivy pretending to use her fake gun to shoot him, Reece was able to seize one of the niggling questions floating around in his head and voice it. "Why would they want the gun? Nivy?" She looked back at him, expression dry. "Got an answer for us?"

"Even if she does, she can't give it to you until I teach her how to write. And she can't very well learn to write without getting some decent sleep, which I am currently prescribing for all of us," Hayden said, taking off his bifocals, stretching out on his bed, and pulling his blanket up over his head with finality. "Doctor's orders."

Reece was the only one with an early class the next morning, so while the others were still traipsing through slumberland, he was packing the datascope containing his class notes into his satchel and hurrying about the suite with his hair standing every which way and only one of his pant legs tucked into his boots. At the last second, he scooped up the mysterious book and Liem's cufflinks. He rarely went anywhere without the cufflinks anymore; any time he noticed their slight added weight, he made himself remember Liem, wherever he might be. The cufflinks felt heavier than usual in his pocket today.

He heard someone stir as he opened the suite door and turned to look at Nivy in her nest of blankets in the corner. Her eyes were open, staring enviously at the book beneath his arm. When she met his stare, she gave her head a short shake and then rolled over in her blankets. He wasn't sure she'd been entirely awake, but the longing in her eyes had seemed lucid enough. He locked the suite door behind him.

Campus was big enough that students in The Owl's crisp black dress were never crowded, but still, there was a distinct feeling of busyness coming back from the holiday, when everyone had new tutors to impress and new classes to tackle. The students Reece walking with on his way to the engineering building hurried as much as he did. As he hurried, he tried spitting in his hand and smoothing down his hair to no avail. All it did was draw revolted looks from some pretty Sixteens who had been smiling at him a second ago.

Airship Engineering III was taught by a papery old lady in an olive drab jumpsuit named Tutor Agnes. Reece had seen her around before, usually in deep discussions with burly mechanics that had come seeking her advice. Her short, curly white hair was tucked back in a handkerchief.

"The airship," she began in a voice like dusty chalk as she circled the glass-walled classroom with her hands behind her back, "is the soul of pioneering, of exploration. And it is the only body that can survive the vacuum of space, which would kill you and me by explosive decompression in a matter of moments. It is a marvelous being, is it not?"

"Yes ma'am," the class intoned, Reece included. He glanced around at his classmates as he tapped his data wand on the edge of his desktop. It was mostly the old crew, students who'd been at The Owl for aviation from the beginning. The Ailey brothers, Silas and Jesse, caught his eye and grinned while Molly Brewer glared over his head, ignoring him.

"Everything we do in this class will be on the clock," Agnes continued, still prowling from desk to desk. "When your crew is depending on you to fix their ship and save their lives, there can be no hesitance. You must learn to deal with the pressure."

Molly raised her hand importantly. "Ma'am? We're not studying to be mechanics, we're studying to be pilots."

Agnes paused, then sniffed disdainfully and raised her reedy little voice so that it carried to the back of the room. "Mark this down, all of you, if you please." There was a soft whirr of datascopes powering up.

"There is a reason a captain is called the captain, not the pilot, when he is in charge of a ship. A captain is not just a pilot. He is the doctor. The cook. The mechanic. He is a chameleon of duties, the paramount of which is understanding the workings of his vessel and not being an ignorant passenger who simply believes a wing will swing to port when ordered to without knowing why. Also, Ms. Brewer? Mechanics save lives every day. It is a noble calling. If you cannot stoop so low as to aspire to be one in my class, you may take your things and kindly leave so that I do not have to get angry every time I look at you."

That was when Reece knew that he and Agnes were going to get along very well. Behind Molly's back, Silas and Jesse gleefully bumped their fists together.

Agnes was a pusher; she expected nothing short of excellence out of her students, even the ones who didn't have a mechanical bone in their body. Reece himself had never been much good at fixing ships, though he understood their workings well enough. Real mechanics, ones like Agnes, were good because they had a knack for it, not just the sense to hook a snozzle to a thrunge plate.

"Mr. Sheppard," Agnes forebodingly clicked her clocker to cut its ticking short, "that was shoddy work, for the time you put into it."

Reece held up the undulator he'd reassembled, squinting at it. "I don't think it looks *that* bad."

"That's because you're an amateur with little aptitude and no flair for the art. I once taught a Twelve who did that in twenty-two seconds."

"Twenty-two seconds? Really? Wow. Give him my congratulations."

"Save your wit for the engine room. And you can tell *her* yourself. She is doing a guest lecture for me in our afternoon session." Agnes smiled; her wrinkles turned into well-used smile lines, and for a second, she looked more like a grandmother than a hard old crow. "Now, let's see you disassemble that in thirty seconds. Remember, at thirty-five, the heat compressor will combust and burn you and your crew alive."

When class broke for lunch, Reece wasn't the only one who stumbled out of the room glassy-eyed and with engine grease on his face. Campus was busier now that it was midday, but most of the students were on their way to the great pillared banquet hall where meals were served four times a day. Reece weighed his hunger against his desire to see how much more Hayden had been able to teach Nivy this morning. He'd probably think clearer on a full stomach.

Rolling up the sleeves of his jacket, Reece merged into the stream of students on their way to lunch.

"There you are," someone with a breathy voice said, startlingly close. "You are a very difficult young man to track down." The hand on his shoulder felt strangely like a restraint.

Glancing up, Reece tried to keep his face from showing the panic suddenly streaming through him like waves of electricity. Headmaster Charles Eldritch, so lean he seemed almost skeletal, had a slight stoop in his back from putting his head level with Reece's.

"Me, Headmaster?" Reece affronted an easy smile. "Sorry about that. With just getting back from holiday—"

"Was it a very eventful holiday, Reece?" Eldritch's lips curved, patronizing. The portly Robert Gustley was shuffling along behind him, scrubbing the sweaty forehead showing beneath the rim of his bowler cap with a handkerchief.

With blood pounding in his head, Reece made himself shrug. "Well, I assume you heard about my brother, Liem."

"Indeed I did." Eldritch gave his shoulder a pat. "A most terrible thing, the kidnapping of the Palatine First. Honora is a sight to behold. Your brother's face is the only thing on the evening wireless waves."

"It *is* terrible," Reece agreed carefully, evenly. With the headmaster hunching over one of his shoulders and Gustley panting like a racehorse behind the other, he was starting to feel a little crowded. "But whoever is responsible will get what's coming to him. The duke will see to it."

Eldritch chuckled as he straightened to his full height. "Alas, but I do not think the duke has much power there, my boy. Not anymore. Perhaps back in the day when we had kings, not dukes, but these last eleven generations, Parliament and its democracy have been Honora's origin of power."

They were coming up on the banquet hall and its tall white steps, where several dozen students were spread out with books or trays of food in their laps. Reece stopped walking to face his stalkers with a frown.

"Why were you looking for me?"

"I wanted to congratulate you on your induction into the Honoran military," Eldritch crooned, extending a slim hand with a gaudy ring on one of its fingers. "I just heard this morning. You must be thrilled at your luck. It seems you'll be piloting a ship after all."

After a pause, Reece shook the hand. "Thank you, Headmaster." He tried to release the handshake, but Eldritch clung to it, covering Reece's hand with both of his.

"The final stretch of a student's career at The Academy is pivotal, Mr. Sheppard. Often, he or she is tempted to let…distractions…hinder their focus. But distractions can be dangerous." Eldritch's eyes suddenly flashed, and he gave Reece's hand a cold, unwelcome squeeze. "For your career, I mean. The last thing you want to do is disappoint your parents."

"Well," Reece freed his hand, "I'm wouldn't say the *last* thing. I mean, it's down there, but certainly not below becoming a traveling mime, or eating someone I know."

Eldritch's smile tightened impatiently. "Then your friends. The Rices, the Creeds. It is sadly true that the ones dearest to you are the ones hurt the worst by…bad choices."

He was threatening. Threatening Reece's friends. Stepping up toe-to-toe with Eldritch, Reece glared into his face, his sunken eyes and sunken cheeks, imagining how Hayden would bemoan this story when he heard it.

"I will protect them from the consequences of my choices."

Gustley paled. Students did not speak to the headmaster in that hostile tone.

Eldritch's eyes narrowed, looking strange paired with his amused smile. "You are a fascinating specimen, Reece Sheppard. I wish you the best. I will grieve the day when no one is there to protect *you* from the consequences of your choices."

I bet you will, Reece thought.

"Sorry," interrupted a Westerner voice, sweet and soprano. "But did you just say Reece Sheppard?"

Gustley, spluttering his objections, was pushed aside by a wink of a girl with a face that tickled Reece's distant memory, with freckles and white-blonde hair braided over her shoulder. Her cheek was smudged with the same black oil peppering her grey jumpsuit.

"Oh, there you are!" She beamed at Reece. "Almost didn't recognize you. Agnes told me to introduce myself, said you're really clever with engines. Well, Agnes don't say that about nobody, so I thought that even though we've kinda already met, there wouldn't be no harm in meetin' again."

"Er—" Reece glanced sideways at Eldritch, who was gazing down at the Westerner girl in clear contempt. "Hello?"

"Hi!" The girl stuck out a dirty hand. "I'm Po Trimble, remember?"

"Er—"

"Wanna grab some lunch? I hear they're servin' crab cakes today."

"Sure?"

"Swell!" Po faced Eldritch for the first time, and her freckled face turned cool. "You have a nice day now, Headmaster." Then she turned on the heel of her clunky black boot and started up the stairs of the banquet hall, as self-possessed as any lady would have been despite her appearance of having just crawled out of a gut engine bypass.

Watching Po give the Headmaster of The Aurelian Academy the cold shoulder left Reece feeling as speechless as Nivy, so he hadn't quite gathered his scattered thoughts back together when Eldritch suddenly reached out and clasped his wrist.

"Good day to you, Mr. Sheppard," his whisper rattled. He pressed something smooth and rectangular into Reece's captured hand, snapped his fingers at Gustley, and left. Strolling between the students in his tall dark suit, he looked to Reece like a terrible bat trying to blend in among bright birds.

Reece gazed down at his old gun, feeling a jarring spike of alarm as he recognized it, and then shoved it under his jacket. Anger crowded into the space between his scattered thoughts. It had all been a game of wits between him and Eldritch, and he had just lost terribly.

XII

It Only Gets Deeper From Here

Reece caught up to Po in the buffet line serving vegetables, and grabbed himself a plate even though his appetite had sunk to the pit of his stomach. Po saw him, and after spooning herself a glob of orange squash, went ahead and spooned him a helping as well.

"Trust me," she said brightly, "just put a little sweet cream on top'a that, and you've got yourself the healthiest dessert this side of the Epimetheus."

Blinking, Reece said, "Uh, thanks. Listen. What was that between you and Eldritch? You seemed—"

Po sighed and gestured with a serving fork with a carrot skewered on one of its tines. "A mite unfriendly, I know. But with Eldritch, you gotta…what's it called?...establish dominance. You gotta do that straight away, or he'll walk all over you."

She took off again at a brisk, bouncing walk, veering toward the bread line. Reece hopped to stay on her shadow and tried to remember where he'd heard that chirpy voice before.

"Have a lot of experience with him?"

"Not really. Just one really bad one, when I told him I was quittin' The Owl." In the bread line, Po picked out the butt of a greenish loaf of bread and settled it next to her squash, careful to keep the two foods from touching.

"Quitting The Owl?" They drifted toward the pasta line. "You mean you're not a student here?"

"Oh, heck no! Haven't been since I was a Fourteen! I dropped out to help my brothers with their shop in Caldonia. Eldritch didn't like me leavin', to be honest. Agnes had told him I was a prodigy, and he wanted me to be The Owl's prodigy, not nobody else's. So we got in a bit of a spat when I told him I was goin' and he couldn't stop me."

When Po seemed satisfied with the eclectic foods she'd gathered, she led Reece to one of the two-person tables under the hall's tall, pointed windows looking out at The Owl's busy sidewalks. A waitress came and poured them glasses of dark green limeade, and Po said thank you and told her to have a wonderful day. Being with Po, Reece felt as if he'd accidentally fallen onto some other planet. A planet of chirpy birds and meadows and rainbows.

The answer suddenly rang like a bell inside his head. Where he knew her from. He almost choked on his limeade as he realized, "You rode beside me on Bus-ship Ten, didn't you? You were the little mechanic girl!"

Po looked down at her food bashfully, stirring her squash and noodles together. "Is that all you remember me from?" she asked. When Reece said nothing, stumped, she glanced up and blushed. "I sat behind you in class before I left The Owl."

"Which class?"

"Um. Beginner Aerodynamics. Alien Anthropology. Literature and Composition."

"Huh."

"Arithmetic I and II. Honoran Economics. Zoology," Po continued. She put down her fork and narrowed coffee-colored eyes at him as he cringed. "What kind'a person takes eight classes with someone and doesn't bother rememberin' their name?"

"*Eight*? We had *eight* classes together? What were the other two?"

"Piano and Paintin'."

Vaguely, very vaguely, Reece recalled a tiny blonde girl playing a jaunty saloon tune in Amateur Piano and getting rapped across the knuckles by Tutor Clevenger. He'd been a Thirteen then, in the midst of turning his parents and Liem against him. He'd burned most of the memories from that period out of his mind.

He and Po proceeded to talk mechanics and aviation over first and second helpings and then dessert. Being an airship mechanic, Po had a natural affinity for ships, but she hadn't flown on much but bus-ships, so begged Reece for story after story about Nyads, Dryads, Furies, Kraken, and even the mysterious Spectre ships of the Veritas. To Reece's great envy, she and her brothers had been hired three times to run diagnostics on Aurelia, and had even done work on the Afterquin.

"I don't care if she's the oldest ship there is. Engines like Aurelia's can't be duplicated. The Afterquin's just..." Po groped for words, gesturing. "Honestly, I don't know how we ever made it to begin with."

Gnawing on the end of his fork, his forehead gathered in concentration, Reece asked, "Po, how much to you suppose Aurelia's been altered since she was decommissioned?"

"Altered? Wha'dya mean?"

Reece put a foot up on the windowsill and glared into the sunshine. "Don't you think it's strange she never had escape capsules? If she's the elite, why didn't she have a way to save her crew in an emergency?"

Po chewed on this for a moment, slowly dragging her fingertip over the whipped custard left on her plate and then sucking it clean. "Well," she drawled, "here's what I think. You know how Aurelia's designed to look so pretty? She ain't like them heliocrafts with all their unnecessary bells and whistles. She's simple. Well, all the ships that came after her had capsules, but they were the exterior kind that fixed under the wings and hugged the sides of the ship like leeches or somethin'. Aurelia wouldn't'a had that design, because it wouldn't'a been keepin' with her simplicity. But she could'a had pods inside'a her to be shot out the hydraulic hatch on her belly. We always assume that that hatch is for loadin' cargo. But it could'a also been for *sendin'* cargo, primarily escape pods, out in a hurry. Hey, where are you goin'?"

As Reece pushed in his chair and started pulling on his jacket, he said, "It was really good meeting you again, Po, but I've got to go."

"Where?" She checked the unwieldy watch on her wrist that looked like it had been crafted out of scrap metal. "We've got class in ten minutes! Reece? Reece!"

But Reece was already jogging out the door, leaving her alone with a frown, two trays, and a pile of dirty dishes.

Reece had been right in assuming Gid, Hayden, and Nivy would return to Praxis—he'd figured Hayden wouldn't keep Nivy at the dormitory for a second longer than he had to. He found the three of them in Mordecai's small backyard, surrounded on all sides by a fence of unkempt hedges. Gideon was kneeling with a piqued face beside his bim, trying to fix a new rear tire to it, while Hayden and Nivy were sitting in a hazy patch of sunlight, sharing Hayden's datascope.

Reece stopped before Gideon and his bim and frowned. "Is she salvageable?"

Gideon grunted as he jimmied the rear rotational pin with a clock wrench. "She'll run. But those bleedin' sisquicks did her a number."

"They did you a number, too."

"Yeah," Gideon smirked, "but *I* heal."

Hayden joined them, running his hands through his hair tiredly. Reece peered over his shoulder at Nivy, who was manning the datascope on her own, tapping its screen and every once and a while shaking her head with a silent sigh.

"So. Can she spell 'troll' yet?"

Folding his arms over his chest, Hayden mustered up a stern look, pointedly ignoring Gideon's chuckle. "Probably. She's doing well, considering your unreasonable expectations. I mean, we have no idea where she comes from, let alone what the typical means of communication is there. For all we know, her people may be accustomed to…to drawing on cave walls or—"

"*Drawing!*" Reece shouted, startling Hayden as he grabbed his shoulders. He turned about and barked, "Nivy, come here!" Catching Hayden's disapproving look, he exasperatedly added, "Please!"

Taking her good old time, Nivy moseyed over, handing Hayden his datascope so he could check her work. The glance she cast Reece had the look of a challenge; it made Gideon return to working feverishly on his bim, and Hayden focus on the datascope with undue amounts of concentration.

"Don't give me that look. You brought this on yourself. Just as soon as you can tell me what I want to know, you're free to go wherever you want."

Nivy stopped him with a short flick of her fingers, then started signing, one gesture at a time, until he figured out what she was trying to say. She wanted to strike a bargain. Her answers, for—

"A ship?" Reece repeated incredulously. "You're kidding, right? A ship? Can you even fly?"

She pointed at him, pretended to steer a yoke.

"Me, fly you? If that's your asking price, you'd better have *a lot* of answers for me. First I'd have to find a ship, and then I'm not even licensed to fly in the Streams, so…" Rummaging around in his satchel, he produced a piece of carbon paper and a quill. Nivy gazed at them suspiciously. "It doesn't have to be anything fancy."

With a sigh that picked up and then dropped her shoulders, Nivy took the quill, flattened the paper out on her palm, and gave him a look.

"Okay," Reece began, scratching his head. "Uh, tell me where you came from."

She stared at him, flatly disbelieving, then put her pen to the paper, drew a circle with some blotches on it, and shoved it back at him. A planet.

Reece made a face as behind him, Gideon snorted. "Very informative, thanks. What Stream is it near?"

Nivy scrawled a big X on the paper.

"None?"

Reece was a little skeptical about that. The Streams went everywhere in Epimetheus. There were several that were popular—the one that lanced around Honora, the one en route to Oceanus, Castor, and Apollon, and the handful that looped around the sun—but there were hundreds more that weren't as well traversed, Streams that could be dangerous, Streams that pulled unwary travelers into the Voice of Space and left them stranded. Planets that weren't near Streams typically weren't inhabited.

"How's that work?" Gideon wondered aloud from under his bim.

"Well, Atlas's coordinates could have been preprogrammed into her capsule by its operating ship. Then there wouldn't necessarily have been a need for a Stream to carry it in the right direction," Hayden explained, glancing at Nivy for confirmation. She nodded.

"Did your capsule somehow come from the Aurelia?" Reece butted in. The emblem on the capsule, the book, the cufflinks—that was the thread that ran through all the puzzle pieces, the one thing that connected Nivy to Liem to Eldritch.

After a pause, Nivy shook her head, but stopped him with a sharply-aimed finger when he tried to go on. She put on a very pointed expression, willing him to continue on the path he'd started down.

"Did it come…" Reece squinted, concentrating. "…from Aurel*ius*?"

The expression grew more pointed, and she stared into his face in her intense way, as if trying to burn her thoughts into him.

"Not from either of them, but from a ship like them? *Exactly* like them?" More yes's. That shouldn't be possible. *The Aurelia* and *The Aurelius* were the original airships, the only two of their kind, more mother and father than brother and sister. There couldn't be another. "Where, Nivy? Where is the other ship?"

Knowing this was a climactic moment for Reece, Nivy dramatically pointed at the drawing of her planet.

"But if your ship is just like Aurelia…and it came from *your* planet…"

Nivy set to drawing again, connecting quick, sketchy lines, sweeping the quill in a loop. She thrust her hand out and presented her finished piece to Reece.

After he had looked at it, he turned to sit on the house's back stoop, dropping his head into his hands. Aurelia was Honora's. She and Aurelius were cornerstones in Honoran history, the blueprints for every Honoran airship. But Nivy's drawing of Aurelia's famous emblem had been connected to her planet by a thick, resolute line.

"Aurelia and Aurelius came from Nivy's planet." Saying so aloud felt like a betrayal of everything he'd ever believed.

"You sure?" Gideon muttered, and Reece heard the insistent flapping of Nivy's drawing as she shook it for him to see. "Yeah, but how can you *really* know that? Those ships are a couple thousand years old?"

His hope snagged by the question, Reece dragged his head up to see Nivy's response. Glowering at Gideon, she pointed at herself, pointed at Aurelia's emblem, and then made her hand soar like a ship till her finger came down and landed on the depiction of her planet.

Hayden made a fascinated noise even as he sat by Reece and put a consoling hand on his shoulder. "She came here to retrieve *The Aurelia*. To take it back where it belongs." He peered up at Nivy, squinting as if he were examining her through a micro lens magnifier. "I assume that's why you were on Aurelia two nights ago. You were seeing if she could still fly."

"Just a bleeding second." Reece's heart did a strange upbeat number in his chest, undecided between nervousness and excitement. "You said you wanted me to fly you back to your planet. You didn't mean...on *The Aurelia*?"

Hayden gasped. "Reece, you can't!"

"How would he get back?" Gideon asked Nivy darkly, as if that was the biggest hitch in her plan. "That's not the issue!" Hayden exclaimed, voice as tight as a piano string liable to snap at any moment. "She could send him back in an escape capsule, but Aurelia, the single greatest artifact of Honoran history, would be left there. Reece could be executed for a theft like that!"

"He'd have to get caught first. I wouldn't let him get caught."

"That doesn't change anything. What we're talking about...it's practically treason!"

"Not if Aurelia wasn't ever ours to begin with. Sounds like we might'a stole her first."

"Oh, *now* you want to be all noble—"

"Shut up, both of you!" Reece shouted, making them jump. "Nivy?" She glanced at him, seeming a little frazzled by the intensity of Gid and Hayden's argument. "Would you walk with me?" She nodded and squeezed between Gideon's broad chest and Hayden's red face, which were at a level.

There wasn't enough yard to walk to find privacy, so Reece led her around the building and onto the pedestrian walkway, teeming with shoppers in their garish hats and bustles and men in their shirtsleeves and suspenders. They walked in silence for a time, Reece entertained by Nivy's absorption in the bright things she saw in the storefronts, bells and baskets for push bikes, top hats in all colors, antique bound books, all sorts of automata...he was going to guess that wherever she was from, it wasn't like this.

They stopped at a frozen dairy stand, and Reece ordered them scoops of vanilla and ginger melted over apple pie, his favorite. Nivy stared down into the tin bowl cupped between her hands with a look of pure rapture.

"Okay," Reece began, waving with his spoon for her to join him on a bench tucked around the corner of the red and white striped stand. "Have I earned the right to start asking questions again, or do I need to get you some more ginger for that?"

With an almost-smile and a mouth full of white cream, Nivy nodded for him to go ahead.

"Look, just need to be clear..." Reece searched her face. "I don't trust you, and I know you don't trust me. You ran when I would have asked you to stay, and it's made things difficult. Maybe that's on me. I haven't exactly been Captain Courteous these last two days; I know that. But I'm going to tell you everything now, Nivy, because I'm making the choice to believe you. You're going to have to believe me too, alright? I need you to. I can't help feeling like we're running out of time. Both of us."

Though Nivy seemed engrossed in cleaning the bottom of her bowl, she gave a jerk of a nod. So he told her. About everything from Bus-ship Ten to meeting Po Trimble. Laid out, the story sounded fragmented, holey, because he was still missing pieces. The question was, *which ones*?

"...Hayden and I have been drafted to be cleanly disposed of at war. Eldritch has probably figured that no one will notice if Gideon gets killed the old-fashioned way, being a Pan and all."

Thoughtful, Nivy tapped the back of her spoon against her bottle lip, staring over his head at nothing.

"So that first capsule," Reece continued after a lapse of awkward silence. "Was that from your planet too?"

Still staring blankly ahead, Nivy nodded.

"What do you think went wrong that first time? Do you think it was *The Aurelia* not being able to fly?"

Nivy glanced at him as though surprised he had to ask, held his gaze until he figured it out.

"Eldritch," he guessed. "Why? And how would he even know what the capsule was? Why the cover up, unless he knew the truth and wanted to hide it? Nivy…" Reece turned sideways on the bench, forcing her to look at him. "Who is Charles Eldritch?"

Nivy seemed to be suffering from an internal battle of the wills, biting her lip, glancing at him, then shaking her head as if arguing with a voice only she could hear. Finally, she reached into her pocket and pulled out the piece of parchment already decorated with the sketch of her planet and Aurelia's emblem. She turned to its clean side and stared at it.

"Nivy?" Reece leaned down to look up into her face.

Without meeting his eyes, she put a hand on his forehead and pushed him away. He waited.

Suddenly, she began scribbling furiously, her eyes screwed up in concentration. When she had drawn a new planet, she tapped it madly with her pen until Reece nodded in understanding, then started writing in an unpracticed, childlike scrawl, E—L—R—I—C—H. She was missing a few letters, but he wouldn't dock her points for that.

"Okay, okay." Reece rubbed his hands together eagerly. "Eldritch and a planet. Not Honora? Your planet? No? Okay. Uh. He…"

Impatient, Nivy kept tapping the nib of her pen against her drawing. She drew an arrow from Eldritch's name to the planet and darkened it with a few fevered strokes.

"He is going to another planet? He's a spy?"

Nivy paused on the second question and tipped her head uncertainly. Seeming to decide to leave that question be for now, she continued rapping her pen on the planet, waiting for him to try again.

"He's…*from* another planet?"

Nivy pointed at his face and nodded enthusiastically. He'd struck gold.

"He's an alien? Eldritch is an alien?" Reece repeated. He was sure Eldritch was registered as Honoran-born—otherwise he wouldn't be allowed to be headmaster—but him being an alien wasn't otherwise fishy. There were loads of non-natives living on Honora. "What planet is he from?"

Nivy began drawing slapdash circles around her first illustration, and after several guesses, Reece worked the word "galaxy" out of her frantic gestures.

"Nivy, you're losing me," he admitted, rubbing a hand through his hair.

Throwing down the parchment, Nivy put her chin in her hands. If Reece felt frustrated, he couldn't imagine how she felt.

After a moment of sitting in restless silence, Nivy looked up at him, studying him intensely. And somehow he knew, without any certain proof, that she was trying to decide whether or not she really could trust him.

Nivy carefully picked up the parchment and angled it on her leg so he couldn't see what she was drawing. After a moment, and another scrutinizing glance, she extended her work. Scratched in the margins of the cluttered page were two words.

The Kreft.

Reece opened his mouth to read them aloud, but Nivy put a finger to her lips and shook her head frantically.

"I don't understand. What is it?"

She pointed to Eldritch's misspelled name.

"Is it something he's after?" She shook her head. "Is it his planet? His…his race?" Finally, she nodded, and visibly shivered.

So there it was. Eldritch was an alien, something called a kreft, or a kreftite, or what have you. How did that help Reece? What was in Nivy's head that she couldn't draw or spell? Why was she shivering?

Someone cleared their throat, and Reece jumped and looked up.

"Sorry," Hayden uncomfortably said, scuffing the toe of his shoe against the road. "I didn't want to interrupt."

"What is it?" Despite Hayden's apology, Reece couldn't help but feel annoyed by the interruption. He'd finally been making headway. *The Kreft.* What were they?

"It's just, Scarlet's at the house, and—"

"Scarlet? At Mordecai's?" Somehow, the picture of the upstanding young lady in petticoats and the one of Mordecai's grungy workshop clashed in Reece's head.

"Yes." Hayden played with the buttons on his shirt. Always a bad sign. "Reece, she has a message from the duke. And she's asking questions. About Eldritch."

Standing, Reece took his and Nivy's dessert dishes and lobbed them into the open-mouthed garbage digester rolling on wheels down the road. It beeped at him, registering his contribution, and he suddenly had the urge to kick it. A message from the duke. That could only be bad or worse.

"I'll deal with Scarlet. You take Nivy and get her some new clothes. Something frilly and normal. Take Gid with you, just in case." Digging into his pocket, Reece pulled out a fistful of crumpled shields and slapped them into Hayden's hand. "We're going to need her to blend in a little better until we can get Aurelia operational."

Hayden stared at the marks in his hand, left momentarily more aghast by the amount of money he was holding than by what Reece meant. Then he looked up abruptly, paling in the bold sunlight.

"You don't mean...you're not going to...but you can't!"

Meeting Nivy's eyes—which looked almost as surprised as Hayden's—Reece said, "I don't break my promises. We have a deal. If Nivy helps me find out what happened to Liem, I'll take her and Aurelia back where they belong."

His own words sank in belatedly, surreal. He'd be flying Aurelia. Across the galaxy, through Streams and into The Voice of Space. How was he supposed to keep his motives straight? He couldn't be driven to solve this mystery because the end of it was a means to taking Aurelia to freedom. He still had Gid and Hayden to look out for.

And Nivy, too.

"You've been drafted."

"I hope that's not the duke's message. Because I found that out yesterday."

Scarlet stood in Mordecai's kitchen, amidst the pyramids of canned foods and dirty dishes, twisting her white gloved hands. It was the twisting hands part that worried Reece. Scarlet always kept her emotions so in check; if something had spooked her to the point of public hand-wringing, he had good cause to be nervous.

"Scarlet?"

Without warning, Scarlet threw her arms around his neck, her golden hair springing into his face. "Reece," she said in a fierce but quiet voice. "It's so much worse than you know."

Startled, Reece awkwardly closed off the hug, let her settle in his arms as she drew a tremulous breath. "What is?"

"Everything."

"Could you be more specific?"

Pulling back with sudden steam, Scarlet said in a clipped voice, "You told me to watch Eldritch, and I did."

"I know," Reece hurried to say. "I'm sorry. Go on."

Scarlet composed herself with a deep breath, smoothing down the front of her bright blue skirt. "There's something *wrong* about him. Everyone in Parliament is scared of him. He's been at The Guild House every day for the last week when his place is at The Academy, but no one will question him. They daren't."

As she talked, Reece dragged a rickety stool out from the pantry and held it as she collapsed onto it, her skirts blowing out with a puff of air. Tea. That's what Scarlet needed: a little tonic for her nerves. She had to become Scarlet again, no more of this anxious girl prone to spontaneous bouts of hugging.

Scarlet wrapped her hands gratefully around the dented tin mug that Reece had filled with one part herb and two part Burnthroat. "Parliament is calling summit after summit these days, and all the buzz coming out of those summits is the same. They're building up our military, using the draft. A third of all Honoran men over the age of fifteen will be required to receive training in firearms, tactics, and aviation."

"So many."

"I know."

"What else?"

"Eldritch. He's mysterious. Elusive. He's been at The Academy for thirty-five years but has never had any close colleagues, excepting maybe his secretary. Mr. Rice and I even tried to look into his file, but—"

"You and *Mr. Rice*?" Again, two images collided in Reece's head: Scarlet, regal, composed, stately, and Hugh Rice, quiet, untidy, forgettable. He caught a glance of Scarlet's smile before her raised teacup hid her lips.

"Ugh." She lowered the cup again, grimacing. "This stuff is ghastly. Yes, Mr. Rice and I. Why does that surprise you? He *is* the Chief Librarian."

"Ah, right. And you wouldn't associate with him otherwise."

"Yes, because despite all outward appearances suggesting that I've risked my whole career for you, I really am quite shallow." Scarlet snapped her cup into its saucer and gave him a wry look. "A little credit, if you please. Mr. Rice and I realized that the two of us had drawn similar conclusions about the headmaster and thought to look into his personnel file. I was thinking of you. I imagine Mr. Rice was thinking of Henry."

"Hayden."

"Whichever. Anyways, the only copy of Eldritch's file in existence isn't being kept in the archives as it should be." Scarlet gathered herself up with a significant pause. "It's locked in your father's desk."

Reece felt like he'd stepped in a hole as his stomach dropped unpleasantly. "You don't think the duke—"

"—knows who Charles Eldritch really is, yes, and is possibly protecting him."

Nivy's information and this unpleasant news aligned perfectly in Reece's head. Eldritch was masquerading as a Honoran citizen when he was really an alien, apparently with something to hide. Reece considered telling Scarlet what he knew...asking her if she'd ever heard whispers of a people called The Kreft...but she breezed on before he could decide.

"It gets worse. There are numerous suspicious deaths linked to Eldritch. He has no alibis that anyone can recall, and has never been called to court for questioning. Rumor is it's because he is in direct control of The Veritas themselves. Reece?" Scarlet pulled up short on her tirade to touch the back of her hand to his cheek. "Are you alright?"

The coolness of her skin shocked him back to reality, like a spark of static. "What about The Veritas?"

Scarlet studied him. "I don't think they answer to Parliament. I think they answer to him."

Reece caught himself before he cursed in front of Scarlet. Hayden wasn't the only Honoran with a Vee phobia; their methods of truth-seeking were the nucleus of almost every good horror story Reece knew. How could something so feared answer to an oily old thing like Eldritch?

"Since when?"

"Since always." Lacking her usual poise, Scarlet tugged her fan out from the belt of her dress, cracked it open like a whip, and beat it before her face so the tiny ringlets hanging like bells over her ears fluttered. "The Veritas were formed just over thirty-five years ago. The same year Eldritch was elected to headmastership by Parliament."

"So he created them. What's the duke *doing*? Eldritch might be some kind of crooked politician, but the duke is...*the duke*. The people answer to him, not the bleeding headmaster."

Her fanning slowing down, Scarlet said on a different, quieter note, "He caught me at The Guild House and told me to tell you...to *ask* you...to return to Emathia soon."

Wrapped up in dark thoughts, Reece answered her with a grunt. Her hazel eyes steadied on his face, like drills ready to break the surface and dig beneath.

"Reece, I've been to Emathia twice since holiday, once with my mother, once with my etiquette tutor. Abigail is devastated, thinking about you being drafted. She begged the duke to exempt you. You should visit her. I know your relationship is—"

"Stop." Reece lifted his head. It felt like lifting a rock. Cold. Heavy. "She asked the duke to exempt me?"

Scarlet warily shifted her fan before her face. "Yes?"

"And he didn't. Does he have that power, as duke? Could he have exempted me?"

"According to the dukeship's Rite of Imbuement…yes."

"Then it's worse than both of us thought, Scarlet," Reece said as he pushed the heels of his hands into his eyes. "He isn't protecting Eldritch. He's *taking orders* from him. He must be. If it had been up to him to exempt me, his Palatine Second… Palatine First, as long as Liem's not around…he would have. Not out of fondness for me, his own bleeding son. Just because he had to."

No, there wouldn't have been any partiality in the duke's decision. Not after their last fight, after the words that were exchanged. Reece had told the duke he hated him. And the duke…he hadn't even cared.

With a smart click, Scarlet slapped her fan closed in the palm of her hand. "I'm going to allow myself this one indulgence and be frank with you, Reece. Quit pitying yourself."

It went without saying that those three words were not the ones Reece had been expecting.

"Don't you see? You're in danger, I know that, but with Eldritch in power, *all of us* are in danger. The difference is that you are in a position to act. It would serve us all well if you remembered that, with what's coming."

Count on Scarlet to make Reece feel like a total numpty. Not to mention present a speech compelling enough to guilt a room of Guild House advisors. Reece bowed his head, trying to look meek when he really just felt bothered. Something in her words stuck with him like a bad itch.

As Scarlet got ready to go, crowning herself with a brimmed wool cap, she said, "There's to be a masquerade at Emathia. You would know if you'd been around. All the members of The Guild House are going to be in attendance, and all of Honora's most prestigious families. You should come. For your parents." As Reece opened his mouth, his disdain plain on his face, she added, "Also, Eldritch is going to be there. If he's planning something, that night would be the ideal time to spring it. The publicity would be astronomical." She straightened her hat with a small grin. "Make sure to bring a date."

Reece escorted Scarlet outside, filing her latest information away in the already cluttered stacks of his mind. Afternoon was getting on, and the light over Praxis was the warm golden kind that brought out the deep, true colors of everything, the punchy red of the brick building faces, the edible-looking hue of the sky, like icing. Reece soaked it all in with a sort of grim readiness. Liem's prophetic words hung on his mind: *It only gets deeper from here.*

"What did you mean," Reece asked Scarlet as he walked her to The Iron Horse platform, "when you said 'with what's coming'?"

She looked at him as if it should be obvious, and it made what she said that much worse.

"We're going to war, Reece."

XIII

Pour the Burnthroat

There were certain things that made Hayden uncomfortable. Raucous laughter when he was trying to study. Being too close to undomesticated animals. Gideon teaching Sophie how to juggle knives.

This experience, new as it was, trounced them all.

"Tea, dears?" Madame Maraux held out a tray on white gloved hands. She batted her fake eyelashes at Gideon, who shook his head no and went back to tinkering with some gun part, a chamber, it looked like.

Hayden accepted a porcelain teacup with two hands, squinting at its color, a pink that put the other pinks in the shop to shame. And there were many other pinks. In the curtains, in the velvet upholstery, in the throw rug on the wooden floor. Madame Maraux herself modeled a peach-pink beaded gown that burned the eyes a bit.

How funny he and Gideon must look, sitting at opposite ends of the small pink couch surrounded by dresses and gloves and ribbons that went to who-knew-what. There were three young ladies flipping through the gowns racked against the mirrored wall, giggling to themselves. Once in a while, Hayden would glance up and catch their eyes reflecting back at him, and he would go as pink as the upholstery, and the girls would giggle again.

What he wouldn't give for a book to close his head in.

"Take it easy, Aitch," Gideon said as Hayden slouched low in the couch. "It ain't so bad."

"I find it really unsettling that you're more in your element here than I am."

With a shrug, Gideon admitted, "I've been here before."

"You've been in Madam Maraux's Magnificent Misses before?"

Flipping the chamber from one hand to the other and then pocketing it in his leather waistcoat, Gideon shrugged. "Sure. Came once or twice with Ariel. I'll tell you how it works." He pointed at the curtained stalls where Nivy was currently detained, trying on the garments that the Madame had picked out (or more accurately, forced upon) her. "Nivy's gonna come out from there wearin' somethin' frilly and bright and possibly unflatterin'. All you gotta do is smile, nod, and tell her it's your new favorite every time she comes out in somethin' new."

"Lie?"

Gideon nodded sagely.

"Oh darling, don't you just look lovely!" Madame Maraux cooed, clapping her hands delightedly. "That fabric just makes your form...pop!"

Looking as mean as a waterlogged cat, Nivy dragged herself out of the curtained stall. The dress she wore had short puffy sleeves and a high waist tied off with a ribbon. It didn't make her form pop so much as it made her look skeletal, all bones and cotton dress.

Taking his cue, Hayden faked a smile and nodded. "That looks nice, Nivy."

Nivy menacingly shook her head at him and sank back into the stall. Hayden and Gideon sat in silence while Madame Maraux tended to the other ladies, who were holding dresses up to their shoulders and twirling around, still throwing frequent glances at the couch. Time had never gone slower.

The little golden bell over the shop door tinkled, announcing new customers. Hayden grimaced. More girls come to make him squirm, he shouldn't wonder.

"Welcome, welcome!" the Madame sang, bustling across the store. "What can I—oh my."

The steps on the floor were heavy and clodding, not like a woman's. Hayden started to curiously lift himself to see over the back of the couch, but Gideon caught his shoulder and forced him to stay down. He gave his chin the slightest of shakes.

A deep, hollow voice—like wind blowing through bare trees, somber and wintry—said, "Gideon Creed?"

Gideon stood, leaving Hayden doubled over on the couch, hidden. Hayden's heart increased its tempo. The girls across the room were clinging to each other's arms with faces as pale as the lace they'd let fall to the ground. Then Hayden saw the mirror behind them.

The men stood in identical poses, shoulders squared, hands clasped before them, their sickly white skin bright against the black of their jumpsuits. Both had shaved heads and sharply-boned faces, temples that jutted out just a little too far, eye sockets like caverns, hiding eyes with pupils so dilated they seemed mostly black. That was from the serum they lived on. A steroid treatment replacing the need for vitamins, protein, calcium, food and water. It turned them into wraiths, the addiction for the serum, in exchange for the tools they needed to do their job. Strength, speed, stealth. Hearsay had it that it also gave them an unnatural proclivity for hurting things, but then, that was part of their job as well.

On the right lapel of their black jumpsuits, the letter V was embroidered in scarlet thread. The Veritas. Truth seekers.

Hayden couldn't see himself in the mirror, because Gideon was standing between him and his reflection, but he was sure he looked as ill as he suddenly felt.

Gideon didn't answer to his name, just frowned a little deeper and folded his arms over his chest. In the mirror, Madame Maraux was trying to fix some extra tea for her distinguished guests, and her hands were rattling the porcelain.

One of the Veritas flowed gracefully forward, discernable from the other only by the shape of his nose, bowed like a beak.

"You are a Pan, are you not? Yes. Most cases of treason involve Pantedans. Disloyalty to the Honora. The very hand that feeds them."

"Mr. Creed." The other Vee had a silky tenor voice that made the hairs on Hayden's arms try to stand. "We are going to recite our terms as granted by Parliament. Please understand. If at any time you wish to interrupt us, you abandon your right to hear what we are and are not allowed to do to you to ascertain the truth." Gideon said nothing. "Very well. We are The Veritas, appointed by Parliament to seek out the truth, to discern evidence without need of a jury, to determine sentencing as is due the party at question. In the course of questioning you may or may not be burned, cut, shocked by means of artificial photon pulse, struck repeatedly, subjected to extreme temperatures and conditions—"

"Extreme temperatures? You mean like hot and cold?" Gideon asked, mocking.

Madame Maraux stole the chance to jostle her female customers into a back room and out of sight.

"Yes."

"Kinda weird."

Hayden tried thinking like Reece, but that made it impossible to devise a plan that didn't count on violence, law-breaking, cunning, and a fair bit of luck. Gideon had told him to stay down. It was the best plan he had, for now.

"We've broken Pans before. When the frost builds on their cheeks and they begin to lose fingers, they wonder how many fingers they can make do with, and by the third finger, they're broken."

"The eyes always yield the quickest results," the Vee with the bird's nose added. Neither of them sounded angry, amused, or even eager. Their voices didn't go up and down, and the eyes hidden in the hollows of their faces held no expression. "Pans are always so proud of their eyes. They set them apart from the Honorans. Threaten to take those away, and—"

"We must not get carried away prematurely," silk-voice purred, making a peaceful gesture with two fingers. "This does not have to be your fate, Gideon Creed."

Gideon snorted; his eyes flickered, briefly, down toward Hayden. His hand was sliding slowly down his arm, toward the back of his hip and his hidden sheath. Customers weren't allowed to carry guns on the premises, but knives...

Across the room, Nivy pushed through her dressing stall curtain, holding The Madame's clothes in a ball at arms' length, her face disgusted. When she saw The Veritas, a curtain of ice seemed to fall over the room. She froze, Gideon froze, the Vees froze. Hayden was the only one who moved, triumphantly throwing himself to his feet with a surge of courage. The Veritas, whether because they were preoccupied with Nivy or because they had always known he was there, paid no attention to him.

"The girl," one Vee said, lips parting with a hiss. He started to reach into his black jumpsuit.

Gideon's knife flew like a sleek silver bird. The Vee's face contorted with a grimace, but he didn't yell or jerk as the knife burrowed into his wrist, merely reached with his other hand and wrenched it free. Nivy's reaction was as instantaneous as Gideon's had been. Lunging forward, she thrust the tangled dresses into The Veritas' faces, blinding them with layers of cotton and silk.

"Aitch!" Gideon bellowed as he stamped a hand on the back of the couch and vaulted over it. "Get clear!" One of the Vee's faces peeked out from the fabric, and he threw a fist into it with a grunt of surprise for just how hard the face hit his hand.

Fumbling, caught between wanting to obey and wanting to help, Hayden grabbed for Nivy, pleading, "Come on, Nivy!"

Nivy's bony wrist slipped out from between his fingers as if oiled. Her hand closed on his sleeve, yanked it till he jerked about, and then shoved him from behind, sending him a few tumbling paces toward the door and safety. As if she was going to stay and fight while he went and hid with Madame Maraux and her girls!

With a shout of willpower, Hayden picked up the unwieldy wrought candlestick sitting on Maraux's counter. He could do this. All it took was a tap on the temple…or the mandibular nerve….

He turned. Gideon was fighting Beak-Nose, holding his own. If by a hairsbreadth. Hayden cringed as the Vee caught Gideon by the jacket and heaved him off his feet, landing him with a creak and a thud on a wooden countertop. Gideon rolled from the counter and came up with a stool, which exploded into splinters against the Vee's guard a second later.

Where Gideon's strength was in his raw power, Nivy's was in her speed. As long as she couldn't be caught, she couldn't be touched. Her Vee flailed, batting open space with arm and leg trying to catch her as she ducked and dove and skipped.

Hayden's candlestick pulled down on his hands heavily. His eyes twitched as he tried to decide, Gideon or Nivy, Gideon or Nivy. It was Nivy's Vee who made the decision for him as his arm struck like a snake through her defenses and landed a fist in her side. Nivy spilt onto the floor with her face screwed up in pain.

Gathering himself, Hayden gave a shout and charged the Vee. There was a flash of movement, and then a strange pressure on his throat. He dropped his candlestick to clutch the arm connected to the Vee who was choking him. Oh, bloody—

"Hayden Rice," Silk-Voice sighed. "There are questions we could ask of you as well. But I think you would be too easily broken."

Hayden shuddered as his body begged for air he couldn't give, and for the first time, he saw a Vee smile, a curve of white lips that narrowed the eyes.

"Mmm, Hayden Rice," he said thoughtfully, and to Hayden's wonder, eased up on his grip so Hayden could draw a wheezy breath. Not half a second later, the Vee had pulled out a small silver pistol and placed its barrel firm against his heart. "You will come with us. To make everything less painful for your family. Because you don't want to hurt anyone, do you? You don't like hurting people. We're not like you, Hayden—we will hurt them. Understand. Sophie is just another child to us."

Sophie. Gasping and groaning as air scraped down his battered windpipe, Hayden forced his head to nod. Satisfied, the Vee, holding him by the arm to ensure he didn't run, turned and brought his ALP up to a level with Gideon, who had the bird-nosed Vee pinned to the wall. Hayden's Vee adjusted his aim for a nonfatal shot and closed one eye.

A gunshot snapped, filled the air with a smell like hot metal. The Vee on Hayden's arm staggered uncertainly. Another *snap*, and he dropped to his knees, releasing Hayden. One more snap. He rocked and then fell to his face, blood leaking out about him.

Reece rushed into the room, face drawn of color, his old hob raised in both hands. "Hayden?"

"F-fine," Hayden reassured him, backing away from the dead Vee until his knees involuntarily folded and he collapsed onto the couch.

The shop was mangled. The bottles of perfume shelved against the wall where Gideon was holding Beak-Nose were shattered, filling the room with the reek of lilac and peppermint. Madame Maraux's counter had a crack down its middle from Gideon's weight being dropped on it, and her stool was nothing more than two legs and some unidentifiable shards. Thin streams of blood were dribbling down Gideon's forearms. Yesterday's injuries had broken open.

Stepping over a dented hat, Reece crouched down to feel for the Vee's pulse. His fingers came away red. The doctor in Hayden felt a deep, cold horror, looking at the body. Everything else he was remembered what the Vee had said about Sophie and wanted to hate them all, and for a while, he let himself, blankly watching the way the swinging photon chandelier overhead made ruby jewels out of the blood on the floor.

Reece and Gideon's words suddenly came to him, subdued.

"What about this one?"

"Let's take him to Mordecai's—put the questioner to the question. Scarlet thinks the Veritas answer to Eldritch. He probably sent them after you. They were probably the ones on the road loast night."

"Makes sense. They seemed downright surprised to see the girl though."

Reece glanced at Nivy, who was massaging her side and staring at the dead Vee with her eyebrows drawn together. "They recognized her?"

"Seals the deal, don't it? If they were Eldritch's hands, they'd be on the lookout for her."

Reece was silent a moment; there was a scuffling as the Vee against the wall squirmed and tried to speak.

"Mordecai's," Reece repeated, voice hard. "We can't let him go back to Eldritch with what he knows."

"You think Parliament is gonna overlook a couple'a their truth seekers goin' missin'? Or one of them turnin' up dead? We've got four witnesses who knew the Vee's were lookin' for me."

"If I'm right," Reece said as he stiffly tucked his hob behind his belt, "Parliament knew nothing about today's little rendezvous. This is all Eldritch. Let Eldritch deal with it."

Hayden came out of his reverie, and didn't like what he saw around him, the bodies, the chaos, the faces of his friends, Gideon's, focused and intense, Reece's, quietly outraged, his brown eyes unforgiving. Inside, he felt empty, like if he swallowed a coin, it would bounce to the bottom of his stomach.

A hand stole into his and held to it tightly before he could register the feeling of soft cold skin and too-skinny fingers. Nivy looked over at him, eyebrows tilted to make her expression inquisitive. Too taken aback to do more than nod that he was alright, Hayden let her pull him out of the shop after Reece, Gideon, and the captured Vee, wondering when along the way Nivy had decided to become his friend.

Evening at Mordecai's was a sober affair. Last night, he and his grandson and his grandson's friends had sat around his table and laughed at stories and shared bird-on-a-stick. Today was a bim crash and a Veritas attack later, and tonight they ate dinner in silent shifts, with Mordecai, Reece, or Gideon always off watching the Vee that was locked in Mordecai's storage room.

Hayden stirred his limp green vegetables in circles on his plate as Gideon left and Reece took his place at the table. All day it had been the same. Hayden had had two late classes to attend, and had suffered through them, biting his nails and watching the slow circuit of his pocket watch's hands. He'd been so preoccupied with imaginings of Vees coming for his friends or visiting Father and Sophie on Honora, he'd actually drawn a blank when Tutor Macintosh had asked him to determine the kinetic energy of an electron with a wavelength of 2m.

Across the table, Reece served himself a cold slab of buttered pork, cutting into it with a vengeance. Mordecai was at the foot of the table, making mellow hooting sounds over the mouth of his burnthroat bottle while Nivy looked on in interest.

"Here," Reece suddenly said, and slapped a thin wad of shields down on the table, rattling the silverware. "For the job, Mordecai."

"You mean the job you just hired me for a day ago?" Mordecai pulled the money toward him and glanced his thumb across its edges. "Sittin' around doin' nothin' pays pretty good nowadays."

"It's not just for putting up Nivy. It's for letting us keep that lunatic in your basement."

"You think he's a lunatic?" Hayden asked.

Reece snorted to himself and gestured with his carving knife. "They're *all* lunatics. It's a wonder Parliament ever agreed to put them to use."

"They barely did," Hayden recalled. "The vote almost didn't pass. There were worries about the science of the serum...the ethics of it."

"But it did pass. Because Eldritch has Parliament under his thumb." Reece shook his head scornfully. He'd told them about Eldritch being an alien, but none of them were sure how that figured into his goings on. "I bet if you checked the transcript from the Guild meeting where The Veritas were voted in, you'd find that it was his proposal to begin with. I wonder if that's how the rumors started...about the Vees being used by certain members of Parliament to bully Westerners...to torture them..."

"Supposing Eldritch came here thirty-five years ago and created The Veritas. Why would he do that?" Hayden rubbed his temples. "Why would an alien spy do that? The Veritas are terrible, I realize that, but they don't weaken Parliament...they reinforce it." Seeing Reece's look, he added, "I hate their methods too, Reece, but they do what they were made to do. They keep the Honoran people suppressed. Crime is practically nonexistent. Regular Honoran sentries couldn't guarantee that."

"So Eldritch is just protecting Honora from itself? He doesn't really seem the humanitarian type."

"No, but don't you see? The crime rate is so low because The Veritas *frighten* people. They're the most dangerous tool Eldritch could have at his disposal. The Vees have power over the people, and Eldritch has power over them. So I don't think Eldritch is a spy, not unless this is all some complicated plan to prepare Honora for a quiet invasion. He's certainly doing more than just gathering intelligence."

Reece folded his arms over his chest and looked down with a frown. "Honora doesn't have the kind of enemies who would do that." He abruptly glanced up at Nivy, who had been staring at a spot on her plate. "Not that we know of."

Nivy raised her eyes, and they stared at each other with a kind of grim understanding. Slowly, Nivy nodded. Hayden thought he knew what about.

"The Kreft?" he guessed quietly, and they both looked at him. "I have a hard time understanding why a people we've never even heard of would single out Honora. Orpheus is wealthier. Oceanus has more advanced automata. What does Honora have that Eldritch's people could possibly want badly enough to manipulate the political environment for thirty-five years?"

Reece looked again to Nivy, but she just spread her hands helplessly and shook her head, as lost as they were. "They don't want Aurelia? That's what brought you here." She shook her head again, but more uncertainly, and with a thoughtful, even worried frown.

"That doesn't fit. Eldritch could have taken Aurelia any time. And what about the war?" Hayden went on. His brain was whirring like a datascope, sifting through facts faster than he could compute. "What about Parliament boosting Honora's armies?"

"You're right. Eldritch and The Kreft wouldn't build up Honora's armies if they were planning to invade. That's being done for something else. But what?"

For a second, Hayden could have sworn Nivy had been about to say something. But when she saw him staring at her, she lowered her eyes to her lap and clenched her hands tightly together, as if forbidding herself from hand-talk.

Mordecai, who Hayden had completely forgotten was at the table, quietly mused, "Always knew the establishment couldn't be trusted. Crooked is as crooked does."

Their conversation dropped out, leaving only the sounds of Reece's fork ticking against his plate and Mordecai's resumed jug playing to take the edge off the silence.

For the sake of having something to do, Hayden began clearing the table around Nivy, Reece, and Mordecai. He used the quiet to replay the conversation he'd had with Sophie over Mordecai's log interface.

"Hayden! How's school? How's Reece?"

"Fine…they're all fine. We're fine. How…how are you?"

"Good! Guess what? You'll never guess. I found an owlet with a broken wing behind the house today and I'm fixing it a splint. Um. I borrowed some of your supplies. I hope that's okay."

"That's fine, Soph, but listen. Are you home alone?"

"Yup. Father's working late again."

"Why don't you go to the Adams' for the night? Take the trolley. Use the money hidden in the hollow leg of my bed. I'll send Father a log and tell him."

"Oh, I don't know, I really need to watch Ben. That's the owlet. I named him Benjamin."

"So take him with you. Charity keeps an owl, doesn't she?"

"Yes, but—"

"I'd really like you to, Soph. It would make me feel better."

"Why? What's wrong? You sound…are you sick?"

"No. Everything's fine. But promise me you'll go, alright? Promise me you'll stay there."

"Hayden—"

"Promise?"

"…I promise."

He'd warned his father about The Veritas, though he wasn't specific as to how he knew what to warn. Hugh had been less than pleased and more than a little anxious, but he had promised to lie low with Sophie at the Adams's. Mother's parents. They would probably be glad of the extra company.

The night grew heavier as it stretched on. Hayden and Reece had brought their schoolwork, and plunged themselves into catching up on it while Nivy, faithful to her promise to Reece, worked her way through vocabulary graphs that Hayden had brought from The Owl. Mordecai swapped duties with Gideon, disappearing into the tunnel as his grandson emerged, convulsively rolling his revolver around his finger. His forearms were still shiny with the fresh coat of medical glue Hayden had reapplied to the scrapes from his bim accident.

"If you're gonna question the Vee," he said to Reece, "I think now's the time. He's actin' kinda funny. Might be sick."

"Sick?" Hayden raised his eyes from the screen of his neurosciences lapbook. "How so?"

"Shakin'. Sweatin'. Actin' like he's run a race or somethin'."

"It sounds like he's going through withdrawal."

"From the serum," Reece guessed, scratching the dark stubble that had dusted his cheeks these last few days. "I hadn't thought of that. How often do you suppose he's used to getting it?"

Not sure, Hayden shrugged. The exact formula behind the Veritas's serum was protected by Parliament, but it was easy enough to speculate on its properties. "As much as three times a day, maybe? To replace the standard meal? It's hard to say. A compound like the serum's is *extremely* unforgiving on the body. I mean, from what we know if it, its effects are instantaneous, and no drug should be able to work with that kind of speed. So it must create a sort of fake internal system—" He stopped when he saw Reece's vacant look, and went back to his lapbook, trying to immerse himself in its simple, familiar words. Adrenergic, amygdala...

"So how are we going to do this?" Reece wondered quietly, standing.

"Figure it should be just you and me. You ask your questions, and I'll make sure it answers." Gideon gave the revolver an extra energetic spin.

It had never bothered Hayden to be excluded from talks like this…before today. Today, in every way, all his studies and good marks had failed him. He'd let Gideon hide him, Nivy push him to safety, Reece save him again. He felt like a shelved book that never got read: full of good information, but in the end, useless.

Nivy tapped his arm, and he tore his eyes away from a diagram to look at her. Her face impassive, she handed him a scrap of parchment. In her lopsided, messy hand, she'd written, "ask", and then, puzzlingly, "pun".

"I…don't understand," Hayden admitted, embarrassed. "What pun?"

"Someone's making *puns* right now?" Reece asked incredulously from above where they were sitting. "Seems kind of inappropriate."

Nivy was at work again, scribbling out her mistake and replacing the word "pun" with a drawing that Gideon recognized before anyone else.

"*Gun*, not pun," he grunted. "She wants us to ask about her gun."

"Oh. Nivy, G faces the other way, see? And it has a fishhook on its bottom, like this…"

Reece and Gideon left the room, one behind the other. Hayden followed the sound of their footsteps down the dimly lit hall, Gideon's a heavy march, Reece's a brooding stamp. A door opened with a rusty groan, then closed with an ominous squeal and a click.

"I wish you could speak," Hayden told Nivy earnestly. "I hate the quiet."

Quirking her head to the side, Nivy studied him in her not-quite-smiling way.

"Sorry. I suppose you're use to it. It must have been very quiet, coming across space in that pod. How long did the journey take?"

Nivy shrugged one shoulder and laid the side of her face down on folded hands. She shut her eyes.

"Oh. They put you in a sleep stasis." Hayden considered for a moment. "It was probably months, then, especially if you didn't travel by Stream. The Streams intrigue scientists, you know. We couldn't dream of getting to even Cronus Twelve without them, at least not in any reasonable amount of time, and yet we haven't a clue where they came from or how they were formed. They—what?"

Nivy was staring at him with an amused if slightly mystified smirk. She put her pen to her parchment and thoughtfully tapped its nib a few times, spotting the page, before shaking her head and giving up.

"What? What is it, Nivy? Is it about The Streams?"

"Aitch," Gideon's voice boomed down the hall, interrupting. He followed it into the room a second later. "We need you."

"What did you do?" popped out before Hayden could stop it, and he flushed deeply.

Unfazed, Gideon said, "Nothin'. It's havin' some sort of fit. You better have a look at it."

It being the Vee. Hayden made himself stand on legs that kept trying to lock in place. A person needed his help. He was a doctor; it was his duty to treat any patient entrusted to him to the best of his abilities. Even a Vee.

"You too," Gideon said to Nivy, jerking his chin at her. "You're still our prisoner. Can't leave you alone."

As calm as ever, Nivy set her things to the side and followed him and Hayden down the poorly lit hall with its dingy, flickering photon globes hanging by chains from the ceiling. Ocher lamplight framed a door at the end of the hall, and as someone started choking and coughing beyond it, Hayden walked faster. He rubbed his sweating palms down the sides of his pants.

He hadn't given Reece and Gideon much credit. Here he'd been expecting a dark and empty cell when they had set the old storage room up with some civilized albeit small comforts. A canvas cot and a tub of clean water, an ancient oil lamp, a plate of food. It wasn't so different from the detention rooms at The Owl (which he'd only ever seen from the outside looking in).

With a scream and a kick, the Vee sent his plate of food flying into the wood-slated wall, narrowly missing Mordecai, who straightened up from dodging with a low, impressed whistle. The Vee was crouched in the far corner like some kind of wounded rodent, hiding in the shadows that the guttering orange light couldn't reach. Hayden inspected him from a safe distance. Pallid and yellow, shaking, sweating, his eyes ticking back and forth wildly. There was vomit on the floor by the bed.

He hesitated only a second, and then something in him took over his body and directed it forward. It was hard to be frightened of someone who needed your help. "Can you tell me exactly what you're feeling?" he asked as he knelt.

The Vee's eyes rolled to him, bloodshot. He did not answer.

"Do you have a name?" Hayden asked instead, tentatively reaching for the Vee's arm.

Behind Hayden, someone shifted uncomfortably.

"Careful, Hayden," Reece warned. "Don't get too cozy."

"I'm going to have to, if you want him to live out the night," Hayden said evenly as he closed his hand about the Vee's wrist. The skin's sticky coldness made him shiver.

"I don't necessarily need him to. I just need him to answer my questions."

Hayden looked over his shoulder, alarmed. "I'm not going to help him live just long enough for you to—"

The arm in his hands snapped to life and roped him about the shoulders in a flailing sort of hug, trying to drag him, thrashing and shouting, to the floor. Quick as a blink, Gideon and Reece and Mordecai were there, Mordecai and Gideon towering with their revolvers trained on the Vee, Reece untangling Hayden from his trembling captor.

"The serum, we beg you," the Vee rasped, lathering like a rabid animal. "If you will just give us the serum—"

"Keep dreamin'," Gideon growled. "And quit talkin' like that. It's creepy."

As Reece helped Hayden up by his elbows, he said loudly enough for the Vee to hear, "Come on, Hayden. He had his chance."

"But—" Hayden started before Reece gave him a look that cut the appeal short.

"Burn you all!" the Vee despaired loudly, ripping at his clothes. "We will make you *bleed* for this! Bleed until your life…slowly…seeps….out…" His words gave way to horrible, hacking laughter.

"Shut him in," Reece snarled at Mordecai and Gideon. "He'll cave, when the thirst gets too much for him. Everyone out."

Hayden had never seen him in such a temper. He knew it was bad by the quietness of it. He didn't shout, just glowered and burned and twisted his fingers into fists as he marched out into the hall.

"I told you to be careful," he muttered in Hayden's direction.

Surprised, Hayden turned his back to the cobwebbed hallway wall and observed Reece over the tops of his bifocals. "You're mad at *me* for this?"

"No...no. I just wish you'd been more careful. I know when you go doctor on us, you get tunnel vision, but that's a Vee in there. He could've snapped your neck, did you think of that?"

Hayden had, actually, in passing. But the Vee would never have *really* hurt him with Gideon and Reece in the room—not unless he'd had a death wish. He told Reece so and tried to push back into the Vee's room, but Gideon stopped him with a one-handed shove to the chest while Nivy caught him by the sleeve.

"Hayden," Reece was trying not to smile, "he *does* have a death wish. He *wants* to die. He was trying to make us help him."

The hallway got very hot then, and Hayden had to excuse himself to get a drink of water, and also a tall glass of burnthroat.

XIV

A Deal, a Caper, and…Oops

Personally, Gideon kinda just wanted to shoot the Vee. He wouldn't, not without Reece's say-so, but that didn't stop him from wantin'.

It was about midnight, and the house was hushed in its creaky old buildin' way, meanin' there were unaccounted-for squeaks and groans regularly breakin' the quiet, makin' him edgy. Everyone was sleepin', except for the Vee, who he could hear whimperin' through the cell door. His brain felt heavy, stuffed full'a thoughts without an end. Reece had a heckuva mystery on his hands. Gideon felt the weight'a it for him, once he sat down alone and listened to the Vee's shrieks.

Speakin'a which.

Gideon leaned up outta his slump and listened. The Vee was quiet. Then, *tap tap tap*, knuckles on the door. He looked to the door like he could actually see the sound when it came again, *tap tap tap*.

"We know you can hear us," the Vee's voice rasped.

Gideon grumpily knocked the door with the heel'a his boot. "Remember what I said about talkin' creepy?"

The Vee's broken laughter sounded like weepin'. "Oh, we remember everything. The serum lets us. We never forget a face, a voice, never forget a past. We know you, Gideon Cephas Creed. Pray tell us…was the war terribly hard?"

Gideon braced himself. It'd been like this all night, the Vee pushin' everyone's buttons, tryin' to get outta livin' without his precious serum. Reece got a whole earful about his mother likin' Liem more than him, and Mordecai had had to sit through reminiscin's about Esther…his wife, who'd died durin' the war.

"Did Reece Sheppard tell you?" the Vee purred softly. "There's a war coming here. A grander war than little Panteda ever saw. Reece Sheppard and Hayden Rice will both go to fight…and both will die…and it will be like Panteda all over again, won't it? Losing everyone, unable to do anything but watch."

The Vee paused, and Gideon tried to focus in the quiet, shuttin' his eyes, pullin' in slow breaths. His hands were crampin' from holdin' them in tight fists.

"No one who understands, do they, Gideon Creed? How you saw your mother die. Out your ship window, as she suffocated trying to reach you. You did not see your father die, but you were given a ribbon for his valiant war efforts…a little green ribbon…"

Gideon had risen to his feet and was methodically unlockin' the door, not knowin' what he was plannin' to do, but knowin' what the end result would be. He was gettin' ready to pull the door open when an arm shot out and barred his way.

"Don't give him what he wants," Reece said, and despite Gideon's growl'a protest, started slidin' the locks back into place to the sound'a the Vee's fresh bout'a mournful wails. "If he dies before he breaks, he won't have failed the other Veritas. We can't give him that."

For a minute, Gideon stood chest to chest with Reece, feelin' his anger crawlin' over his skin. Then he remembered who he was angry at—not Reece, but the Vee behind the door—and the steam went outta him. His shoulders dropped as he turned away and let Reece finish boltin' the door. The Vee's words were sittin' in the bottom'a his stomach like a hard, cold rock.

"He said there's a war comin' here, and that's why you and Hayden were drafted."

Reece hesitated. "That's what Scarlet overheard in The Guild House, yeah. Parliament is buffing up our military for some sort of attack, reforging alliances with the outer planets—"

"Attack from who?"

"No one seems to know."

Gideon sat down, his back against the wall, and hung his arms limply over his knees. The Vee's despairin' noises had faded into the night, maybe because he'd given up, maybe because he was eavesdroppin'. Let him. Not like there wasn't anythin' he didn't know anyways.

"I uh…" Reece gestured mutely, fumblin' for words. "I *do* know about your parents, Gid. Mordecai told me and Hayden pretty early on how it happened. We figured you'd say something when you were…ready, I guess. But eight years went by kind of fast."

"Well." It was Gideon's turn to fumble as he pulled a trigger outta his pocket and twiddled it between his fingers. Somethin' to look at besides Reece. "I still ain't ready."

Reece made a noise that Gideon couldn't quite read. He looked up to see him smirkin' and shakin' his head.

"What?" Gideon snapped, and for good measure, flung the trigger at him. It bounced off the wall by Reece's head with a metallic *ping* and chattered to the ground. "Ain't nothin' to be smilin' about."

"It's not that. Listen."

Gideon did, squintin' his eyes as if that might make him hear better.

There was a whisper, faint like the scufflin'a mice's feet, comin' from under the Vee's door. "Please, we will tell you…we will speak …please…"

Reece and Gideon locked eyes and stood up with purpose, grim though the purpose was. Reece muttered to himself, "We've got him," as he started undoin' the locks he'd set in place moments ago. Pullin' out his revolver, Gideon took a ready stance and waited till Reece had his hand on the door handle to nod his go ahead.

When Reece turned the handle, the door burst open, and the Vee tumbled into the hallway, scramblin' to get past them. Gideon caught him by the back'a his jacket, propped the revolver's barrel against the small'a his back, and steered him back into the storage room.

"Take a load off." He thrust the Vee onto the cot.

"Please…please…the serum…"

Standin' beside Gideon with his arms crossed and his face set, Reece informed him, "We don't have any serum for you. But tell us what you know, and we might see if something can be arranged."

The Vee hissed, spit dribblin' from his chin, as his black eyes burned up at Reece. Gideon added a decisive click to the conversation by loadin' a bullet into his revolver's chamber. Those unnatural eyes flinched at the sound, as if it had been all that loud.

"No no no," the beak-nosed Vee panted and waggled an admonitory finger back and forth. "We will not let you let us die. For you will. We will give you everything, and you will not repay us. We think not."

Frownin', Reece looked at the Vee like he was actually considerin' its crazy talk. "What do you suggest?"

Gideon glanced at him sideways, keepin' his finger a smooth twitch away from his trigger. "We bargainin' with it now?"

"I'm hearing my options."

Mightn't have been the smartest thing, but Gideon was feelin' a might tense, and he didn't like bein' talked down to, not even by Reece. He split his glare between the Vee, who was smilin' craftily at him, and Reece as he snapped, "Burn it, Reece! We've only got one option! *It's* the bleedin' prisoner here, let's just get what we need outta it and be done!"

The look Reece shot him was so packed full'a heat, it was a wonder Gideon's eyebrows didn't singe. "If you don't like how I'm handling things, you can leave me the gun and get out."

Simmerin', Gideon grunted and swallowed down a couple'a choice words that Reece wouldn't'a understood anyways, because they were in Pantedan. Would'a made Mordecai's eyebrows go up, though.

"Good Pan," the Vee tittered. "Knows when to stop barking."

The finger slipped into place almost on its own, and Gideon let it pull the trigger. The *boom* sounded loud in the confined space, more like an explosion than a gunshot. Plaster rained down the ceilin', a white dustin'.

"*Gideon!*" Reece shouted, livid, as he grabbed the front'a Gideon's waistcoat in two angry fists.

"It was just a warnin' shot!" Gideon yelled back, gesturin' at the cowerin' Vee and the dinner plate-sized hole in the wall a foot above his head. "Elsewise I wouldn't'a missed!" He knew it wasn't really necessary to add that last, but he didn't want anyone misunderstandin'.

Reece shoved off his jacket, leavin' his hands up in surrendered disbelief. Like he didn't know what to do with him.

"What the heckles is goin' on down here?" Mordecai bellowed, comin' into the room at a jog with a hob in either hand. He was wearin' a striped dressin' gown and a long nightcap.

Hayden and Nivy slid in behind him, Hayden totin' his medical bag. "Is anyone hurt?" he added, blinkin' heavily because he wasn't wearin' his bifocals.

Reece looked liable to combust at any second, though his voice was deceivingly calm. "Out. Everyone out." He swung a finger up and pointed at Gideon's face. "You too, you bleeding trigger happy pirate. Give me the gun."

When Reece had shut the lot'a them out in the corridor, Gideon sat his back down against the door and tried to listen in on the negotiations, but they were too quiet to hear. The others hung around too. They played jacks and laughed (Nivy just smiled) when Hayden blindly bounced the rubber ball at nonexistent jacks. Gideon didn't ask to play. He could shoot an egg off a pole from a hundred and fifty yards, but bouncin' a stupid rubber ball at a jack was somethin' else altogether.

Could'a only been fifteen minutes before Reece rejoined them, face hidin' all hints'a what'd gone on in the storage room. He tossed Gideon a look'a lingerin' disapproval along with his revolver.

"Well?" Mordecai asked, catchin' two jacks in his hand without lookin' at them. "Did you strike yourself a deal?"

"Yup."

"What kind of deal?" Hayden asked.

"The only one there really ever was to make. Our answers for his serum."

Mordecai's bushy mustaches twitched. "In what order, pray tell?"

Reece crouched down to be at a level with the rest'a them, his elbows on his knees, and let his face answer for him. Mordecai grunted unhappily while Hayden sighed and Gideon glared. Seemed wrong to him, givin' the Vee what it wanted. Wasn't like they could let it go free after it met its end'a the bargain.

Runnin' his fingers tiredly through his yellow hair, Hayden wondered, "How are we supposed to get him the serum? It's not exactly stocked at the local apothecary."

Reece answered matter-of-factly, "A heist," and Gideon sat up straighter, finally hearin' somethin' he liked. Reece saw the movement and nodded at him. "Gid and I will do it."

Hayden was a step behind the rest'a them. "What are you heisting?"

"The Veritas' base of operations. Our friend in the storage room gave me the coordinates."

"*The Veritas' base*? Are you out of your mind?"

"I hear I wouldn't know if I was."

"Reece, they're not going to let you just walk in and take some of their serum so you can make a traitor out of one of their own!"

"Which is why," Reece said dryly, "they call it a heist. It's also why you're staying here with Mordecai and Nivy."

Nivy clicked her fingers to get their attention, then pointed insistently at herself. Reece started shakin' his head before he even looked at her.

"Sorry, Nivy, this trust thing is still a work in progress, and I can't be watching my front *and* my back."

Wearin' her unreadable pokerface, Nivy stood, stepped over the scattered jacks, and sauntered off down the hallway. Sulkin', likely as not.

"Hayden," Reece said, starin' after her. "Go with her. Make sure she stays put."

After openin' and closin' his mouth in mute protest for a minute, Hayden obeyed, feelin' his way down the hall with a hand on the wall. He paused before he sank too deep into the shadows to call back over his shoulder, "If you can, try to get the components for the serum, not just the finished product."

"Why?" Reece asked.

Aitch's voice was quiet. "Because some good might come from figuring out how the serum really works. Who knows. Maybe it can be used to help people, someday."

Then he was gone, and Mordecai, Reece, and Gideon were left sittin' in a triangle, starin' at each other blankly.

"Well, don't just scratch yer head about it," Mordecai finally said, tetchy. Gideon knew what about. He wanted to come on the heist too. Just wasn't humble enough to say so. "Give me the burned coordinates and I'll figure out how'ta get you off Atlas and where ya need to go. Bleedin' ginghoos…" he mumbled as Reece passed him a folded piece'a parchment. "…be chasin' yer tails without me. Heist…peh! This'll prolly be a slice'a pie compared to the capers I've seen."

It was near on four in the mornin' planet time by the time Gideon and Reece arrived in Caldonia in the cargo hold of garbage transporter, which meant they had little more than an hour to get in and outta the Veritas' base before dawn lit up the city.

They were standin' in an alleyway between The Pantheon Theatre, all its gaudy showbiz lights dimmed for the evenin', and a tavern with some muffled burlesque music singin' out into the night. Gideon handed Reece his hob and strapped his revolver into the holster on his hip before slidin' extra rounds into his chest pocket. The only thing he could make outta Reece was the outlines'a his face caught in the green light'a the tavern's alleyside window.

Not too many folk were out this late (or this early, however you preferred it), but that didn't make the city quiet. There was always the distant hum'a the public locomotive or the whiz'a ships overhead, the burr'a photon energy, an undertone to everythin'. And the owls that quietly observed the city durin' the day owned it at night. Like black kites, they floated from rooftop from rooftop, sittin' on buildin's like rows'a gargoyles.

The area the Vee's directions led them towards was about what you'd expect. Brick warehouses with outdated advertisement projections flickerin' reluctantly on their broadsides, tight-fittin' alleyways with rundown fire escapes. The light'a the projections was made misty by the thick smoke pourin' outta a couple'a the warehouse's smokestacks.

Reece stopped abruptly at a crossroads in the alleys and gestured for Gideon to block the glow'a the photon wand that he used to light up the face'a his wrist compass. A warm wind chased paper trash up one'a the other alleys, rattlin' it.

"One more block. The back entrance will be on our left at number three twenty-three. He said we'll know it when we see it. The word to get us in will be *charter*. Huh," Reece grunted as he slipped the photon wand back into his coat pocket and rustled his hand about. "Weird."

"What?"

The hand rustled some more. He shook his head. "Just…never mind. Let's keep moving."

They continued, Reece leadin' the way, Gideon watchin' their backs. At number three oh two, he called Reece to a halt with a hiss, sure he'd seen a flicker'a somethin' on a rooftop behind them. They briefly waited for the flicker to turn into somethin' more, but Reece was impatient, and dawn wouldn't wait on nobody. They went on, runnin' now.

Turnin' one last corner neck and neck, they skidded to a stop, blinded by the white light pourin' into the alley outta a storefront ahead. Gideon stared. All the other stores down this way had been stripped bare and taken to with bricks and paint. This one looked like it should'a been on Main Street. The bright gold numbers on its window sparkled like fresh gilt, and there was a little bell and a pristine green and white striped canopy over its rotary door.

"He said we'd know it when we saw it," Reece whispered, and Gideon heard a smile in his voice.

"It's creepy," he decided. "Gives me a feelin'a wrongness."

Once they were close up on the window, they could see how the glass was milky so as to make the store light soft like a candle's under a blanket. It was hard to see much past the empty white display case. Gideon figured that was on purpose.

Reece didn't dawdle. He drew a hard breath, lifted his hob, and stepped into the rotary door, which spun him out into the store with well-oiled ease. When Gideon had popped out after him, they stood and stared about together. Closest thing Gideon could compare the place to was a toy shoppe. Its marble floor was black and white checkered while its walls were hidden by dense strands'a colorful marbles like strung-up rainbows. There were no shelves, but model airships, Furies and Harpies mostly, dangled from the ceilin', spinnin' in lazy circles. In the middle'a the room was a single writin' desk— one'a the dainty kinds with curvy legs and clawed feet—and on it, a display'a beakers with a wide spectrum'a liquids, bubblin' blue, goopy green, steamin' scarlet.

Gideon was so caught up in studyin' the weirdness of it all that he almost missed the hatch liftin' up outta the floor near the back'a the room.

"There," Reece hissed, and snapped his gun to the ready a beat behind Gideon.

They watched as the hatch opened, listened to the dull sound'a footsteps comin' up the wooden stairs beneath it. A head as white as snow appeared first, followed by the body'a the tallest, skinniest fellow Gideon'd ever seen. He wore green pinstriped trousers with suspenders, a crisp white shirt, and a funny green bowtie. As if oblivious to Reece and Gideon, the old geezer came up outta his hole, shut the hatch after him so it blended back into the pattern'a the floor, and dusted his hands.

"Just take it nice and slow," Reece began, and the old man jumped about a mile high. "We're not going to hurt you."

"Dear me, who's there?" the man blustered, lookin' all around as if followin' a fly with his eyes. White eyes as milky as the store window.

"Blind," Gideon grunted, and Reece nodded to show that he had seen.

"Why don't you come sit down?" he suggested kindly.

The old man hesitated, twistin' his long fingers into knots. "Oh, you shouldn't be here…you shouldn't be here at all…"

"We were sent. Sent with the word 'charter'."

Sighin', the green-clad man walked unsteadily to the desk, felt about for its chair, and sat down heavily. "No, you weren't. You aren't one of *them*. I can hear it in your voice. Oh, you shouldn't be here. This is terrible. I can't let you go on, you know. They'll stretch my ears, if I do."

"I could knock you unconscious." The old man and Reece both looked in Gideon's direction, and he explained impatiently, "Least then it would look like you went out with a fight."

The man's narrow face brightened. "A fascinating proposition! Yes, yes, quickly, a blunt object!"

Gideon was gettin' ready to oblige when Reece asked the fellow, "Who are you?"

"I—" The man started, and then stopped to look surprised. "You mean you don't know? Why, I thought it would be obvious. I am the apothecary!"

The hairs on the back'a Gideon's neck shifted, his skin pricklin'. He swung about and brought the revolver up on the rotary door, sure he'd see a silhouette on the other side'a it, watchin' them. Nothin'. So

far as the eye could tell, they and the old man were the only folks about
for at least a mile. So far as the eye could tell.

"You mean...*you* make the serum for them?" Reece said, like it
was too good to be true. Gideon heard him sheathin' his gun and made
a disapprovin' noise that was ignored. "Do you have some? Here?"

"Oh no, that would be most forbidden. All completed droughts are
confiscated immediately. I simply work from here. *They* wish me out
of the public eye, you see, for my own safety. If the public knew who I
was, I'd be hounded for the serum. No, it's better I stay here
altogether. That's better for everyone, you see."

After a thoughtful pause, Reece answered, "Well then. I'm
assuming the way to the Veritas's base of operations—" The old man
made a chokin' noise at the name. "—is through that hatch. So Gideon
will be knocking you unconscious now, maybe even tying you up for
effect. Are you ready?"

"Y-yes, of course."

"Gid. *Gideon!*"

Hesitatin', Gideon pulled his eyes and gun from the door. The
feelin'a bein' watched came back as soon as his back was turned. He
sauntered over to the old fellow and popped him on the back'a the
head with the revolver without puttin' any real heart into it. As he
pulled retractable rubber coil outta his jacket and bound the wilted
man's wrists together, he grumbled, "There a plan if this turns out to
be a trap, Cap'n?"

Crouchin' by the trapdoor, Reece cheerfully shrugged. "Hope for
the best?"

Gideon snorted.

The stairs beneath the hatch stretched down into darkness in a
tunnel'a wooden crossbeams. They must'a been climbin' down them
for a good quarter mile before the stairs leveled out into packed dirt
floors and the ceilin' lowered so that Gideon felt the subconscious
need to stoop.

It was a few minutes' walk in the dark before they saw the lights
up ahead, three dozen'a the dingy red sort, arranged in a curious six by
six pattern. In another minute, their tunnel drained out into an
underground cavern the size'a one'a the warehouses above ground.
Square in its middle was a bronze dome with six terraces, with six
arched doorways on each level and a red light over each door. Tippin'
his head one way, Gideon could see it as a rust-colored honeycomb.
And the lean, graceful shadows glidin' in the inner depths'a the
dome—those were the bees.

"Finished serums are fourth row up, third row in, second door on the right. The components are first row up, second row in, seventh door on the left," Reece murmured.

Gideon felt him tense when the dome suddenly emitted a shrill, mechanical whistle. Steam flushed outta small fissures in its body. The whistle dwindled; a scream echoed through the cavern, long and pain-ridden and human.

When the scream faded out, Gideon and Reece leaned back on their haunches and looked at each other in the panes'a red cast by the dome's lights.

"Well," Gideon rumbled, "don't say I never did nothin' for ya." Still in his crouch, he started to edge outta the tunnel and into the cavern. Only, somethin' caught him by the back'a his jacket and gave it just enough of a backwards tug for him to tip and sit down hard on the dirt floor. "What the heck, Reece—"

He stopped when he saw that Reece was sittin' too, and lookin' sour besides. He pointed. Gideon turned to find Nivy stooped with her arms roped around her knees, smilin' smugly at the two'a them.

"How the bleedin'—you been stalkin' us, girl?"

"Mordecai." Reece stood. "He put you on the garbage transporter too, didn't he?"

Nivy simply nodded.

"I'll kill him," Gideon grumbled. Reece was too busy tryin' to beat Nivy in a starin' contest, a real battle'a the wills by the look'a it, to pay him any attention.

"Stay here," he ordered her, deadpan. "Don't follow us, don't leave...just *stay here*. Got it?"

Gideon couldn't say how he knew what was comin'—maybe it was that understandin'a Nivy he thought he had—but when she started runnin', he was ready. Didn't make much of a difference, because *dirt*, she was quick, but he was. She slipped outta his hands like a bar'a wet soap and charged into the cavern with long, determined strides that made less sound than an autumn breeze.

Reece grabbed Gideon around the middle before he could take after her, gruntin' as they wrestled, "Wait!"

Their arms tangled together, they froze and watched as Nivy went at the dome in a wild sprint. Gideon was all ready for a collision when she leaped, kicked off the base wall, and grabbed the railin'a the first terrace to pull herself to its level.

Stumped, Reece and Gideon watched her disappear into the terrace shadows and reemerge again a second later, wavin' for them to come on already.

Reece made a reluctantly impressed sound. "Mordecai must've known what he was doing."

"The old man's a numpty," Gideon said harshly. "His job was to watch Crazy, not send her out so he can live vi...what's the bleedin' word...*vicariously* through her."

As Reece started forward, he clicked his tongue and said somethin' like, "Sure you're not just jealous?"

Gideon gave him a dirty glare and said nothin'. No need to defend himself against total bogrosh.

They jogged to the brass dome, and Gideon gave Reece a boost up to the railin' before jumpin', grabbin' the ledge with the tips'a his fingers, and pullin' himself up after him. Nivy was waitin' for them, her face an irksome blend'a amusement and patience. She pointed at them and jabbed her thumb at the dark corridor mouth at her back, pointed at herself and nodded upwards, and then finally waved at the tunnel leadin' to the apothecary's.

"You get a sample of the finished serum, we get the ingredients. Meet back at the tunnel." Reece didn't sound too thrilled about his own interpretation, but if he wanted to argue, he didn't take his chance. Nivy's feet were already disappearin' as she pulled herself up to the next terrace and outta sight.

The strange sudden absence'a the Vees had Gideon tryin' to look every way at once as Reece led the way down the red-lit corridor that had been bustlin' five minutes ago. Where'd they all gone? And, the more pressin' question, when were they gonna be back?

Reece stopped at the seventh door down and punched a few numbers into its access panel as Gideon prowled around him. As the door rushed back into the wall, warm air curled out into the corridor, carryin' with it the clean, sharp smell'a chemicals. The room's auxiliary lightin' was an underwater blue that backlit the glass aisles neatly linin' the room. Aisles'a endless tiny beakers and bottles, all'a them unlabeled.

The shadows on Reece's face took on a hard edge in the room's light. "Take some of everything, as much as you can carry."

The bottles were so small, rollin' in the flat'a Gideon's big, callused hand, he had to move extra slow so as not to accidentally crush them. Reece's pockets filled up twice as fast as his, bulgin' with the bottles that rattled when he walked up and down aisles. Always, under the sound'a clinkin' bottles, they could hear the dome hummin' like it was breathin'.

"I think that's everything," Reece said when they'd finished their rounds about the room.

"Good. This place puts an itch down my back."

Noddin' as if he was familiar with the sensation, Reece reopened the door and ducked into the corridor, which was still as silent as a cemetery, and in the same sorta eerily restless way.

It was a second before Gideon realized they'd turned left, not right, outta the door, and that it was gettin' darker and darker. The corridor ran doorless and lightless in this direction; the auxiliary lights were distant, hazy suns at their backs and just pinpricks'a red far ahead.

"What—"

"We're never going to have this chance again, Gid."

"What chance? The chance to get ourselves dead? I dunno, I see lots'a opportunity for that in the near future. Don't think we need to rush into it now."

"Well, I doubt you're helping our chances any by *talking so loud.*"

Gideon checked himself with a scowl and lowered his voice. "Don't have to get snippy."

Reece made a noise—sounded like a muffled laugh. Gideon couldn't make out the details'a his face, only the outline'a him walkin' funny to keep the bottles on his person from chimin'. This whole ordeal was sourin' Gideon's stomach. He hadn't strictly been keepin' track'a time, but it felt like there was a big clock in his head, tickin' off the seconds loud enough to bring the Vees runnin' to investigate.

Turned out there *was* a door in this corridor. It was the only one, and the hallway ended at its threshold, like it was presentin' the great steel hatch to Gideon and Reece. It was open just a hair; scarlet light and a deep, lecturin' voice both squeezed out into the corridor as Reece crouched at the foot'a the hatch and Gideon kept watch from behind.

"...the time grows near, now. Our next task will be the last before the truth is drawn to light, once and for all. We will install the new order of justice. We will..."

Gideon started as Reece tugged on his jacket, and crouched down beside him to see what he could see. The door was attached to an amphitheater, a great domed room that was the beatin' heart'a the hive. There were no seats. The hundreds, maybe thousands'a Vees inside all stood shoulder to shoulder, jammed for space around the circular platform where the speaker Vee stood in a fall'a red light. There was nothin' in particular that distinguished it from the rest'a the Vees. Gideon wondered if any one'a them coulda been the speaker, if there weren't any ranks among the creatures. Or if there were...what rank'a Vee they'd left with Aitch and Mordecai...

Catchin' Gideon's attention with a wave, Reece nodded back the way they'd come, and they hurried to put distance between them and the hatch and what it hid. Gideon'd seen a lot in his short twenty-one years. Nothin' compared to lookin' into that amphitheater and feelin' like he'd stuck his head into a nest'a evil.

They reached the outer terrace, and after checkin' to make sure there weren't no stragglin' Vees about, climbed down into the cave and sprinted to the tunnel without worryin' about the noise their bottles made.

"Nivy?" Reece called softly into the tunnel. He glanced at Gideon, eyebrows bunched together. "She's not here."

"Unless she got back and then left again...made a run for it..."

Reece's glance lengthened and hardened into a stern stare. "If she was going to run on us, she wouldn't have bothered following us all the way here."

"Unless she wanted the serum."

"Why would she want the serum?"

"Makes you stronger, doesn't it? Faster, smarter, and all that? Who wouldn't want it?"

The conversation froze as together they spotted Nivy makin' her way down from the upper terraces. The way down looked harder than the climb up. She had to let herself over the edge'a one terrace, hang, and then drop, catchin' the railin' below with just her fingertips—like one'a them street acrobats they have on Orpheus, that scale buildin's and run on rooftops. When she reached ground level, she crouched in the dark, catchin' her breath. Lookin' straight at them, she nodded. She had it. The Crazy had the serum.

Reece smirked at Gideon, who bristled.

"Yeah, whatever. This only means she won't have the chance to run off without us catchin' her."

"No, this means you'll have the chance to apologize to her."

"Aw, comon', Cap'n..." Gideon gulped down his words as he glanced a bit'a movement outta the corner'a his eye. He looked up.

On the dome's topmost terrace, a lone Vee was standin' at the railin', starin' out into the cavern. Dirt if it didn't make Gideon feel like its creepy black eyes were right on him and Reece.

Reece had gone utterly rigid—he had seen, too. "Stay put," he murmured, barely movin' his mouth. Gideon knew he wasn't talkin' to him. He was willin' his words on Nivy, who across the cavern, was gettin' ready to run.

She sprang outta her shadow, flyin' at them with a will. At the same time, a terrible siren started in the dome, an endless mournful wailin'. Nivy didn't look back, just kept sprintin', her face too focused to look afraid.

"Burn it!" Gideon shouted, the siren gobblin' up the volume'a his voice. "She ain't gonna make it!"

Half a dozen Vees were spillin' outta the base'a the dome, runnin' so fast they were blurs'a black jumpsuits and pale white skin comin' up hard on Nivy's heels.

"Cover her!" Reece barked, aimin' his hob and fannin' its hammer with his left hand, sendin' bullets singin' over Nivy's head. Two'a the Vees staggered.

Fingers curlin' into their familiar restin' places on the revolver's three triggers, Gideon took a step outta the tunnel and picked out three targets. Left, middle, right. The gears'a the gun worked, pullin', pushin', clickin', and the barrel rolled on its ball three times, to three angles. The recoil ran down his arms as revolver jumped in his hands and the bullets fired.

The two Vees that Reece had started on collapsed and skated to stops on their stomachs. A third, on the right flank, twisted on a leg he suddenly found a lot less functional without its knee.

Nivy was almost in the clear, about twenty yards out from the tunnel, when she suddenly surged forward, thrown by the extra momentum'a somethin' hittin' her in the back. Gideon couldn't tell if it'd been a bullet or somethin' else, but it hurled her onto her stomach and left her unmovin' and wide open. He and Reece ran outta the tunnel in tandem, shootin', reloadin', and duckin' under what must'a hit Nivy, small, blue electrical projectiles that fizzed as they were shot from the terraces above.

Reece swerved between Nivy and the gunfire, planted his feet, and kept up a steady discharge'a bullets as he ordered, "Get her up!"

Without slowin' down, Gideon slid to one knee and started grabbin' Nivy around the middle.

The weirdest thing happened. She was movin, tryin' to help him help her up, and he could'a swore…she spoke. Looked right at him and said in a liltin' kind'a accent, "I'm fine!" And, odd as anythin', she looked as shocked about it as he felt, with her eyes goin' as big as saucers. There wasn't time to make sense'a it. Reece had gunned down the rest'a the first batch'a Vees, but more were startin' out from the hive, and the sizzlin' blue bullets were fallin' like rain.

Nivy's legs wouldn't hold her weight, so Gideon stooped and brought her up across his shoulder roughly. They ran for it, him and Reece takin' turns shootin' and rechargin'.

At first, it seemed they might make a clean if narrow escape. But comin' up on the end'a the tunnel, Nivy was startin' to feel mighty heavy, Reece was lookin' green in the face from sprintin' the whole way, and Gideon had his doubts.

"This...should be...good..." Reece panted, reachin' into his jacket as they dared to slow to a gruelin' jog. He pulled out an egg-sized silver contraption with a corkscrew-shaped stem. A burstpowder shell.

"Where the bleedin' bogrosh did you get that?" Gideon growled at him, shiftin' Nivy's bony body over his shoulder.

Reece grinned and used his forearm to scrub sweat outta his eyes. "Mordecai...left it in my...coat pocket. Thinks of...everything."

Gideon rolled Nivy off his shoulder. She staggered dizzily, and he and Reece grabbed her arms and pulled her up against the wall, where they crouched.

"How close are they?" Reece asked, thumb propped under the curled pin, ready to pop it off.

"Few more seconds," Gideon guestimated. "Wait..."

They held their breath, trustin' their ears to infiltrate the dark before their eyes. Gideon counted four seconds off before the first echoes'a footfall reached them. Not a heartbeat later, a spray'a blue electric charges struck the wall above them.

Windin' back his arm, Reece pitched the burstpowder shell into the black ahead. The pin *pinged* as it hit the ground.

"Heads down!" Reece shouted, then yapped, "Bloody—" as a streak'a blue struck his raised arm.

The shockwave rolled under their feet, a second ahead'a the white flash that shook the tunnel. Dust curled around them in the sudden burst'a hot air, and Gideon and Reece coughed into their sleeves while Nivy tried to guard her eyes against the driftin' dirt.

They waited a long minute for the air to settle before helpin' each other stand.

Gideon strained to see if the rubble and wreckage had properly clogged the tunnel mouth behind them. "Think we managed to kill a few?" he asked hopefully, keen on the thought.

"As long as they can't get through, I'm happy," Reece muttered, massagin' his throwin' arm. "Those blue charges pack a sting. I feel like I've stuck my finger in a panel feed fixture. Nivy?" She looked at him, her face smudged with dirt. "Do you have the serum?"

Nivy considered for a moment, pattin' her trouser pockets. She suddenly went still, the way a person goes still when they realize somethin's gone terribly awry. Her eyes widened in confusion; she flushed bright red. Then, without so much as a warnin', she lunged at Gideon and shoved him hard in the chest.

"What?" he snapped, and would've shoved back if Reece hadn't caught his arm.

Shakin' her head furiously, Nivy pulled her fist outta her pocket to present the splintered remains of a glass capsule that would've been about the size'a her little finger. Purple liquid stained the palm'a her hand, bled outta the broken beaker.

"How's that *my* fault?"

Takin' a step toward him, Nivy demonstrated heavin' somethin' over her shoulder, simulated crushin' it with her arm.

Now it was Gideon's turn to go red in the face. Mindlessly reloadin' his revolver, he growled at her, "Well, you could'a said somethin'!" She made an exasperated face, wrinklin' up her nose. "Hey, I ain't stupid, I *heard* you!"

"Heard her?" Reece interrupted, cuttin' between them with his hands raised. Well, one raised. The other kept fallin' down on its own accord. "What—"

"In the chamber! She bleedin' spoke! Looked right at me and said she was fine! Now, tell me that don't sound like she's been playin' us like a couple'a burnin' fools!"

Even though Nivy looked like she wanted to shake her fist at him, she looked at Reece, whose face had darkened, and appealed to him with a gaze to make a fellow feel like he'd just been hit with one'a those blue charges. All big-eyed like.

Maybe Reece bought it, maybe he didn't—it was hard to tell. He'd been takin' leaves outta Nivy's book when it came to hidin' his thoughts lately. Frownin', he said slowly, "Let's save that particular explanation for later. We've got to get to the garbage disposer." With a glance at his watch, he started joggin' backwards toward the stairs. "Post haste."

Gideon grouchily picked up his revolver to eye level and followed. And tried to keep a good safe distance between himself and Nivy, who was still lookin' mighty hostile.

XV

The Longest Day in the History of Longest Days

Reece could list everything that'd gone wrong with the heist. Nivy, the serum, making it back to the garbage disposer by the skin of their teeth...but he was just too tired. Besides, there wasn't room in the cramped cargo bay for another bad attitude. Gid was grumpy enough for all three of them.

The garbage disposer landed on Atlas just as the grey and yellow dawn started outshining the stars. Reece and Gideon's bims were parked in the vehicle stables next to the massive white building that was the midway point for garbage disposers on their way to collect new batches of dumpsters. Reece's legs felt like flimsy wires supporting his body as he and his companions climbed the stairs to the bims, and he yawned a yawn that stretched the already too-tight muscles in his face. None of them spoke, just doggedly climbed onto the bims, Nivy doubling with Reece.

Mordecai was waiting for them outside the shop, smoking a cigar. His bright Pantedan eyes twinkled as the bims' engines roared and then sputtered to a stop on the pedestrian walkway before him.

"Lookie there! Not a bullet hole to be seen in one'a you!"

"Only because they weren't using bullets," Reece told him dryly, stretching. "They preferred some kind of...I don't know. Appendage-frying electricity."

"Eh. Lightning caps. They would." Mordecai paused, chewing on his cigar and watching them lift their sorry selves off the bims. "Hayden's already left for The Iron Horse. He'll be sad he missed ya...don't think he slept more than two winks. Left you all breakfast, though."

Gideon paused, glanced around with a frown, and asked suspiciously, "Who's watchin' the Vee?"

"No one. Fella's been out cold for about two hours now. Hayden managed to get some water in him, but he ain't doin' so good. Likely will be needin' that serum before another day goes by, elsewise we'll have a dead body to account for. You got some you can give him?"

Cringing, Reece heavily sat back down on his bim so that it bounced on its wheels. Bed and breakfast were going to have to wait.

He needed to fetch Hayden and put him to work on the serum before the Vee keeled over…though, truth be told, he didn't feel so far from keeling over himself.

"Here," he grumbled, shoving handfuls of bottles at Nivy and Mordecai as he pulled them out of his pockets. "Get down there and try to get the Vee lucid. But don't let him get his hands on any of these. And don't leave him alone anymore. Stay put till I get back."

Mordecai and Gideon both opened their mouths as Nivy raised her hand to be heard, but Reece was already kick starting his bim and switching into second gear. He peeled off the walkway, spraying pebbles in his wake.

In the distance, The Iron Horse's kettle-like whistle sounded, and he grouchily stomped on the clutch to shift up again. He could see the locomotive chugging into the distance, a mile or two ahead of him, too far gone to be stopped now. It looked like he had a half hour drive back to The Owl to stay awake for, and nothing but a splitting headache to keep him company on his way.

Steering with one hand, he reached into the leather satchel slung behind his seat to retrieve his wireless earpiece. As he let it cuff the rim of his ear, he caught the crackling sounds of the morning public wireless wave, and settled back to listen, hoping the brisk morning wind would be enough to keep him conscious.

Guy Clark was heading the broadcast this morning, in a smooth, chipper voice that made Reece mash his molars together irritably.

"Day two-hundred and eleven of the Epimetheus's solar cycle promises to be lovely. The Honoran Airway Sentries ask for your caution flying in Caldonia today, as it is the biannual equestrian march, and access to ground roads will be limited. In addition to our daily log, today we will be hosting an exclusive interview with Hester Knight, event planner for the Grand Duke's upcoming masquerade. This interview is sponsored by Mister Mortimer's Old Thyme Carriages, and…"

Reece made it back to The Owl in record time, though not entirely on purpose. His foot had been heavy without his help, heavy like the rest of him, particularly his eyes.

The Owl's oak trees and picket fences were swathed in mist; students hurried along under shared parasols, teeth chattering. Guy Clark's weather predictions apparently didn't cover Honora's moons.

Aware that he was entertaining stares from all directions, Reece looked down at himself, and in spite of how bone weary he was, snorted. He was still in his heist clothes, dark and filthy and stinking of garbage. And he could feel that his crop of brown hair was standing on end, sticky with sweat and slicked with rain. Oh well. If he had a reputation to look after, he *might* care, but as it was…

He beat The Iron Horse to its station just east of the Airship Command Center, parked his bim, and sat sideways on it to await Hayden's arrival. The rain didn't bother him. By this time, he was so tired that someone could have turned a bucket of water over his head, and he would have thanked them for their contribution.

There weren't many people on the platform—mostly just girls who were painfully obvious about waiting for some boy or another to return from a night spent in Praxis. They milled about restlessly in their prim black uniforms…Reece's eyes started to close as he listened to the soft *chhh* of the rain…there was one girl in brown, one out of a dozen in black, walking toward him…

"Reece!"

The buoyant voice startled him. He rocketed up off his bim, slightly frantic, swallowing hard, and looked around. Someone giggled.

"Well, that's what you get for sleepin' on the platform," Po gently admonished.

Reece sat down again. "It wasn't my first choice, believe me," he told her as he shook out his rain-dappled hair.

"I do." Po tipped her head to the side. She leaned across his handlebars to look him in the face. "Everythin' alright? I was kinda worried, you just up and disappeared yesterday."

Reece navigated carefully. "I had some business in Praxis. What are you doing here?"

"Oh. Me and Gus are shoppin' for undulator parts." She waved a dirty hand at a man in a jumpsuit with a mop of bleached hair and a small, clever face, sitting on one of the platform's black benches. Too young to be her father. He had to be one of her brothers. "What are you—"

"Waiting for a friend."

Teeth catching her bottom lip, Po considered him. "Don't know what it is," she said after a moment of thought, "but you've just got a look about you today. Somethin' that wasn't there yesterday. You're all…feverish."

Pushing up the cuffed sleeve of her jumpsuit, she pressed the back of her hand to his forehead, like Abigail would have done ten years ago. New though Po was to Reece, this didn't feel odd or unfamiliar in the least. He wondered if Po ever made anyone feel out of place, or if she was like one of her beloved engine parts that could be jimmyrigged to fit wherever it needed to fit to make the engine run smoothly.

"I haven't slept," Reece admitted, because there was no harm in saying that much, and because lying to Po felt twice as wrong as lying to anyone else.

"Maybe you shouldn't be drivin' a bim around The Owl then, Cap'n." Po smiled bashfully; it might've been a trick of the dull morning light, but Reece thought she had gone rather red behind her freckles.

Right on time, The Iron Horse noisily slid in on its tracks, breaks shrieking, chimney coughing. Shapes milled behind the milky glass of the carriages, ready to spill out onto the platform. Hayden was probably one of the smallish shapes getting crowded further and further back in line.

"That's me, then," Po said as she stood and dusted at dirt on her filthy jumpsuit that Reece got the feeling was there to stay. "I'm off to see a man about an AX734 crude undulator refinement cap. Don't be a stranger, alright, Reece?"

Reece watched her skip away and almost trip on one of her straggling boot laces as she joined Gus in the boarding queue. She said something to Gus, turned, and waved enthusiastically at Reece one more time while Gus glared over her head broodingly. So, probably not a member of the Palatine Second fan club, then.

"Who was that?" Hayden asked as he joined Reece by the bim, a little breathless.

Reece started to answer before he noticed Hayden's face—tight, discolored, and tired. His stomach clenched in guilt. If there was a way he could do this on his own, he would do it. In a second, he would do it. The hard fact was, he couldn't. A captain wasn't much of a captain without a crew.

"Hayden...don't take this the wrong way, but you don't look so good."

Hayden smiled and said, "It could be worse. I could smell like I spent the night in a garbage disposer."

"That *would* be worse."

"Did you get what you needed? Are Nivy and Gideon alright?"

"Er...in a manner." Hayden's face spasmed in alarm, and Reece hurriedly amended, "I mean, we got what we needed in a manner. Crazy and The Grouch are fine. It couldn't have been easier."

Hayden eyed Reece doubtfully as he hefted his leather bookscrip from one shoulder to the other with a grunt. Reece tried to keep his face cool, but even his cheek muscles were too tired to cooperate. His attempted smile felt like a lopsided grimace.

"Something's wrong," Hayden guessed with a sigh. Distantly, The MA Building's bell began tolling, counting off the seventh hour as Reece scrubbed his bleary eyes.

"Our sample of the original serum was destroyed. We need you to recreate it from the ingredients we got you. From scratch."

Reece expected a lecture about safety first and taking risks, but Hayden just stared at him like things couldn't get any worse, and sighed again.

"As soon as possible, I'm assuming?"

"You're the doctor. You think our friend the Vee can afford a few hours?"

Making a face, Hayden looked back at The Iron Horse. "I'll need to swing by the dormitory...collect some of my supplies."

"I'll meet you back at Mordecai's."

"You're skipping class again?"

"Let's put it this way," Reece said as he sagged onto his bim. "Given my options, I'd rather sleep on a cot than a desk."

Reece slept for a whole twenty minutes on Mordecai's patchy couch before Hayden gently shook him awake, his apologetic eyes made huge and comical by the magnifying lab specs he wore.

"I'm sorry, Reece. I'm going to need your help."

"It's fine, it's fine," Reece mumbled as he unwillingly came to, leaning up on his elbows. His hair hadn't even had time to dry from his stand in the water closet not half an hour ago.

Nivy came into the room through the kitchen's swinging doors, artfully balancing a triangle of mugs in her hands. After handing one to both Hayden and Reece, she sat her chin on the rim of the leftover, letting the steam of the chocolate tea (Reece could recognize that smell anywhere) soak her face. Of the three of them, Reece had to say she looked the best. She had her natural wildness to help cover up her sleeplessness, but she still seemed genuinely, bafflingly, somehow alert.

Reece felt worn thin, as if he could stand in front of a light and be translucent.

They did what they could with what they had. The shop upstairs was better lit, but rather less discreet, so they had to make do turning Mordecai's kitchen into Hayden's makeshift laboratory. That meant boxing up Mordecai's junk and sanitizing the whole room to Hayden's very fastidious satisfaction.

Hayden was spreading a drop cloth over Mordecai's counter as Nivy and Reece scrubbed at the gritty floor with the sponges bound to their hands. Standing on a chair in the middle of the room, Mordecai worked to fasten new photon globes to his hanging chandelier.

Mordecai coughed as he inhaled dust. "All this cleanin'…it ain't gonna look like home in here anymore."

"We're almost done, now," Hayden promised. "If you want to go keep wa—"

"Nah. I'd rather be in here, in case somethin' goes wrong with the serum and it explodes or somethin'."

Reece thought it would make more sense to want to be out of the room pending a chemical explosion; going by Nivy's small smile, she would say the same, if she could. If she could. His grin faded.

"What happened to the serum, anyhow?" Mordecai asked. "Thought you were gonna at least try to bring back a copy of the original?"

Nivy's scrubbing turned violent, and she cringed unhappily.

"We did," Reece said on her behalf, "but it didn't make it back."

"It's unfortunate," Hayden sighed. He picked his black satchel up off the floor, clicked it open, and spread it out on the counter like he was unfolding a book with pages made of tapering metal tools. "Anything I make will be more or less a rough mock up. I would've liked to see the serum in its purest form." He paused, appraised the room, and declared, "I'm ready to start. Let me grab the rest of my tools."

Mordecai started whistling cheerfully to himself as Hayden disappeared into the living room. The sudden privacy Reece and Nivy had down on their hands and knees made Reece feel slightly self-conscious. It was the first chance he'd had to ask her alone—*almost* alone—about what Gideon had said in the tunnel last night.

"*Can* you talk, Nivy?" he asked in a whisper so low he almost didn't hear it himself. Mordecai went on whistling, as chipper as a spring bird.

Nivy didn't look up until her scrubbing brought her so close to him that their heads nearly touched. Then she raised her eyes, and with that odd power of hers, forced an answer on him in the silence.

Relief made his words come out as a sigh. "No, you can't."

But there was more to it, he could tell, because Nivy's eyes narrowed slightly, and then her gaze intensified.

Reece shook his head helplessly. "I'm not asking the right question."

"Or maybe yer just askin' the wrong person."

Nivy and Reece both jumped, startled, at Mordecai's interruption. He didn't look down at them, just kept screwing in the photon globes, touching them with only his callused fingertips.

"I know I don't look it," Mordecai drawled, "but I have been around the bend a few times. Seen a lot, you know. Been to nearly all the planets this side of the Epimetheus, one way or another. One planet in particular, I'll never forget. Not one of Honora's ally planets, nosiree. Big slave tradin' planet, enforcin' all kinda laws over the lower class. Ever heard'a Zenovia?"

Reece leaned up off his knees, flexing his pruned hands, and shook his head speechlessly. Nivy remained prostrate on the kitchen floor, bowed over her scrubbies with her blue eyes sharp on Mordecai. She looked wary.

"Figured you hadn't," Mordecai continued, still intent on his work with the chandelier. "Ugly planet. Ugly government. Cruel place to live, 'specially if you get lotteried into the slave class. Zenovia's slaves have less rights than a bucket'a fish bait. Speech is forbidden to them, you see. They couldn't talk back if they wanted to, because as soon as they get lotteried, they're collared."

A bad taste had settled in Reece's mouth. "Collared?"

"Mmhmm. The collar the slaves wear is some kinda impairment technology that shuts down their vocal chords so long as they're worn. And here's the kicker. The slaves can't take them off, not even off'a each other. Only their master can remove them. Fair as dirt, if you ask me."

A voice spoke up from the doorway, cutting through Reece's speeding thoughts. "Her necklace..." Hayden suddenly joined Reece and Nivy on the floor, wearing a lab coat, his goggles, a pair of tight rubber gloves, and an expression that looked ill. "Nivy, is that...is that what happened to you? Are you a...slave?"

That image felt off, skewed. Nivy, a slave forced into silence by a lottery and a master and a piece of shiny new technology—Reece didn't believe it, even before Nivy started shaking her head. She stuck up her chin proudly, and there, around her neck, Reece saw the black ribbon she never took off. It had never been particularly pretty, but it had never struck him as ugly, as it struck him now.

"You're not a slave, but the collar works the same," he said darkly. "It keeps you from speaking. It cuts off your voice."

Abigail and Liem's voices in his memory: *"Nivy doesn't speak."*
"She's a mute?"
"She doesn't speak."
Had Liem known?

Nivy hesitated, then nodded, running her thumb over the band above her collarbone without any particular fondness.

Hayden seemed stricken, staring at her throat. "Can we take it off you? Is there a way?"

"Seems to me," Mordecai said dryly, "if she'd wanted you boys to try, she would've told you what that collar did from the start in her own way."

"Why? I'm sorry, Nivy, but...who chooses not to be able to speak?"

"Someone with something to hide." Nivy frowned at Reece's tone of voice. "Your own people collared you in case you were captured by Eldritch. So you couldn't speak about who you are or why you want Aurelia back."

Reece had never dreamed that not being able to talk was *convenient* for her. What better way to guarantee her secrets' safety than to wear one of those bleeding collars? What sort of person...he stopped that thought. He was overreacting because he'd started counting Nivy as a sort of tenuous friend, a surrogate crew member. A crew didn't keep secrets of this magnitude from each other.

Even as Reece simmered at her, Nivy cautiously reached out a hand and touched the top of his head, then brought the hand back to her chest to cover her heart. The gesture didn't make sense, but Reece knew what was at the heart of it. She was sorry.

Nivy repeated the gesture to Hayden, who was like putty in her hands. "I understand, Nivy," he said with feeling. "Well...as much as I can, I suppose. We really have no idea who you are, do we?"

Nivy outright grinned at him as if to say, "No idea at all."

The kitchen fell uncomfortably silent. Mordecai occupied himself with disposing of old photon globes while Hayden, seeming embarrassed, returned to arranging beakers, wash plates, and crucibles on the counter. Reece realized they were waiting for him to say something.

Standing on legs bruised from scraping over the hardwood floors, he studied Nivy's earnest expression and sighed. "I guess you didn't mean anything by it."

Nivy rolled her eyes, and Reece read in her face, Of course I didn't.

"I just thought we were going to start trusting each other."

She started reaching for his head again, and he batted her hand away, trying not to smile, now. "I guess it's a good thing you can't be bought with apple pie alone," he allowed grudgingly.

An acrid smell made Reece's throat sting, and he looked over at Hayden, who at the counter, was transferring droplets of green liquid from one beaker to another filled partway with purple. As green curled into violet, the liquid sizzled angrily, and the smell grew more defined, almost rubbery.

"Should we leave you to concentrate?" Reece asked, hoping for a yes as he covered his mouth and nose.

It was a minute before Hayden replied, he was so focused on those tiny green droplets. "It doesn't matter either way. I'll be experimenting for quite some time to even figure out what half these chemicals are. I mean, doesn't this look like hydroburotane to you?" He picked a yellow bottle up between his thumb and forefinger and showed it to him, his magnified eyes widening to disconcerting proportions.

Reece stared at it. He didn't want to say what he thought it looked like. "Sure, yeah. Hydro…burrow…tang."

Hayden turned back to the counter and started working again with feverish but precise speed. "Get some rest, Reece. I'll wake you when I have something."

It was three hours before Reece rolled off the couch, startled awake by the sounds of frantic shouting and Pantedan curses. He opened his eyes regretfully and stared up at the ominous purple cloud clinging to Mordecai's low ceilings.

"Cap'n!" Gideon roared as he rushed through the room with a pail of dirty water in either hand. "You'd better come quick!"

Clumsy with half-asleepness, Reece tripped to the swinging kitchen door and hurled himself through it. It would have been better if he'd waited for his feet to come to their senses—there was an ankle-deep layer of yellow foam covering the kitchen floor. With a wordless scream, Reece slid through the foam, crashed into Gideon's wall of a back, and fell.

"Get up, get up!" Hayden shouted from where he was trying to stop a strangely endless flow of foam from erupting out of an impossibly small beaker by cramming a dinner plate over it. "It will eat through your clothes!"

As Reece thrashed, Gideon doubled over and grabbed him by the front of his waistcoat, heaving him to his feet. Reece could smell the singed threads of his shirt. What was worse, his back was startling to prickle.

"Water!" he bellowed, trying to peel his shirt off before the foam ate through to his skin.

Skidding in the foam, Gideon grabbed a bucket of water and turned it upside-down over Reece's head.

And that was just the first incident.

After the foam, there was the concoction of liquid that froze Hayden's hands together. Next came the black goop that bubbled like tar. At one point the kitchen started smelling like an old shoe, and it turned out the smell was from an airborne chemical that had traits similar to a hyperactive compulsor's.

"Open the vents and try to flush it out!" Hayden said shrilly upon realizing what the smell was. He fanned a glove before his face. "Where is Gideon? Probably off polishing his guns somewhere—no no, I didn't mean that! Hurry up with the vents!"

Reece, standing on the counter and trying to open the airvents that had long since been rusted shut, snapped, "You *could* get up here and help instead of waiting uselessly on the sidelines like you always— ugh, I'm sorry, that's not—"

"Uselessly! I'm tampering with dangerous chemicals for you while you sit back and get your forty winks! I didn't sleep at all last night either, you know!" Hayden violently smacked his glove against the counter, stared at it, and then whispered, "I shouldn't have done that."

As Nivy leaped up onto the counter with a butter knife to help Reece with the vent, she looked at him, opened her mouth, and then closed it. He saw her throat constrict as if she'd had to swallow her words. He could have asked her anything, *anything* right now if the collar wasn't doing its job to a T. In Gideon speak, it was fair as dirt.

"Reece," Hayden suddenly cried, throwing himself into a kitchen chair, "I *do* get airsick, I'm sorry I never told you! I'm a liar! A terrible liar!"

Reece held out his hand for Nivy's butter knife and started wrenching the creaking vent out of the ceiling before Hayden could altogether lose his head. Relief washed over him as the vent split and fresh oxygen replaced the old in his lungs.

"That's not all!" Hayden bemoaned, dramatically dropping his head into his hands. "Do you remember when we were Thirteens, and you and Gideon were going to skip our Honoran History class but Tutor James caught you? I ratted on you! I'm sorry! I didn't want you to go to the Mead Moon Festival and leave me behind!"

"We weren't going to go to the festival without you."

Hayden raised his head. "Really?"

"No, that was a lie. I was testing to see if the chemical's gone. I think it's clearing out." Reece hopped down from the counter and wiped his rust-stained hands down the front of his shirt with a sigh. "Look—"

"I know." Hayden started straightening his goggles and pulling his gloves back on, avoiding meeting Reece's eye. Reece thought he was just embarrassed over what had been dredged to the surface (he didn't bother confessing that he and Gideon had always known about the airsickness and the ratting) until Hayden looked up with a deeply troubled frown. "I don't know if this is going to work. The formulas I've tried so far have had fairly harmless results—"

"I almost died in acid foam."

"Well, there's that." Hayden pinched the bridge of his nose and shut his eyes. "Reece...I can't make that serum. Someone's going to get hurt if I keep trying."

"What if you had some help?"

"From who?"

Reece's eyes wandered in the direction of the back tunnel, and Hayden made a thoughtful if uneasy sound.

"The Vee?"

"If anyone knows something about the serum, he does. And I think he'll be eager to save his own neck, if we gave him the chance to try."

"Gideon won't be happy."

"Lucky we're used to working without Gideon's stamp of approval. Nivy," she looked up from the empty beaker she was turning over mindlessly with her fingertips, "go get Mordecai. We're going to need a little extra supervision."

The Vee had to be roughly shaken out of the comatose sleep he'd been in all day. The expression, if that's what you could call it, that flashed across his face upon realizing he was still alive was, Reece thought, the equivalent of human disappointment. Every time the Vee spoke in his withered-snakeskin voice, he had to pause and gulp as if his throat were unbearably dry.

"You should kill us now," he panted as Gideon, who'd gone to new heights of sourness at hearing Reece's plan, pulled him to his feet. "It would be a mercy."

"Right, because you've got a whole lot'a that comin' to ya," Gideon muttered.

Mordecai raised his gun as Reece stepped forward to cautiously wrap one of the Vee's arms over his shoulders.

"Walk with me," Reece ordered, recoiling at the Vee's rattling breath, so close to his ear.

The Vee took an unsteady step forward before his knees bowed inward. Slouching heavily against Reece, he chuckled hoarsely. "We feel death's nearness. Shall it take any of you with us, we wonder?"

"Gideon," Reece choked, and Gideon, grumbling, came and took the Vee's other arm and draped it across his back.

"Rather cuddle with a spider," he complained under his breath.

As Gideon and Reece carried him down the corridor, the Vee's pained groans faded into murmurs. Reece tried to ignore them, tried to think of daylight and laughter and bubbly little Po and anything but the Vee's chilling whispers, which burrowed deeply, twisting the pit of his stomach...

"Spiders. An interesting tool, to those with the fear of them. Anything can be a tool, of course. Fire...heights...darkness...we wonder, Reece Sheppard, what your tool might be. What could be used to bring you to the brink? You become a different man, at the brink. We have seen it. It is...a wonder."

Mordecai beat Gideon to cutting the Vee short. Rarely had Reece heard his accent with the gruff edges that Gid's had, or seen his whiskered face look so menacing. "You'll do best to keep walkin' and save your strength, stranger. Young Mister Sheppard here is tryin' to save yer sorry life."

The Vee let out a breath from between his teeth. "To bring us to the brink."

Gideon grunted. "What's he goin' on about now?"

Reece could guess. These last few days, he'd wondered about The Veritas, about their reason for existing. They were still human, in a sense; surely they had some sense of what *life* was. The serum didn't change the fact that they were sentient beings. They had to have goals, ideals (twisted ideals, granted), memories. Limits.

"Caving into questioning. Betraying the Veritas. That's his brink."

Blinking, Gideon eyed the Vee, who was staring numbly ahead, and barked a pleased laugh. "It's *scared*?"

The Vee looked at him sharply, and again, Reece saw not emotion on his face, but the impression of emotion. Like it was there inside, but he didn't know how to shape his face to match. "Fear is our greatest ally. We admire those with the skill to use it."

If ever Reece wondered if he was making the right decision, it was then.

As soon as they reached the kitchen, the Vee had to be allowed to rest; he was too weak to even keep his head erect so that Hayden could check his dilated pupils with a photon wand. All they could do was wait for him to recharge.

"Let us begin," the Vee finally said. His eyes scanned the kitchen without blinking, passing with interest over Nivy, who was propped on the empty end of the counter behind Reece. "Bring us what you have."

"Remember, nothin' funny," Gideon warned cheerfully, hefting his revolver. He and Mordecai were standing on either side of Hayden, managing to look like grandfather and grandson, for once.

"Your understanding of fear is trite, Gideon Creed." The Vee's white fingers danced over the mouths of Hayden's beaker collection. "There is no art in your method. Hayden Rice—" Reece saw Hayden stiffen. "—we will begin with the polythermatine. Next, the…"

Afternoon dragged into evening in the longest and most confusing chemistry demonstration Reece had ever endured. Hayden started out fumbling and nervous, paling whenever he was forced to hand off a beaker to the Vee, but by an hour into the serum's preparation, he had come into his prime. Reece would venture that he might actually be enjoying himself if it weren't for the Vee's routine comments about death and pain and fear and so on and so on.

As for the Vee…he was fading. Every hour, the paleness grew paler and the shaking grew shakier while sweat soaked his filthy jumpsuit. Reece thought he was willing himself to stay alive only because he knew the serum was on its way.

"We have come to the final element." The Vee's voice would've been carried away by a slight breeze, it was so thin. Doubled over in his seat, his eyes level with the meniscus of the brew in the beaker, he nodded once, then let his forehead rest on the edge of the table.

"Hurry, Hayden," Reece felt the need to add.

Hayden didn't need the reminder. He already had the hydrogen ready, and added it with steady hands to the serum, which settled into a creamy purple color.

"I-I don't know how much you need…"

The Vee was so quiet and so still, for a moment, Reece wondered if he'd already passed.

"All of it," he finally gasped out, and Hayden quickly transferred the serum from a beaker to a syringe, felt his way to the thick vein in the fold of the Vee's pallid arm, and nudged the needle in.

It was a long time before he gently pulled the empty syringe away. The Vee didn't raise his head, just kept opening and closing the fist of his injected arm, allowing the serum to pump through his bloodstream. Reece felt like the room was holding its collective breath.

"Well," Gideon started impatiently when the silence stretched, "did it—"

The Vee was a blur of movement, standing, grabbing Hayden by the throat, hurling him across the room and into Gideon and Mordecai. Mordecai shouted something, but the words rushed past Reece as he hurtled after the fleeing Vee. The Vee couldn't reach the surface. Everything they'd worked for, everything they'd learned, it would all come to nothing if he escaped now.

It didn't occur to Reece until he had reached the stretch of tunnel between Mordecai's living area and the toolshed behind the shop that he didn't even have a gun. Huh. Maybe that's what Mordecai had been shouting about.

He faltered slightly as he stepped into the dark tunnel, and something invisible crashed into him and drove his back into the wall. It felt like a bleeding battering ram.

"Did you really think," the Vee jeered, his beakish nose inches from Reece's face, "that we would be so easily controlled? That our secrets could be bought?"

Again, the Vee became a blur. One second he was latching onto Reece's arms, and the next, Reece was airborne. The hard stone floor flew up to meet him as he landed in a rolling sprawl, his bones seeming to shiver with the impact. His left wrist was definitely out of commission, he knew that right away.

Everything went out of focus when he tried to sit up. *Concussion.* Again. He couldn't make sense of what he was doing or why; his body was following old orders while his scrambled brain tried to make new ones. As the Vee started to pass by, Reece lunged and wrapped his arms around his legs. Pain that was realer to Reece than anything happening in the tunnel raced like fire through his wrist, and he put his chin down to his chest and screamed and held on.

XVI

1,201 Confessions

"Cap'n! *Reece!*"

Reece peeked between his eyelids and up at Gideon. The big Pan's eyes were pinched at their corners, worried.

"What happ—arrrggghhh!" Reece curled his body around the wrist that he'd tried to move.

"Busted?" Gideon said with interest.

"I think it's just a sprain. A…really bad sprain."

"How's your head?"

Reece tried to gather his scattered thoughts and remember why his head would be anything but fine. His brief flight down the tunnel swam slowly into his memory. He touched the back of his skull with his good hand and found a patch of wetness.

"I would've come sooner," Gideon said, somber, "but Hayden hit the counter pretty hard. There was lotsa blood."

"What?" Holding his wrist against his stomach to keep it steady, Reece leaned up and looked around, feeling weirdly sluggish. He and Gideon were alone in the dark tunnel, but there were voices, presumably Hayden's and Mordecai's, coming from the kitchen. "He's alright, then?"

"He says so. Apparently head wounds bleed a lot, or somethin'. Mordecai insisted on gettin' him stitched back together before he saw to you. Still, I think you're gonna want to have a straightener on that bone sooner rather than later. Think you can stand?"

Reece considered. Bracing his back against the tunnel wall, he pushed himself to his feet and was pleased to find that his body still worked like it should, even after the whack to his brainpan.

As he started walking, Gideon at his elbow like a loyal wolfdog, his memories filled out.

"The Vee?"

"We've got him." Hesitating, Gideon admitted, "Nivy clubbed him from behind while you were wrestlin' with him. Didn't think you'd want me to shoot him after she knocked him unconscious."

"Wouldn't have been very sporting," Reece agreed dryly. Not that hurling your opponent through the air was exactly fair play. "Where is he now?"

"Tied up in the kitchen. Still under."

"And Nivy?"

Gideon grumbled, "Except for bein' all cocky about gettin' the Vee, yeah, she's fine."

Stepping into the kitchen, squinting because the light made his head buzz, Reece looked around and flinched. There *was* a lot of blood. On the counter, on the floor, in a handprint against the wall. Even though Gid had said Hayden was alright, Reece's eyes jumped to find him.

He was sitting at the kitchen table, staring sideways into a handheld mirror to watch Nivy's hands work a needle through his tangled hair. In the corner of the room behind them, the Vee was trussed to a kitchen chair that faced the wall, like they had tried to put him out of sight, out of mind. Except a rare unsmiling Mordecai was in the corner too, and his revolver said he wouldn't be forgetting any time soon.

Hayden glanced up from the mirror, saw Reece's slightly nauseated expression, and mistook it for worried. "It's not as bad as it looks. Just a surface scratch."

"Right."

"Is your wrist—?"

"Just sprained, I think, but I'm not sure."

"Your head is bleeding, too."

Nivy tapped Hayden on the shoulder and presented him with her needle, finished. Her fingers, stained red, pushed a strand of sweaty hair out of her eyes. Maybe she hadn't been as collected as she looked.

"What happened?" Hayden asked, in full doctor mode as he held out his hands and let Reece sit his ruined wrist on them.

"He lied to us. He was never going to tell us anything."

Pursing his lips, Hayden mumbled, "There was always the danger of that, I suppose."

There was. And Reece had still dragged the lot of them into this mess, despite that danger. It had been a head-graze and a sprained wrist this time…what would it be the next time he put so much at stake for his precious answers?

He didn't think there was going to be a next time. He'd forgotten about the cufflinks, about why he had carried them, was carrying them.

"We're done," he announced grimly, and they all looked up at him, Hayden, Nivy, Gideon, and Mordecai. "We're in too deep. It's time to pull back."

It came down to this: sacrificing the safety of his crew wasn't going to save Liem, it wasn't going to change Parliament, and it wasn't going to keep him from being sent off to war. It wasn't going to reverse time and start things over the day before Reece, Hayden, and Gideon had snuck out into the Atlasian Wilds and seen Eldritch combing over Nivy's crash site.

It wasn't going to get him his captain's wings. Funny, that that was buried deep in the core of all of this, the seed that everything else had sprouted from.

All it was going to do was cost him the things he knew that selfishly, he couldn't give up.

Suddenly, Hayden *tsked*. "It looks like this has a slight fracture, Reece. I'm think I'm going to put a straightener on it, just for a day or so—"

"Didn't you hear me?" Reece snapped, exasperated. He tried pulling his hand away, but Hayden grabbed his arm with the gentle firmness of a doctor and held it in place.

"I heard you. It doesn't change the fact that your hand is broken and needs to be treated."

"How long is that gonna take?" Gideon complained from the doorway. "I'm hungry enough to eat a Freherian boar. Heck, I'd eat Nivy."

As Nivy made a face at the chuckling Gideon, Mordecai thoughtfully scratched his beard and bent over a cracked cupboard. "Think I've got some bird-on-a-stick stashed somewhere in here—burn it, never mind, the foam got it."

With his good hand, Reece slapped the table and growled, "Don't any of you automata have an opinion? I said it's over. It's time to pull back."

There was nothing uncertain about the pause, this time. Hayden kept working diligently on his wrist, but his eyebrows crinkled together as his look of concentration deepened, and Nivy went so far as to shake her head at Reece like she refused to believe him.

"I think you got it backwards, Reece. See, once you're in this deep, you don't pull back. If you want out, you see it through. All that pullin' back is gonna do is leave a messy trail and a lot'a unfinished business," Mordecai said gently, all the while hitting upon a hidden stash of black plums under his kitchen sink and tossing them one at a time to Gideon.

"The old man's right," Gideon added before Reece could get one syllable in. As he caught the plums, two, three, and then four, he juggled them in a complicated cycle he made look as easy as breathing. "Comon', Reece, you know you ain't givin' up on this, not really. You're just tryin' to do what you think is right by your reckonin' and put the rest'a us outta harm's way."

"That's not—"

"It is." Hayden smiled without looking up. "You're very transparent."

"Alright, so what if that's true? Anyone remember Gideon's bim accident? Do you realize how many close shaves we've had recently? Eldritch is on to us. He's controlling Parliament *and* The Veritas. How long do you think we're going to last if we keep sticking our noses where they don't belong?"

Gideon finished out the juggle, catching the four plums in one hand. "S'not as though you ever cared about takin' the safe way out before."

"And I don't see how that will solve anything, anyways," Hayden added in a milder voice. "Our sudden uninvolvement in this isn't going to protect us from what Eldritch already knows about what we know. Nivy, could you hand me that cellophane tape and canvas bonding? Thank you."

"You're unbelievable. All of you. Even you," Reece accused Nivy. She smiled and passed Hayden his torture devices. "This isn't going to end well."

With a chuckle, Mordecai twirled one of his mustaches around a finger and said, "Well, I suppose that's true for *somebody* out there, but heck, someone's gotta win. Might as well be us."

The discussion was far from over for Reece, but his chance to pursue it came to a dead halt when the Vee began to writhe in his chair in the corner, flexing against his bonds. As one, Gideon and Mordecai took up stations on either side of the chair and brought out their revolvers.

"Easy now, stranger," Mordecai warned. "My grandson and me, we're not too impressed with your shenanigans. Gideon here was trigger happy *before* you tossed around our friends, so just imagine how heavy his finger is on that trigger right about now."

"It's real heavy," Gideon clarified helpfully.

The Vee was silent for a moment, listening, perhaps, to the sound of Reece crossing the room, holding his half-braced wrist at an odd angle away from his body.

"So this is how it will be," the Vee quietly speculated. "You will try to press us, but your endeavors will get you nowhere. You are eager for failure, Reece Sheppard."

As Reece circled the chair, he caught Gideon's eye and nodded just slightly. He would have been lying if he had said his stomach didn't clench when Gideon sheathed his revolver in favor of his long belt knife. This had always been the plan, hadn't it? To put the questioner to the question?

There wasn't a trace of hesitation in Gideon's movements as he bent over with his knife angled to carve.

"Wait!" Hayden suddenly barked. "Gideon, wait!"

"If this is gonna make you squeamish, Aitch—"

Hayden broke through the circle that Reece, Mordecai, and Gideon made around the Vee, holding a small stopped tube that looked empty. "There's another way. Please. Put away the knife." When Gideon did no such thing, Hayden turned and appealed to Reece, his face drawn of color. "Reece, I saved a sample of the chemical we concocted earlier. The one that works like a compulsor. It's at least worth a try, isn't it?"

The Vee laughed. "Indeed, proceed with the compulsor, if you wish to waste your time. But you will find that this body is immune to such primitive devices."

It came as a surprise to Reece when Hayden mustered the courage to look the Vee right in the eye and say evenly, "I said *like* a compulsor. But the standard sentry's compulsor is liquid-based. This chemical is gaseous in form, unique in every way. It's probably the first of its kind. I doubt your body, perfect though it may be, will have the defense capabilities to fight it yet."

As soon as Reece saw that flicker of almost-emotion in the Vee's black eyes...almost-uneasiness...he said heatedly, "Do it." And if his relief was written all over his face as he stepped back from the Vee and slumped against the wall beside Nivy, oh well. "The rest of you should all clear out. He's not going anywhere, and the chemical's affects are a little, uh—"

Blushing a bright tomato red, Hayden put in, "Mortifying."

"One'a us oughta stay behind with you," Mordecai said. "'Cause obviously, accidents happen."

"I'll stay. Can't be that bad. Besides," Gideon twirled his knife around his fingers and grinned toothily down at the Vee, "he might still need persuadin'."

"Alright, me and Gid, then."

After snapping her fingers to get their attention, Nivy pointed to herself. Reece didn't have a problem with her staying. It didn't get much safer than sitting in a room with Nivy and an armed Gideon—provided they were on your side.

Ten minutes later, Reece, sitting between Gideon and Nivy, faced the Vee on what felt for the first time like even ground. They were all under the influence of the airborne compulsor that Reece had unstopped from its bottle after Hayden and Mordecai had gone, but the Vee was clearly feeling its effects most keenly. He didn't know the trick was in not thinking about everything you had to hide. His black eyes kept twitching like they were reading a datascope's memory archive.

"Let's start out simple. Do you have a name?"

The Vee's adam's apple bobbed as he tried to swallow his answer. "Yes," he hissed contemptuously, against his will.

"What is it?"

"One Thousand Two Hundred and One."

"Your name is One Thousand Two Hundred and One?"

"There are only numbers to distinguish the one from the many."

"Does he have'ta talk like that? It spooks me out," Gideon complained beneath his breath before clearing his throat. "I mean, it's annoyin', is all."

Reece heard a grunt and assumed Nivy had elbowed him. "That's a mouthful. You'll have to make due with a nickname. Oh-one. Owon, if you will."

There was a long pause as the Vee dropped his eyes to his lap and closed them as if in meditation. Reece leaned back, and folding his arms over his chest, waited. He tried to breathe shallowly, but he could still taste the compulsor on his tongue, like an aftertaste of sugar water.

"Kill us now, Reece Sheppard," the Vee designated Owon finally whispered. "If you have an ounce of pity, you will. There is no life after betrayal for The Veritas."

Again the words *life* and *Veritas* mingled strangely in Reece's mind. Maybe somewhere behind those depthless eyes, there was a humanness the serum hadn't touched. Or maybe the Vee was just playing him.

"I'm going to start asking questions now. You can try to fight the compulsor, or you can—"

"We hope we are among the brothers who bring you to the brink, Reece Sheppard. A broken bone is but a small sampling of *that* pain. We regret that we could not do you more harm with the chance we had."

"Alright then, your choice. Who controls The Veritas?"

The Vee's forehead crinkled as all of his concentration went into deflecting the question. His jaw went taut; his long, spidery fingers curled around the edge of his chair and clutched it angrily.

"Owon," Reece persisted, "who controls The Veritas?"

"Headmaster...Charles...Eldritch."

Reece hadn't realized, but his heart had been thudding unevenly, anxious. Now it did a merry skip out of pure relief. It wasn't as if this news was actually good at all—but bogrosh, did it *ever* feel nice to get a straight answer, no strings attached.

"Since when?"

"Our conception," Owon gave haltingly as a bead of sweat slipped down his sharply-boned face. "Thirty-five years past."

"He created you?"

"Yes."

"To help him get a foot in the door of Parliament...or to keep the people suppressed..." The Vee said nothing, so Reece appended, "Is that why he created you?"

His teeth clenched together, Owon raised his head, found Reece's brown eyes, and stared into them fiercely. "He created us to uphold peace and truth, to seek out those—"

"Well, that ain't what you do," Gideon snapped, leaning into Reece's peripheral vision. "What you do is tromp around and abuse folk and leave them with nightmares'a you comin' to—"

"That is part of our purpose." The Vee was losing the cool grip he had on his voice, and sounded all the more frightening for it. "Fear is the motivator we use, a tool of power. A man who has nightmares of being punished will avoid being caught in the wrong at all costs. The easiest way for him to do so is to *not do wrong to begin with.*"

"Do you really believe that?" Reece asked before Gideon could get in another angry word. "You think that's your purpose? You think that's why Eldritch created you?"

"Yes. Justice is our highest priority."

It seemed that unless Owon had broken through the compulsor's spell, he really believed that. Reece's dilemma took on a horrible new light.

"Don't you think it's hypocritical to claim justice as your highest priority when Eldritch has done so much wrong to get to his place of power...and you've helped him?"

The Vee hesitated. "We...do not understand the question."

"Eldritch has killed. He's stolen. I have reason to think he's kidnapped. Everything The Veritas do helps him get a firmer footing over the Honorans. How can you call that justice?"

There was an air about Owon as he gathered his answer that Reece didn't like at all. He wanted Reece to hear this, wanted him to feel its sting deep between his lungs.

"When Charles Eldritch rules Honora, he and The Veritas will rewrite the law. Democracy leaves opportunity for corruption and private agendas...we will cleanse Parliament of these things. We will establish a kingship and a king, and The Veritas will be handed the power to properly flush out the disease that erodes Honora's foundations, the criminals, the lies, those dark places where the Pantedans hide and live off the work of society..."

Reece's chest, his stomach, his head, they all felt empty, like his feelings had just dropped dead at his feet. Distantly, someone touched his arm, and he knew it was Nivy, but that meant nothing to him, because Owon's words were turning spirals in his head, and he felt dizzy. Charles Eldritch ruling Honora. Not a duke—a king.

"And the Grand Duke?" he asked hoarsely.

Owon gave a wicked smile, and there was no "almost" about the emotion in it. It was spite, pure and simple. "He will be...removed."

Reece's chair toppled as he jumped up and began pacing, breathing hard. Here it was, then, the pinnacle of Eldritch's plan. An assassination. For a second, Reece was able to look past everything the duke had and hadn't done to him, was able to push aside the terrible night of their last fight, and imagine a world without the man who had taught him all about airships and flying.

"So naïve," the Vee suddenly cackled.

"What's that?" Reece said, turning.

The Vee shook his bald pate, clearly savoring the moment. "Reece Sheppard, these things must happen. Can you not sense it? These times are truly bigger than the life of one forgettable duke. Things are happening, things that—"

Reece took two steps forward, wound back his good fist, and punched the Vee squarely in the mouth. The Vee's head snapped back and smacked the wall behind him. Very satisfying.

"Hey, are we gonna—" Gideon began, sounding excited, and then cut off with a grunt that suggested Nivy had elbowed him again.

Refusing to massage his raw knuckles, Reece stood before Owon and glared down at him. "What do you know about The Kreft?"

The Vee froze, contemplating Reece through eyes that were little more than dark slits. "You know of them?" His eyes flickered to Nivy; he seemed surprised.

"Answer my question," Reece demanded, stepping to the left to bar Nivy from the Vee's stare. "Why are they trying to take over Honora?"

"They are not."

Pausing, Reece studied the Vee, not entirely convinced he wasn't somehow fighting the compulsor. "But Eldritch…"

"Naïve," Owon repeated, very nearly snorting. He shook his head disdainfully. "Reece Sheppard, you think through the lens of your lifetime. These things that happen, they feel important to you, but they are not. Thaddeus Sheppard will not be the first leader to die for the advancement of mankind. There have been a hundred deaths spread over a dozen planets. All according to The Kreft's design."

Deciding to be more direct, Reece asked, "Who *are* The Kreft?" He sat down between Gideon and Nivy, glancing sideways at the latter. She seemed engrossed in the Vee's words, as if trying to glean some information from them for herself.

"The Kreft are an ancient collection of beings who have been the political power in The Epimetheus Galaxy for nearly a thousand years," the Vee calmly answered. His lips curled as Reece fell back in his seat as though slapped.

"That's—"

"It is very possible," Owon cut him off. "They are artists at manipulation, thriving in the shadows of ambiguity. A duke who came to know too much of them might indeed find himself tangled in a web of conspiracy. He might perhaps find himself with a target over his heart."

It was more than Reece could comprehend, much more than he should believe. He felt like he should be shouting, or laughing, or running, afraid. This eerie calm was much worse, because it meant that he *did* believe.

"Tell me more."

The Vee smiled mirthlessly as he stared defiantly into Reece's colorless face.

Gideon stepped in, his voice gruff. "So why is this all happenin' now? All the plottin' and—"

"It is not happening now, Pan. It has been happening for a thousand years. For every planet, for every prime minister or duke or king, there is a strategically-placed Kreft. Every political move…every civil war…" The Vee's eyes took on a decidedly wicked glint, and he chuckled throatily. Reece heard Gideon draw a sharp breath. "…all pioneered for their purposes. They are marauders, conquerors, as ancient as The Voice of Space itself. This is not the first galaxy they have conquered, and it will not be their last."

It was Reece's turn to cover for Gideon as his friend stared, poleaxed, at the Vee, clearly gathering up the steam for an explosion. If the Vee wasn't somehow lying, then the massacre of Panteda likely hadn't been a violent, unstoppable accident—it had been a ploy, manufactured. All those hundreds of thousands of Pans, dead because of a strategic move in someone's idea of a game.

"So you're saying The Kreft just came to Epimetheus and set up camp for the long haul? According to you, they have it conquered. Why stay? Why not move onto the next galaxy and start reupholstering that one?"

In the chair next to Reece, Nivy stirred uncomfortably, frowning. The Vee's eyes narrowed in on her, cold and studious.

"True, Reece Sheppard, but The Kreft do not yet consider this galaxy conquered, for it is the only galaxy they have encountered true opposition in. As long as there are those who rebel, as long as there is something left to overcome…" Again, the Vee gave Nivy an almost pointed look. "…they will not leave. All opposition must be destroyed. An interesting dilemma, is it not? They cannot be conquerors without something to conquer. While a rebellion provides them that, it also holds them here. The alternative to rebellion is lying down and allowing subjugation. There can be no winner until one has destroyed the other."

Suddenly, Nivy stood and walked calmly from the room, hugging herself. The curtain of her hair hid her expression, but there was something in her walk that suggested she was feeling very deeply, almost as if her emotions were too much to carry.

Reece knew this much: he might not understand who Nivy was or where she had come from, but what she did, she did to fight these beings known as The Kreft.

And he knew this: he was going to help her.

It was after midnight when Reece finished with the Vee and called a conference in Mordecai's sitting room. Mordecai, Hayden, Nivy, and

Gideon sat staggered about the room, all of them with bleary eyes and cups of tea and burnthroat steaming in their hands. Reece paced before them, hands behind his back.

"So Eldritch established The Veritas thirty-five years ago, meaning to use them to build up his power over the people," Hayden typed into his datascope, balanced on his knee. "He wants to reinstate a kingship with him as king so he can have the absolute power of a monarch to weed the Westerners and Pantedans out of Honoran society. All in accordance with The Kreft's grand plan for the Epimetheus." He looked up. "How...how could we have never known?"

"Because they didn't want us to." Reece's face and voice were both utterly deadpan. A stillness came over the room when he spoke, as if they were all wary of his mood, or lack thereof. "Because they've been in control the whole time. The duke was unfortunate enough to catch onto Eldritch, and now he'll die for it. The Vee said The Kreft exist in the shadows. The Epimetheus is just their puppet box, and us, we're just the puppets. All of us."

"Bad stuff, that," Mordecai murmured, brushing his thumb over his mustache. "Makes a man want to spit."

"But I don't see how Honora will ever stand for a kingship," Hayden said quietly. "We haven't had a kingship in nine, maybe ten generations—"

"Eleven," Reece corrected without feeling. "Eldritch told me in passing, that day we spoke and he gave me back my hob."

For a time, they sat in near silence, listening to the wind hoot as it whirled down Mordecai's chimney. That's what Reece felt like. A hollow space with a cold storm trapped inside.

"You'd be surprised how many folk will jump at the idea of a king," Mordecai finally said, sighing as he hoisted himself up off his couch, mug in hand. "Lotsa them don't like havin' to think for themselves, just wanna be safe, protected. Havin' a king does that. Makes a person feel like the responsibility is on someone else's hands if somethin' goes amiss. Makes them feel like they've got a hero if nothin' does."

"You know," Hayden said after a pause. "I bet that's the real purpose of The Veritas. To sedate the people enough so that when...when a change in rule happens," he glanced uncertainly at Reece, "they'll accept it without putting up a fight. The Kreft might have been planning to use them for that from the beginning."

"Peh." Tipping back his head, Gideon finished his tea with a noisy gulp and then clapped his empty mug triumphantly onto the end table. "We won't go for a king meanin' to kill the rest'a us off." It was clear that by *we* and *us*, he meant Pantedans. "There're enough'a us. Paired with the Westerners, I bet we could give the bleedin' Kreft a heckuva time with it."

Reece pivoted on the spot, facing Gideon was a hard stare. Nivy was already shaking her head at him. "You'd start a civil war. Innocent people would die. And in the end, you'd be wiped out...because if it comes to choosing sides, the Honorans will side with their own."

For the briefest of seconds, something unfamiliar flickered in Gideon's eyes. Reece almost wondered if for the first time in ten years, he'd gotten through that thick Pantedan skin and cut him to the quick.

"The Vee did say there was a war comin'," Gid grumbled.

"But he doesn't understand what it's over any more than we do. Eldritch only trusts The Veritas so far. They know about The Kreft, but they aren't part of them." With a heavy sigh, Reece stopped pacing and sat down next to Nivy, leaning his back against the cold, potbellied coal stove and looking at her. "I wonder if this is what Liem knew."

Nivy looked up at him slowly, her mouth drawn thin. His eyes slid down her neck, hesitated on the collar she wore, and then jerked away. He very likely could have asked the Vee about where she had come from and why Eldritch wanted her, but, as much as he disagreed with her people's methods, Nivy wore her collar for a reason. And he wanted her to be able to tell him herself.

"Somehow, all this ties in with you, Nivy, and with Aurelia." The others were quiet, straining to hear him. "I asked you before who Charles Eldritch was...but I think I should've asked who *you* are. Eldritch is the most powerful man on Honora, and he wants you. Because you're fighting him. Your people...whoever and wherever they are...they're resisting The Kreft, aren't they?"

Nivy smiled at him, then dropped her shoulders in a heavy, silent sigh. It felt like they had come to an impasse, and yet Reece couldn't sit still. He studied her for a moment longer, then stood and started pacing again.

"I have to go to Honora. I have to speak with the duke."

"Are you sure that's a good idea?" Hayden doubtfully frowned. "The Veritas will be on the lookout for whoever broke into their base. And The Kreft...Eldritch—"

Reece cut him off. "Eldritch thinks he's dealt with me by getting me drafted. If he was really all that worried about what I'm up to, it's well within his power to have done something else with me."

"But The Veritas that came for me and Gideon..."

"That doesn't mean he doesn't have questions. It just means I'm not his biggest priority. Look, out of all of you, I'm the best off. I'm Palatine Second...or First, I don't even know which anymore. My father's the grand duke. That gives me protection that the rest of you haven't been afforded."

By the others' uncomfortable silence, he knew they knew he was right. He was the only one who would be missed if he suddenly and conspicuously disappeared.

That should've made him feel better, but it didn't.

XVII

Up in Flames

Bright and early the next morning, while it was still misty and blue outside, Reece got up, pulled on his riding jacket and goggles, and took a piece of marmalade toast to eat on his way to bus-ship docks. Gideon and Hayden were still sleeping, but Mordecai and Nivy were awake, sitting on the back stoop of the upstairs workshop with a chess board balanced across their knees. Mordecai was teaching her to play, but Reece wasn't sure he was being exactly fair: she was down to her king and knights while he'd held onto everything but a few expendable pawns.

Mordecai looked up at the sound of Reece's boots squelching in the dewy grass. There was nothing crazy about his bright blue gaze this morning, just a level shrewdness.

"Well, I'm off." Reece's mouth felt dry, and he swallowed.

Without looking at the board, Mordecai reached over and swept up one of Nivy's knights. "You be careful, Reece. I don't think Eldritch can be the only Kreft hidin' on Honora. And if The Owl's headmaster can be one…anyone can."

Nivy looked up at Reece, worry plain on her face. He knew it was a gesture of friendship, but someone needed to tell her that sometimes the best thing a friend could do was *not* show how worried they were. Things were going to be fine. He was going to confront the duke with what he knew, warn him that his life was in danger, and then book it back to Atlas before anyone was the wiser.

"Things are going to be fine," he repeated out loud. "Nivy…walk with me for a minute?"

Nodding, Nivy scooted her legs out from beneath the wooden chess board and walked with him across the yard, leaving Mordecai to lazily slide his last bishop into check. They turned the corner of the house, and Reece sat on the front step, patting the place beside him. Nivy sat down, her face curious.

Reece had made up his mind last night, when he'd sat beside her and faced the Vee and realized that no matter what else she was, she was on his side. He trusted her. Maybe it was reckless of him, maybe he was setting himself up…but he didn't think so. The trust came too naturally for that. He didn't have to choose to trust her. He just did.

"I think I'm right in saying this belongs to you." Reaching beneath his jacket, he pulled out the ancient tome Liem had left behind and offered it to her.

Nivy stared at it for so long, he wondered if maybe he'd imagined the aching in her eyes every time he'd had the book out around her. Then she took the book and hugged it tenderly to her chest, hiding her face behind her long black hair. He was startled and embarrassed by the intensity of her emotion.

"Nivy?"

She looked up at him and smiled. She shook her head to dismiss his concern.

"Did you bring it with you? Did it come with you to Honora?"

She shook her head again. Sniffing, she gestured slowly, almost sluggishly, without raising her eyes.

"The book came with the first capsule?"

Nivy nodded, but seemed too absorbed in the gentle perusing of the book's thin pages to give him much more. That was alright. His pocket watch said it was time to go anyways.

As he stood, Nivy glanced up at him sharply, her question plain on her face.

"Not a chance. The only thing we have up on Eldritch is the fact that he doesn't know we're hiding you. I'll be back."

Nivy watched from the step as he rolled out his bim and let its engine warm up in the cool air, its exhaust curling into the fading fog. He sat for a minute on the bim, his hands on the handlebars, and returned her unreadable stare with a small smile. Then she bowed her head once more over the book, and he slipped away and didn't look back.

Emathia shone in autumn. Her oaks were orange-tipped, her fields tall and yellow, her apple trees plump with fruit. There was an orange and gold wreath the size of a carriage horse over the front doors, and candles wrapped in marigolds and firehearts in all of the mansion windows. Reece paused as he handed his bim off to a black-clad servant who didn't meet his eyes, and sniffed deeply. He'd almost forgotten what food *not* bird-on-a-stick smelled like, fresh out of the oven—warm rolls, cinnamon turkey, spicy hot cider poured over dessert scones…

Before he even started up the stairs, one of the purple front doors burst open, and Abigail stepped out into the bracing sunlight, her skirt gathered in two fists. Her peppered hair was down about her shoulders, looking wispier than usual. With pursed lips, she swept down the front stairs and threw her bony arms around his neck.

Too shocked for words, Reece dumbly patted her on the back. The last time he'd seen Abigail, she had been watching him leave from the bay window just after she'd thrown a picture frame at him and very nearly taken off his nose, furious slash distraught over Liem's disappearance. Maybe, having been allowed to sit for some weeks now, those emotions had turned into—

The whole left side of his face was suddenly prickling and stinging and—he dazedly felt it—hot to the touch. He looked at his mother, standing back with her fists on her hips, and realized she had slapped him.

"You selfish, incorrigible boy!" she seethed. "If you had any idea—how worried—how upset—we thought—"

Hearing rather than seeing her arm swing again, Reece ducked. "I've been busy—"

"You could have sent us a log!" Abigail shrieked.

"There wasn't an interface—"

"Scarlet said she gave you our message!"

"She did, but—"

"You knew I wanted you home!"

"School was—"

Baring her teeth, Abigail reached behind her back and pulled out a parchment envelope with a bright gold seal. "This is a personal note from Headmaster Eldritch himself." Heart thudding in his ears, Reece made a grab for the envelope, but she held to it with fingers of steel. "'*Reece has shown worrisome neglect toward his schoolwork*'," she quoted, "'*he spends more time off campus with his comrades than—in—class*'!" She slapped the envelope three times against Reece's chest, punctuating her words. "I have half a mind to lock you up at Emathia, like he recommends!"

She suddenly spun, muttering to herself, and started marching back up the front steps. There was nothing for it but to follow and let her slowly run out of steam.

In the sitting room, they sat across from each other in matching scarlet armchairs, and Abigail had a servant bring tea, as if all her screaming had been just another detail of her schedule. Reece thought it was safe to take Eldritch's note off the table between them and flick it open with a finger. There wasn't much to it that Abigail hadn't already recited, just Eldritch's angular signature.

He looked over the top of the letter at Abigail, who was tipping back her second cup of tea like a shot glass. "Did the duke see this?"

"Not *yet*," Abigail snippily emphasized. "It just came today. The headmaster delivered it himself, rather than sending a log."

A chill rushed down Reece's back; goosebumps pebbled his skin. "How long ago did he leave?"

"Not long before you arrived. He had business at The Guild House with your father." She looked up as Reece jumped to his feet, almost toppling the table and their tea platter with it, and then smashed her cup down with an angry clatter as he pulled on his jacket and gloves. "Don't you dare—"

Reece raised his voice over hers. "I've got to see the duke."

Abigail stared as if he'd grown a second head right in front of her.

"I—that's—" She hesitated, clearly suspicious. Then she huffed, "You're not going like *that*, are you? You look like something the wolfdogs got into. For goodness sake, *at least* put a comb through your hair. I'll have the servants draw a carriage for you, you can't go The House on that horrendous—"

But Reece was already walking out the parlor door, mussing up the back of his hair as he went.

By this time, he was so full of angry nerves that when Guy Clark started chirping over the wireless about the Grand Duke's masquerade ("The gala of the solar cycle! Academy students are invited to volunteer for serving duties for a once in a lifetime chance to see The Estate of Emathia at its very blah, blah, blah!"), he yanked the earpiece off and threw it into the wind.

Caldonia traffic, both ground and air, was a nightmare. It seemed the biannual equestrian march was still going on, so the streets were crammed with horse-drawn carriages and automobile drivers who were impatiently drumming on their horns, while the skyways between buildings were packed with overflow from the road, hovering aethercopters and Dryads. His bim was narrow enough to carve its own path between carriages, but it was slow-going, and he didn't much like getting called a gingoo by drivers stuck in line.

Fortunately, access to the cobbled lane leading to The Guild House was restricted. As Reece pulled off Mablethorpe Road and up to the tall iron gate, a sentry with a baton and an ALP strapped to his belt came to run his classification card through a datascope.

"Reece Sheppard," the sentry said, surprised, as Reece's information blinked red on his screen. He tilted back the black visor of his cap to get a better look at Reece, simultaneously nodding for the other sentry on post to open the gate.

Reece didn't wait around. He revved his bim's engine and shot through the small opening in the gate while the sentry was still cranking it open.

The road ran in a straight, stark line, pinned in by a fringe of trees on either side. It made Reece feel like he was moving down a tunnel of mirrors, because everything looked the same for so long, until the House suddenly loomed before him, six stories of white stone and column and black roof. Having no windows but seven whole smoking chimneys, it resembled a very fine, very neat factory.

The sentries posted at the wide black doors, wearing green jackets with black tassels on their shoulder guards, double-checked Reece's classification card before bowing him in with a synchronized, "Sir."

As a child, Reece had been scared of The Guild House; a bit of that feeling hung with him now. His confidence wavered as he stepped into the marble entrance hall, looking up at the green and black banners hanging down from the ceiling, each the size of his suite back at The Owl. A white staircase curled around the cavernous hall five times, up all five stories.

When someone called his name, he had to hop to catch the bust of some scholar or another he had accidentally elbowed off its pedestal.

Hugh Rice was hurrying across the entrance hall, from this far away, looking uncannily like Hayden, right down to the mousy hair and off-kilter bifocals.

"How are you?" Mr. Rice clasped one of Reece's hands, smiling in his distracted way. "Come to see the duke?"

Nodding, Reece looked about the hall again, vast but strangely emptied of the green-robed figures that usually busied it. "Where is everyone?"

Mr. Rice cast a sad gaze around. "Where they always are, of late. In a summit. I've never seen the House so quiet, and at the same time, so very busy." As if seeing Reece clearly for the first time, he started, caught up Reece's arm, and started pulling him none-too-casually toward the vertical translocators at the foot of the stairs. "You can just, eh, wait in the library until the duke is free. Don't...don't want to be idle."

Reece let himself be hustled onto the translocator platform, which had a clear glass bottom. The translocator ran smooth and silent, letting off only the occasional spout of steam, like a soft sigh under their feet, as they rolled up and were deposited onto the fourth floor.

"Who called for the summit?" Reece asked even though he was sure he already knew. He would eat his bim, starting with its tires, if the suspenseful quiet laying over the House wasn't Eldritch's handiwork.

Hugh played restlessly with the lion heart pin on his collar as he gave Reece a sidelong glance. "One of the members of Parliament, I'm sure. But then, what do I know, I'm just the librarian. Here we go, let's use the back way. It's quicker."

Reece wasn't sure that it was. Squeezing down the cramped little hallway, he felt like he was back in Caldonia traffic, only instead of dodging carriages and automobiles, he was edging around dismantled library pulleys and kinetic book carts that needed new wheels.

Hugh kept apologizing for the mess and pausing to wipe dust off his bifocals. "So sorry—Advisor Kirkland, he thought I was a bit overstaffed, and Parliament cut my help. Haven't really had the hands to get this all in order—keep meaning to bring Hayden and Sophie to work with me. Almost there now."

At the end of the hall, they came to a single door that didn't want to open even when Reece wedged himself in next to Hugh and helped push.

"Sorry—sticks sometimes, I've been meaning to fix that—"

Working together, grunting loudly, they managed to throw the door open and spill out into the foyer of the Grand Duke's Ancestral Library, the single grandest collection of antique books and datascope drives on planet Honora. The sound of their forced entry echoed from wall to distant book-filled wall. The library gave Reece the feeling that he wasn't as alone as he thought, that if he strained hard enough, he might hear dusty whispers coming from the dark aisles of books that spiraled into the center of the library like a circular labyrinth. When Reece and Hugh walked forward, they walked on black marble painted with webs of constellations and galaxies and Streams. The ceiling somewhere high overhead was lost in darkness.

"Have you never been in here before?" Mr. Rice asked, surprised. He paused to take down the oil lantern hanging from a bookend, pull a spark-starter out of his pocket, and put the two together. He and Reece were suddenly standing in a bubble of orange, flickering light.

Reece made himself stop gaping up at the shelves that were taller than the oaks at Emathia. "Not since I was five or six."

"Well, I suppose it *is* rather hard to gain access to, usually. I wish Parliament would open it up to the public, some of these poor books haven't seen daylight since before even I was born. I'm just going to send a log to Sophie, let her know I'll be late for dinner. Would you like to see my office?"

They entered the aisle of shelves, making frequent right-hand turns as they spun deeper and deeper into the labyrinth, every ten or so steps passing flickering datascope screens referencing where in history they were. It was terribly tempting not to pull over and innocently browse *The Knighting of the Dukes, An End to Monarchy.*

Hugh's office, lit by a pair of dim photon stands, was at the eye of the spiral. Or rather, his office—which wasn't much more than a small writing desk and a filing cabinet—was *on* the eye of the spiral. Steady vibrations ran through Reece's boots as the massive gold clock face underfoot ticked loudly; every time the second hand as long as he was tall snapped into place, the pens on Hugh's desk rattled.

"That's not distracting?" Reece wondered, walking the circumference of the clock and pausing over the stout hour hand.

Hugh chuckled as he sat down behind his desk. "It's actually quite relaxing. I'll be done in just one moment."

As he sent his log to Sophie, Reece idly wandered into the labyrinth, brushing the dusty spines of books that looked worse for wear. These were the oldest books in the library, dating back to L.F. 327. They'd be dust themselves if it weren't for librarians like Hugh who dedicated their lives to the gentle rebinding and repairing of covers and pages.

So why did Reece feel like Nivy's strange book was so much older? It certainly didn't look that old, not compared to these relics. The rule of antiques was, the older, the more important—so maybe Reece thought that because Nivy's book was very important, it must be very old.

Which made less sense than Mordecai's bird-in-a-cake recipe.

From Hugh's office came the sound of a ringing bell. Slumping against a bookshelf, Reece listened to Hugh's low, hurried voice, sounding decidedly relieved. When he came to find Reece in the labyrinth a moment later, he looked ten years younger. Well, maybe five.

"Headmaster Eldritch has left. The House should be a good deal safer for you, now."

His odd behavior and their trip down the library's unlikely back way suddenly made a lot more sense.

"Mr. Rice." Reece exasperatedly dropped his hands. "You don't have to protect me. If Eldritch thought you were helping me sneak around behind his back—"

Hugh made a quieting gesture. "I merely thought it would be better for you not to have a run-in with the headmaster on his ground."

His ground. So The Guild House was his ground now, not the duke's, not Parliament's. It was starting already.

"Look, I appreciate it, I do. And I appreciate what you did with Scarlet. But you don't have to—"

"She told you about that, did she?" Mr. Rice nervously looked around, as if the books might have grown ears while his back was turned. "Reece, these are dangerous waters we're treading. I'm not going to deny there are dark things underfoot, but at some point, you have to weigh the potential risks."

It was like hearing his own thoughts read back to him. "I have. And, for what it's worth, I tried to keep Hayden from getting any more involved."

Mr. Rice's smile was difficult to read. "Much as I wish he would listen to you, I am perhaps a little glad to know that neither he nor Gideon will." He put a hand on Reece shoulder and looked down over his bifocals at him. "It's alright to ask for help, sometimes."

Both of them jumped as an echo of footsteps carried to them, a quick, confidant march.

"Probably someone coming to fetch a record out of the archives," Mr. Rice said uncertainly. "I'll just—just go see who it is."

Thinking about waiting in the clock-office with nothing but its ominous ticking to keep him company, Reece picked up his feet and followed. For some time, there was only the combined sound of their footsteps and the footsteps coming toward them to allay the silence.

The footfall of their visitor grew to its loudest yet, and then stopped so abruptly that Hugh and Reece both skidded to a stop, Hugh clutching Reece's shoulder.

"Hello?" Hugh held up his lantern up a little higher.

Just as Reece started to reach a hand under his jacket for his hob, the duke stepped into the light. While Hugh almost collapsed with his heavy sigh of relief, Reece suddenly felt like getting seriously lost in the labyrinth.

"Mr. Rice," the duke greeted in the deep, rich voice that called to mind memories of being read mysteries in front of a fireplace on cold winter nights after Abigail and Liem had gone to bed. "Tell me, who is that gangly young man behind you with the unsightly hair?"

As Reece unconsciously stooped a little, Mr. Rice laughed nervously. "I'll, uh, I'll just leave you to find out." Reece shot him a desperate look, but Hugh made an apologetic face and handed him the lantern. "I have…some books…yes, some books to…read."

Hayden's father shuffled away, leaving Reece to stare catatonically at the duke, feeling strangely disembodied. His father began circling him, hands clasped behind his back.

"It is not particularly pleasant," Thaddeus Sheppard began thoughtfully, "to hear news of my son visiting *someone else's* father while I am but a corridor away."

Reece found his voice in a key too high. "I came to see you."

The duke said nothing, keeping enough distance to leave his face in uncertain shadows. He was big-chested, if slender, taller than Reece by some inches, all sharp lines and hard panes. The right breast of his dark green jacket glinted with medals and ribbons and honors.

"Have you swallowed your tongue, boy?"

Reece double-checked to make sure he hadn't and nodded. Something horrible was creeping over him. Here he'd taken every painstaking precaution to avoid this confrontation for two years, and now that it was here, instead of laying on the duke like he deserved, he was getting an uncomfortable lump in his throat. He did what anyone would have done. He panicked.

"I came to warn you," he said quickly. "I know about The Kreft. Eldritch, he's rotting Parliament from the inside out. He's in control of the Veritas. He wants to get rid of the dukeship."

The duke listened to his rant passively, his frown deepening ever so slightly. When Reece had finished and drawn a shaky breath, he calmly reached and took the rattling lantern from him with a white-gloved hand.

"I'd rather you not drop this," he said. "You would send the whole library up in flames. Walk with me."

Reece didn't let himself feel relieved. Instead, when he felt a small stab of frustration over the duke's coolness, he latched onto it, let it carry him away. Anger. *That* was what he wanted to feel toward the duke; *that* was what he deserved.

"I would ask how you've come to such fantastical conclusions, but I'm certain you would not do the story justice with our unfortunate time constraints. So I will make this brief, and you will listen to me." If the duke's face changed at all as he spoke, it was about as much change as a rock went through when it turned into a stone. "When you leave The Guild House shortly, you will go home to Emathia and write me a detailed account of whom you have been talking to and what questions you have been asking. Then you will pack your things, take the Dryad, go to your Uncle Uriah's house in Olbia, and stay there."

Reece didn't have to work at all to feel angry now. This was just like what had happened two years ago—the duke had tried to ship him out of his and everyone else's life then too. "Until I go off to war, you mean. The Kreft's war, whatever it bleeding is."

"Until I tell you otherwise is what I mean," the duke replied evenly.

"If I'm going to war, I'm going to spend my last few months at The Owl with my friends, not at Abigail's loopy brother's house on the other side of Honora."

"An understandable sentiment, but the order remains the same. The headmaster and Parliament are none of your concern."

It was more than any sane person could take, and Reece wasn't entirely sure if he was completely sane anymore anyways. He stopped walking and shouted at the duke's back, "They're going to have you killed!"

Ten paces away, the duke paused and slowly turned. Reece had thought his expression had been serious before, but he had been wrong, because this new one made Gideon's meanest face look totally benign.

Reece plunged ahead blindly, not knowing what he meant to say until it was out of his mouth. "If you want to abandon Mum and me, *fine*, but you can't leave Honora to Eldritch—I won't let you!"

Slowly, like a statue melting out of its stiffness, the duke lowered his lantern arm. As he walked toward Reece, he said thoughtfully, "You really mean that, don't you?"

Reece studied his father's face. "Yes."

The duke's lips stretched into a tight smile that filled Reece's mind with more misty, almost-forgotten memories. He clasped the back of Reece's neck with one hand. "Good boy," he said quietly. "Good boy."

It was a small thing to completely shatter Reece's composure, but there it was. His throat made a strange sort of choking sound as it constricted, and he jerked away from the duke before he could make any more of a sod out of himself.

After a moment, he and the duke began walking again, closer together than they had been before, but still with a certain distance between them that had nothing to do with proximity.

"What happened to your hand?" the duke asked, managing to sound not the least bit curious.

Distracted, Reece glanced down at the straightener on his bad wrist and caught himself before he snorted. This probably wasn't the time or place to mention that he had tried to take on the Vee that he was holding captive in his friend's grandfather's basement.

"I sprained it. Listen, you *are* going to do something, aren't you? About Eldritch? About...*them*?"

"I will do what I judge to be right. That will have to do."

"So you have something planned?"

"On the contrary, my lack of planning is very contrived."

"What does that even mean? You're going to do *nothing*? Didn't you hear what I said before? You're in danger. The Kreft want you out of the way. Eldritch is planning to—" Reece couldn't even say it aloud without cringing. "—to assassinate you!"

There came a deep, throaty sound from the duke, and Reece realized he was chuckling. "Do not underestimate your old father, boy. Mr. Rice."

A flustered-looking Hugh sank out of the shadows as if he'd been waiting for them just out of earshot, holding a stack of books. "Sir?"

"Escort Reece to the road. I imagine you are still driving around that loud contraption?"

"It's called a bim. But I don't understand—"

"I want it to be known," the duke smoothly continued overtop of Reece's complaint, "that if you choose to disobey me and return to The Aurelian Academy, I will have a public log put out to Caldonia's Sentry Center with an order to bring you under immediate house arrest if you are seen setting foot on Honora."

Reece thought the pop of his eyes should have been audible. "*What?*"

"Mr. Rice, if you will."

And then the duke started to turn away, leaving Hugh and Reece at the end of the labyrinth, a short walk from the library's oval front doors.

"You can't—The Kreft—why should—I *am* going back to The Owl!" Reece yelled, straining against Hugh, who was holding fast to the back of his jacket.

The echo of the duke's voice, bouncing back to them as he disappeared, sounded amused. "Then I suggest, this time, you stay there."

XVIII

Captain Pleasant's Hairstuffs for Gents and Other Dangerous Things

"I'm not going."

"Well, if he's not going, I sure as heck ain't."

Glowering down at Gideon and Reece, who were sitting on Mordecai's back lawn watching the sun rise over the trees, Hayden crossed his arms and sighed, "He *is* going. We all are."

With an exaggerated yawn, Reece spread out on his back and closed his eyes. It didn't matter that he'd gotten a full night's sleep; early was early, and a sleep full of bad dreams wasn't much of a sleep at all. "Be reasonable, Hayden. With everything else we've got on our plates, can you really expect us to take class seriously? Besides, it's Honoran History. Point of interest," he held up a finger, "we've just recently learned that our history is totally wrong."

"Peh." Gideon coughed a laugh as he tore up a handful of yellowing grass and tossed into the breeze. "Count me out."

Swelling up indignantly, Hayden said, "We agreed last night that one day of classes would throw some suspicion off us. And we're going to have to be eligible to graduate whether there's a war coming or not!"

"The Vee—" Reece began.

"Mordecai and Nivy will watch him, and if it really makes you so nervous, we can check back on break. Please?"

Groaning, Reece lifted his pocket watch and glared blurrily at its face. The only bright side to Honoran History was that it was the GR the three of them shared. That meant that on a normal class day, they could all sit at the back of the classroom so Gid and Reece could play paper rockets under the radar while Hayden took enough notes for all three of them (not on purpose—he would be caught smuggling Freherian Tobacco with Mordecai before he was caught cheating). Today, that just meant none of them had to worry about being upbraided in front of class alone.

Hayden must have sensed he was winning Reece over, because he smiled and started for the workshop door. "I'll grab our books."

Gideon glared over his shoulder at Reece. "We really doin' this?"

"I don't know what else we would do today," Reece admitted. "Plus, we might be able to use the school library to cross-reference clues about The Kreft—where they've been, what they're ultimately up to. Get a better handle on what we're dealing with."

"Soundin' a little like Aitch, there, Cap'n."

Reece hesitated. "I think there's a chance some of the tutors might be Kreft. It's all about making the population subservient, isn't it? So who better to pollute the minds of the next generation?"

Gideon just stared at him, bored.

"We might run into Eldritch."

"I'd like that." Gid nodded pointedly at his holster. "But you don't sound exactly hopeful."

Sitting up with effort and dusting damp grass off the back of his untucked uniform jacket, Reece shrugged. "Much as I wish Eldritch would spend his free time wandering around campus rather than furthering his people's nefarious plans of world domination, I doubt we can count on it."

Gideon thought on this a moment, and then, as if just seeing the dark humor in it, laughed. Until a grinning Hayden came out to them carrying three stuffed leather satchels—then he cut off abruptly.

Because they had spent so much time arguing, they were already running late when they pulled into The Owl and hurriedly parked in the motor vehicle stables. With the Social Economy Building on the other side of the lake, a half a mile from where they were standing when they got off their bims, they would have to sprint to make it to class before Tutor Flint shut the classroom door. Which was alright for Reece and Gideon, but Hayden kept tripping on his pant legs and losing his bifocals and consequentially going blind.

Sliding to a noisy, panting stop in the handsome corridor outside Flint's classroom, they paused to smarten up, Reece pushing down his hair, Hayden smacking dust off his shoulders, Gideon grumblingly tucking in the loose tail of his undershirt. The door was shut, but not all the way, not yet. Reece did the honors. Drawing a breath, he knocked once and pushed the door open into the circular wooden classroom with vaulted ceilings and stained-glass windows.

Standing beside the podium at the front of the room, Tutor Flint turned to inspect him through horned bifocals. He'd forgotten how much like a bird she looked—a bony, sharp-nosed bird, with cheeks that were always a little puckered.

"Well, if it isn't our very own Mr. Sheppard come back home," she said in the dusky voice that had lectured Reece to sleep many classes before. "Mr. Ailey, Mr. Ailey, if you would move to the back, I think Mr. Sheppard and Mr. Rice would both benefit from a front row seat."

Silas and Jesse stared at Reece in wonder as they scooped up their things and went to the back of the class to fill two of the three empty desks that were usually Reece and his friends'. Trying to smile at the old vulture charading as their tutor, Reece slid into Silas's desk and started setting up camp, plugging the power cord of the desk's recording mechanism into his datascope. Hayden had unpacked into Jesse's desk before they both looked up and saw Gid waiting at the door with a strange look on his face.

Written across the blackboard, big and bold and unpleasant, was the headline, "The Battle of Eudora and The Pantedan Massacre, L.F. 1283".

Tutor Flint descended upon Gideon as Reece ducked out from behind his desk and hurried after her. The classroom was positively hissing with whispers.

"I don't think today is perhaps the best day for you to be here," Flint said, her cheeks sinking deeper as she frowned.

Gideon just kept staring at the blackboard, a vein ticking in his jaw.

"It's not as though he hasn't heard it all before," Reece told her quietly. He wondered if there was a way to tell if a person was Kreft or not. Flint and Eldritch didn't have many physical similarities apart from their skeletal height, but…

If Flint *had* been a bird, she would have huffily ruffled her feathers. "Take a seat, Mr. Sheppard."

"I just don't see why—"

"I will not tell you again!"

There was a moment's silence after Flint's shrill shout, and then Gideon turned to leave, the back of his neck an angry red. His pulse beating in his ears, Reece swept everything from his desktop into his arms and glanced over at Hayden, who looked frozen to his desk.

"Hayden?"

With a start, Hayden glanced from him to the unsmiling Flint and the blackboard, and then dropped his eyes to his lap. Reece got the idea. Following in Gideon's footsteps, he left the room and made sure to pull the door shut hard enough to rumble some eardrums.

He found Gideon standing by the lake with his hands in his pockets, watching the indigenous blue swans of Atlas glide around on the slate-colored water. Not far from him, a group of well-dressed girls in bustles were setting up some sort of booth. The flag on the front of it read, "Masquerade Volunteer Committee".

Shifting his feet, Gideon muttered, "Didn't want to go to class anyway."

"Me neither," said Reece honestly. He dug up a small flat stone with the toe of his boot, dusted it off, and spun it into the lake, where it skipped and startled the swans into flight.

"You think Tutor Flint could be Kreft?"

"No," Gideon said simply. He didn't look at Reece. "She's Honoran. You can tell."

"Reece! Gideon!"

They looked over their shoulders at Hayden as he tripped off the front step of the Social Economy Building and came running to join them. Reece had to cover his laugh with a cough when the Masquerade Committee saw him as an excited student rushing to volunteer and bombarded him with posters and even a few artful invitations to send a log if he had any questions. When Hayden joined them, there wasn't a bit of skin showing on him that hadn't gone as red at the swans were blue.

"Stop laughing," he pleaded, mortified, and shoved some of the duplicate posters at them. Gideon promptly started folding his into a hat. "I managed to get all our homework from Tutor Flint. I was going to stay, but that…that wasn't very good of her, was it?"

Reece just shook his head and stared out over the lake again. Angry though their clash with Tutor Flint had briefly made him, he welcomed the normalness of it; it felt like stepping back into sync.

"What other classes do you have today? I want to take a look at as many tutors as possible."

Hayden checked his schedule on his datascope. "Botany. But Tutor White is an old friend of my parents'…he was born down the road from my mum."

"Ship Repelling. Tutor Rowe is a real numpty, so I guess he could fit the profile. I'll check him out," Gideon answered as he twirled his hat around his finger. Looking past Reece, he raised an eyebrow and quirked his head to the side. "You know her?"

Reece glanced at the slight blonde figure bouncing his way. Po walked right through the middle of the Masquerade Committee's posters and bustles and insulted gasps and joined Reece and the others at the water's edge with a freckly grin.

"Heya, Reece!" She blinked at Gid and Hayden. "Hi! Reece's friends?"

Reece didn't appreciate how they looked at each other for confirmation before nodding. He rolled his eyes ungratefully. "Po Trimble," he gestured to Po, "Hayden Rice, Gideon Creed."

"Hi!" Po repeated, and shook Hayden's hand so hard that his bifocals fell off one ear. Her eyes honed in on the paper hat in Gideon's hands and twinkled. "Did you make that? Clever! You'd prolly be good with engines too, you know, because'a all the geometry that goes into it. Oh wow!" She moved as fast as a hummingbird, from Gideon's hat, to Hayden's auto-encrypting journal. She doubled over with her hands on her knees to look at the book in his hands. "I ain't never seen one'a those before, not outta a store window, anyhow. You know that chip technology, that's some'a the same stuff that's used in the smallest engine there is, the Flutterbee—but you prolly already knew that."

Straightening up, Po sighed happily and looked around at the three of them. "Well, I'd better go. I'm workin' on the bus-ships today, all ten'a them. Don't wanna get a late start!" Spinning to face Reece so quickly that her white braid swung over her shoulder, she told him earnestly, "Your friends are real nice, Reece."

When she had gone, Hayden and Gideon turned to him with looks of complete bewilderment.

"She seems...nice," Hayden said.

"She frightens me," Gideon decided, staring at the hat hooked on his finger with a thoughtful frown.

They had an hour to kill now that they didn't have Honoran History and the lovely Tutor Flint to enjoy, and they spent it walking around the lake, joking like this was two months ago and they didn't have a hundred worries to go home to tonight. They didn't talk about the Vee, Nivy, or Eldritch, about The Kreft or going to war or Liem, even though Reece's fingers were secretly wrapped around the cufflinks in his trouser pocket. He could really only forget for so long.

It was over lunch in the banquet hall that it all came crashing back into focus.

Reece was sitting down with his third plate of lunch, making up for all the meals he'd had to substitute bird-on-a-stick for real food, when his eyes landed on the masquerade poster that Gideon had been using for a placemat. There was a black and white drawing of Emathia on it, accurate except for the miniscule little figures in ball gowns and top hats depicted wandering around the grounds.

The picture disappeared as Gideon arrived and covered it with his fifth or sixth plate (Reece had lost count) of poached eggs, sausage sandwiches, and smoked apple pudding.

Hayden was stirring a mug of chocolate tea and saying exasperatedly, "—but you see, that's the point of poached eggs, to—" He stopped and grimaced as Gideon began violently scrambling his eggs and pudding together.

But Reece's mind wasn't on lunch anymore.

"I think I've just realized something," he said dazedly, falling back in his chair with a thud.

"What is it, Reece?" Hayden asked, still watching Gideon make mush out of his food, looking horrified.

"The masquerade. Scarlet said the most prestigious members of Parliament are going to be there, along with Eldritch. She said if he had something up his sleeve, he'd pull it out then, when it would make the biggest waves."

Tearing his eyes away from the catastrophe on Gideon's plate, Hayden frowned at Reece. "You can't be thinking of going. You know your father wants you away from Eldritch and Parliament. If you show up at the masquerade, he'll have you arrested and taken to your uncle's before you can say—" He glanced sideways as Gideon began spooning his creation into his mouth. "*Disgusting.*"

"I know."

"I mean, Emathia is the last place you should go right now."

"I know. So does the duke. That was his plan." Everything was falling neatly and disastrously into place. Reece pushed the heels of his hands into his eyes. "I thought maybe he was protecting me from Eldritch, but that's not it. He's keeping me out of the way."

Gideon and Hayden still didn't understand, though they were both alert and listening; Gideon had even stopped tormenting Hayden and put his plate to the side.

"He told me his plan was to do nothing. He's going to let himself…let himself…but why would he do that?"

"I'm sure you're just misinterpreting," Hayden said, trying without success to mask his worry. His fingers were gripping the table's edge very tightly.

"I'm not." Reece felt like someone had opened a trapdoor under his stomach. "My father is going to let himself be assassinated by The Kreft. And I know where it's going to happen."

When Reece, Gideon, and Hayden banged their way into Mordecai's, arguing loudly, they were covered in dust and sweat and their hair was standing up, wind-slicked. They'd driven their bims into the ground to get here as fast as they had, but now that they were here, Reece was drawing a blank. He paced around the sitting room, madly clicking his fingers as Nivy and Mordecai stuck their heads in from the kitchen to see what all the noise was about.

"It takes three hours to fly from here to Emathia…I've got to get a ship, and not a garbage disposer, either. I need—what do people wear to masquerades? I'll need one of those…my hob…maybe a backup ALP…"

"What the bleedin' heckles is goin' on?" Mordecai demanded loudly.

Reece was too busy talking to himself to answer, so Gideon covered for him from the corner of the room, where he was pouting and not bothering to hide it. "Reece thinks The Kreft's gonna try to off the duke at that fancy masquerade tonight."

Mordecai whistled through his front teeth and rubbed his hands together. "Now, that's what I call a job! Guns, assassins, and free food, I'd wager!"

"That's the thing," Hayden unhappily explained, collapsing onto the sofa. "Reece has it in his mind that he's going alone."

Reece took a break from his monologue to snap over his shoulder, "None of you will make it past the front gate! You're too recognizable!"

"And you aren't?"

"I know every servant's name at Emathia—I'll have no problem talking myself in a side gate. Once I'm inside, I can blend in. None of you can."

"What are you doin' now?" Gideon mumbled as Reece threw open the cupboard concealing Mordecai's outdated log interface.

Reece flicked on the small screen, transmitter, and audio box, punching in a four digit code that started the interface up with a protesting hum. "Scarlet said I would need a date. She's right. I'll be too conspicuous on my own."

Beet.

"This," Scarlet said gravely, "had better be important."

The black and white image of her kept fading in and out of focus, but it was plain to see that her hair was in a tower of strange rods that Reece couldn't begin to imagine the purpose for outside a torture chamber, and her face was caked in something that looked like it had been dug up from the bottom of the lake.

For a second Reece was too stunned to speak. "Oh—uh—it is," he said quickly, avoiding direct eye contact with the creature on the screen. "I need you to come to the masquerade with me."

"The masquerade that is less than six hours away?"

"Yes."

"I see." Scarlet's muddy face lurched closer to the screen (Reece unconsciously leaned backward), and she glared. "Did it occur to you, Reece Sheppard, that I might already have a date, seeing as it *is* six hours away?"

It really hadn't. He'd actually been under the impression that she might be waiting for him to ask her to go.

Reece blurted out dumbly, "Who?"

"Lucius Tobin, if it's any of your business."

"*Him?*" It'd been six years since Abigail had forced him to one of her dreaded "most important families in Honora" tea parties, but the name Lucius Tobin brought to mind a picture of a porky boy with hair parted right down the middle under a straw boater. He had to shake his head firmly to dislodge the memory.

"Look, I really need—" In a warped reflection on the screen, Reece saw the answer to his troubles. One of them, anyways. "Never mind."

His last glimpse of Scarlet before he ended his transmission was not a happy one. He turned around. Before he had even opened his mouth, Nivy started eagerly nodding her answer.

"*What?*" Gideon barked when he realized what the nodding meant. "You're takin' *her*, but you can't take us?"

As Reece began punching a new code into the log interface, he said dryly, "Don't be jealous. If you could fit in a dress, you could come too."

Beet.

He had called in to the bus-ship housing units at The Owl, and the face that greeted him, while not covered in mud, looked as menacing as Scarlet's had. Tutor Agnes was wiping her oily hands on a rag and scowling as if Reece was an unexpected blip popping up on her radar.

"Yes, Mr. Sheppard?"

"Hello, Tutor Agnes, may I speak with Po Trimble?" A little extra manners couldn't go amiss, afterall.

"She's currently wedged between an Axil 11-Seven engine and a bypass funnel," Agnes told him curtly, slinging the rag over her shoulder. She put her hands on her hips and scrutinized him through the lens of her interface. "Is there something I can help you with?"

"I...really just need to speak with Po, actually."

"Well, I'm afraid you'll just have to wait, Mr. Sheppard, seeing as Ms. Trimble—"

"Mr. Sheppard?" Po's voice squeaked off-screen before she pushed her way into view. Her grubby jumpsuit managed to make Agnes's look clean. "Hey, Reece! Long time no see!"

Reece waited to speak until, grumbling mutinously, Tutor Agnes picked up a wrench and prowled out of sight. "Po, I need a favor. A really big favor."

"Short of fixing a Bylink 12-Twelve to run smooth—because you *know* that'll never happen—you got it!"

Uncomfortably aware that Hayden and Gideon were closing in on either side of him, Reece leaned closer still to the screen. "You see, there's this masquerade tonight," Po's expression brightened, "and I need a ship to get there," and then fell a little.

"Well, that's not such a big favor. You can prolly take Tilden's Nyad back planetside. Him and Gus and me have to ride the bus-ships down anyway, just to make sure they're all in order."

They made arrangements to meet on the landing dock where the Trimbles' Nyad was stationed, and then Reece signed off the interface and turned to face Gideon and Hayden, who were standing identically, arms crossed, frowns deep, eyes dark. The only difference was that Hayden had to work at it while Gid was a natural.

"Seems like everybody's gettin' to help but us," Gideon mused to Hayden.

"I have that feeling as well."

"You can help me," Reece said sharply as he impatiently pushed his way between them, "by letting me focus on what I'm trying to do."

"That ain't helpin'! That's just stayin' outta the way!" Reece shot Gideon a pointed look over his shoulder. "Aw, comon', Cap'n—"

Nivy stepped out of the kitchen and met Reece in the middle of the room with a grim smile. She plucked at her frayed shirt with meaning and then turned around with her hands spread to show him exactly what he had to make presentable and essentially unrecognizable in less than two hours. Skinny, rings under her eyes, lank hair. Not that he was the foremost expert on grooming.

"We need a dress," he decided, quickly losing confidence in his plan. "Probably a...really poofy one."

"Leave me to take care of Nivy Girl," Mordecai announced. "Gideon, get in here and keep your eye on the Vee so I can take Nivy to Madame Maraux's."

Hemming and hawing and stomping louder than was necessary, Gideon disappeared into the kitchen; by the sounds of his muffled growls, he was taking out his irritation on their trussed-up prisoner.

"Maraux's won't work. The Madame won't have forgotten what happened last time Nivy came for a visit." Reece was starting to feel a sort of hot panic boiling in the bottom of his stomach. There wasn't enough time—they'd already lost twenty minutes just standing here!

"Oh," Mordecai chucklingly put Nivy's hand on his arm and led her from the room, "Hettie Maraux is an old acquaintance...you leave her to me."

After they'd gone, and it was just Hayden and Reece in the sitting room, Reece lowered himself onto the sofa and put his face in his hands. A plan this slapdash *couldn't* go smoothly—he was sure there was a rule somewhere that said so.

"What are you going to do?" Hayden asked quietly, sitting down beside him.

"Get as close to the duke as I can and stay there all night. At the first sign of trouble, I'll just..." Reece shut his eyes. "I hope I'm wrong."

"So do I."

"But it makes too much sense. A public assassination on this scale would throw Honora into panic...and set up the perfect atmosphere for The Kreft to step in with their monarchy and save the day. The Vees will be the ones to do it. You didn't hear them, at the dome. Talking about their last task before bringing their new order of justice to the light...this will be it."

"And the duke? He's just going to...let it happen?"

That was the question of the hour. The duke was the hardest, shrewdest person Reece had ever known; he wasn't the type to roll over for anyone, even under (or *especially* under, in this case) threat of death. The duke Reece knew would have fought back hard after learning who Eldritch was and what The Kreft were doing. Not taken a bullet for their plan's sake.

Maybe Reece *was* wrong.

Please, please let me be wrong.

The minute hand on Reece's pocket watch seemed to move forward in leaps and bounds every time he glanced at it. How could jumping in Mordecai's water closet have taken five whole minutes? Did using a thermal press on the breeches Hayden had fetched from the gentlemen's clothing emporium really take twenty? That was nearly one half hour down already!

Embarrassingly enough, he had to have Hayden show him how the different pieces of his evening suit worked. Cotton undershirt, white dress shirt, green waistcoat, frock coat, handkerchief, breeches, stockings, boots, spats, funny little neck scarf that he learned was called a cravat…by the time he'd finished attaching Liem's silver cufflinks to his sleeve, he was sweating. Hayden suggested getting undressed so he wouldn't sully the suit before the masquerade, but he was kidding. Reece hoped.

At last, feeling like a clown and a half, Reece took his stand in the middle of the room and turned around under Hayden's studious eye.

"You'll pass," Hayden said as if he was a great expert on this sort of thing. He was holding something behind his back—going by his face, something he knew Reece wouldn't like. "But you'll need to do something with your hair." He held out a tonic in a red glass bottle, and Reece took it hesitantly.

"*Captain Pleasant's Hairstuffs for Gents*'," he read, revolted. "I am *not* putting anything on my head that's made by a man named Captain Pleasant."

He heard a muffled snorting from behind the kitchen door and imagined Gideon pressing his ear up against it, laughing.

Hayden refused to take the bottle back, crossing his arms mulishly. "It's that or a top hat."

"And I'm not wearing a top hat, I told you—"

"You're the one so concerned with fitting in."

"I'm going to stop an assassination! I think I can afford to be a little underdressed!"

"If you're not going to let me help with anything else, you can let me do this much right!"

"Then do it right! Get me something that wasn't made for *girls*!"

As Hayden fumbled for a comeback, Reece pulled his pocket watch out of his waistcoat, examined it, and swore. They needed to meet Po at the docks outside The Owl in less than an hour, and he couldn't ride his bim there unless he wanted to show up at the masquerade wearing a film of dust, so that meant catching The Iron Horse's late afternoon run. In fifteen minutes.

Nothing seemed to be where he had left it as he dashed around Mordecai's. He wanted to wear his flight wings (still his bleeding "first feathers") and was sure he'd left them on his morning jacket, but he'd seemed to have misplaced that too. Hayden removed his wrist straightener as an afterthought. Even though it still twinged to flex, Reece couldn't afford to wear something that would set him apart from the other guests.

"Hey," Gideon called from the kitchen door during one of Reece's frantic passes, "here. These oughta help you some."

He stretched out the most un-Gid-like thing Reece had ever seen him handle: a netted bag filled to its drawstring with colorful marbles. Gideon gently tipped some of the marbles into his hand. They were decorated with swirls like miniscule galaxies.

"Your generosity and resourcefulness is truly humbling," Reece said dryly.

"They're full'a burstpowder, genius." Gideon put the marbles back into their pouch one at a time, his big fingers cautious. "One'a Mordecai's oldest tricks. The marble masks the metal in the powder, makes it undetectable by magnomiters and the like. Throw one'a them and you'll get about half the result of a regular burstpowder shell. And there ain't no reason an upstandin' citizen like yourself shouldn't be carryin' a bag'a marbles on his person." He handed over the gift with a leer for Reece's attire. "Just be sure to bring back the spares, Cap'n Unpleasant. Mordecai'll be put out if I go givin' away all his tricks."

Mordecai and Nivy returned with only six minutes to spare. At least, Reece *thought* the girl with Mordecai was Nivy, but there wasn't much to go off. The only similarity between the girl they had caught on Aurelia and the one in the silver gown on Mordecai's arm was their black ribbon necklace.

"Go ahead darlin', give us a spin!" Mordecai said as he backed away from Nivy and stood in line with Hayden, Reece, and Gideon, who had a foot stopping the kitchen door from closing all the way. Mordecai, Reece noticed, smelled suspiciously of lilac perfume.

Looking like she wanted to laugh at herself, Nivy spun with faked enthusiasm. Reece wasn't going to pretend to understand the dynamics of her dress or what this part or that part was called, but he knew pretty when he saw it. The gown had laces up its back, short sleeves that sat on the edges of her shoulders, and little pearls around the neckline. Her hair, curled and pinned over her shoulder, had not a lank strand to it.

Hayden gasped as Reece offered Nivy an ALP.

"If you can find someplace to keep this, you can carry it."

Nivy stared at the gun thoughtfully, chewing the inside of her cheek, and then reached for it. Reece pulled back slightly and added, "I want your word. No unpleasant surprises," before he let her take it for good.

"It's just like one'a those stories," Mordecai said dreamily. "Where the urchin gets to go to the ball and act like a princess." He pulled out a celebratory cigar and struck a match against the wall. "Makes a man tearful."

Po was waiting at the docks, sitting cross-legged on the rusty roof of her brother's Nyad. She pushed her goggles out of her eyes and slid down onto the nose of the ship to get a good look at them—at Nivy in particular, Reece thought.

"You two look clever," she called, swinging down to the ground with a sigh. "A smart match." Her eyes lingered on Gid and Hayden. Mordecai had stayed behind to guard the Vee. "Are you two not goin'?"

Reece made his way under the Nyad's wing and opened her creaky sliding door. For being a family of genius mechanics, the Trimbles' sure had an old lugger for a ship.

"We weren't invited."

"You weren't?" Po sounded delighted. "Oh, phew, I was scared I was the only one!"

"In you get, Nivy," Reece said, waving Nivy into the leather co-pilot's seat. "We've got a tight schedule to keep."

Struggling with her dress, Nivy hopped up into the Nyad and sat down with an explosion of air from her poofy skirts.

Reece turned to face his friends. "Well, if all goes well, I'll be back by morning. If it doesn't—"

"Just be careful, Reece," Hayden interrupted with a frown, unamused. "I mean, I know you will be, but I guess I mean—don't be reckless. We don't know for sure what Eldritch is planning."

"We know enough." Pasting on a smile, Reece added, thinking it would be good to give Hayden something to distract him tonight, "You should send your father a log. He's been pretty worried, I can tell." He started to say something equally heartening to Gideon, but it turned out Gid didn't need it.

"Remember what I said about the marbles," he whispered. "I mean, about bringin' them back. Mordecai's gonna spit like a cat when he sees they're gone."

"Yes, I promise to bring *the marbles* back safe and sound."

As Nivy and Reece started buckling in, Po came to the door and began relaying instructions and ticking points off on her fingers.

"Now, she shakes real hard when she's breakin' atmosphere, but that's totally normal, and if you hear a clickin' sound, that's just one of the propellers that's got a nick in it. You'll want to ease up on the levelers when you take off, because if you overdo it, you'll burn the system out and then you'll have to fly without your artificial gravity, and, well, you saw all the junk we've got in the back, that wouldn't be good—"

When she had run out of fingers, she wriggled them and backed away from the Nyad, which made less of a purr and more of a whine when Reece rather nervously started it up.

"You'll do fine!" Po shouted, waving happily as the Nyad rattled and drifted upward.

Looking out his window, Reece watched her put a hand on Hayden and Gideon's shoulders as if she had known them for years, saw her moving her mouth as if she was saying one last thing. The Nyad was too bleeding loud to make out what she was shouting; hopefully it wasn't important.

As the Nyad gradually became a speck in the very distant sky, Po shook her head. "Well," she said to Gideon and Hayden, "if he doesn't figure out that the clamp's been modified to roll right instead of left, I expect we'll be seein' them again *real* soon."

XIX

Brainstormin'

Reece and Nivy stood at the foot of Emathia's long drive, staring down a tunnel of oaks draped in innumerable strands of tiny photon globes. The sun had gone, but it wasn't quite dark yet; there was a blue sort of tinge to everything that made the orange in the oaks and the red streamers braided up the estate's closed iron gate burn brightly. Reece could hear, beneath the crickets and the chatter of other guests lining up for admittance, a stringed orchestra playing Abigail's favorite movement of Vorherr's "The Chrononaut's Last Voyage". The hulking dark mass on the far reaches of the grounds was the Kraken-class heliocraft the masquerade would relocate to after the guests had all been fed, for the skywaltz.

Nivy looked ready to scale the gate, she was so eager to get in. Reece caught her elbow and steered her around the gatehouse where servants were matching invitations to names on a long scroll of parchment. There were two well-dressed sentries on either side of the gate with metal-detecting wands, checking guests and occasionally confiscating a sidearm, tagging it, and placing it into a brass box already filled with delicate-looking ALPS that Gideon doubtlessly would have melted down into something more useful.

"Bag," Reece whispered as he and Nivy slipped furtively between two large shrubberies.

Nivy handed him the beaded silver pouch concealing their guns. He placed it on the ground and used his foot to nudge it under the gate.

"Ready?" he asked, looking over her head at the long line of carriages and guests afoot.

Chin held high, Nivy nodded. It was lucky Mordecai had thrown a white fur stole at her at the last second; the night was crisp and sharp and smelled of coming winter, and her teeth were chattering as it was.

"You look very pretty," Reece said.

Nivy smirked, pointed at him, and made a "so-so" gesture that he laughed at. This was good—keeping things light, staying confidant, remembering to smile. They weren't even inside the party yet, and Reece's stomach was already performing back flips.

Sliding out from the shrubberies to a few disparaging stares, he tapped on the back door of the gatehouse.

The door opened a sliver, and a spotted face peered out, saw him, and gasped.

"Mr. Sheppard?"

"Lionel!" Reece pretended to be just as surprised. "I was expecting one of the senior servants, maybe Watkins, or Grim."

Lionel, who was a redheaded boy a year or so Reece's minor, slipped out of the gatehouse and closed the door behind him, looking smug. "The Duchess herself assigned me to the guest list, as a matter of fact. Hey, I didn't know you were coming tonight. You're not on—"

"Actually," Reece lowered his voice, "I wanted to surprise Abigail…I mean, The Duchess." Stepping out of Lionel's way, he gestured at Nivy, who affected a shy smile perfectly on cue. "This is…my friend. Orpha." Luckily, Lionel bowed just as Nivy cringed. "She and The Duchess haven't been properly introduced; that's why I'm keeping a low profile. To keep the surprise intact, as it were. You know how this lot—" Reece jabbed his thumb at the guests in waiting. "—can gossip."

Lionel frowned thoughtfully. "Would you like me to call you a private carriage to take you up to the mansion?"

"No, no," Reece said quickly. "We'd rather slip in quietly, if possible. Is there a side gate being used?"

"Well…" Lionel uncertainly glanced at the gatehouse as if wondering whether or not he needed approval from some higher power. "There's one over by the duck pond, but it's just for servants—"

"Excellent. Could you take us there? I'd make sure to mention your help to The Duchess."

Lionel hesitated, scratching one of his too-big ears. "I suppose that might be alright."

Reece impatiently glanced at his pocket watch. The guest line was going down more and more; he needed to get in there!

"Lionel," he said firmly, trying to give his voice the duke's velvet edge. "This *is* my house, you know."

Flushing, Lionel stammered, "Oh, right sir, I mean, I know sir! This way, sir!"

Without further ado, he grandly waved them away from the gatehouse and set off at a slightly-harried march. Nivy flashed Reece a congratulatory grin behind Lionel's back and, when prompted, linked her elbow through his.

Reece recognized the duck pond gate, but he remembered it being overgrown and rusted, not neat and trim like it was now. Servants in dark green livery were rushing in and out of the gateway, narrowly avoiding collisions while balancing silver trays laden with drinks. Lionel led Reece and Nivy right up to the gate and then held them back with a hand and an apologetic grimace.

"All the gates have been rigged with magnomiters to check for automata and weapons."

"I'm not carrying any."

"Right, well, then you should be able to go on through. It's just, with all the members of Parliament in one place, the sentries and The Veritas wanted to take extra care…"

Nodding, Reece began pulling Nivy toward the duck pond gate. "Thanks again, Lionel, I'll—"

A terrible blaring alarm suddenly started wailing, causing both Reece and Nivy to leap back from the gate and jump apart from each other, ready for the worst. Reece's heart felt like it was trying to batter its way through his ribs. Servants were stopping to cover their ears and stare as if the horrible noise was coming directly from him.

The shrill wail slowly faded out, leaving a warm ringing in Reece's ears.

Lionel made a confused sound. "That shouldn't have happened if you're not carrying anything. Did you leave a wireless in your pocket, maybe?"

Thoroughly confused himself, Reece turned out his pockets for all to see. "Nothing. I think you might have a loose wire."

Looking as though this was the worse news he'd heard all night, Lionel shouted across the gate to a fellow staring servant, "Call Watkins! He'll want to hear of this! No! I said *call him*!"

Reece cleared his throat uncomfortably. "Can we…?"

"Oh, yes. Go on through, we'll take care of it, sir!"

Exchanging a puzzled look with Nivy, Reece walked through the gate, this time not stopping when the alarm went off, though he did wriggle a finger in his ear. So much for keeping their heads down.

Hugging the shadows of the hedges, they snuck back around the estate wall, watching their feet for signs of their bag. When Nivy saw it, she scooped it up as if she'd only just dropped it, and placed it under her arm again. They merged into the incoming traffic from the main gate, carefully keeping one eye on the sentries until they were behind and out of sight.

As the mansion grew larger and the music louder, the guests around Reece and Nivy started gasping and pointing, beside themselves. Reece didn't know what about. He thought the mansion looked rather eerie, lit up in colored spotlights, outlined in more of those tiny photon globes. The water in the tiered fountain the carriages were pulling around glowed a bright, bloody red.

The colors danced on Nivy's awed face, reflected in her eyes. Reece elbowed her pointedly.

"Mask?" he asked.

Without tearing her eyes from the mansion, Nivy pulled up the silver mask that had been hanging around her neck and fixed it over her nose. Reece followed in suit with his green mask and felt instantly better, having some of his face hidden.

"Remember the plan," Reece whispered, and saw Nivy nod confidently out of the corner of his eye. There wasn't much to be confidant about; it wasn't much of a plan. He was going to cover up her muteness by being exceptionally rude all night, which he didn't think would be too hard, considering the wide supply of pompous people at hand he would enjoy being rude to. If someone said something to Nivy and expected a reply, it was his job to cut in and answer on her behalf. He could do overbearing. What he couldn't do was waltz. But he'd deal with that later.

Gideon and Hayden had picked up a third mouth, and it didn't want to go away any more than it wanted to stop runnin'. Po followed them right onto campus, chatterin' like a wind-up doll with an endless lifespan.

"So what're ya doin' now?" Po asked with her hands in her pockets as she bounced along between them.

Catchin' Hayden's eye, Gideon shrugged. He wouldn't say no to another lunch; he hadn't quite maxed out his capacity his first go around, and he had the sinkin' feelin' it was gonna be a long night, waitin' on news from Reece.

"I was thinking of stopping by the nearest log interface and calling home," Hayden admitted. "I think there's—"

"Oh, the nearest's at the bus-ship housin' units. I was just goin' that way myself. I can take you there, if you like."

Another glance passed over her head as Gideon shrugged again and Hayden hesitated. Wasn't like they were in any real hurry.

Gideon had been to the housin' units for a couple'a odd jobs, but not in a year or two, and he'd never been there when there was work bein' done on the ships themselves. The big warehouse was one-roomed, with all the bus-ships suspended at different levels on thick metal planks, the highest goin' right up to the ceilin' some hundred feet overhead. He liked the feel'a it right away, the flyin' sparks, the smell'a hot metal, the dusty glimmer lyin' over everythin'.

"Gus! Tilden!" Po called as she skipped over a tool box lyin' open on the cement floor.

Gideon recognized Gus as the lanky blond fellow sittin' on a chain swing thirty-some feet above them, a thermal torch in hand. Tilden was even higher up, hangin' in a harness from the ceilin'. He'd heard'a the Trimble brothers, even seen them around Caldonia, but they hadn't looked quite so hostile then. Aitch took a carefully measured step away from their little sister.

"I brought friends!" Po announced, like it was a great surprise for them.

Gideon could see Gus strokin' his thermal torch fondly.

"Maybe we should come back later," Aitch began, but Po made a snortin' noise and blew him off with a wave.

"Don't you mind them, they're always mean when I bring boys around. Just look out and make sure they don't drop a wrench on your head. Comon', the interface is this way!"

Gideon left them to it and wandered around on his own, curiously lookin' up into the underbellies'a the bus-ships. He wasn't much of a mechanic, or into ship lore like Reece, but he could appreciate the skill behind a thing all the same. Stoppin' under Bus-ship Fourteen, he peered up into the mess'a wires that had been laid bare, hearin' rather than seein' the little old woman deep at work in the engine. Until her head popped out from the wires, upside-down and wrapped in a red handkerchief.

"You, there," she barked, and a hand rose outta the wires. "Hand me that rotator pike."

Gideon flipped the spindly metal tool up to his hand with his boot and passed it along to the woman, who he now recognized from the interface at Mordecai's. The woman scanned him, made a disapprovin' sound, and then sank back up into her bog'a wires.

Po appeared suddenly at Gideon's elbow. "I see you've met Agnes," she said brightly. "Agnes," she called up at the wires, "this is Gideon!"

"Pleasure," came the dry reply, not soundin' at all pleased.

Po shrugged at Gideon and smiled so that dimples showed around her mouth. "Hey, want to come see where the magic happens?"

"Er—"

She hooked his hand and started draggin' him to the next bus-ship over, narratin' as they went.

"People don't think much'a these old luggers, but they've got a lot'a character. And they're downright hardy. Know how old this one is?" Po asked as she stopped and patted the hull'a Bus-ship Sixteen like a faithful pet.

Gideon, squintin', inspected the rusty ship and guessed about three hundred.

"Almost fifty!" Po boasted. "Sure, bus-ships take a lot'a maintenance, but what can you expect, you know? They've got a big job, transportin' all those kids back and forth safely. Can you imagine if one'a them went wonkers between here and Honora?" Twinklin' brown eyes goin' wide, she leaned alarmingly close. "It'd be like what almost happened on me and Reece's bus-ship when we were Tens. You ever hear about that?"

"Er—"

"It was just lucky he was so quick on his feet. He saved a kid, you know." She bit back a smile, sighin' so theatrically, she blew a wisp'a hair outta her face.

Gideon really wanted to go find Aitch, but Po had moved on past talkin' about ships and now wanted to know all about him, which made him plain uncomfortable. There was no good way to talk about himself without breechin' subjects that made most people nervous, subjects like the war and workin' illegal jobs and bein' Pantedan. Much as he tried to bring the conversation to a dead halt, Po wouldn't let up. It was like tryin' to stop the rain.

"I've heard all about that shop!" Po exclaimed, hangin' by her knees from a taut chain under the bus-ship. She swung down, lookin' so impressed Gideon felt himself goin' red in the face. "Your lot makes the best guns this side'a the Epimetheus—Tilden has been wantin' to put in an order, but Mum always gets nervous when he brings it up."

"My lot?" Gideon repeated edgily. He scowled from where he was sittin' on the floor beneath her, polishin' his revolver on his pant leg.

"Oh," Po looked briefly stricken, "I mean the lot'a you in that old house in Praxis. I wasn't talkin' about Pans." Tiltin' her head one way so that her braid swung like a pendulum, she frowned. "I've gotta get down, all the blood is rushin' to my head. A little help?"

Thinkin' that a drop on the head might do Po more good than bad, Gideon got up and grabbed her stiffly around the biceps so she could lower her feet one at a time to the ground. They opened their mouths at the same time, Po about to start chatterin' again, Gideon about to lose his temper, and were both cut off by the anguished cry that echoed jarringly through the warehouse.

Recognizin' it immediately, Gideon dropped Po (she landed with a grunt on her backside) and sprinted out from under Bus-ship Sixteen with his revolver drawn and ready.

"What was that?" Tilden shouted from way overhead.

"Where did it come from?" Gus added.

The log interface. Gideon tore across the warehouse, leapin' over pumps and ramps and scattered engine parts. He could see Hayden's haggard shape slumped against the wall by the interface. He was on his feet, but he was holdin' his head in his arms like he was in pain.

"Aitch!" Gideon half collided with him, takin' him by the shoulders and shakin' him. "Aitch, what's up, what's goin' on?"

He heard a racket behind him and glanced back to see Po, Gus, Tilden, and Agnes all hurryin' to join them at the interface, their faces showin' everythin' from worry to confusion to annoyance.

"Gideon," a kindly voice crackled outta the interface.

Still clutchin' Aitch's arm, Gideon glanced over at the small screen to see Mr. Adams, Hayden's baldin' grandfather, starin' at the lens with a shockgun held across his chest. The room in the background'a his picture looked like a Freherian boar had torn through it.

"What happened?" Gideon asked, releasin' Aitch, who crumpled to the floor, rockin' back and forth. Po dropped to her knees beside him, her face pale beneath her freckles.

Mr. Adams swallowed a few times, his Adam's apple workin', before replyin'. "The Veritas…they came…took Hugh and Sophie…"

It took a minute for what he said to fill Gideon with the dread it deserved—his brain, his heart, his breathin', everythin' had slowed down to the point'a stoppin' completely.

"Were they—did they—" He couldn't say what he wanted to aloud, not with Aitch in a wreck at his feet.

Tremblin' as he wiped his brow, Mr. Adams shook his head. "They were arrested, I don't know why, but I don't think they were harmed. They had been staying with us these last few days…I think Hugh might have known this was a possibility, but all the same…"

Down on the floor, Hayden's voice hitched in a sob. "He knew," he said hoarsely, not lookin' up. "He knew because I told him it was a possibility. *I* knew it was. This is my fault."

Gideon started pacin', blockin' out Po's brothers' whispers and Agnes's perturbed stare. He didn't even care if they were listenin'."What did the Vees say? Tell me exactly what they said."

"They just recited their terms," said Mr. Adams as Hayden let out another low moan. "And said to let Reece know—"

"Reece?" Gideon barked. "Not Aitch or me?"

"They just said Reece."

For the first time, Hayden glanced up, his red eyes clearin' as he realized, "Eldritch. This has to be Eldritch's doing."

Still pacin' with his arms crossed, Gideon did some quick work in his head, thoughtfully tappin' the barrel'a his revolver against his side. Truth be told, it was hard to think when his mind kept gettin' caught up in fantasies'a huntin' Eldritch down with a bucket full'a that flesh-eatin' acid foam.

"Reece was right. Tonight's the night Eldritch is gonna try to off the duke." Someone behind him gasped. "Eldritch knew there was a chance Reece might guess as much and wanted to distract him. Give him somethin' else to do tonight. So he sent the Vees after Sophie and Hugh."

Mr. Adam was starin' into the lens with a frightened and befuddled expression. "I don't understand, what do you—"

As he passed the interface, Gideon reached and shut it off so that Mr. Adams disappeared with a beep and a blink. It was for his own good.

"Only the Veritas were too late," Hayden croaked despairingly. "Eldritch didn't know Reece had already left for the masquerade."

Somethin' seemed off about that, Gideon thought as he scratched his head. He was missin' somethin'. Brainstormin' like this was Reece's strongpoint, not his.

"The Veritas are never too late," Agnes suddenly said in a grim voice.

Gideon paused and stared slowly back at her as the cogs in his mind lumbered into place and the wheels started turnin' a little faster. She returned his stare with a kind'a subdued alertness, her mouth pulled tight so the wrinkles around her mouth tripled in number.

"She's right," he said. "The Veritas could'a taken Sophie and Hugh any time today if they wanted to occupy Reece. The Vees came when they *did* because they did know he'd already gone."

Hayden said in a tired voice, "That doesn't make any sense."

"Yeah, it does," Gideon snapped. "If Eldritch found out he would be too late to stop Reece from bein' at the masquerade, he would try to put somethin' in place to distract Reece *at* the masquerade."

"Following that train of thought, if you should try to contact Reece and tell him your friends have been taken, you will be serving the headmaster's plan," Agnes said darkly. So much for keepin' everythin' quiet.

Findin' some strength, Hayden stood, holdin' the wall for support. "We have to! We're three hours away from Emathia—we'll never make it in time ourselves! Who knows what the Vees will do to Sophie and Father if Reece doesn't go for them!"

"That's leadin' Reece right into a trap," Gideon argued.

Glarin' at him, Hayden staggered over to the log interface and started dialin' it up. Gideon lunged for him and caught his jacket up in two fists.

"Think, Aitch! You'll be givin' Reece into Eldritch's hands!"

"I'm not letting them be taken to *that place!*"

"We don't know that'll happen!"

"I'm not willing to take the chance!"

Growlin', Gideon roped his arms around Hayden to heave him bodily away from the interface. It worked for a second—then Hayden wedged a hand up between them and dug his thumb into Gideon's arm just below the elbow, and then that whole arm went totally limp, like it'd been struck by a lightnin' cap.

"What the bleedin'—" Gideon roared.

As Hayden tried wrigglin' out from under his good arm, he brought up his knee and let him ram himself into it in his scramble for the interface. Gideon would'a thought that'd be the end'a it, but he was wrong. Doubled up and wheezin', Hayden whirled around, lookin' slightly crazed, and lashed out with just his fingertips. The fingers hit the soft spot between the shoulder and collarbone'a Gideon's good arm, and then that went limp as a rag too.

"Quit doin' that!" he yelled as his revolver clattered uselessly to the floor.

Hayden turned once more toward the interface. Gideon stuck out his leg and swept both his feet so that he landed with a shockin' *smack* face-down on the cement.

"Stop it right now!" Po suddenly shouted, hurryin' into the empty space between them. Her brown eyes had gone as big around as cricket balls. "Shame on you both, fightin' when your friends are in trouble. If you lose your wits now, Reece isn't gonna have no one to help him!"

Flexin' his stubbornly-numb fingers, Gideon scowled down at his feet. He could see Aitch at the corner'a his vision, nursin' a bloody nose and lookin' meek.

"Now," Po went on in a timid voice, hands still raised as if to deflect any blows that might fly her way, "I can get you to Honora in under two hours."

For the first time, her brothers spoke up from the background, soundin' none-too-happy.

"What are you bleedin' goin' on about now—"

"Po, don't be a ginghoo, you ain't—"

"And just how do you propose to do that, Miss Trimble?" Agnes asked, puttin' her fists on her hips. "Do you happen to have a Trixt 2-Four hidden in your jumpsuit? Perhaps a lattice power conduit in your braid?"

At first Po gulped, but then she dropped her hands and pushed back her shoulders like she was ready to fight for her territory. "The emergency modifications we made on Bus-ship One could do it."

Agnes laughed a cold laugh. "Oh, they could do it alright, if they don't make your engine combust first!"

"They'll hold, I know they will, I ran the simulations myself."

"You're not goin'," Gus said right over top'a her, Tilden noddin' his agreement. Tilden was the older'a the two, shorter and stockier, but anyone who thought they could push Gus's buttons had another thing comin' to them.

Flushin', Po turned to her brothers with her hands on her hips. "You can try and stop me if you like, but I'd bet if Da was here, he'd say I was right. And don't think one'a you is gonna volunteer for the job," she added when Tilden opened his mouth, lookin' cross. "I made the mods, I'm the best one to fly it, and you both know that's a fact!"

Buttin' in, Gideon grunted, "Bus-ship One?"

Agnes shot him a witherin' look. "For carting The Owl's staff from Caldonia to campus."

"They call it The Tutor Taxi," Po explained in a gentler voice. "And I *know* it can get us there in under two hours."

"Two hours is still a long time," Hayden whispered from the floor.

Gideon glanced at him, saw his head bowed in defeat, and decided that for now, he would forgive him for the temporary paralysis in both his arms.

"It's less than three," Po said firmly as she turned and started climbin' the ladder stretchin' up to all levels'a the warehouse.

Tilden and Gus moved forward as if to stop her, but Gideon took a step in their direction, glarin' threats. He wasn't gonna shoot them— after all, he didn't have any hands just this second—but he could always get in the way. He was a pretty big obstacle, even rendered armless.

"I'm sorry about your arms," Hayden said quietly, comin' to stand beside him as they waited on Po, a scrap'a handkerchief up either nostril. "They should be back to normal shortly."

Gideon made a noise'a sorts and wasn't sure whether there was goodwill behind it or not.

"Do you have a plan? Are we going to the Veritas's base?"

"We're goin' to the masquerade." Seein' another outburst gatherin' power on Hayden's face, Gideon added, "Because that's where I think they'll be, Aitch."

Hayden blew out a breath'a relief, but Gideon couldn't hear it; somewhere in the warehouse, an ancient engine was grumblin' loudly to life.

"Why wouldn't they take them to the base? That's where they...they..."

"Listen, you gotta understand how a brain like Eldritch's works," Gideon said impatiently, followin' the Trimble brothers and Agnes as they started marchin' toward the source'a the grumblin', their heads together. "I think I've got his number. He can do torture, yeah, but that's not why he took Soph and your da. He took them on impulse, to use them to get Reece's attention off the duke. He's too...dirt, what's the word...he's too practical to torture just to torture, he's gotta have a reason for it. The thing is, he knows Reece too well. Reece would fly off the handle if he found out Soph and Hugh were bein' hurt at all. Eldritch doesn't want that, not at the masquerade. He wants him distracted. On top'a that, Soph and your da are no good to him damaged." Pausin', he added in an undertone, "I ain't gonna let anythin' happen to them, Aitch. They're like my family too."

Hayden smiled gratefully and apologized again for the state'a his arms.

They paused and stood back as the rectangular bus-ship nearest to the ceilin' backed outta its spot. Dust eddied around them, blown by the ship's burners. As they watched, the bay door on the warehouse's roof scrolled back to show a square'a inky blue sky.

Po's voice, amplified by the ship's exterior megaphone, called, "Come on up the ladder, I've got the hatch open for ya!"

Gideon nodded at the nearest ladder and had Aitch start up first, to give his arms that much more time to recuperate. He'd gotten the grip back in his hands, that was what mattered most.

"Allow me to be candid," said Agnes as she, Tilden, and Gus surrounded Gideon at the foot'a the steel ladder. The boys' freckled faces were hard as thunderheads and made him readjust the weak hold he had on his gun. "If Po returns in less than perfect condition, I will personally weld you to the hull of a garbage disposer and send you out into the Voice of Space, understood?"

Outta Gus, Tilden, and Agnes, Agnes was the one Gideon would least like to meet in a dark alley, even if he had his revolver, *especially* if she had a thermal torch.

He climbed the ladder as fast as he could so his hands didn't have to think so hard about holdin' on. All the way up at the ceilin', Bus-ship One, which looked newer than all its brothers with a fresh black paintjob, hovered a foot above the top'a the ladder. Aitch stood in the mouth'a its open hatch, already a mild green shade. Gideon kicked off the top rung and landed with a few stumblin' steps as Po heard him arrive and started pullin' the ship outta port.

"You'll want to get up here and strap in," Po called, her white head visible through the circular window in the cockpit's door.

Staggerin', Gideon and Aitch joined her in the smallish room, Gideon takin' the co-pilot's chair, Hayden sittin' in the spare pull-down seat against the wall. As soon as they were in place, Po flipped a switch on the flightpanel that turned off the overhead photon dome and left them with only the colorful scatterin'a lit buttons on the panel to dampen the dark.

"Seal and bolt the door," Po instructed as she fastened a harness over both her shoulders. "If the engine *does* combust, we might be able to coast out the crash in here and let the rest'a the ship burn up."

Gideon spun the handle on the door till he felt the sealants lock in place with a soft hiss. Hayden was goin' back and forth between puttin' his head between his knees to fight his oncomin' airsickness and leanin' it back to slow his nosebleed.

The bus-ship vibrated without stop as it began tiltin' its nose toward the ceilin', fillin' the canopy window'a the cockpit with a view'a the blue-black sky they were about to go crashin' into (hopefully not literally).

"This is gonna be rough," Po said quietly. Her throat sounded dry, and she swallowed. Gideon glanced at her hands, grippin' the yoke as if afraid to let go. "But I know the mods will hold."

"Take us to the lake before you take us into space."

"Why?" Po and Aitch said together.

Gideon pulled the paper hat he'd crafted outta poster earlier in the day and sat it on the flightpanel. "I've got a plan, is why."

XX

The Gala of the Solar Cycle

Reece and Nivy allowed themselves to be ushered with all the rest through Emathia's front door and down one of the side corridors that Reece knew led to the ballroom. Every surface in the mansion shimmered under candlelight, polished to the very last mote of dust. Abigail's extravagant flair decorated everything. A red carpet had been laid like a road to the ballroom, tall antique candle trees rooted on either side. Paintings of past dukes loomed in the shadows, fifteen feet tall.

The ballroom itself, while better lit than the rest of the mansion, had a sort of gauzy golden glow cast by the photon chandelier hanging from the domed ceiling. The air was warm and sleepy, helped on by the burning hearth dominating the far wall of the room. A stringed orchestra played to the left of the fire in matching gold masks that made their faces identical, impassive. To the right of the fire was the grand staircase that spilled out onto the black marble floor from the balconies above.

"Stay close to me," Reece said to Nivy in an undertone as he led her to one of the circular tables set about the room. It was draped in white and set with crystal goblets, plates, and an unrealistic amount of forks in all different sizes. "We'll stay put until the duke and Abigail make their appearance, probably there." He pointed at the staircase. "Then it's just a matter of—ow! What?"

Nivy, who had kicked him none too gently in the shin, pointed with her eyes. A square-shouldered man with a ruddy, boyish face was heading their way with a blonde in a viciously red gown on his arm.

"Oh, bleeding—" Reece began and then swallowed dryly, grabbing for his goblet, which a waiter in green had just topped off with something blue and steaming.

"Reece," Scarlet greeted pleasantly enough. The eyes behind her feathered mask flitted to Nivy and back. "How wonderful to see you. I believe you remember Lucius Tobin?"

Lucius smiled and snatched Reece's limp hand out of the air, shaking it wildly. "Good to see you, old boy, good to see you! It's been ages, what? You're looking swell!"

"Yes—it—so are—" Reece blundered. His hand felt like it'd been caught in a clamp. "Scarlet, Lucius, this is Orpha. Orpha is from Olbia."

"Orpha from Olbia," Scarlet repeated thoughtfully. "What's your surname, Orpha? My family has a vacation house in Olbia, I wonder if—"

"Trimble," Reece blurted. His hands were sweating; the one that Lucius had returned felt like it was swelling. "We met through my uncle. She's in the theatre." He winced as Nivy kicked him in the shin again.

"An actress!" Lucius exclaimed. "How positively novel!"

"Quaint," Scarlet agreed. Was it Reece's imagination, it did she sound unconvinced? "I wonder if we might join you for the dinner. Are these seats taken?" Before Reece could say yes, she had circled the table, pulled out a chair, and sat down beside him.

"It's funny," she murmured as Lucius sat and helped himself to a steaming crystal goblet. Her voice was nearly lost in the rambling monologue he was cheerfully delivering to Nivy. "Last I heard, you had a notice on your head and a warning not to return to Honora."

He should've known better. Nothing escaped Scarlet—she was like a bird ferreting in the dirt for worms. "Is that common knowledge?"

Scarlet studied him from behind her red mask before slowly shaking her head. "No. I only heard from Mr. Rice. When you sent me that log this afternoon, I didn't really think you were serious about coming. What are you doing here, Reece?"

It was Lucius who saved him from answering. As he finished telling Nivy an apparently uproarious story, he turned to Scarlet and put a comfortable arm around her shoulders, still chuckling. "Scarlet, darling, I was just telling Orpha about the time we were out nightcat hunting and old Mr. Drummond fell off his horse, do you remember?"

"I remember," said Scarlet tonelessly.

"Oh, it was just wild, *wild*! Poor fellow, but of course, he should have known better than to try to take that jump, he hadn't nearly the experience for it. I told him, I said, 'Ambrose, this is really for the more experienced rider, perhaps you should just watch this go around', but wouldn't you know, he scoffed at me and went ahead and tried it anyways. Got what he deserved with that broken tailbone, didn't he! He'll leave the difficult stuff to the real riders next time, won't he?"

Scarlet glared at Reece as he raised his eyebrows at her. Nivy looked a bit shell-shocked, and was gripping one of her forks as if taking a necessary precaution.

Oblivious, Lucius tipped back his goblet and finished out his draught with a gulp. He smacked his lips contently. "I do say, this is good stuff, really classy, don't you think? I'll go fetch a servant to bring us a bottle."

"Spiffing," Reece said, suppressing a laugh, and winced as Nivy and Scarlet tag-teamed and kicked his throbbing shin one after the other.

Lucius hadn't even pushed back his chair before the photon chandelier dimmed and the orchestra died out on a high, suspenseful note. Reece craned his neck to get a clear view of the staircase as a globe of light appeared on the steps.

"My, but they look marvelous!" Lucius loudly exclaimed as the duke and Abigail stepped into the light to thunderous applause. He, along with all the other guests, had pushed back his chair to stand as he clapped, hailing the High Duke and Duchess, both dressed in a deep, almost-black green. Reece rose after a moment's pause with a strange heat rushing in his ears: adrenaline. As he clapped halfheartedly, his eyes started a circuitous sweep of the ballroom, looking for a hint of out-of-placeness to warn him of danger.

The duke gave a brief welcome, then descended the stairs with Abigail and started for the elevated table on the other end of the room, greeting guests along the way.

"You know, Reece, I'm quite surprised you're not sitting with them tonight," Lucius mused. "But I suppose it must be exhausting, being in the spotlight so. Especially since Liem disappeared. Big shoes to fill, isn't that what they say?"

Reece made a noncommittal noise, staring fixedly at his parents as they shook hands and nodded respectfully here and there. As they passed by a few tables to their right, he dropped his fork and spent a moment doubled over by his feet, waiting for them to move on. When he resurfaced, Scarlet was watching him, tapping her lips with a finger.

Every course of the meal dragged. The cranberry custard salad tasted like weeds in Reece's mouth, the warm sourdough bread like a sponge. He put away a considerable amount of food nonetheless, just to have something to do with his fidgeting hands.

Halfway through the third course (stuffed cream chicken that tasted like rubber), golden hoops were lowered from the ceiling bearing girls in white leotards who twisted around the hoops as if they had no bones to bend. Reece watched only the duke, who seemed quietly focused on his plate and unaware of the daring acrobatics being performed overhead. Even when one of the performers dangled upside-down by a single foot, he paid her only a glance.

His chin on his fist, Reece frowned. Respect had snuck up on him before he'd realized what was happening. The duke knew tonight was the night he was to be assassinated. For whatever numptified reason, he was willing to let it happen, and this was how he faced it. The man was either brave or out of his bleeding mind.

There was a slight pressure on Reece's arm; he glanced at Nivy, whose brow was furrowed in question. Seeing how Scarlet and Lucius were engaged in a heated argument over which candidate should be elected to represent the southern district of some county or another, Reece asked, "What is it?"

Nivy pointed at the duke, pointed at him, and spread her hands "why", or maybe, "what".

A suddenly tired smile pulled at Reece's mouth. "What happened, you mean? Between the duke and me?"

Nivy nodded patiently, her blue eyes on the duke.

"We had a fall out a few years ago. He wanted to send me across Epimetheus, to a planet called Leto, to study politics."

Scarlet stopped midsentence to turn and stare at Reece, leaving Lucius gazing at the back of her head with a sleepy smile. "Leto? I never knew that. That—"

"Is halfway across the Epimetheus," Reece finished for her. "I know."

Scarlet pursed her lips. "I was going to say that would have been a great opportunity. Leto has needed political intervention for decades now, it's on the brink of uncivilization."

Reece wondered wryly how that factored into The Kreft's plan for Epimetheus.

"Great opportunity for you, maybe, but I was studying to be captain, remember? My life was at The Owl. I would've disappeared from everyone's lives; they all would have gone on without me. That's how I saw it. That the duke just wanted me out of the way."

Reece shuddered as if the old memories he drudged up brought a chill with them. He clenched his eyes shut and remembered. Sitting at the clawed feet of a chair, playing with a wooden replica of Aurelia as his father read *Legends from the Voice of Space* aloud. Two or three years later, the duke taking him to The Guild House, telling him how one day, when he and Liem governed Honora, he would be in charge of managing Emathia. A few years further on, Reece begging to be allowed to study aviation at The Aurelian Academy, not Interplanetary Politics. That's when the chasm between them had started to grow, when the duke had stormed out of Reece's bedroom and left him standing there, alone...

He'd met Hayden and Gideon not a year later. For the longest time, the duke had pretended this didn't concern him. The chasm stretched. Reece got older, saw the duke less and less. Imagined more and more how he must resent him for choosing becoming a captain over becoming Liem's second-in-command.

Then there was that fateful day in late winter. Reece could remember just how it felt, standing in the doorway of the duke's office at Emathia, staring at his father's back as he poured over notes on his desk.

"I've decided to send you to Leto," the duke had rumbled without turning, jotting something down with an eagle-feather quill. "You'll finish out the rest of your schooling there."

It had taken Reece a whole minute to stop staring and demand why.

"Experience. Practice. The planet is in need of strong political faces. If you assert yourself properly, I expect you'll return to Honora in a few years time ready to take a stand in The Guild House."

"But I'm not...The Guild House..." Reece had tripped to his father's desk and planted his hands to support himself. "I'm studying to be captain! These last six years, that's all I've worked for! For what, if you're going to send me to Leto now?"

"You will be Liem's right hand. You will manage the estate and *do as you are told.*"

"But classes—"

"An end must be put to your juvenile fancy with flying. It's time to grow up, Reece."

"Six years!" Reece had yelled. "Six years, and you never once told me this was the plan. Liem doesn't need me! He's going to be the bleeding duke, he could care less what I do with myself!"

"This is hardly about you or Liem. It is about duty, about obligation." Frowning, the duke had bent over his desk, checked a schedule projected on his flat datascope screen, and added with finality, "You leave tomorrow at noon."

Reece flinchingly remembered kicking the leg of the desk as he shouted, "It's the middle of the school year! I have friends here! Hayden...Gideon!"

"As I said, it's time to grow up. Your friendship with those beneath your station has been encouraged for too long."

"Encouraged? Mother won't even let me bring them in the front door! And you, you haven't cared a scrap about who I spend my time with, you've never even asked, you never ask *anything*! You haven't been here—*you haven't cared*!"

The knuckles gripping the duke's quill had gone white. "A man in my position can't often afford to expend himself upon caring. You'll want to start packing."

Reece often wondered when this memory came back to haunt him if he and the duke might've recovered from their fight if he hadn't had a total lapse in judgment and shouted at the duke, "I hate you!"

The duke's response, given calmly, without looking up from his work, had been, "Then perhaps it is fortunate I cannot afford to care."

That had been two years ago. Reece had left Emathia on his bim, gone to Atlas, and stayed with Mordecai and Gideon at the workshop for the rest of the school year. When he returned to Emathia months later, the duke said nothing about Leto, their fight, or their parting words—which had made Reece that much angrier. As if the duke could just pretend he hadn't meant to ship Reece out of his and everyone else's lives! Well, if that's what he wanted, Reece decided he would give it to him until he acknowledged he'd been wrong.

Only the duke never came to set things right, and after the first seven or eight months of waiting, Reece knew he'd gone too far to ever turn back. And the regret he felt was never enough to drive him back to Emathia when he knew the duke would be home. They both knew the chasm could never be closed again.

Reece swiftly ducked his head as the duke gazed briefly in his direction. "We fought. I waited for him to apologize, but he never did, and by the time a year had gone by, I knew I never could either."

"That's a little petty, Reece," Scarlet said sagely.

"And you're a little nosy," he snapped. "Seems we all have our little faults."

"Come now, Reece old boy," Lucius chuckled good-naturedly. "Scarlet does have a point! It's time to bury the hatchet! Why, I used to resent *you*, if you can believe it—thought you had everything. Well, now I see how miserable you are, I can't find it in me to resent you in the least!" He half choked on his drink and sat up straighter, looking over their heads. "I say, I think that's Hogarth Boyle over there, I simply must say hello. Please excuse me."

As Reece, Nivy, and Scarlet watched him walk a little crookedly to a neighboring table, Reece said, "Wow. I'm really warming up to him."

Nivy laughed silently into her hand, but Scarlet scowled reproachfully.

"Be nice. He means well, and he's right. The duke's your father, Reece...you only get so much time to enjoy him." Her look added, *I would know.*

"Enjoy him," Reece repeated dryly, watching the duke as he scanned the dessert menu on a wide datascope a servant was holding before him. "It's hard to enjoy someone from a distance."

Lucius returned, bubbling with gossip fresh from the mouth of Hogarth. They all selected their desserts, except for Reece, who despite never having felt emptier, couldn't make himself eat one more bite. Nivy still picked one for him, clearly with the intention of eating it herself.

"Orpha, I don't think I've heard you say one word," Lucius said thickly, through a mouth of cheese and red fudge.

Reece very unsmoothly intercepted the attempt at conversation. "She has to save her voice for the theatre." He lifted up off his seat slightly as a waiter blocked his view of the duke. What was he going to do if someone pulled a gun? He couldn't outrun a bullet.

He was just considering moving closer to the duke's table when Lucius gave a dramatic gasp and exclaimed in a hoarse sort of whisper, "Stars above, is that a Vee?"

Reece spun so quickly, his back cracked twice. He, Scarlet, and Nivy followed Lucius's startled stare to its target and saw a thin, sallow figure observing the ballroom from one of the box seats in a balcony above. Its bald head and dark eyes were visible even from this distance.

"They are a work of modern man, aren't they?" Lucius said in awe. "Here to keep a special eye on things, no doubt."

No doubt.

Face grave, Nivy started digging in her handbag; Reece caught her wrist before she could draw her gun.

"Not—yet," he said through his teeth, wary of Scarlet, who at the moment was staring at the Vee with cold, stiff composure. A few other tables had noticed the Vee, but the general consensus seemed to be in agreement with Lucius's thought that the Vee was here for everyone's protection.

Reece had subtly gestured for Nivy to join him in trying to get
closer to the duke and was starting to stand when a hand appeared on
his shoulder and shoved him back into his chair. Out of the corner of
his eye, he glimpsed a servant's dark green sleeve, but it seemed
strangely matched to the hand attached, a hand both callused and dirty.
He about had a seizure when he twisted his head and found his
mysterious waiter was Gideon.

Gid was dressed in the servants' livery right down to the napkin
draped neatly over his forearm, but his jacket was tight in the
shoulders, and his sleeves showed too much wrist. It said something
that it was seeing him dressed like this that had Reece gaping like a
fish out of water, not the fact that one of his cheeks was turning the
royal purple of a bruise and his bottom lip bore a fresh red cut.

"Splendid timing!" Lucius declared, very pink in the face. He held
up his empty goblet. "I was just about to go get another! Good help
here tonight, what?"

Gideon shot Lucius a look of the deepest contempt before
kneeling beside Reece's chair.

"What the bleeding bogrosh are you doing here?" Reece hissed,
not dumb to the fact that Scarlet was staring at the both of them with
puzzled interest. She knew Gideon well enough to know that his
hobbies didn't exactly include volunteering for servant duty.

"We've got a situation," Gideon mumbled.

Nivy leaned forward to hear better, her second helping of dessert
pushed aside. Lucius also leaned forward, and in full view of all,
dragged Reece's mostly full drink toward himself and knocked it back.

"What kind of situation?"

Hesitating, Gideon opened his mouth, but it was Lucius who
spoke. Or, more accurately, sprayed his drink (which was actually
Reece's) everywhere.

"Bleeding bogrosh!" he exclaimed in a slur. "There's s-something
in my drink!"

As his tablemates stared, Lucius used his fork to dig in the dregs
of his glass and fish out a small red trinket. He pinched it between his
thumb and forefinger and went cross-eyed holding it before his nose
and mumbling, "It's some sort of pin...dropped by a servant, I
suppose...*hic*...I shall most a-assuredly be having a word with—"

Feeling as if someone large had just trodden on his lungs, Reece
snatched the red lion head pin out of Lucius's hand and held it up to
the light. It was Mr. Rice's pin. The one he always, *always* wore, had
worn as long as Reece had known him...it had been his wife's...

He instinctively glanced upward and froze as if caught in a spotlight. The lone Vee remained seated in his lofty box, staring down at Reece with that sinister emotionlessness. As anger seared Reece's insides and turned his look of shock into a glare of hate, the Vee's lips parted in a smile.

"That's what I'm tryin' to tell you," Gideon said, his voice low beneath the babble of busyness all around them. "Eldritch is onto you. He's got a hold'a Mr. Rice and Sophie and is likely gonna—"

Reece tried to stand only to find himself being slammed roughly into his seat again.

"That's what we're here for." Gideon sounded half irritated, half amused. "Eldritch is gonna try to distract you from doin' what you came to do. You keep your mind where it's been and let us deal with the rest."

Then tonight *was* the night, if Eldritch wanted to distract him. Well, the plan was working. Reece felt as though a seam down the middle of his chest was being pulled from either side, ripped painfully in two.

"Reece, what's going on?" Scarlet leaned around Gideon. She was having another rare wringing-of-the-hands moment, looking anxious behind her mask.

Nivy had her own questions. Forgetting or maybe not caring any longer about their charade, she gestured at Gideon, pointing at him and then at the empty spot beside him, wondering—

"Who is *we?*" Reece asked aloud for her.

"Aitch, me. Er...Po."

Reece choked as if he'd gotten a lungful of bad air. Now wasn't really the time to lecture Gideon on getting Po involved, but he felt like a parent who'd just found out their child had been snuck into a raucous party.

"You'd better go, we're drawing looks," he told Gideon as he glanced around and met a few too many curious eyes.

Peevishly straightening his napkin, Gideon nodded and turned to go. Then Reece was struck by a sudden inspiration.

"Waiter? Excuse me, *Waiter?*" he said a little loudly, in a voice he hoped was sufficiently pompous.

Gideon paused and turned very slowly, giving Reece a look that promised physical harm should he ever call him that again.

"Would you see these are put in my carriage? I hadn't realized I'd brought them in." Reaching into his jacket, Reece pulled out the netted bag of burstpowder marbles, first making sure to tip a few loose in his pocket. "Do take care, won't you? They're my uncle's."

Gideon bowed deeply, hiding his dark smirk, and accepted the marbles smoothly. They disappeared into his jacket as he crossed to one of the corridor mouths attached to the ballroom, where Reece could see Po daubing Hayden's bleeding nose with a handkerchief as they waited in matching green uniforms.

Po just had time to wave and smile before she was sucked out of sight by an impatient Gideon yanking on her hand.

"You know," Lucius mused dazedly, "I don't think that man is really a waiter at all!"

XXI

Gid Makes a Promise

Hayden had decided. Of all the things in the galaxy he could hate, the thing he knew for certain he hated the most was feeling helpless. Knowing that Sophie and Father had been taken by The Veritas, knowing how powerless he was on his own to do anything for them…that's what he hated.

He, Gideon, and Po made it to Emathia in record time. Po hadn't been exaggerating about the modifications she had made to The Tutor Taxi, or about how rough a ride it would be. They'd been rattled so badly putting down on Emathia's back meadow, Hayden had bitten down on his sleeve to keep his teeth from chipping together, and Gideon had had a case of emergency medical supplies fall on him.

Somehow, in all the hubbub of servants rushing in and out of the side gate with candlesticks and fresh flowers and replacement strings for the cellist, Gideon, Po, and Hayden managed to slide in unnoticed, just another cluster of servants on their way to work, thanks to the uniforms Gideon had appropriated from The Owl's Masquerade Committee. They had a brief scare when an alarm started peeling shrilly, but then a red-haired servant hurrying in the opposite direction impatiently waved them on, shouting for the alarm to be shut off.

"I thought we had that fixed! Someone get Watkins! *Get Watkins!*"

They entered the mansion through the back door Reece was in the habit of using whenever he brought Hayden and Gideon home, followed a line of servants pushing dessert trolleys to the ballroom, and then ducked into a dark sitting room to catch their breath. Then Gideon left to warn Reece.

Hayden's feeling of uselessness was climaxing.

"What now?" he asked when Gideon rejoined him and Po. Gideon hauled them through the sitting room and out into the corridor intersecting it, which was dark and marked off-limits by a thick velvet rope that he stepped over without a second glance.

"Where do we go? Do you think—"

"There was a Vee on one'a the balconies overlookin' the ballroom. Watchin' Reece, likely as not. It'll know where Soph and your da are."

"Is that supposed to make me feel better?" Hayden's voice cracked as it rose hysterically. He had never been in this wing of the mansion before. Being here now, when it was dark and eerie and there were Vees to face, made him feel like there was a rock bobbing at the bottom of his stomach."Is that supposed to—"

"Burn it, Aitch!" Gideon hissed, slapping a hand over his mouth. "If you can't stay calm, you're gonna have to stay here!"

Po circled around them and looked anxiously into Hayden's face. "Close your eyes, Hayden," she said with a tremor in her voice. Without knowing what for, Hayden obeyed. "You just gotta think about…about puttin' all your thoughts into one tiny seed in your head. Focus really hard on not thinkin' at all. Take a deep breath."

The dark clouds Hayden could feel cluttering his brain receded slightly, and he gave a small shiver as he pushed out his breath and opened his eyes. Gideon watchfully peeled back his hand.

"We get to the Vee on the balcony. I say where there's one, there'll be two," he continued as he stripped off his undersized jacket with some difficulty. He pulled his revolver out from behind his belt and began neatly loading it. "I'm gonna try not to have to shoot them. A shot would be loud. Might draw unwelcome attention."

"How big is this place?" Po wondered as they turned down a hall lit by the frail blue moonlight falling in through its row of oval windows. The light turned their faces blue, made it seem as though they were underwater.

"Four stories, a dozen and some suites, two kitchens, a half a dozen offices and music rooms…" The numbers helped Hayden focus. He rambled them off and felt the dark clouds scroll even further back, till his panic was a quiet buzz in the back of his head. "…then there's the library, with well over twenty thousand titles, the sunroom, the—"

Gideon suddenly threw out his arms to stop Po and Hayden and backed them up into a stretch of wall between two windows with a shushing sound. On the ground at their feet, the shadow of a tree swayed and convulsed in the wind. And then three shadows, lean and human, glided across the moonlight, as silent as the tree.

Hayden heard Po gulp as she ducked her face into Gideon's back. His own throat felt like it was sticking when he tried to gulp away the lump that had risen in it.

They waited for some time like that, but there was no more sign of The Veritas than that quick march of shadows. Hayden supposed it might not even have been Vees…but he doubted it. He'd never known a normal human to bring that pins and needles feeling into a room with them.

"Let's move," Gideon said, and started walking again so abruptly, Hayden and Po fell against the space where he had been.

They climbed a set of winding stairs, doubled back down a hall on the third story, and then cut through two sitting rooms to reach the collection of curtained doors hiding the balcony box seats. There were a dozen on this floor alone, their black curtains furling and unfurling in the breeze flowing in through the open window at the end of the hall. Hayden clutched his arms around himself, his teeth chattering. It was getting colder outside.

Gideon signaled for him and Po to stay put as he checked the box seats one at a time, using the barrel of his revolver to nudge each curtain aside. His footsteps sank into the mansion's thick carpets; the only sound was the muffled echo of the orchestra drifting up from the ballroom.

There was a flash of darkness at the edge of Hayden's vision, where his bifocals stopped and the blurriness began. He swung to the left and blinked down the dim corridor.

"What is it?" Po asked, seizing his hand so suddenly he jumped.

"I thought—I thought I saw—" The curtains shifted in the breeze again, and he relaxed. "Never mind. It was nothing. Just the curtains."

"There's nothin' here," Gideon called as he thrashed the last curtain aside and disappeared into the box stall. He made an impatient noise. "Wonder where it got to."

Po, still clutching Hayden's hand with both of hers, suddenly jerked, yanking his arm hard enough to make his bifocals bounce off the bridge of his nose and dangle from one ear. Her fingers slid out from his, raking the back of his hand on their way out.

Fumbling to right his bifocals, Hayden turned and found himself alone in the hallway. Gideon was in the box stall. Po was simply, inexplicably, gone.

"Gideon!" he called in a hoarse whisper. "*Gideon!*"

Something bumped at the other end of the hallway, so softly, it shouldn't have been frightening at all—but Hayden found the quietness of it terrible, because it left so much to the imagination. His heart hammering, he groped inside his jacket and pulled a small photon wand out of its inside pocket. He aimed with a shaking hand, flicked on the wand, and gasped as the beam grazed a gaunt white face and a pair of black eyes.

With a yelp, Hayden dropped the photon wand. The light swept across Po in its downward spiral. The Vee had her from behind, his spidery fingers over her mouth, his pale lips close to her ear.

Several things happened at once. Moonlight seeped between the cloud coverage and struck the corridor window, turning the hallway blue. Gideon emerged from the box stall, started as he saw the Vee and Po, and snapped his revolver into position. And a nervous-sounding voice called from somewhere nearby, "Is somebody there?"

A second later, a sentry with a shockgun tucked in his shoulder stepped from one of the sitting rooms into the corridor, halfway between Gideon and his revolver and the Vee and Po. He spotted Gideon first.

"Lower your weapon!" he shouted quaveringly, hefting his gun. "I said lower it!"

"Behind you!" Hayden tried to say, but the lump in his throat seemed to be stopping up his voice.

The Vee was pulling Po backwards into shadow; her feet were kicking, dragging, but her hands were pinned against her sides.

"Stay where you are!" the sentry barked as Hayden took a reflexive step after Po. "Just—just stay there!"

"There's a Vee—"

"I said *stay there!*"

Po gave one last kick and a stifled scream through the Vee's hand. The sentry turned toward the sound…Gideon tilted the revolver resignedly…and Hayden leaped forward with one hand taut and outstretched—

As the knife edge of his hand chopped across the cluster of nerves under the sentry's chin, the man's eyes rolled back into his head, and he slumped forward like a puppet cut from his strings, landing facedown with a dull thud. His shockgun went off with a deafening bang as it fell beneath his hand. Po screamed.

It might have been the only time in Hayden's life he ran as fast as Gideon, tearing down the hall, his bifocals jumping on his nose. Po's supine shape materialized through the darkness, curled into a ball with her arms wrapped around her head.

"I'm—I'm alright," Po said without uncovering her face as Hayden knelt and touched her shoulder. "I'm fine—the shot hit his leg—h-he went through there—" She pointed her little finger at the cupboard door at waist height on the wall above her.

Gideon bumped the door open with his knee, frowning. "You recognize this, Aitch?"

Gently prizing Po's arms apart, Hayden said distractedly, "It's the chute that goes down to the stream, isn't it? For the servants to send laundry to the washers? Po, are you sure you're alright?" he added as Po emerged from behind her guard with quivering eyes and a dazed expression. She nodded unconvincingly.

"Aitch," Gideon suddenly said, "don't ever do that again."

"Do what?"

"Jump out like that when I'm gettin' ready to take a shot. Could'a hit you. You think'a that?"

Swallowing dryly, Hayden tried to sound as if he had. "I'm sure you wouldn't have."

A reverberating *crack* cut through the silence. Hayden's ears rang dully as he yelpingly ducked down next to Po, who was covering her face again, this time with good reason. As shockgun pellets splattered the wall above them, plaster and dust puffed out into their air, blinding, choking.

As he crouched against the baseboard, Gideon shouted angrily, "You didn't kill him?"

The "him" was pointed at the sentry down the hall, who was wrestling with his shockgun, trying to reload with shaking hands while shouting into his wireless. The sound of his approaching reinforcements rumbled down a nearby hallway like thunder.

"Of all the ludicrous—of course I didn't kill him! Why would I kill him?"

"Maybe," Gideon yelled as he dove, picked the unmoving Po up around the waist, and stuffed her unceremoniously into the chute, "so somethin' like *this* wouldn't happen!" As Po leaned her head out of the chute, mouth open, he snapped at her, "What are you waiting for, burn it? *Get down there!*"

White faced and startled, Po disappeared again, her clunky boots clanking against the sides of the dark tunnel.

"You there! Halt!"

Uniformed sentries were pouring into the corridor, organizing themselves into two rows, the front most on its knees. It reminded Hayden of a firing squad, but...oh.

Gideon roughly grabbed the back of his neck, doubled him over, and pushed him into the chute. His knees smashing against the floor of the tunnel, he rolled once, holding his bifocals against his face, and then shouted as the floor fell out from under him. His heart flew into the region of his adam's apple as he slid down the steep chute, his jacket occasionally squeaking over the tin flooring. He could hear

Gideon crashing down behind him, curse words interspersed with thuds, but he daren't open his eyes. His stomach was rebelling as it was.

The tunnel spat him out abruptly. It was a moment before Hayden's head stopped spinning and he trusted it enough to look around. The night was cold and black, its starlight blotted out by scudding silver clouds. Tufts of snow peppered the air, made prisms out of the distant lights of the mansion, and laid a fuzzy carpet on the frozen stream beneath his back.

Po, nearly to the river bank where there was a line of stout stools for the washers, twisted her neck to look at him. She was sprawled on her stomach, dragging herself along by her elbows.

"Hurry, Hayden," she whispered as if her voice alone was enough to shatter the ice. "It's real thin…you can see the water runnin' underneath…"

Hayden's stomach flip-flopped as if he'd missed a step. He couldn't swim.

He had just touched one tentative hand to the stinging ice when Gideon shot out of the chute. There was a sound like a muffled gunshot—a shudder ran through the ice, he felt it in his legs—and then he was sinking, and Po was screaming, and the water was so cold that his brain went utterly blank.

His feet dragged against the bottom of the stream as it pulled him downriver, and he tried to plant them and push up, to get back to the surface, but his muscles were oddly unresponsive. *That'll be the early onsets of hypothermia*, he told himself, like that was any reassurance. He started to panic; his throat worked compulsively, trying to gulp air. His heart was plodding very quickly in his ears, like the fast, wet footsteps of someone running.

Something caught him under the armpit; it felt like he'd collided with a steel bar. He tried to use it to pull himself toward the ice, toward air, to find it was the bar that was doing the pulling, not him.

His head scraped over the top of the water, and he sucked in a breath that tried to fill his lungs with frost. Coughing, he let himself be dragged out of the water and dropped, sodden and shivering, onto the crunchy grass.

He opened his blurry eyes. His bifocals had managed to cling to the very tip of his nose during his underwater tumble.

"G-G-Gid—" he stammered in time with his shivers.

"He's alright," Po said from somewhere beside him, sounding uneasy. "They pulled you both out."

Hayden tried to ask, "They?" but he'd begun shaking so wildly, he didn't trust himself not to accidentally bite off his tongue if he unclenched his teeth. Lifting a hand, he shoved his bifocals up his nose. The scene slid into focus, and despite his shivering, he managed a sort of tremulous groan.

An unaccounted-for silver and blue glow was giving everything a curious backlight. He'd drifted maybe fifty feet downriver—he could see the mouth of the chute in the hillock behind Po, the two Veritas holding either of her arms, and the dark mound on the grass at their feet. The mound seemed to coughing up a pint or so of water. Gideon.

There were four other Vees. Two had sleeves that were wet up to their shoulders, but for all the care they showed, you would have thought the air quickly crusting Hayden's clothes felt tepid to them.

"We recognize them," one of the Vees said to the others, voice flat and unfeeling.

"Reece Sheppard's companions," supplied the Vee who had Gideon's revolver dangling on his hooked finger.

"How curious."

"Shall we question them?"

"Time. There isn't enough time. Reece Sheppard has not taken the bait as expected. He must not be allowed to interfere."

One of the Vees made a thoughtful noise as he stalked in a circle around Hayden. "Even now, he speaks with Thaddeus Sheppard. Our plan goes awry." He glanced toward the grey garden hedges made small by the short walk across the grounds.

"Charles Eldritch knows this. He has plans to deal with Reece Sheppard accordingly. But what of these?"

Behind Po, who was sagging between her captors as if her knees had gone slack, Gideon raised his head. Hayden caught his eye and tried begging silently, *Please don't try anything, please…*

"Take them to the rest. We shall speak to Charles Eldritch, see what he doesn't want done with them."

Gideon must have understood Hayden's pleading stare, because when a Vee tried pulling him to his feet, he shrugged off the Vee's white, spidery hands with a snarl, but otherwise came quietly. He didn't seem to be shaking as much as Hayden, despite the fact his hair had frozen into tiny curlicue icicles on his forehead.

Though it was true Hayden didn't like being touched by the Vees, he couldn't have stood without their help—the joints in his knees felt like they had rusted into place.

"Take my jacket," Po said quietly as she pulled her arms out of her sleeves. She laid it across his back as they walked, three Vees before them, three behind. Hayden didn't say so, but if the jacket added any warmth, he couldn't feel the difference.

The source of the mysterious blue and silver glow came into sight as they circumnavigated a copse of evergreens and stepped into a band of white light. The Kraken-class heliocraft loomed like a huge wooden monster rearing over the tops of the trees. Its balloon alone was as big as the mansion, straining lazily against the chains tethering it to the wooden mass of the round-bellied ship. The wintry light beaming from the ship's every porthole, every open door, made Hayden feel, if anything, colder.

The Vees led them around the back of the silhouetted ship to avoid the crowds streaming from the estate gardens to the wide gangplank being lowered down onto the snow-dashed lawn. Hayden, his numb hands balled under his armpits, tried lagging behind, wanting desperately to be noticed by even one of the ladies complaining that their fur stoles weren't thick enough.

No such luck. The Vees frog-marched Gideon and pushed Po and Hayden around the hull of the ship and in through a steel hatch without even the nearby lantern-bearing servants glancing their way.

One of the Vees punched a sequence of numbers into a panel on the dirty metal wall next to a bolted door. The steam and noise and smell of metallic heat made Hayden think they were close to the engine room. Sure enough, when he glanced at Po, she was staring straight up, her eyes narrowed in study. He followed her gaze and through his foggy lenses perceived a room-sized block of metal with squiggling wires and gaping funnels pointing off it in all directions. It was suspended above them in an extensive spider web of brass tubes that now and again spewed jets of steam at the junctions where two or more tubes met.

"The Quadrant 7. Pretty, isn't it?" Po said under her breath with a nervous smile.

She jumped as one of the Vees seized her arm and guided her and Hayden through the now-open door and into some kind of furnace or boiler room. Pot-bellied stoves crowded the corners while cylindrical tanks topped with gauges lined their walk into the heart of the room, where a low fireplace provided flickering orange light. The two people seated on the ragged blanket before the hearth looked up.

"Hayden!" Hugh let out a gasping sigh of relief, and Sophie hopped up, her feet twisting the blanket awry.

Hayden felt a swooping rush of relief at the sight of his family. Forgetting where he was for a moment, he clumsily squeezed between a Vee and a rusted boiler and rushed Sophie with his arms out.

"You're drenched—and you're freezing!" Sophie said, pulling back hurriedly. "What happened? What did those monsters do to you?"

"Silence, little girl," one of the Vees ordered coldly. His arm flashing out like a snake, he caught Sophie's cheeks in his bony hand and touched her top lip with one long fingernail. "We have ways of sealing your pretty little lips."

Gideon lurched against his captor's hold, growling murderously as Hayden wrapped his stinging arms around Sophie, pried her from the Vee's grip, and backed into his father, who had jumped to his feet. The Vee left his hand outstretched, his unsightly fingers still positioned for cupping Sophie's face.

"They are a prime selection, are they not?" the Vee crooned, his thin lips curling. "A perfect sample of humankind at its most endearing." There was a *pinging* noise as one of Gideon's thrashing feet nicked an iron stove. Looking suddenly bored, the Vee dropped his hand, peered over his shoulder, and frowned. "We should put that one in irons."

"And station a pair of watchers on both sides of the door," contributed another Vee.

"Agreed."

"Agreed."

Hayden blocked their cool voices out as best he could as he turned and faced his father with Sophie. Up close, he could see purple bruises flowering up the side of Hugh's face; his bifocals' left lens had a crack down its middle.

"Are you both okay?" From behind him came sounds of rustling movement and the hatch closing with a *clank* and a *hiss*.

"We're alive, in any case," Hugh said, sounding exhausted. "Sit down next to the fire, Hayden, we need to start warming you up. And take off your jacket."

Hayden did as he was told, though he already felt better. He could tell the boiler room was actually quite hot—there were beads of sweat on his father's forehead—and a soothing heat had been spreading inside him like a warm cough syrup since he'd first seen Sophie and Hugh's whole albeit slightly worse-for-wear faces.

As he self-consciously peeled off his wet undershirt and allowed Sophie to spread it out before the hearth, Po timidly sat down beside him, and Gideon, his balance impaired by his wrists being locked together at the small of his back, more or less fell down beside her, muttering mutinously.

"What now?" Sophie asked, turning Hayden's shirt like a hotcake.

"What now, indeed?" Hugh ominously shook his head. Sighing, he eased his face into his hands. "This is my fault. I should have protected you from this. All of you. I saw the signs…I knew Reece was digging too deep…if only…"

Gideon, having a private wrestling match with the irons behind his back, grunted exasperatedly, "Can't see how you can blame yourself. You're prolly the only one who didn't have a hand in this."

Pushing a white strand of hair behind her ear—her braid had a distinctly mussed look about it now—Po said, "But Reece…he's out there all alone now…"

"He ain't alone," Gideon snapped, and Po jumped, not knowing what Hayden did, that Gideon was frustrated with the cuffs, not her. "He's got Nivy, don't he?"

"He could have an army of you, Gideon, and it wouldn't make a difference. You saw the Vees. There are at least twice that many on this ship, along with Eldritch himself," Hugh said grimly. "Hayden, you're still shaking. Wrap in this blanket, here."

Hayden was preoccupied, staring into the guttering fire with his mind someplace else. Only when his father shook the blanket at the edge of his vision did he raise a hand to accept it. "Do you know about The Kreft?" he asked suddenly.

Hugh looked startled. "What—"

"You do," Hayden realized as he lifted his eyes from the fire. Gideon was still twisting his hands into grotesque shapes, trying to slip them out of their cuffs, but he was listening, same as Po and Soph, whose expressions of wide-eyed curiosity were almost identical. "How did you find out about them?"

Hugh grudgingly sighed, then staried long and hard in the direction of the hatch, where Hayden could only assume two Vees were standing—it was too dark beyond the ring of firelight to know for sure. He pulled the blanket tight around his arms, hording his warmth.

"I didn't know for sure until I overheard Reece and the duke's discussion in the ancestral library. I had only suspicions before then. The headmaster's personnel file being personally detained by the duke made me curious. You heard that Ms. Ashdown and I tried to requisition it?"

Hayden nodded.

"Yesterday afternoon, the duke had me in his office for a debriefing on some cuts that are being made to the library's funding.

While I was there, the duke was called out and I..." Hugh looked ashamed.

Gideon had stopped tangling with his irons. "You got into his desk, didn't you?" He grinned wolfishly at Hayden. "Knew you had to get your unruly streak from somewhere, Aitch."

"Yes, well," Father didn't seem to like that, "Eldritch's file revealed that he had no history on Honora prior to his promotion to headmaster. He clearly wasn't Honoran born. And there was something else in the file. Here I thought the duke had been guarding Eldritch's secret by keeping his file locked away...but he'd really been guarding a secret of his own. He's done meticulous research into The Kreft's activities in The Epimetheus Galaxy, cross-referenced and mapped every major political move, every suspicious disaster, every civil war...he even traced The Kreft back to L.F. 709. I think he must have been trying to find their weakness. The man is a genius."

"That's what Reece wanted to do," Gideon said to Hayden. "That day we went back to The Owl. He wanted to go the library and do that kinda research. He must'a been thinkin' the same thing."

The hatch in the darkness suddenly burst open with a resounding crash. Po spun and crawled backward; Hayden unthinkingly shrunk back until his father put a hand on his back to keep him from scrambling into the fire. Gideon remained the only one in the foreground, and even he had jumped at the sound.

As if rising up out of murky waters, the colors and outlines of a tall, thin figure surfaced out of the darkness. Charles Eldritch stopped just beyond the edge of light, so that his sunken cheeks and deep eyes gathered shadows beneath them.

"Well," he said simply. "Well." His hands behind his back, he began circling their little area, his dark eyes contemplating each of them in turn. He was dressed as he had been at the crater on Atlas: all in black, from his silk neck scarf to the gloves stretched tight over his skeletal hands. "Are we all acquainted, then? Mr. Rice and I know each other from The Guild House, of course. And your daughter, Sophie...forgive me, but she looks just like Juliet. Sophie..."

Sophie cringed as Eldritch crouched down beside her. Folded up as he was, Eldritch looked to Hayden like a bat hiding his height in his wings.

"I knew your mother, did you know that? Yes, she was a student at The Aurelian Academy, much like your brother is now, near the start of my term as headmaster. She was such a beauty. Boys used to memorize her schedule just to watch her walk—" he mimed walking with two of his fingers, "—from one class to another. Mmm."

There was a meaningful pause, and Hayden's stomach boiled with anger, hating the fondly reminiscent expression on Eldritch's face.

Licking his lips, Eldritch looked at Gideon, who returned the stare with a soundless snarl, and seemed to deem him unworthy of comment. He passed over the Pantedan and turned his attention to Po instead. He gazed at her for a moment and then suddenly stood and pointed. "This one."

A Vee appeared at his side and reached for Po with traces of eagerness on his wan face.

"No!" Hugh said loudly as the Vee's hands closed around Po's forearms. Po seemed to have fallen into a terrified sort of trance, her brown eyes fixed wide and unblinking, her mouth a little O. "Headmaster, please—"

Eldritch held up a hand, and the Vee straightened, releasing Po. "Yes, Mr. Rice? Would you rather I take Sophie? Either will serve my purpose well. I merely need someone whose screams Mr. Sheppard would be loath to ignore. You may choose."

Hugh drew Sophie closer into his side, whitening. "I—there's no reason to—"

Eldritch smiled unpleasantly. The ground, the walls, the hearth—everything gave a terrific lurch, and Hayden had to stamp down his hands to stop himself sliding. A steady vibration rumbled through the wood under his skin while nearby, a whine started out low and then gradually grew to a high beyond hearing. A familiar and not altogether agreeable jolt in the bottom of Hayden's stomach told him that the heliocraft was taking off for the skywaltz.

"I have an appointment to keep," Eldritch said, as if the ship's movement had reminded him. Hayden felt sick, and not airsick, either, as the headmaster's eyes travelled from Po to Sophie and back again. "Ah, it is like choosing between two beautiful flowers...the choice doesn't matter, in the end. The frost has no favorites when it comes time to turn that which was once beautiful..." He swept the back of his hand over Po's cheek, so that she came out of her trance with a shudder and turned her flushed face away. "...into thistles and weeds."

Hayden was not the only one who jumped when Eldritch suddenly clapped his hands together and smiled. "I believe I *will* take Sophie, after all. Bring her to me on the bridge."

"No!" Hayden cried as Sophie gave a dry sob into Father's coat.

But Eldritch had already turned and dissolved back into darkness, leaving the Vee to turn his attention onto Sophie. He started to extricate the weeping girl from Hugh's arms without a glimmer of guilt in his black eyes, and shameless anger and hate reared in Hayden to the point he was surprised there wasn't steam coming from his still sodden trousers from all the heat in him rising to the surface.

Behind the Vee's legs, Gideon was staring at Hayden with the sort of fevered concentration Nivy showed when she wanted to be understood. He made a little jerking motion with his chin. Hayden nodded.

Dropping onto his back from his kneeling position, Gideon kicked with all his might, his feet connecting with the small of the Vee's back. Hayden dove forward and braced himself, and the stumbling Vee kneed into him and took flight, tumbling over into the hearth.

Hugh, Sophie, and Po leaped out of the way with cries of alarm as the Vee flailed around in the flames. A high keening cut the air—all the small hairs on Hayden's arms stood on end, every last one of his goosebumps aroused by the scream that was terribly and unquestionably human.

The second Vee erupted out of the darkness, a strange silver-antennaed gun in his hand…there was a sizzling noise, like bacon cooking in a pan…a blue streak shot out of the gun and as Hayden tried to dive out of its way, struck his leg. He felt a burst of tingling in his knee before it became as unresponsive as the leg of a stranger.

As the Vee leaped over the handcuffed Gideon, Gideon pounced, his hands miraculously unbound, and roped his arms around his white neck, wrestling him to the ground. Hayden's attention zoomed from the tussle to the Vee with the half-charred face, who had pantingly dragged himself out of the fireplace. There were still-smoldering ashes clinging to his black jumpsuit, though parts of it had been entirely peeled away by the flames to show scraps of white skin covered in blisters and black, bleeding sores.

Hugh tackled the Vee around the middle and rolled him away from Hayden; the Vee screamed in agony, a scream that Hayden knew would call in the others posted outside the door.

"Po! Po, seal the door!"

Scrambling, her boots sliding and screeching over the wooden floor, Po threw herself toward the hatch as the burned Vee screamed and wailed, pinned by Hugh to the blood-smeared ground.

"Shut him up!" Gideon growled through gritted teeth, pulling the flat of his forearm up against the throat of the Vee he had from behind. The Vee's eyes kept rolling back into his head as he dithered between consciousness and the alternative.

Looking disgusted with himself, Hugh covered the Vee's mouth with a hand. "H-Hayden—"

Hayden crawled to his aide, dragging his still-tingling leg. The sores, the blisters, the blood, none of it bothered him—he'd seen burn victims before during his practicals at The Owl—but he couldn't stand the thought that he had done this, even to a Vee. The hate and anger had all trickled out of him and left him with a feeling of blank shock. He pressed steady fingers to the side of the Vee's throat and held them there until the Vee stopped fighting and appeared to fall asleep before their eyes.

It had fallen quiet in the boiler room, so that the crackling fire sounded loud. Gideon leaned up from laying the other seemingly sleeping Vee on his stomach, breathing heavily through his nose. Hugh folded Sophie, who was rocking back and forth with her glazed eyes staring over the tops of her knees, into his chest and murmured gently into her hair, which he stroked with a trembling hand.

A *thump* that sounded twice as loud as it should have made Hayden's hands slip as he gently inspected the Vee's burns.

"They're tryin' to get in," Po's voice called nervously. She reappeared, twisting her hands over her stomach. "I sealed it and locked it as many ways as I knew how…it should hold, at least until they get a thermal torch on it."

Gideon, Hayden noticed, was handling the Vee's silver lightning gun with the hand still trailing his irons. His other hand he held away from himself, his thumb jutting out at a crooked angle. Dislocated.

"How well do you know this place?" he asked Po as he let Hayden examine the displacement of his thumb.

"What, *The Jester?*" Po sounded surprised. "I ain't never been aboard her, but she must be about the same as any heliocraft fitted with a Quadrant 7. You know, back pipings and about four boiler rooms like this one to generate heat enough for the balloon." She nodded vaguely upward.

Another time, the faces Gideon was making as Hayden realigned his thumb would have been comical."Is there another way outta here?"

Po looked around for a minute and jumped when another thump sounded behind her. "Just the pipes. They'll all have ladders runnin' up them, for maintenance."

"That's where we'll go then, Aitch," Gideon said, and Hayden looked up with raised eyebrows. "What, you fancy waitin' around for the Vees to bust in the door and Reece get himself killed? You and me'll shimmy up the pipes, circle back behind the Vees and hit them with this—" he waved the silver gun, "and then while you get Soph and your da into hidin', I'll run and help Reece."

Something seemed suspect about that plan, Hayden thought as he chewed his lip and with a final, capable twist, returned the thumb to its place. Po confirmed this as she sat down by Gideon and stared intently into his face.

"*The Jester's* airborne now, you can't get up those pipes! The air that goes through there is hot enough to flay a flea off a rat's back…if you got caught in the draft…"

"So turn it off."

"It's not as easy as turnin' it off!" Po looked upset. "That air is keepin' *The Jester* airborne. If you cut off that feed, the balloon—" She quailed beneath the Gideon's glare.

Intervening, Hayden suggested, "Maybe you could shut down just one pipe?"

Tilting her chin and staring thoughtfully into space, Po murmured, "I guess I could tamper with the gauges and change the timin' on the heat discharges…it'd prolly give you a five minute window to get up to the next level and get clear."

Hugh spoke up for the first time, his voice slightly muffled in Sophie's hair. Sophie still hadn't surfaced from his jacket. "Hayden, I want you to stay here."

"What?" Hayden looked over at his father, his eyebrows drawn together. "But Gideon—"

"I think Gideon's proven himself capable," Hugh said dryly, clearing his throat. He raised his chin over Sophie's blonde hair, and Hayden saw the kind of sternness in his face that meant Hayden wouldn't be getting his way no matter how he hemmed and hawed. "And besides, your leg won't be ready to climb anything for some minutes yet. Gideon?"

Gideon shrugged one shoulder as if he couldn't see how it mattered either way.

"You shouldn't go alone," Hayden stiffly insisted.

Po had been staring at her lap, concentrating on her fidgeting hands, but now she suddenly stood. "I could go," she offered a little apprehensively. "In fact, I think I should. I'm used to climbin' through engines. You might need a guide to get outta the Quadrant. And if *he* wakes up…" she jerked her head without looking at the unconscious Vee Hayden had been tending, "…you'll need to put him under again, Hayden."

Gideon and Hayden stared at each other for a moment. Unable to find an argument, Hayden finally, unwillingly, nodded. Useless, again.

"Just take care'a your family," Po said gently as she led Gideon off into shadow, clinging to the wrench she had procured from an old toolbox in the corner of the boiler room.

Hayden watched them go and felt the fight fizzle out of him; his shoulders slumped, and he looked glumly over at his father and Sophie to find their eyes on him.

"They'll be alright," Sophie peeped as she eased herself out of the protective cage of Hugh's arms and took one of Hayden's hands in both of hers. Hayden gave her warm hands a squeeze as if trying to press more certainty into her words.

In the darkness, the hatch continued to thump.

Po weaved confidently between boilers and cylinders, keepin' just barely in sight, her shape a blur through the sticky steam shootin' in continuous jets from trappin's around the room. Much as Gideon was glad'a somethin' useful to do, of bein' able to put a plan into action, he had his misgivin's, largely owin' to Po. His parents were prolly rollin' in their graves, seein' him draggin' a girl into this sorta danger. Though it really felt like Po was doin' the draggin'.

"Here!" Po had stopped at the very back'a the deceivingly large boiler room.

Two steps in front'a her, the floor dropped down into a deep basin. At the bottom'a the basin was a mammoth black pipe mouth, gapin' wide, lookin' hazy in the heat it was puttin' out. Above the basin were three smaller pipes. Laced together like a braid, they spiraled up through the ceilin' and outta sight. It wasn't hard for Gideon to think'a the big pipe as a mouth, and the other three as a set'a panpipes that were waitin' to be blown on to make a sound.

Po scooted closer to the edge'a the basin and put her hands on her knees to look down into it. She had to wipe sweat from her forehead before she straightened again not five seconds later.

"This is gonna be tricky."

"Can you do it?"

In answer, Po circled the basin and went to the metal power box built into the snakin' tubes that hid the walls. She pried it open and started tinkerin', mutterin' too quietly for Gideon to make out any particular words, her hands flutterin' over the box controls.

A few moments later, she scurried back around the basin to the sound of a fan powerin' down, a little too close to the edge for his peace'a mind. Flinchin', he grabbed her arm and yanked her a few steps to the left. She hardly seemed to notice.

"That wasn't so bad. I programmed a release'a cool air to flush all the heat outta the pipe so's we don't scald ourselves." She thrust a pair'a thick mechanical gloves at his chest. "Expect we'll still need these—the metal is likely to be a little toasty."

With a wild howl, air started pourin' outta the leftmost pipe, pleasantly cool on Gideon's bruised face. Dust scampered and whirled across the floor while Po's braid flopped against her back.

Diggin' into her back pocket, Po pulled out a junky watch. She tapped its face. "Soon as that air stops, we'll have six minutes and forty-three seconds to get up the tube before..." She faltered and snapped the watch around her wrist.

"You could stay here," Gideon suggested, uncomfortable.

Po looked up and braved a smile. "So could you. But Reece needs us."

The wind cut off with one last gasp. Together, they hurried to the edge'a the basin, where the lowest rungs'a the three ladders runnin' up the tubes were barely visible.

"Boost?" Po asked.

Gideon cupped his hands, accepted her foot, and lifted till her head disappeared inside the tube and her feet started kickin' as she squirmed up the ladder. Hands gloved, he leaned and grabbed hold'a the rung. His feet dropped from the ledge and dangled as he pulled himself up the tube, which was just tight enough for his elbows to scrape the sides if he didn't keep them tucked into his chest.

They climbed without talkin' the first three or so minutes. The sound'a their breath came back to them louder than it should've. All the metal was biscuit-pan warm, and added to the feel'a them being in a giant oven. Sweat trickled down Gideon's face, burned in his eyes.

"We nearly there?" he grunted, lookin' down between his feet. There was a coin-sized drop'a orange light far below; all else was black.

"Should be." Po sounded uncertain. "Maybe another fifteen—" She stopped suddenly. "Do you...hear somethin'?"

He did. Somewhere—overhead or down below, the tunnel's reverberant length made it hard to tell—a fan had started purrin'.

Gideon was grippin' the rungs so hard his fingers felt numb. "Move!"

Po's clothes rustled and her boots clanged as she continued upward. Gideon stayed close behind her, hampered by how slow her fastest was.

"I see the fork in the tubes!" Po suddenly shouted, her relief echoin' four times over. "It's just—ARGH!"

Gideon looked up in time to catch a boot with his face—goin' by the squeak'a rubber on rung, Po's foot had slipped. Gideon followed up her scream'a alarm with a growl'a pain and took her flailin' boot in hand before she knocked out his teeth.

"I'm sorry, I'm sorry!"

"Bleedin'—just forget about it! Keep climbin', we're runnin' outta time!"

"I...Gideon, I'm stuck!"

Gideon squinted up, barely able to make out Po wigglin' violently as she tried to free her other boot. It was wedged between the ladder rungs and the wall.

Spurred on by the thrummin'a the fan growin' persistently louder, Gideon squeezed his shoulders up into the gap by her feet and tried reachin' a hand into the tight fold'a space. His arm wouldn't go in past his wrist, his fingers just brushin' her bootlaces.

"How'd you—"

"I don't know, I just slipped. I can't hardly move it—it's too tight around my ankle."

"I can't reach it," Gideon said through gritted teeth, stretchin' his fingers as far as they would go.

Meanwhile, the hummin' was gainin' power, and the tube was gettin' hot. Gideon's back prickled as sweat rolled down his neck.

"You gotta pull harder!"

"I'm pullin' as hard as I can!" Po said loudly, her voice crackin'. The rung strained against her struggle.

Face screwed up in effort, Gideon managed to wring another tenth of an inch outta his arm. His forefinger hooked one'a Po's laces, and he yanked. The knot fell apart in his hand, undone.

"Gideon...the fan—"

"*I know!*" He pressed a forearm to his eyes. The heat felt touchable, like a dense bog all around them.

"Y-you should go! You should go on!"

"I can't fit around you, burn it, and I don't got time to go back...you just gotta pull harder!" Spewin' a stream'a Mordecai's favorite Pantedan curses, Gideon twisted Po's bootlaces and tugged till they snapped. He stared at the outline'a the broken strings in his hand as if not believin' what he was seein'.

Po suddenly made an exultant noise, and Gideon felt the rung rattle madly as she went at the boot with fresh determination. "My foot's comin' outta the boot!"

Breathin' in was like takin' a hot drink, so Gideon didn't waste the breath talkin'—he attacked the shoelaces with his fingertips, rippin' them as often as not. Po kept pullin', and it occurred to Gideon that even over the sound'a the fan, he could hear her watch tickin', tickin' away their last few seconds...

There was a jerk, a change in balance on the ladder, and then Po screamed, "I'm out!"

"Well, don't just sit there singin' about it!" Gideon shouted. "*Move!*"

They clambered up, blinded by sweat, darkness, and the thick steam coilin' up around them like snakes in a race for the surface. As the fan grumbled loudly, the tube began to shake, and Gideon could sense the hulkin' body'a air rushin' up from below, about to overtake them and melt them both into nothin'—

The dark lightened; there was an openin' to Po's left, the mouth of an intersectin' tunnel. She yelled somethin' and dove, but Gideon couldn't make out her words because the grumble had turned into a roar like a waterfall's. He scrambled into her place. She grabbed his shirt and helped him jump into the tunnel, and they both fell to their stomachs, and not a second later, felt the explosion'a hot air rush past their splayed feet.

After a moment'a layin' in shock, wonderin' if he was really alive, Gideon opened his eyes. This new tunnel was lighter than the last. He could make out Po's freckles as she slowly leaned up, starin' without blinkin'.

"My boot," she whispered. "This was my last pair."

"I'll buy you a new pair," Gideon promised as he started crawlin' forward on his hands and knees. A gust'a fresh air swept down the tunnel; he could've drunk it in, it smelled so good.

The tunnel ended not a minute later in a hatch with a small round window. Orange light shone in through the window like a spotlight, lightin' Po's hands as they blurred over the knobs and buttons on the hatch, which eagerly sprung open at her touch.

They climbed outta the tunnel and into a different world, Po's world. They were on a railinged wire bridge connected to the oversized cube that was the Quadrant 7. There were gaps in the walls'a the cube, places where the metal didn't fit together, and through them, Gideon could see cogs and wheels workin' together in perfect sync, like clockwork, like a giant heart.

Po suddenly grabbed a fistful'a his shirt and gasped. Far below, beneath the tangle'a tubes, wires, and bridges, two Vees were furiously tryin' to jimmy their way in a door she and him had already been through once that night. Gideon's hand closed around the hot silver handle'a his stolen gun, and he wriggled his fingers awkwardly, tryin' to find a better grip that wasn't there. The gun felt uncomfortable in his hand, wrong.

"Get me closer," he ordered beneath his breath. "And be quiet about it."

Noddin', Po bent over, pulled off her remainin' boot so that she was stockin'-footed, and set off on tiptoe. There was nothin' for it but to follow and hope, different gun, same aim.

XXII

One, Two, Three, Traitor

Reece wondered if his nerves had overextended themselves. They had been sputtering wildly only minutes ago, and then suddenly flatlined, leaving him with an empty sort of calm. He supposed he preferred the calmness—he could think clearer this way—but he missed the adrenaline. As the night progressed and guests began to mill around the grounds, waiting to board the heliocraft, he felt almost stupid with tiredness. And irritable on top of it.

Upon being dismissed from the ballroom, Lucius had tipsied over to join some friends at the bar, but Scarlet had been harder to lose, sticking to him and Nivy like thermosphere gnats stuck to warm engines. How much she had figured out, Reece couldn't tell. She didn't ask questions. She was just there, a supervising presence trailing him and Nivy as they clung to the edge of the duke's social circle.

"They're going to notice you," Reece growled at her.

"Why should they notice me?" she said crisply. "I have every reason to be here. You're the one who stands out."

It didn't help that Nivy was too fascinated by Scarlet to take his side. She kept tipping her head and peering at her like something she'd found under an upturned rock. Reece half expected her to poke Scarlet with a stick.

They moved in their small, awkward pack through the crowd, never more than twenty yards from the duke and Abigail. The Vee on the balcony had disappeared, but that didn't mean anything. He, or one of his brothers, would be back.

The duke, Abigail, and their procession of fans left the ballroom through a pair of elegant glass doors leading to one of the estate's gardens. This one, called The Shifting Green, literally revolved around its centerpiece, a tall brass statue of a buck rearing on its hind legs. All the different hedges of midnight black roses, blue fairy bulbs, and emerald nevermore blossoms were on their own track, and the tracks orbited the statue, shifting and working together like clockwork. It could be quite disconcerting, looking down at your feet and seeing the different planes of grass moving every which way.

Nivy almost tripped coming onto the first plane of moving grass, but Reece and Scarlet simultaneously caught either of her arms. For whatever reason, this irked Reece further.

"Go away," he said acidly.

"I can help you, if you'd just let me." Scarlet irritably smoothed back a wave of her cornsilk hair. The night had gone from brisk to chilly to downright cold, and there was a kind of stillness to the air that made Reece think they might be in for snow. "I've made enough sense of what's going on."

"You don't know anything about what's going on."

"Why are you being so stubborn?"

"Because this is already complicated enough without adding the help of a pampered politician with no grasp on the real world."

Scarlet's green eyes flashed as she, Nivy, and Reece stepped together onto the next track of grass, shifting now to the right, scrolling past the nevermore blossoms. "This coming from the boy who fell off the MA Building's roof because he was playing Airship Captain in the bell tower!"

"Scarlet," Reece groaned, "I need to focus. I can't fight with you and protect them." He jerked his chin pointedly at his parents.

"And how to you propose to keep them safe, hiding behind a rosebush? What are you going to do against a knife hidden in a handshake, or a gunner a quarter of a mile away?"

Reece just shook his head. Because he had a bigger problem. With the duke determined to let this happen, he was working against Reece as much as Eldritch. Why?

Nivy snapped her fingers to get Reece and Scarlet's attention, then gesticulated an idea, keeping her hands close to her body so no one else would see. It looked like she thought they should shoot the duke themselves, to get him out of the way.

"Clever," Scarlet said dryly, "but rather counterproductive."

Reece caught on quicker. "If we took him out of the picture ourselves...just a leg wound..." The idea clicked as Nivy tried to finish the sentence with her hand motions. "Everyone would swarm around him. It'd be hard for the assassin to get in close or get a clear distance shot."

Scarlet's face cleared, and she began nodding. "I see. Get him out of danger tonight, then—"

She jumped with everyone else in The Shifting Green as an unmistakable *boom* rattled the mansion's upstairs windows. It sounded like someone had set off a firework indoors. A few people, who like Reece and Nivy had recognized the sound of a gunshot, gasped.

Reece instantly looked for the duke and Abigail, but his parents were staring at the mansion with everyone else. The duke, looking especially solemn, bent over his wife's shoulder and whispered something that she nodded to with pursed lips. She began hurrying away with her skirts drawn up in her hands.

"I believe that is the signal for us to move ourselves to the heliocraft for the duration of our evening," the duke announced. He gestured toward a silver gate lodged between two hedges. "If you will kindly gather yourselves aboard the ship, the crew should be waiting to accommodate you all."

A pair of flustered-looking sentries hurried up and started speaking to him in hushed voices as everyone in the garden drifted toward the gate, nervously chuckling at their jitteriness or frowning at the mansion over their shoulders.

Nivy grabbed Reece's arm and turned him to face her, eyes beseeching.

"That didn't sound like a revolver to me, and you know Gideon will always get the first shot out," he told her. "I'm sure they're fine."

He winced as if he could feel the pain of the seam in his chest straining. One gunshot. It could've been meant for any one of them—Gideon, Hayden, Po, Hugh, Sophie. He braced himself as if waiting for four more shots to tear him apart.

"Reece, you need to do whatever it is you're going to do before the duke boards *The Jester*," Scarlet murmured, drifting to join the guests en route for the airship. Lucius was already at the gate, hiccupping and beckoning for her to join him. "If nothing has happened before now, it's because the assassin means to act during the skywaltz…when the duke has nowhere to go." Her hands clutched over her stomach, she let the track carry her to Lucius, and then disappeared through the gate.

She was right. No matter what Reece did to save the duke once they were airborne, until they landed again, there was nowhere to run that an assassin couldn't run also. Now was the time to act. The garden was emptying, the duke was occupied, Abigail had already gone—he was never going to get a clearer shot.

He reached for Nivy's bag and was surprised when she swatted down his hand defiantly and pointed at herself.

"Don't be stupid," he told her, exasperated, and reached for the bag only to have his hands land on air. Nivy had put it behind her back. "Give it to me, Nivy."

She gestured furiously; Reece caught only half of what her hands said, but he got the point. If he shot the duke, he'd be arrested, and then what good would he be? Let her do it. She could outrun the sentries.

"*No.* Now give me the bleeding bag before—"

Neither one had noticed, but as they'd argued, their track of grass had made a full rotation around the buck statue and was now passing within ten feet of the duke and the sentries. Reece made a garbled sound and on instinct, shoved Nivy with all his might into the fairy bulbs. The sound of rattling bushes drew the duke and the sentries' eye.

Any other night, it would've been funny—Reece standing there alone, gliding slowly past his father, who looked positively nonplussed. Reece lifted a hand and sheepishly waved as his track bore him silently on. The duke's expression turned murderous.

"Arrest him," he said to the sentries. The sentries were so astounded by this sudden development that he had to say a second time, in a much rougher voice, "I said *arrest him.*"

There was no point in running, so Reece didn't bother. He even met the sentries halfway, hands raised.

"Foolish, headstrong boy," Thaddeus Sheppard growled as the sentries brought Reece before him. He threw a glance around the garden, which had emptied quickly after the mysterious gunshot. "See to the ship," he ordered the sentries. As they disappeared beyond the hedges, he began, his voice a dangerous sort of quiet, "I warned you against coming to Honora, and this is what you do."

"You know why I had to come."

It was odd, but now that the sneaking around was over, now that it was just him and the duke, Reece felt calmer than he had yet. It wasn't the empty kind of calm he'd felt before. This was readiness.

Considering him, the duke moved onto the next track over, the one that rolled by the firehearts dangling like little red and orange bells from their bushes. "I should've had you arrested on the spot when I heard you were at The Guild House. I should've known you'd never do the unthinkable and actually obey your father." There was a trace of grim humor in his voice that made Reece smirk. "You've done a very stupid thing."

"Not nearly as stupid as what you are about to do," Reece retorted. It began to snow, glittering flakes softly kissing the ground. "Why are you letting this happen? Why are you letting The Kreft have their way?"

"I have my reasons."

"It's suicide!"

"It's sacrifice."

"For the good of Honora? Is that what you think? That letting The Kreft keep playing their game with our lives is—"

Another gunshot rumbled distantly, from somewhere deep within the house. Before he could stop himself, Reece twisted and looked up at the big bay window overlooking the garden. The seam gave slightly to one side.

Following his gaze, the duke murmured through a sigh, "I suppose you have something to do with that."

"With what?"

"The Veritas are in a state. Their presence tonight was supposed to be minimal, discreet, but there must be at least a dozen on the grounds, and I've never seen them unhappier. Supposing, of course, those things can be unhappy."

"You know why that is?" With effort, Reece tore his eyes from the mansion. "It's because Eldritch knew I was coming and tried to distract me by using Hugh and Sophie Rice as bait!"

"Mr. Rice? Got him tangled up in this, did you?"

"That's the last thing I wanted," Reece said defensively. He pointed up at the mansion, and out of the corner of his eye, saw a troupe of armed sentries rush by the bay window. "My friends are in there trying to save them so I can be here to save you—please! I *know* there are others out there in the Epimetheus who are fighting The Kreft, who are refusing to let them have their way. We can fight! We don't have to keep letting them win like everyone who came before us has! *Don't let them win!*"

His father paused, and then as he had in the library, reached out a hand and clasped the back of Reece's neck. Reece got the feeling it was supposed to be a paternal gesture, but the hand gripped hard, stiff and cold.

"Reece," the duke shook his head, "they already have."

Quicker than Reece could react, the duke shoved back from him and brought up a sleek bronze hob. Reece stared down its barrel, almost cross-eyed.

"Get out," the duke said. "Now. I don't care where you go, but leave, leave before it's too late."

Angling his head so the gun wasn't pointing quite so directly at his forehead, Reece snapped, "No! There's never going to be a winner between The Kreft and everyone else if someone doesn't take a stand.

I'm not letting you die so they can take Honora and do whatever they please with her! That's not sacrifice *or* suicide...it's stupidity!"

As the track carried them past the fairy bulbs, Reece chanced a sideways glance. Nivy and the bag were nowhere to be seen.

"You know nothing of sacrifice." His father scowled, his hand white on the grip of the hob. "I had to watch Genevieve die because I took the kind of stand you're talking about. *Watch her die*, Reece. I as good as killed her! It's the sort of pain no person should ever have to suffer, the sort of pain I would do anything to never feel again."

The gun in Reece's face slid out of focus as he stared blankly past it. But...Liem's mother had died from a virus...something she'd contracted off-planet...she'd never—

More of The Kreft's games.

"Now I've lost Liem to them...and you and Abigail are all they have left to use against me. I tried to spare you Liem and his mother's fate...I tried to send you away. But you wouldn't go. I had to protect you. If you were of no value to me, you couldn't be used, you see?"

Reece felt as though the duke's words had to travel a long distance to reach him; they sank in slowly, as if soaking through all the layers he'd built up. The duke gradually pulling out of his childhood...wanting to send him to Leto...never coming to apologize, letting the chasm between them stretch. All to protect Reece.

"Honora will do alright. It is the control The Kreft want, not the power of one planet, *the control*. It's their whole purpose. It is who they are." The duke suddenly shook himself and tightened the slack in his arm so that his hob was held level once more. "This is much bigger than the life of one duke. Much bigger than the fate of one planet, even. I am one of the only unfortunate ones. I was born into this position of power, and therefore I am either useful or expendable. Most people will never know the true power in Epimetheus. They will live. They will be happy. The world will go on."

Reece's thoughts came crashing back to Honora, to his father and the hob and the moment. Snow had gathered in the folds of his jacket, accumulated in his hair.

"You think that's living?" he asked quietly. "You think they prefer to live in ignorance, never knowing that their sons and fathers go off to die in a war that's all part of someone's machinations? You think they're really happier, not knowing?"

The duke was looking at him, not with surprise, but something close to it. "I think they're safer."

Reece shook his head. "They should have the choice. Being safe and being happy aren't the same thing. They should be able to trade one for the other, if they want. They should be given the chance to fight."

"Charles was right about you, young Mr. Sheppard," someone behind Reece said ominously.

Reece twisted, and with a kick in his gut counted four armed Veritas blocking the garden gate. The portly Robert Gustley stood in their midst, looking grim but satisfied, his enormous mustache twitching.

"Arrogant, predictable, and too nosy for your own good," Gustley finished.

"Mr. Gustley," the duke began, but Gustley cut him off with a swift, chopping gesture. The duke darkened angrily. A Vee stepped forward and confiscated his hob.

"Duke Sheppard must make his appearance at the skywaltz. Escort him there," Gustley instructed the Vee to his right. "As for the Palatine Second, Charles wishes to see him on the bridge."

"Good," Reece snapped, and Gustley blubbered in surprise at the interruption. "I want to see Charles too, Ghastly."

The duke growled in his throat and made a move in Reece's direction, but what he'd intended, Reece would never know. The Veritas moved forward, dividing the two of them with easy, reptilian grace. His arms in the clutches of two towering Vees, Reece watched as his father was led from the garden, despite his "escort", looking completely in control. He never looked back.

He had been trying to protect Reece all along. It would take time for that to sink in…time Reece might not have.

Now it was just him, his two Vee guards, and Gustley. Gustley seemed downright gleeful about what Reece was sure he thought a daring capture. He bounced on the fronts of his feet, his hands behind his back, the cupped rim of his bowler catching snowflakes like a gutter.

"Come along, Mr. Sheppard," he said.

Reece went peacefully, following the secretary across the twilit grounds. He cast around in his mind for a plan only to come up empty-handed. It felt like he was back at The Owl on a testing day, staring down at a blank piece of parchment and trying to conjure an answer to an essay he'd forgotten to study for. Try as he might, he couldn't invent something out of thin air this time. He needed something, anything to work with. Nivy was a start. She was out there, and she had a gun.

Gustley and the Vees took him to the bow of the ship, where a hatch opened into a vertical translocator lit by soft golden light. Reece stepped onto the translocator platform and looked up the long, narrow shaft that climbed to the bridge of *The Jester*. Soft cello music played out of a gold phonograph horn attached to the platform's handrail. As Reece, the Vees, and Gustley began their ascent, Reece recognized the last few chipper bars of "Dr. Silverbee's Danger Emporium" and, looking at the straight faces around him, had to fight the insane urge to laugh.

The translocator rattled to a stop at the top of the shaft with a final gush of dewy steam. Gustley opened the hatch with an effortful grunt and stepped onto the bridge, chest puffed out and straining against the buttons of his waistcoat. The bridge was a luxurious oval room, its front wall a domed oval window, like a bubble containing the sprawling flightpanel where four more Vees were seated. Reece's shoes sank slightly as he stepped onto the plush scarlet carpet. He glanced up and saw his own face, slightly warped, staring back at him from the mirrored ceiling.

"We have him," Gustley declared to the room at large. He jerked his chin at Reece's guards, and they shoved him into one of the crew chairs lining the back wall. "Take the ship up."

The Vees at the flightpanel made no sign they had heard Gustley, but one began toggling controls on the panel nonetheless. The sparkling chandelier hanging from the ceiling gently jangled as the heliocraft's engine began to wake.

Jaw clenched, Reece stared out the bulging bridge window, watching trees sink out of the picture as stars slid in. He jumped slightly as the door beside his chair groaned open, a set of bony fingers curling around its edge. Charles Eldritch quietly entered and closed the door behind him with a gentle push. This was the first time Reece had faced him knowing what he truly was. An alien, a tyrant.

"I am impressed, it is true," Eldritch began without preamble. He turned and faced Reece with his hands clasped together in front of his chest, as if he might begin singing. "I might have known you'd be like Liem, thirsty for knowledge to the point of recklessness."

At Liem's name, something inside Reece burned. He leaned forward in his seat, following Eldritch with his eyes as the headmaster moseyed across the bridge. "And you had him killed for it."

"Killed? Hardly. The Kreft never waste their resources, Mr. Sheppard." Eldritch held up his hands and made a shushing sound as Reece opened his mouth. "Oh, I'm not going to kill you either." Crossing the bridge, he doubled over and tapped a long fingernail against Reece's forehead. "First, we must mine, mine the recesses of your brain for...what?"

Reece stared.

"For memories!" Eldritch answered himself with relish. "Knowledge in the form of sweet, unblemished memories. You see, you, like Brother Liem, are a resource of the most distinct sort. You are a recording device that I have been eagerly awaiting to reach its capacity. I dare say we are nearly there. Gustley."

Gustley waddled forward, digging in his jacket. He snuffled his mustache and then made a noise of victory as he pulled from the recesses of his pockets a coin-sized brass disc with six crooked arms. It looked like a tiny insect—the kind you'd rather not find in your bed sheets. Reece leaned back in his chair, trying to make the motion look nonchalant.

"As with any mining expedition," Eldritch gingerly took the disc in hand, "there are tools we must exploit to achieve maximum efficiency. This Spinner is the first. With it, we brush aside the dirt that hides, reveal the shape of our prize. But for the second stage of mining, we require a more precise tool."

Reece felt the air leave his lungs in a rush as Eldritch said quietly, "Sophie Rice will be our second tool if you should fail to be generous with what you tell me, Reece."

Anger and desperation and panic fell on Reece all at once; for a moment, he wanted to run, to not have the chance to sell anything he knew to Eldritch. But the last two emotions must have cancelled each other out, because all he felt was anger when he said in a clear if strained voice, "I have no idea what you're talking about."

Eldritch smiled blandly. "You will."

He took the disc and pressed it to Reece's temple.

The pain was dull but ongoing, the throb of a needle in a vein, pulsing and aching. Reece lost awareness of his body—he didn't know whether his hands were trying to rip the golden bug off his face, or if he had slumped unconscious in his chair. In contrast, he was certain he'd never been so aware of his mind before, of all its sparks and emissions and messages. It was as though the bug on his temple were a drain, and all his memories were being sucked out of their crevices and swept into a whirlpool he watched swirl past in a blur.

He saw Nivy's crash site as if peering again through the boughs of an evergreen; he relived racing through the Atlasian Wilds and realizing his hob was gone. The twenty minute conversation he'd had with Liem in the tower streamed through his mind's eye in mere seconds, and then he was remembering finding Liem's bedroom and study in ruins. He watched his hand pick up the curiously-placed cufflinks. He felt like a small force, powerless to the flood of memories.

The memories took on a theme: Nivy. Every conversation Reece and Nivy had shared zipped through Reece's brain like someone was pulling them by a string. In the sped-up memories, Nivy's gesturing hands were a smudge of movement.

Something stung Reece's temple, and his awareness of the pain brought him back to the present, to the bridge of *The Jester* and Eldritch. Gasping as if he'd been holding his breath—he might've been—he sagged forward in his chair and propped his arms on his knees. The spot where the gold bug had fixed itself throbbed like a swelling bruise.

Eldritch was turning the bug between his fingers, studying Reece with a frown. As Reece pantingly peeled his sweat-soaked shirt from his skin, Eldritch raised the device and pushed it against his temple like he was pressing a button. His dark eyelashes fluttered over the whites of his eyes; his mouth fell slightly open. After a full ten seconds, the bug popped off seemingly of its own accord and plopped neatly into Eldritch's ready hand.

Reece's thoughts felt scattered, as if a whirlpool really had passed between them. But there was an upside to the mental chaos. By picking and choosing between Reece's memories, Eldritch had left him a clear trail.

"You'll—never find her," Reece said, still trying to catch his breath. "Whatever it is you think you can get from her, I hope you can live without it." He chuckled hoarsely. "Well, on second thought—"

Something hit his cheek; the blow felt like it should've unhinged his head from his neck. He toppled right over the arm of his chair and collapsed to the ground. If his head had hurt before, now it felt like someone had taken to it enthusiastically with a hammer.

Groaning, he rolled onto his back and stared up at Eldritch. It couldn't have been him. One of the Vees must have dashed in and struck. Eldritch's two skinny arms combined shouldn't have been able to deliver that much force.

Then Eldritch reached down, tsking, and took Reece's jacket in a fistful. He jerked. Reece not only rose to his feet, but beyond. His toes dangled over the carpet as Eldritch held him aloft. By one hand.

"Charles Eldritch," the Vee at the flightpanel said in a scratchy voice, "there has been a malfunction in one of the heat vents. The pipes—"

Eldritch's gaze twitched to the window and back. "We do not seem to be losing altitude."

"No."

"Then I do not wish to be interrupted." Pausing, Eldritch looked around the room, ignoring the hand holding a stunned and struggling Reece. "Hmm. Miss Sophie should be here by now. Gustley, toddle off and see what's keeping our little friend, won't you?"

Nodding his many chins, Gustley scurried to the translocator hatch and disappeared down the shaft.

Reece's heart was pounding at unprecedented speeds. Choking, he gasped, "Been taking the Vees' serum, Eldritch? Still power-hungry, after everything?"

Eldritch threw back his head and laughed. For an instant the laughter sounded dual-toned, harmonized, as if there were two different people laughing together inside Eldritch's one body. It sent goosebumps rioting down Reece's arms.

Eldritch suddenly heaved him across the room; he crashed to the floor in a rolling sprawl, knocked breathless. He felt two of the burstpowder marbles tumble out of his pocket and skitter across the carpet.

"Is that really necessary, Headmaster?" a familiar voice said from the doorway.

There was a cold, plunging sensation in Reece' stomach. The voice. He'd thought...but hadn't the duke said...

His elbows shaking, Reece rose to his hands and knees and dragged up his heavy head. The man standing in the doorway wore a golden mask that covered his full face, but he had familiar eyes, brown eyes, eyes like Reece's...only blacker. He was holding a windswept Nivy pinned with her arms behind her back.

Eldritch gasped with delight, clasping his hands together. "Nivy! My dear! Well, doesn't this make short of our chase?"

Reece was still staring at the golden-faced man, thunderstruck. He could be hallucinating, he supposed. His head *had* suffered enough recent trauma.

But no, when the man reached up a gloved hand and pushed the mask to the back of his head, it was *Liem* looking down at him. Reece's brain was still muddled; he couldn't make out individual emotions anymore, just feel the wild rush of them all, like a torrent inside of him.

"She must have somehow recognized me as I boarded the ship," Liem was saying in answer to a question Reece hadn't heard. "She pulled me aside and asked for my help. For him, I assume," Liem nodded at Reece. The offhand acknowledgement twisted the imaginary knife stuck in Reece's back. "She didn't seem surprised to see me. I suppose she must have suspected I was being kept alive as a tool against the duke."

"Perhaps," said Eldritch thoughtfully, stroking his chin. He seemed amused. "Or perhaps not. Nivy always was admirably clever. I would not be surprised at all to learn she revealed herself to you because she knew you would bring her here, to me and to Reece."

Reece met Nivy's urgent stare. He couldn't put the energy into reading her thoughts. He was confused to the point of lightheadedness—though again, that could be the head trauma—and all his willpower was going into containing the storm building power inside of him.

"My plan hasn't gone too far awry after all," Eldritch mused. He suddenly chuckled to himself and performed a little pirouette. "Oh, Nivy, Nivy, *Nivy*! I should never have doubted you! Bring her in, Liem, I want your brother to see something."

When Nivy and Liem drew close enough, Eldritch reached out his bony but, as Reece vividly remembered, unnaturally-strong hands and caught her by the shoulders. He turned her to face Reece. She was snarling, her teeth bared.

"As you have deduced, Mr. Sheppard, Nivy is not from Honora, nor any of our near-lying neighbors. Her people are from The Ice Ring, an outlying cluster of frigid planets on the other side of the sun. They call themselves The Heron. And allow me to say, Nivy, that your audacious people have been a thorn in The Kreft's foot since the first day we crossed into The Epimetheus Galaxy."

"Headmaster, is this the time?" Liem asked, throwing an unreadable look at the Vees by the flightpanel. With his eyes roving, Reece was able to study him. He looked thinner, paler, his unkempt hair longer, though it seemed to be falling out in places. Good. Sleepless nights were the least of what he had coming to him.

Eldritch's attention wasn't on Liem, but on Nivy's neck, and the ribbon ringing its base. His fingers skimmed across it, and Reece's anger flared up out of the mass of his other emotions, sharp and invigorating. He sat up a little straighter.

"You once wondered, Mr. Sheppard," Eldritch said breathily, "if Nivy was a slave. You concluded that she wasn't. That she had been Collared by her people—the Heron—to protect their secrets. You were correct."

Reece didn't ask how he knew this. Eldritch had browsed his memories of Nivy, but Reece was certain he'd eavesdropped on his conversations before now. Kneeling, Reece grabbed hold of the silver cufflinks on his sleeve, ripped them off, and cast them at Liem's feet. He should have realized when the alarm had gone off at the gate— those cufflinks Liem had left behind hadn't been a clue, they'd been a trap. They were broadcaster links, relaying everything they heard to a receiver likely in Eldritch's possession at this very moment. Reece scanned Eldritch through squinted eyes, and honed in on the gaudy ring on his middle finger.

"Ah, very good," Eldritch praised, not at all thrown by the interruption. He lifted the bejeweled hand and twisted the ring's gem like a dial so that it gave off a whistling white noise like a wireless trying to tune in to a station.

Liem looked duly mortified. He gave the cufflinks a wide berth as he nervously took a seat.

"As I was saying," Eldritch continued after he'd switched off the receiver ring. "Nivy's collar was my very quandary. Nine years ago, an escape capsule identical to hers crashed on Atlas…as you are well aware, I know. But I wonder, did you make the connection that Liem himself witnessed the crash?"

Eldritch waited for a long moment for Reece to reply. Finally, Reece nodded, his stare still divided between his stepbrother and Nivy.

"Very good. Liem, perhaps you would like to…?"

Paling visibly, Liem shook his head. "I'd rather—"

"Tell him, Liem," Eldritch purred. "It is only fair he should know the full truth, for what you have done to him. It is a tenuous balance The Kreft always observe in dealing with our enemies. Your brother has earned the right to hear how you have bested him. You are showing your superiority in telling him."

Swallowing silently, Liem nodded. He raised his eyes and stared at a spot over Reece's head.

"It was the year you came to The Aurelian Academy. The escape capsule disrupted the bus-ships' engines as it passed in close proximity to them—The Academy almost suffered several crashes. As it was, my bus-ship was knocked so off course that we landed in the Atlasian Wilds and had to be retrieved by automobile. The students explored the area while waiting on our transportation. I wandered and stumbled upon a crater in the woods."

Liem glanced at Eldritch, who nodded encouragingly, still stroking Nivy's necklace. Nivy was maintaining an aloof posture, standing stiffly with her hands in fists at her sides.

"It all happened so quickly," Liem went on, picking up speed. "The capsule opened, and a…a man came out of it. He saw me, and I was so frightened I started to run, but he followed me. Chased me back into the woods. Then The Veritas came out of nowhere…they took him to the ground. He didn't even cry out as they beat him."

Nivy shut her eyes, and Reece felt his insides lurch for her. He wondered for the first time if that person in the capsule had been someone of special significance to her.

"I thought my presence had escaped The Veritas' notice, but I was wrong. They came and found me at The Owl and…" Liem trailed off, mouth opening and closing without sound.

Eldritch swooped around Nivy and knelt beside Reece, still smiling. "The Kreft offered him a future. We made a deal, him and I, a pact." He popped his P loudly.

It was enough to turn Reece's stomach. He glared at Liem, watching him squirm. "Coward. What did you have to gain?" he demanded. "You're the bleeding Palatine First. You were going to be duke! Why—" He choked as Eldritch elbowed him in the chest, and coughing, doubled over.

"Come, you're cleverer than that, Reece. Did you really think *I* would be king over this self-important planet?"

Wheezing and clutching his chest, Reece lifted his head.

"It is the control The Kreft want, not the power of one planet. The control." The duke's words. And then the Vee's: "They are artists at manipulation, thriving in the shadows of ambiguity." Reece had assumed Eldritch would set himself up a throne after the duke's assassination, installing The Veritas' new order of justice in exchange for their loyalty to The Kreft. He'd been wrong. That had never been Eldritch's plan. Eldritch, who intimidated Parliament from the wings, pulling political strings from the shadows. By putting a king of his choice on the throne, he could fashion The Kreft another puppet. And if that king was someone who had been heir to Honora anyways, well, that just guaranteed the approval of the Honoran people.

This way both The Kreft and Liem got what they wanted. The Kreft the control, Liem the spotlight.

"You see it now, don't you?" Eldritch stood and sauntered in a circle around Reece. "Yes. I offered Liem the throne I planned to instate. There were stipulations, of course, but he was amenable. "You see, the survivor of that first crash wore a collar just like Nivy's, so I could not force him to tell me anything, even by torture—which I still tried, of course. That's what killed him, in the end. But he likely wouldn't have broken even if he had been allowed to speak. The Heron have a regrettable inclination for secrecy."

Eldritch's eyes suddenly flashed, and his smile became a wicked leer. "They condition themselves to withstand torture. The collaring of their spies is an added precaution against The Kreft. They've become nearly impossible to break." Following Reece's train of thought, the headmaster held up a finger. "You are wondering, I take it, about the Spinner I used on you. The answer is simple." Despite Reece's noise of warning, Nivy stood still and let Eldritch gently press the golden bug to her temple. It refused to attach, falling to the floor. "Kreft automata doesn't work on The Heron. Not since their rebellion infiltrated our science facilities some two centuries ago and discovered how to make their bodies immune to the three basic elements of our technology. An unfortunate gain for them, one that tipped the scales in the war."

Reece didn't think the answer was simple at all, but he held his questions at bay, in part because he was still feeling the repercussions of the elbow's impact with his sternum. Clutching his chest with one hand, he stood, teetering slightly on unwilling legs.

"What did you...want from the survivor?"

"The same thing I want from Nivy." Eldritch suddenly thrust Nivy forward, sending her sprawling face-down on the carpet. "And what your memories, Mr. Sheppard, will now help me get."

From beneath his jacket, Eldritch pulled out a sleek silver gun: the lightning weapon of The Veritas. He took aim, and before Reece could do more than shout, fired.

The blue fizzing projectile hit Nivy squarely in the back as she was rising to her knees.

She cried out.

Reece dove forward, bent on tackling Eldritch. In the time it took him to take one step, The Veritas were on him. He hissed as they twisted his arms and forced him onto his toes.

"Electrical pulses disrupt the collar's mechanism," Eldritch said calmly, studying the gun as Nivy trembled on the floor beneath him. "I noticed this in your memories of your daytrip to The Tholos Stone...ah, what you would call the Veritas' base of operations. Nivy?"

Nivy's watering eyes rolled up and glared daggers at Eldritch.

"Come now, girl, don't try to be noble. Speak."

There was a pause. Reece thought he could hear the muscles in his arms straining to hold his joints in place.

Nivy abruptly twisted around and looked up at him. "Reece, listen to me, The Kreft, they're not human! They—" She cut off with a gag, lifting a hand to her throat.

Her voice was different than Reece had always imagined it. Low, with a lilting accent. Her words ended on the up, as if she was asking a question. It wasn't that he didn't like the voice, but it made him feel like he knew her that much less.

Tut-tutting, Eldritch gestured for the Veritas to sit Reece down next to his white-faced stepbrother. Not human? Reece had little trouble believing it. There was something eerie about Eldritch— something more than just his Vee-like strength and oily smile. Teeth grit, Reece glared at The Kreft. What *was* he?

"I recognized Nivy's escape capsule as it came through Atlas's atmosphere," Eldritch explained, gesturing unhurriedly. "My first thought, understandably, was to take her and torture her like the last Heron who came to Honora. But she would most certainly have a collar like her predecessor. How was I to learn her very valuable secrets? The Heron and The Kreft have been at odds for millennia, Reece. They are the very reason we were drawn to Epimetheus, following rumors of a great weapon they had at their disposal. A weapon, we thought, that would lend itself to our ambitions in conquering the known galaxies.

"The war began shortly after our arrival in The Epimetheus. We were stronger, but The Heron...they were resilient. In a final, desperate feat of sacrifice, they destroyed their weapon. In return, we enslaved them. But there has always been a strong underground movement against us, and The Heron," Eldritch glared down at Nivy with a pitying shake of his head, "they have a way of breeding rebellion wherever they can. Thirty-five years ago, we received intelligence that the weapon had *not* been destroyed....merely moved, perhaps hidden."

"That's why you're building Honora's armies," Reece realized. His voice sounded rusty. "For your war. In case The Heron bring out this thing...whatever it is."

Eldritch continued pacing languidly across the bridge, shaking his head. "Why, that's not it at all. How much more satisfying—how much more justified!—for The Kreft to use The Heron's own weapon to destroy them. Then we shall have come full circle and ended the war as it should have ended long ago. There is a *rightness* in it, is there not? We simply must find where their foolish ancestors hid the weapon before they do. Mmm. But you are right about one thing. The final battle is coming. It is time for Epimetheus to be subdued, time for The Kreft to finish what we began. We cannot leave until Epimetheus is ours, Reece. It is…how would you say…a part of our *peculiar* genetic code." He smiled unpleasantly. "There is a saying, among Kreft. To conquer in life is life to be conquered."

With a sudden twitch, Eldritch raised his arm and shot Nivy again, so that she crumpled in a shivering heap at his feet. Reece lurched out of his chair, and when Liem caught him by the sleeve, elbowed him as hard in the nose as he could. The crunching crack implied a satisfyingly messy break.

"I sent Liem to Nivy, after her landing," Eldritch continued calmly, with only a disdainful smile for Reece and Liem's scuffle. "She was unconscious when he found her, so he took her back to Emathia. When she woke, he tried to offer himself as a friend, someone she could trust. He kept her safe at Emathia under the guise of being his fiancé. In time, I planned on learning her secrets using Liem as a filter. Only she didn't trust him.

"I knew at this point of your spying, Reece; I had your gun, proof of your eavesdropping at the crash site. How interesting, I thought. Reece Sheppard, the younger, rebellious brother, infamous for his choice in inferior friends. I suddenly knew that where Liem had failed with Nivy, you could succeed. You were known and even popular for collecting friends no one else would claim.

"How true you were to your reputation! That day you came to Emathia and met Nivy, I had already laid plans to have her passed to you. The duke was showing suspicion regarding Liem's involvement, so having Liem fake his own kidnapping served a dual purpose. He could wait in the shadows while The Kreft prepared his throne, meanwhile passing Nivy to you, who had promised she would be looked after. Only Nivy also had her suspicions about Liem—so when she realized he had been taken, she ran. It nearly ruined everything.

"Then," Eldritch sighed almost nostalgically, "by marvelous chance, you met up again on Aurelia. And I began to listen, very carefully, for Nivy opening up to you. You carried the cufflinks nearly everywhere with you—they worked better than I could have dreamed. It was imperative I obtain the information Nivy was hiding within her person. If anyone knew the location of The Heron's weapon, she would.

"I only had three clues to work with." Eldritch counted them out on his long fingers. "One, the ancient manuscript that the first Heron spy had brought with him to Honora, which The Kreft have never been able to translate. Two, Nivy's gun, a broken antique that I knew from an informant had always been carefully guarded by The Heron underground. Three, the fact that both Heron spies had come to Honora. Why?

"I allowed the book to fall into your hands, Reece, so Nivy would find it. I thought perhaps she might be able to translate it. I had no other leads. I had the gun taken from your Pan friend on the road, but it seemed a useless relic, and revealed nothing. But I knew it was important, because twice Nivy brought it up with you, wanting to know what had become of it."

Suddenly, Eldritch reached inside his dark coat and pulled out Nivy's strange gun. In the bright light of the bridge, Reece could see how closely its design imitated Aurelia's. Sleek and classic and one of a kind. In Eldritch's large hand, its bizarre shape looked more than ever like a skeleton key.

"The most important information I have obtained using Nivy's trust of you," Eldritch lovingly ran a single finger down the gun's slender barrel, "lies in the fact Aurelia and Aurelius apparently once belonged to The Heron. We never knew. The two airships were sent out from The Ice Rings before the war was over, before we had fully assimilated ourselves into The Epimetheus's populace. We had always assumed, along with the Honorans, that the two airships belonged to their history. And this curious gun…how would your friend the Pan say it? 'A dead ringer for Aurelia's design'?

"Here is what I am going to do, Reece." Eldritch finally turned and faced Reece, stowing Nivy's gun in favor of the small silver pistol of The Veritas's. Nivy braced herself on the floor. "I myself have an engagement to keep. The skywaltz will not begin until I take my place among the dancers, and the duke cannot die until the skywaltz begins. So I must go, and leave you to do my work for me."

Reece watched, confused, as Eldritch sat the lightning gun down a short distance from Nivy, who stared at it longingly.

"Sophie Rice will be here any moment now. I am going to have The Veritas begin torturing her in slow increments, and you will watch."

Reece couldn't do anything but stare blankly at the gun, a feel of nausea churning in the pit of his stomach.

"And when you cannot take the girl's screams any longer—for she will not die quickly, Reece, I promise you that—you will pick up this gun, and you will question Nivy for me, and you will not stop until you think I might be satisfied. And if I am not…" Eldritch stooped, putting his long nose right up to Reece's, and Reece heard again that strange duality in his voice as he said, "I will bring up Sophie's brother, and I will bring up the Pan, and I will bring up the little mechanic girl, and they will all *suffer*. Acutely."

Straightening, dusting the front of his jacket primly, Eldritch beckoned to Liem. "Come, Liem—you will not want to see this side of your brother, I think."

Without a backward glance, The Kreft glided from the room, and Liem, still clasping his bloody face, stumbled after him. His eyes met Reece's for a split second, and they looked…sorry was too strong a word. They looked unhappy. He didn't like what was being forced on Reece, but he was above helping.

Reece knew this much. Liem may not be sorry now, but he was going to be. That side of Reece Eldritch had mentioned? Liem *was* going to see it.

After a moment of fuming, Reece looked up at the Vee beside him and nodded. The Vee let him slide from the chair onto the floor and crawl to the silver gun. The Veritas closed in around him, too many in number to take with one little lightning cap gun. He let the gun lay on the floor, ignoring it for the time being, though it might come in useful later. Instead, he reached for Nivy.

She shrunk back from him, pulling her knees up to her chest. For the first time in a while, he could imagine her as a wild creature, something untamed. She thought he was going to turn the gun on her; so did The Veritas. Maybe anyone would think that. But it hadn't crossed his mind.

"Nivy," he said quietly. "We're running out of time…both of us."

Looking out from between two lengths of dark hair, Nivy's face, her expression of stunned betrayal, cleared. She shakily rose to her knees, The Veritas crowding her too now, making a tight circle around her and Reece and the silver gun. Reece could feel their eagerness. If he failed to shoot Nivy, they could lay hands on Sophie. Either way, as spectators or participants, they won. Reece's hate gave him steady nerves and a clarity of mind. Everything Eldritch had told him could be dealt with later over a cup of chocolate tea and one of Sophie's biscuits. He smiled.

Sitting knee to knee with Nivy, he stared hard into her eyes, trying to will his thoughts on her, to use her skill against her. Her eyes frantically scanned his face and blinked blankly. Sighing, he nodded sideways at the innocent burstpowder marble sitting on the red carpet a foot behind the nearest Vee.

He was thinking the two of them would count down together and act as one, but as soon as Nivy saw the marble, she sprang into action without him. Falling onto her side, she brought her leg around in an angular kick that cracked the Vee's knee. The Vee didn't cry out, but he did stumble backwards, grunting.

The instant before the Vee's heel crushed the marble, Reece threw himself onto Nivy and buried her head under his arm, closing his eyes.

And then the air exploded, torn asunder.

XXIII

Well Met, Mr. Sheppard

Reece rolled, blown by the force of the explosion, rubble, dust, and torn carpet raining down on him. For a minute, everything was chaos. His ears were humming, his heartbeat too loud in his head. Something was beeping over and over, annoyingly insistent, and there were loud, angry voices, and deep footsteps drumming on the carpet. He cracked an eyelid.

He was staring into the pale, lifeless face of a Vee. The Vee's black eyes were wide open but unfocused. Blood was trickling from the corner of his mouth to the carpet, where it was camouflaged.

Lifting his head, Reece counted three more downed Vees, their bodies thrown to awkward angles on the floor. It was lucky they had been packed so closely together—they'd made themselves a wall separating Reece and Nivy from the explosion, likely saving their lives.

The two surviving Vees were doubled over the flightpanel, looking satisfyingly battered. A large chunk of machinery had been blown off the corner of the panel, laying bare a mess of sparking wires and leaking tubes. The incessant beeping sound was coming from the flashing blue warning button to the right of the pilot's yoke. Bleeding bogrosh. Reece had broken the ship.

When Nivy grabbed Reece's hand, he jumped, inhaled a puff of dust, and choked. He looked at her, sprawled beside him and wearing a loopy kind of grin, and smiled.

"I broke the ship," he repeated aloud, and she nodded, scrubbing a streak of blood from her cheek. The Heron. He knew who she was now. Knew where she was from. He was a long ways yet from understanding it all, but that little knowledge lightened the heaviness in his head considerably.

One of the Vees at the flightpanel swung around as Reece unsteadily stood, murder in his black eyes.

"Kill them both," the Vee still bent over the flightpanel said coolly.

"Agreed," his partner said, and sprung at Reece with frightening speed.

Reece just had time to plant his feet, grit his teeth, and raise his fists.

CRACK.

The Vee pitched forward, stumbling over his own legs, and crashed loudly to the floor. Reece stared down at him without lowering his fists, dumbfounded. Blood was welling up through the Vee's jumpsuit, like slowly-spreading spilt paint.

The translocator door—its circular window shot out—opened with a clang, and Gideon, Po, Hayden, Sophie, and Hugh poured out, Gideon deftly spinning his revolver toward the Vee at the flightpanel. The final Vee joined his brothers on the floor in a pile of pale white death.

It was mayhem. Sophie rushed Reece, and he caught her up in his arms and kissed the top of her sooty hair and clasped Hugh's forearm. The relief had Reece's stomach soaring; his heart was pounding like he'd run a marathon. He could hardly think for how glad he was to see them all alive and well. He looked to Nivy, who had appropriated the lone surviving lightning gun and was holding it ready, waiting beside the door, and smiled.

The relief lasted maybe one minute before reality came rudely butting back in.

Gid had taken the helm and picked up where the Vee left off, and Po was crawling under the flightpanel with an intense expression of focus.

"This is bad," she said, her voice muffled. "This is real bad."

"Are we going to crash?" Sophie asked worriedly, clinging to her brother and father.

Po didn't answer.

"Try to avoid crashing," Reece advised as he knelt beside one of the Vees and dug through its pockets until he found two tiny purple vials. He pocketed them and stood. "Nivy and I are going to go finish what we came for."

"Reece," Hayden began, face pained. "...Be careful."

Reece spun and fled from the bridge at a ground-eating pace, his dress shoes clapping against shiny wooden floors. There wasn't time to look back. There wasn't time to look ahead. He just had to run, run and hope he wasn't too late.

Most of the heliocraft's footage went into its huge, open-ceilinged ballroom, which looked up into a cloudy sky largely obscured by the ship's balloons. Two obtruding tiers of balconies framed the room, held aloft by gilded columns, while an elevated, slowly-spinning stage in its center—like a giant music box—supported the masked orchestra.

With the lights bouncing reflections off the face of the black marble floors, it looked like the dancers were stepping over a dark, quiet sea. The only thing to ruin the illusion was the snow sneaking in through the ceiling and joining the dancers in twirling across the room.

Reece and Nivy tore from the bridge down a tight stairwell lined with black and white photographs of the heliocraft's past captains, and ended up at the southern corner of the first layer of balconies. Reece rushed to the lip of the balcony and folded over it, breathing hard. The dancers spun and laughed and clapped—unaware—oblivious—

He saw the duke and Abigail waltzing together near the orchestra. Abigail tossed her head extravagantly as she turned in a tight spin and then returned to the duke's waiting arms. The heliocraft gave a rebellious little jerk in response to Po's administrations on the bridge, but the only ones who seemed to notice were the waiters as the glasses balanced on their serving trays chimed together.

Nivy gripped Reece's forearm and pointed frantically across the way. Nearly all the balcony box seats were full, but kitty-corner to them and up on the second tier of balconies, there was one that looked empty. Except it wasn't. Looking twice, Reece could just make out the crest of a bald head topping the balcony railing by a few inches…someone was kneeling behind a gun, its barrel propped almost invisibly against the black railing…

He couldn't move fast enough. His body had trouble keeping up with his feet as he sprinted up a winding staircase and leaped over the indignant gentleman he tripped on his way. He reached the second floor and turned right down a corridor exposed on one side to the wintry night and its swirling snowflakes. He outran the snow.

The door to the Vee's box seat was slightly ajar. There was no time for subtly, or even for thought. Reece threw himself through the door and at the Vee, whose eye was pressed up to the scope of his gun. The impact of their two bodies colliding made a sickening thud. Reece's momentum kept him going right over the balcony railing, and he clutched the Vee, as much for stability as to keep him from touching the gun, but the Vee was falling too…they were both of them falling together…

Shouting, Reece desperately flung out his arms and tried to grab the edge of the railing even as it dropped away from him.

With a bone-rattling slap, his arms instead caught the railing of the balcony below. He dangled from his armpits on its rim, his feet wildly trying to run in midair, and heard, even over the alarmed shouts of the couple who were scampering out of the box seat, a solid, fleshy thump as the Vee collided with the marble ballroom floor.

The orchestra's music cut out shrilly as a deep, shocked silence rose into the winter air. And then someone screamed.

Grunting with the effort of pulling himself to safety, Reece looked over his shoulder as absolute panic came over the ballroom's fleeing, yet essentially trapped, occupants. The empty space between his feet turned his stomach. Even though he had a firm grip on the railing, he didn't look down for long. The Vee had landed on his head, and the copious amount of blood did different, even more uncomfortable things to his stomach. He rolled himself over the railing with a grunt.

The Jester gave a frightening jolt, and Reece caught himself against the wall as he overbalanced and staggered. Waiters' trays across the ballroom toppled one after the other, shattered glass and liquor splashing to the black marble, adding to the bedlam.

Making use of his lurch, Reece fell into yet another run, his limbs feeling almost drowsy. He was fading fast; he didn't need Hayden's medical savvy to understand that the human body wasn't meant to run at highs like this. He was going to need something *inhuman* to finish out this fight.

He wheeled around a corner just as Nivy exploded out of the stairwell to his left, her blue eyes wild, her dark hair pasted to her forehead in strips. It looked like she'd done her skirt a savage hemming job; it had been ripped away below the knee, showing her bare feet. Skidding slightly, she fell into step beside him, her wardrobe modifications helping her keep pace.

She had a hard time sprinting and signing in any great detail (Reece kept tripping over his feet just trying to watch her), so she kept it simple. She swept her hand in a wide gesture indicating the airship, then brought her hands together in a resounding clap that imitated a crash.

Reece made a noise halfway between a groan and a growl. "We won't let that—"

She dismissed him with a sharp chop, and as they took another skidding turn, pointed. Reece caught a glimpse of Hayden fleeing up the staircase to the bridge, and realized with a sinking feeling that he must have come from delivering news. Bad news.

They were going to crash. And it was his fault.

He was forced to slow at the last winding stairwell. With all the frightened guests clawing past each other in their haste to clear the ballroom, there was barely space to breathe in the narrow passageway. Reece pressed against the tide of them and wondered with a pinch of panic in his gut if he had doomed them. Killed them like he'd killed the Vee.

"There must be escape pods," he said, desperate.

He and Nivy tumbled out into the ballroom together. She grabbed him by his jacket and pulled him into the shadow of a column that shielded them from the chaos. Panting, she peered intensely into his face and shook her head in answer to his question. He squeezed his eyes shut.

Nivy's grip on his arm suddenly became an anxious vice. Glancing at her, Reece leaned around the column, and despite himself, shivered. Like a tower in the middle of an angry sea, Eldritch stood on the raised orchestra platform over the milling people, smiling an almost feline smile. He was staring right at Reece and Nivy's hiding spot.

Reece had known it would come to this. Just as Scarlet had foreseen, the duke was trapped on the heliocraft, and Eldritch's plan hadn't died with his assassin. He knew Reece would never stop being an obstacle for him now—that he'd have to kill the son before he could ever get to the father.

It just so happened, Reece was coming right to him.

"Nivy, listen to me. You have to find the duke and Abigail. You have to protect them. There might be other Vees, other assassins. I'm going to Eldritch."

Halfway through his speech, Nivy had begun stubbornly shaking her head, refusing to accept what he was saying. Now she shoved him hard in the chest so that his back bumped against the column and all the minor injuries from Eldritch and the burstpowder explosion burned with sudden insistence, as if reminding him of his mortality. Kind of them.

"Stop it, Nivy!" Reece snapped. "If the duke dies tonight, The Kreft win, do you get that? If you want to fight them, you *have* to protect him! Now *do it!*"

After a pause, Nivy—holding him with a fierce stare—squeezed his arm, nodded, and dashed away.

Reece turned and found Eldritch still watching him from the revolving dais, his face…expectant.

Struggling to keep his hand steady, Reece reached into his coat pocket and pulled out one of the small stopped vials. He ducked behind the column, his back pressed against it for support. He didn't know for sure this would work—all he had to go off were the musings of Hayden, like ghostly echoes in his memory. "*A compound like the serum's is extremely unforgiving on the body. From what we know if it, its effects are instantaneous...no drug should be able to work with that kind of speed."*

He lifted the vial to his lips, ripped out its cork with his teeth, and drank.

It was like drinking hot grease. Scalding, thick, gelatinous. It tried to clot in his throat as he alternated gulping and gagging, his eyes clenched closed, his whole body trembling with the effort of keeping the stuff down. He could feel it hitting his empty stomach like a drop of liquid fire. Reece's knees gave way; he crashed to the floor, his arms wrapped around his middle, and dropped the empty vial

Suddenly, the drop of fire in his stomach exploded, and heat shot through all his veins, painful but invigorating. He could feel every sinew in his arms drinking in the explosion, gaining strength from the force of it. As he twisted on the floor, he realized he felt...light. Too light. As if he'd been walking with weights before, weights that the explosion had destroyed. He experimented, lifting a hand, and it moved a little faster than it should have.

The heat lingered in him, like the remnants of a supernova settling into place. He tried to lean up slowly, testing out what felt like a whole new body, but shot up instead, as if jumping awake. He felt spry, flexible, weightless. Also...he still felt a little sick. When he breathed, the air tasted hot.

Propping his back against the column, Reece tucked in his knees, held his breath, and pushed. His back slid up the marble, and he teetered, not on legs that were weak, but legs that were a little too eager to respond to his promptings. He glanced over the ballroom and judged by the slight shifts in the guests' positions that he couldn't have been down for more than a minute.

He would have liked to say that the serum had boosted, more than anything, his confidence, but he felt ungainly and unsure—a little bit like he'd hit puberty again, horrifically.

But he was faster, stronger, aware like he'd never been before. He'd take that, and do what he could with the rest. Clenching his fists, Reece turned to face Eldritch.

Out of the corner of his eye, he saw a streak of black. He recognized the signs from fighting the Vee at Mordecai's, but now saw them clearer, reacted to them better. He spun and brought up his arms to where his elbows could guard his ribs and his fists protect his face, Rule One of his Gentleman's Combat class.

Charles Eldritch materialized to a stop three feet in front of him. Reece blinked. He'd always pictured the headmaster as a stooped bat.

Well, the bat had un-stooped—and now he loomed, towering over Reece with a wide-eyed, feral kind of grin.

"Ah," Reece said.

Eldritch threw a backhanded swing, and Reece was still so stunned that he took the hit to the side of his face without trying to block. Grunting, he stumbled sideways, and his new, untried balance, while catching him, also disoriented him. He spun to face Eldritch and forgot to bring up his hands, and the headmaster's thrusting kick sank into his stomach, sending him soaring backward.

He slid on his back across the marble floor. The serum didn't stop him from feeling the invisible imprint of Eldritch's boot in his gut, or the itching burn on the side of his face, but it did keep those things from overwhelming him. It suppressed them.

It made Reece feel powerful. Not invincible, but definitely a little reckless. With a powerful thrust, he kicked himself up into a crouch, the chaos melting into a blur around him. He only had eyes for Eldritch, who was moseying his way, humming tunelessly. Reece's serum-enhanced ears allowed him to pick up on the eerie sound. His heartbeat, loud and plodding in his ears, sounded strangely in time with it.

Eldritch suddenly sprang forward, seeming to disappear in the second it took for him to close the distance between him and Reece. Instinct, more than experience or training, told Reece to feint to the right and then dodge to the left. As Eldritch followed the feint, Reece brought his knee around in a kick. Eldritch bent his back to an impossible angle, and the kick grazed the air above him. He tried to sweep Reece's standing leg, but Reece spun out of the kick, stepping out of range.

For a while—the serum jumbled Reece's awareness of time—it was give and take, neck to neck. Eldritch's strikes crept in between Reece's defenses because he fought like a snake, his movements sinuous, then snapping. But each of the backhands and knife-edge chops and good old-fashioned punches Reece threw felt as strong as the pounce of a nightcat; there was power packed behind each one, power that, he was glad to see, troubled Eldritch…at least at first.

As they broke off a flourish of attacks and stepped apart from each other, Eldritch spat a broken tooth into his hand and stared at it as though perplexed. Reece tried to play off rubbing his side with a grin.

"I'll clean the rest out for you," he offered. "That way you can replace them all at once."

"Don't trouble yourself," Eldritch said lightly as he tossed the tooth aside and sighed. "This body was beginning to show signs of wear anyways. It's nigh on time I replaced it."

Reece blinked.

With a glint in his eye, Eldritch spun and threw out his long leg in a hooking kick that would've gladly disjointed Reece's head from his neck. Reece leaned back to let the foot brush the air before his face, and then when it had passed, seized it about the ankle. Then he planted his feet, laced his fingers together, and swung the leg like a bat. Eldritch whipped around him, taking flight as Reece released the leg and let him soar like the old bat he was.

He soared, but he didn't crash. Instead, he turned his tumble into an aerial roll and finished it out neatly, the tails of jacket settling back into place as he stood from his landing crouch. Reece wanted to rattle off a few secondhand Pantedan curses, but he settled for grinding his teeth and bringing his hands back up, fists clenched.

"You see our dilemma, Reece?" Eldritch asked, not even winded as he threw a maelstrom of punches that forced Reece to walk backwards as he blocked. "As a force, I am much more powerful than you. Even in this feeble body I wear, I have a natural edge. But now that you've taken The Veritas's drug, we are quite well matched, for while I am still stronger…this body lacks the stamina that yours has in its youth."

Eldritch was just trying to distract him, but he did have a point. Reece hadn't yet wrung all the potential energy out of his muscles, but Eldritch clearly hadn't either. Reece caught one of Eldritch's arms and tried to twist it into a lock. Eldritch, chuckling, wrapped his long fingers around Reece's wrist and threw his guard to the side. Reece barely dodged a torpedo-like punch that he was sure would have shattered his ribs.

"What will happen if you kill me, Reece?" Eldritch asked. "You think only to save your father…to free your ridiculous planet. What of The Epimetheus Galaxy? What of The Kreft? Will they really leave Honora alone? Will they spare the rebels?"

Reece's dress shoes skidded as *The Jester* creaked and leaned heavily to the left. Chairs and abandoned wine glasses skated across the ballroom in eerie imitation of the departed dancers. Just as the lights in glass brackets on the room's columns flickered as if frightened, Eldritch pounced, his inhuman strength giving his jump supernatural height, his expression one of rapture, of bliss.

The lights went out.

It was like before, with Reece's balance. Stimulated by the serum, his eyes made instant, automatic adjustments to allow him to see clearly in the spotted moonlight. The unexpected clarity off balanced him, and he wavered. It was all the opening Eldritch needed. His fist came down like a hammer on Reece's shoulder, and more than the actual impact, Reece felt the grinding snap of his collarbone breaking.

He went down to his knees silently, his brain wiped utterly blank by the hard shock of pain.

Eldritch knelt down beside him, making a quiet, shushing sound as Reece groaned. "Reece, the problem is…you're just like The Heron. Fighting a losing battle." Blinking heavily, Reece raised his head by a fraction and met Eldritch's dark eyes. "If The Heron would just stop fighting, if they could just accept us as their betters—their gods—we would never have to kill again. The war would be over. And yet, they persist. And so we keep killing."

Sighing, Eldritch reached and laid a hand on top of Reece's head, like a fond grandfather. "I'm going to kill *you* now, Reece."

He slid the hand down to Reece's shoulder, and squeezed. Reece screamed.

.

Nivy Noemie heard Reece cry out. She kept running.

This wasn't the first time she had heard someone being tortured, and as long as her people rebelled, she doubted it would be the last. That knowledge didn't make things any better. It didn't soften the sound of Reece's pain; it didn't deaden her emotions.

It just made her run faster.

Reece's parents, the duke and duchess, didn't recognize the scream, but then, they didn't know what to listen for. How did Nivy get here? Her mission had been simple. Retrieve *The Aurelia*. Recover Tolen's stolen book. There had always been a chance The Kreft would find her, as they'd found Tolen eight years ago. There had always been a chance that like Tolen, she'd never return to The Ice Ring, to the planet Ismara, her home.

The one thing she hadn't counted on was friends.

Nivy continued herding the duke and his wife at gunpoint, driving them up to the bridge with the silver weapon of the creatures known at The Veritas. Another clever invention of The Kreft: a people who shared their proclivity for hurting things.

"Eldritch sent you, I take it?" the duke said calmly, studying Nivy over his shoulder. His eyes were the color of his son's, but hard like she had only seen Reece's once. "I have to admit," the duke went on as he ushered his confused, white-faced wife onto the bridge with a gentle hand. "I had expected someone more—" He stepped through the door after Abigail and stopped to stare at the curious crowd that had gathered tonight mainly because of him.

The girl called Po was arguing with Gideon at the flightpanel, waving a wrench and rattling on in airship jargon. Hayden and his sister and father were sitting along the back wall, huddled together, a family that made Nivy desperately homesick. Someone had thought to remove the Vees' bodies. Good.

"What the bleeding bogrosh is this?" the duchess shrilly demanded, recognizing Reece's friends.

Everyone looked over at her, except for Gideon, who cursed as the splintered chandelier overhead went out with a spark and pulled the bridge into the moonlit darkness that had already taken the rest of the ship.

Nivy shoved Abigail aside, ignoring her indignant gasp, and crossed the bridge to Hayden. He stood.

"Where's Reece?" he asked, eying the duke and duchess uncertainly.

As always, Nivy's body tried to respond to her brain's subconscious messages; it tried to open her mouth, tried to draw the breath to speak, even though she didn't mean to. But when asked a forward question, her brain felt the natural inclination to answer, and that's what her body prepared itself to do. The Band constricted around her throat and sent a faint, tickling electric shockwave through her nerves, immobilizing her larynx. She was used to the sensation.

Suddenly, Abigail gasped theatrically and pointed. "*You*! I *do* know you! You're the mute girl from Emathia…Liem's fiancé!"

"What the blazes are you talking about, woman?" the duke rumbled.

Nivy ignored them both, her eyes on Hayden. How could she explain in gestures what she needed him to do? The person he knew as Eldritch—though Nivy knew him by another name—wasn't *just* an alien…he was Kreft. As long as Eldritch held to his human body, and as long as Reece really had taken The Veritas's serum as she'd suspected he would, then Reece had a chance. The second Eldritch decided to stop playing games…he was dead.

Making up her mind, Nivy thrust her silver gun into Hayden's hand, startling him. He took a step backward, staring at the weapon without comprehending. Gritting her teeth, Nivy pointed at the gun, then pointed at herself. *Shoot me.*

"What?" Hayden exclaimed. Looking horrified, he tried to hand her back the weapon. "No!"

Nivy pushed his hand away and gestured again, angrily. *Come on, Hayden!*

"Nivy, I'm not shooting you!" Hayden shouted, dropping the gun, kicking it across the bridge, and holding up his hands in surrender.

Nivy squeezed her eyes shut. Hayden had a good heart. But sometimes the smartest, bravest thing to do was the ugly something nobody else would.

The gun had skipped against the carpet and landed next to Gideon's chair. He glanced at it, bent over with one hand still gripping the yoke, and picked it up. Looking back at her, he raised the gun. She nodded even as Hayden shouted, "Don't!"

The buzzing blue projectile hit her cleanly on her left calf, and she buckled as what felt like a hundred spiders fled over her leg, leaving numbness in their wake. Hayden caught her around the waist, yelling something indistinct at Gideon, who had already returned to piloting the dying heliocraft.

"Hayden," Nivy choked. Hayden dropped her in his shock, and she tottered but mostly caught herself on her good leg. "Reece needs us. He made me bring his parents. He's fighting Eldritch. I need your help." She tried to be succinct, but found the words irritatingly inadequate. There was so much they didn't know! "How would you destroy a Stream?"

Hayden gawked at her, speechless.

"Hayden!"

He started. "A Stream? Why?"

"Just tell me! How would you destroy a Stream?"

"I...I don't know. They're a natural phe—"

"No, Hayden!" Nivy wanted to shake him. She could feel The Band creeping back to life, pressing against each of her words. "They're a thing of The Kreft—please, you have to think!"

"Triphospherine," a quiet voice chirped from behind. Nivy and Hayden both spun—Nivy a little unsteadily—to face his little sister, who was sitting on her knees in her chair, looking nervous. "Triphospherine, Hayden. Remember?"

Hayden's expression brightened, and he began clicking his fingers feverishly, pacing in a tight circle. "Right, of course! The Streams are in space, so there'd be no oxygen to feed a fire or an explosion...unless the explosion came by way of an internal oxidant, like triphospherine has…"

"What's triphospherine?" Nivy asked.

Of all people, Gideon answered, speaking loudly to be heard over the mutinous rumble of *The Jester*. "Burstpowder." He spared a hand and dug into his front pocket, then chucked something over his shoulder that pinged against the wall by Nivy. She stooped and picked up the rounded sliver of silver between two fingers. A bullet.

"Come with me," Nivy ordered Hayden, down to her final seconds of speech. "Gideon, keep them—" she nodded at the duke and duchess as they simultaneously opened their mouths, "here, and don't—"

The band squeezed angrily, and Nivy's voice cut out with a croak.

XXIV

The Kreft

Reece landed in a limp, sprawling roll, unsure which part of his body to hold—the pain was coming from the general vicinity of *everywhere*, and the intensity of it was starting to take an edge over the serum. Eldritch could kick like a Freherian boar in the marsh season.

Panting, he pulled his knees up underneath him, every little jerk of his bad shoulder threatening to pull him under. He didn't know if Eldritch would kill him if he fell unconscious, but he would certainly kill the duke. Probably Nivy, too.

Eldritch landed beside him—The Kreft had a way of leaping about, exuberant in the throes of knocking Reece senseless. "I see why Liem hates you so. So full of character. Even if he had become duke, people would never stopped comparing you two and reaching the obvious conclusion. You are the better brother."

"True that may be," Reece stood, wobbled, and then straightened, "but I notice he's the one you want on your throne."

"Naturally. We need a puppet, not a rebel." Eldritch smoothly ducked Reece's punch and came up behind him, his mouth at Reece's ear. "Though, just between you and me, I really don't plan on keeping him that terribly long." With a cackle, he swept Reece's leg, caught him by the jacket as he fell, and mightily heaved him into the air.

Reece landed with a shout on the rotating dais in the middle of the ballroom, his hands streaking through a thin layer of snow. It was just the chance he had been waiting for. Fumbling, he slid a hand into his waistcoat and pulled out the second bottle of serum. This time, he didn't hesitate. He choked it back without gulping, letting it gloop disgustingly down his throat. The explosion was…milder this time. Like he'd sprinkled gas on the fire that was already there. He could still feel the break in his shoulder; his awareness of it was just suddenly less distinct.

Eldritch regarded Reece with interest as he stood and made a show of dusting his hands. "A rebel indeed! You are a laudable opponent, Mr. Sheppard. If it's any consolation, I will mourn for you after I kill you."

"It is, a little," Reece said, backing up on the dais as Eldritch bounded up to him. He tested the serum's strength by tentatively touching his bad shoulder and finding the bulge of his bone making a tent beneath his skin. It throbbed dully, but was nothing he couldn't ignore. Almost like a splinter.

Eldritch charged, aiming for a collision course with Reece. Grunting, Reece sidestepped, latched onto the headmaster's forearm, and used his momentum against him, swinging him in an arch and letting go. Eldritch landed within a foot of the stage's edge and spun on his ankle as Reece picked up an orchestra chair and swung. The chair exploded against Eldritch's hasty block, powdering the air with chips of wood, sending vibrations down Reece's arms.

"A fair try," Eldritch tsked as he began to dust off his jacket, "but—"

His head snapped backwards as Reece's punch landed dead center of his face. Shouting, Reece plunged his good shoulder into Eldritch's chest, and they toppled off the stage together, tangled.

They rolled, scrambling, out of their landing. Wary of Eldritch's Kreft speed, Reece dove to the side and snatched up a leg of the broken chair, wielding it like a club as he turned and slid on the shavings of shattered goblets. Then he froze, his stomach clenching, and stared.

Eldritch stood not four feet in front of him, gazing down at the long dagger of glass jutting from his chest in disbelief. The shard of broken glass had impaled him just below the heart; it glinted in the moonlight like the fang of some terrible serpent.

Reece lowered his club-arm, and Eldritch looked up. There was something new in his expression as he panted and stared at Reece, something that roused goosebumps on Reece's arms and twisted his insides with dread...hate.

Suddenly, Eldritch drew himself up to his full height, screamed a terrible, dual-toned scream, and attacked. And Reece realized too late...Eldritch's wound should have been seeping blood. There was none.

With a shout of alarm, Reece swung the club. It cracked into two against The Kreft's left side, but Eldritch kept on coming, the shard of glass poking grotesquely from his ribs. Eldritch hit him once, twice, three times in the face before he managed to duck out of range, his nose streaming blood into his mouth. Before, Reece had known Eldritch was only really toying with him, and that he simply meant to kill him *eventually*. Now, for the first time, he was fighting for his life.

Screaming again, Eldritch leaped at Reece with his fingers drawn into claws, and even as Reece dodged, caught him by the sleeve of his jacket. Reece cursed and by sheer luck, ducked and twisted out of the coat sleeves in one quick movement. He brought his leg around in a kick that buckled Eldritch's knee, then spun with his elbow. Eldritch anticipated the move. Hissing, he pushed Reece's elbow past him, roped his arms around him from behind, and yanked. Reece fell backwards into him. The dagger of glass sticking like a spear out of Eldritch's ribs pushed along his side, but he only felt warmth, sticky wetness, not pain.

His head and heart pounding together, Reece stomped and dragged his heel down Eldritch's shin, at the same time throwing his weight to the right. Eldritch's grip around his middle broke. In an instant of blind impulse, Reece grabbed the dagger of glass like a handle, its edges digging into his palms, and pulled.

After a second of resistance, the glass ripped from one side of Eldritch's chest to the other in one quick, zipping movement. Eldritch and Reece fell apart from each other, Reece unintentionally dropping to his knees, Eldritch tipping over like a felled tree, landing with a smack on the marble floor.

There was a long moment of silence. Reece remained on his knees, staring blankly, cupping the tear on his side. *The Jester* groaned like a creature in pain and jumped, tipping over an orchestra chair that had been balanced precariously on the edge of the stage. The clap of wood on marble startled Reece fully awake, and he stood, putting up one tired knee at a time.

Eldritch was breathing.

Reece hesitated, then walked forward. "Get up," he ordered the body at his feet, voice ragged. The slit he'd opened in Eldritch's chest gaped up at him bloodlessly. "No more games, Eldritch. Get up."

The Kreft remained flat on his back on the floor, almost like he'd been laid in an invisible coffin. Reece took another wary step in and leaned over him. As he did, Eldritch's eyes sprang open, but there was something wrong with them...they stared without seeing, blank, deadpan... and a bright white sheen was coating them, like a film of opaque tears. Reece squinted. The same whiteness, only in mist form, was gathering behind Eldritch's lips, swirling agitatedly. Despite himself, he began walking backwards, raising a hand against the swelling brilliance of the mist.

Charles Eldritch's body suddenly arched onto its heels as if an invisible string was being pulled violently through its chest. The gracefully-swirling mist began climbing out of its mouth, its eyes, its nose and ears, moving not like a weather pattern, but like a creature, like a thing with a will. It squeezed itself out of the headmaster's orifices and stretched limbs of shimmering mist, its insubstantial bulk growing in size till it loomed like a ghostly, faceless giant.

And then the featureless mass of white spoke in the deeper of the two voices that earlier had come from Eldritch's one body. Rasping and cold, the voice prickled the little hairs on the back of Reece's neck. Through the serum's muffling touch on his senses, he felt a spike of panic.

"Reece, listen to me, The Kreft, they're not human!"

"Oh, to touch again...to feel...to stretch..." the voice scratched as the white thing continued amassing itself over Eldritch's limp body.

"What are you?" Reece mouthed.

The thing somehow heard his whisper, and though it had no detectable face, it moved in a way that suggested it had turned to look at him. The mist had a multihued sheen, like the colors sitting stagnant on an oil slick.

"I am Kreft," the voice intoned, its white body undulating.

His heart thumping like a trapped bird against his ribcage, Reece said, "A parasite?"

He jumped as the creature cried out, "A parasite!" and then laughed. "We need not your weak human shells to live! We, who alone can survive The Voice of Space! We, the conquerors of the known galaxies!" The creature seemed to regard the discarded human body at its feet with disdain. "Long has it been since I've shed that human hide. Not since my last body was rendered unwearable. I had almost grown accustomed to human flesh. I had forgotten...yes, I had forgotten..."

The thing gave an impression of turning sharply, of looking into the distance, and Reece couldn't help but glance over his shoulder. His heart missed a beat.

Nivy and Hayden had burst into the dark ballroom, and were standing at the edge of the marble with shocked faces that were washed out by the pulsing light of the thing.

The creature that was Eldritch began to laugh, a rumbling, throaty chuckle that turned into a mad roar. Then, with a flash as quick and startling as lightning, it vanished. Reece's hair blew back from his face as something immense and invisible rushed by him.

Across the room, Nivy and Hayden started tentatively toward the place where Reece stood alone.

"No! Stay back!" he shouted at them, spinning. He viewed them through a curtain of oily haze, a trail that had been left by The Kreft's wraithlike body.

They waited, rooted to the ground, looking around in the dark. A wall of wind blasted by Reece again, howling. He tried following it with his serum-improved eyes, but there was only darkness, darkness and that strange, oily sheen...

He paused to look again at the sheen hanging in the air, so familiar. Suddenly, he knew what it was and where he'd seen it before. In school...in books...in a painting in Emathia's library tower...

His eyes raced across the ballroom, picking out the mysterious floating trail. He found its origin point, its head, and determined that that was where—or what—Eldritch was.

It was coming straight at him, like a locomotive with its breaks out.

"Look out!" Hayden cried.

The Kreft reappeared out of the trail like a blinding, hurtling comet and pummeled into Reece, lifting him from his feet. Its white substance streamed around him as the marble ballroom floor dropped away and he soared twenty, thirty, sixty feet up into the air, splayed over the strangely solid surface of the glowing mass, the wind crushing his back.

It deposited him on the observation deck astern of the ship, where several mechanics had been moderating the flow of coal gas rising through the massive pipes at the corners of *The Jester*. Reece landed on his back, coughing. The three pipes joined together beneath the open belly of the heliocraft's balloon, and even this far beneath them, he could smell their fumes, feel their heat. An anchor to the real world. This night was beginning to feel like one long, bad dream.

The mechanics screamed and scrambled as the white being reappeared, bobbing in midair beneath where the pipes twisted together into one enormous gasline. They fled down a hatch and left Reece dragging himself backward till his hands touched the wooden safety rail hedging the observation deck. Only a few dainty shafts of wood divided him from a deadly drop into the ballroom below, and despite the much more pressing matter of the alien set on murdering him, his stomach hardened queasily when he glanced down and saw Hayden and Nivy looking small enough to fit into a matchbox together.

He looked up just as The Kreft shot at him like a flaming cannonball, and rolled, flinching as the rail to his left exploded into splinters. His eyes unwillingly locked onto the telltale oil slick trickling through the broken gap in the safety rail. Little crumbs of refuse—bits of wood, some shattered glass—were sliding across the floor within the slick, as if resisting some distant magnet. He'd eat a hob if he hadn't just discovered how the Streams out in space were made.

Reece shook himself. No time for lollygagging. He could study the Streams later, provided he didn't die a slow, painful, and by all means very premature death.

Hissing laughter gave him a split second's warning; he dove, barely dodging The Kreft as it zoomed past him, a white bolt of power, energy, and heat. If he hadn't moved, he would have been catapulted out into the night. It was kill or be killed, now.

Which begged the question…*could* Eldritch be killed?

Hayden panted, his heart squeezed in his chest. Up above, on an observation balcony jutting out over the ballroom, Reece was fighting a losing battle. His only strength was in his ability to dart in and out of The Kreft's reckless line of fire; attacking was completely out of the question. He had no weapons, no clue of how to fight back. He was dying.

"What do we do, Nivy? What do we do?" Hayden moaned.

She spared him a glance before jogging toward where the weird undulating haze left behind by The Kreft dipped down and grazed the marble floor. Hayden bemusedly started after her, then stopped to uncertainly adjust his bifocals. There was rubble floating in the haze. Drifting along on an invisible current, spinning lazily up after Eldritch.

Nivy's earlier words snapped together in Hayden's head; he felt like the *click* should have been audible. He could suddenly see it all clearly in his head: The Kreft exploring the Epimetheus, setting up their occupation, their vaporous bodies leaving great streaks in the black Voice of Space. A captain would have accidentally happened into one of the streaks and found his ship caught up in a current that sped it across the great gaps of nothingness between planets in weeks and days that should have been months or even years.

"How would you destroy a Stream?"

Hayden hurried to Nivy, and before common sense could catch up to him, thrust his arm into the Stream up to his armpit. He felt a tug on his hand, and a second later, began sliding. Upward. With a gasp, he kicked, but his toes were already the only part of his foot touching the marble, and even though he could feel his arm, he could hardly wriggle it. It was as though he had gotten the arm shut in a translocator door and was being hauled up after it.

Something pummeled into him from behind; arms wrapped around his waist, pulling so hard a seam on his shirt gave a woeful crack. The force of the tackle yanked him out of the Stream's grip, and he fell, skidding on a jacket that had been dropped amongst the litter on the ballroom floor.

Giving Nivy a grateful nod—he couldn't have formed two coherent words just then, not with his breath caught in his throat as it was—Hayden looked down at his feet and the abandoned dress jacket twisted beneath them. Something glinted on one of the splayed sleeves—a pair of flight wings. Reece's. He scooped it up. The fabric was wet, bloody.

Clutching the jacket in fisted fingers, Hayden looked around at Nivy. She was taking aim with the Veritas's weapon—or trying to. The gun was held steady in her hands, but she kept shifting it fluidly, as if trying to aim at a fly. Up above, Eldritch was zipping back and forth across Reece's defenses like a horse repeatedly trampling an animal on the ground, never more than a blurry smudge of white light. Hayden might not know one end of a gun from the other, but he had to believe getting a clean shot off on Eldritch would be next to impossible while he was moving that fast. Nivy's face, furious and desperate at the same time, confirmed as much. There had to be another way.

How would you destroy a Stream?

"Nivy, the bullet! Of course!" Hayden exclaimed. "You were right! We can use the Streams against Eldritch—they all lead to him, right? Don't they?"

Nivy nodded and gave up on the silver gun, tossing it down. She reached a hand into her dress and plumbed out Gideon's proffered bullet, showing it to Hayden on the flat of her sweating hand.

"Crack it open. We need the burstpowder that's inside." Hayden winced as wild laughter and a shout of pain echoed down to them, one after the other. *Hold on, Reece!* "I saw fire in the oil lamps of the servants' corridors—I'll grab one!"

He left Nivy trying to pry open the bullet with her fingernails and dashed away, bringing the jacket without meaning to. His hands simply wouldn't unclench.

He wheeled around a corner, heading for the distant orange glow he had noticed in passing on his and Nivy's mad run to reach Reece. If he could get that fire and set it to the bullet's burstpowder within the

Stream, the resulting explosion should carry to Eldritch, and at the very least…

Wringing the jacket in his fists, Hayden grit his teeth and bore down on the solitary lantern hanging from a hook on the wall with his heart drumrolling in his chest. He reached the lantern out of breath, fumbled trying to lower it from the wall. The hot glass nudged his arm as it swung, smarting, and he jumped and gasped. Reece and Gideon never looked as clumsy as Hayden felt when they were doing something this important.

Footsteps. Behind him.

Spinning, holding up his only defense—the lantern creaking on its iron handle—Hayden shouted, "Who's there?" He cleared his throat as his voice cracked and raised the lantern a little higher, throwing back the creeping shadows.

Someone was there…he could feel them. There was no reason it shouldn't be one of the duke's guests, though most of them had been herded into windowless safety corridors by sentries trying to restore order. But he sensed…no, that was silly. It wasn't possible to tell someone meant you harm without even seeing their face.

Gulping down his terror, Hayden stepped forward, then immediately spasmed to a stop. He was looking at a dead man.

Liem stood blocking the hallway before him, a golden mask propped on the back of his brown hair, his upper lip crusted with dry blood. He looked furious. Calm, unarmed, but furious.

"Liem!" Hayden choked. "What are you—*how* are you—"

Liem's lip curled. He spoke quietly, in a whisper like the rustling of fire. "I sacrifice everything. And then this."

"I—I'm afraid I don't—"

"Why couldn't Reece leave it alone? Eldritch wanted him involved…wanted to use him…but I knew he'd find a way to use us using him! *I knew it!*"

Backing away from Liem, who looked disconcertingly like a wilder version of his brother in the dark, Hayden stammered, "Liem, it's not too late…we can save Reece…we can stop this…."

"Stop it?" Liem began prowling forward. "*Stop* it? Don't you get it? I can save Honora! I can fix her! I can make her better!" Suddenly, he snarled. "But what would you know of that? You're one of *them*."

"Them?"

"A Westerner."

"But—"

"Westerners, Pantedans, they're all the same! They don't belong! Honora could be powerful, rich!" Liem laughed scornfully. "Instead, she's like the purebred wolfdog whose owners let her mix with mutts…producing bad blood, wild, untamable pups who will suck her dry. We have to start fresh, start over. With a king who will do things right. And a justice system to drive the scourge away."

Hayden wanted to run, but something kept him from turning his back, be it habits leftover from Reece and Gideon's example, or just a strain of common sense he hadn't tapped before. *Never turn your back on an attacker.*

"Do you realize who you sound like?" Hayden asked as he continued walking backwards. If he could just back up far enough, he'd reach the crossroad of the corridors. Putting a turn between him and Liem should give him a few seconds' head start. *Then* he would run. "That's what the Veritas believe! But Eldritch *created* them, Liem—he gave them that idea so he could manipulate them! What you believe is a lie! Just another mechanism to get The Kreft more power!"

"Shut up!" Liem screamed, his dark eyes bulging. He came at Hayden with his hands raised, as if to strangle him, and that's when Hayden saw. The eyes. They weren't dark…they were black. And his skin, it was more than just pale—it was the sickly, wan yellow of an addict.

Stumbling backward, Hayden gasped, "How long? How long have you been on the serum?"

"Months, now. In just a few more, I'll have…I will become…" Liem paused and gave his head a shake, as if he were confused. "I had to do it. It was the only way to beat him."

Three more steps. Two. Hayden gripped the lantern harder, the metal handle imprinting in his skin. "Eldritch?"

Something in the pale face snapped. "Reece."

Liem attacked.

Shouting, Hayden dove to the right and tripped into the intersecting hallway, Liem's hands brushing the back of his shirt. Hugging the lantern to his chest so that the heat soaked through to his skin, he ran, refusing to look back. If Liem really was becoming a Vee, he was doomed.

By all rights, that thought should have had him slowing down, giving up. It didn't. He ran faster than he ever had before, not because he was brave…because he was afraid.

The hallway walls flew away as he sprinted out into the ballroom. It looked as he had left it not five minutes ago: Reece was still alive, fighting Eldritch up above, and Nivy was kneeling by the Stream, transferring a teaspoon's worth of burstpowder from the bullet to her hand. She looked over her shoulder at him as he gasped her name, and her eyes widened in alarm. For the first time, Hayden chanced a backwards glance. He wished he hadn't.

Liem was there, not an arm's length behind him, and if he had been frightening in the dark, in the moonlight, he was terrifying. Screaming so that blue veins stood out along his neck, Liem leaped and seized Hayden, pinioning his arms to his sides. Hayden smashed onto his stomach as his bifocals flew from his face and landed chattering against the marble. His ankle wrenched the wrong way beneath him, throbbing.

The lantern fell beside them and shattered; the fire went out with a feeble hiss. Dead.

In a streak of howling wind, Eldritch rushed over Reece, cackling. Something cracked against Reece's forehead, and he flew onto his back, blinking white lights out of his watering eyes.

His body clung to the serum for consciousness as one at a time, his small aches cluttered the front of his brain. His shoulder, his side, his head, plus a half a dozen bruises and the pain behind the effort of just keeping his eyes open. And there was the worry to contend with. He was starting to think he might die, and that his last act would be standing here like a useless lump while Eldritch ground him into dust.

He groaningly rolled onto his stomach, dragged himself up to his knees. Out of the corner of his eye, he saw the white glow approaching, and braced himself for another impact. He was surprised when The Kreft pulled up short to hover over him, a sparkling web of flowing mist, like a nebula.

"Are you finished, Reece Sheppard?" that haunting voice sounded amused.

Reece tried to turn, but all he could manage was a breathless roll that put him on his back, staring up at stars, clouds, and *The Jester's* monolithic balloon. Though his ears felt full of liquid, they caught a muffled shout, and he turned his face to the side to look back over the edge of the observation deck. Dollhouse-sized figures were fighting in the ballroom below, Nivy, Hayden, and…Liem?

"They will not best him," The Kreft said thoughtfully, as if following Reece's bleary gaze. "Your brother has done much growing, these years he's been in my service. I doubt you will recognize him at all in another year." Reece glanced up at Eldritch, who chuckled. "Forgive me, I have misspoken. No, Reece, you will *not* be here in another year, and neither will your friends. But perhaps I shall be merciful. Perhaps I shall let you pick one to save. Hayden, perhaps? He would make a fine addition to The Veritas. Yes."

Reece laughed and went up to one elbow, though the laugh burned in his throat and his arm shook treacherously. "Hayden? Right. Not that this is news, but I think you're a few personnel short of a full crew."

"And I think you underestimate your Hayden Rice. I could make him into a fine tool. A fine tool."

What *was* going on down in the ballroom? Reece risked another backwards glance and licked sweat off his lip. Nivy and Liem were fighting fist and foot—Liem was an impossible blur, gracefully dodging Nivy's punches and kicks—and Hayden was kneeling with a broken lantern next to one of The Kreft's Streams…though there really was only one, wasn't there? Sinuous and wandering, The Stream started where Eldritch had first left his human body, and ended where he floated above Reece in a cloud of brilliant light.

"What is he doing?" Eldritch suddenly said, voice sharp.

Reece cast The Kreft a quick look. It was impossible to pull emotion out of its faceless white mass, but by the way The Kreft's misty tentacles were twisting and jerking, he thought it was agitated. He looked back at the miniature Hayden. He held something in each of his hands, too small to make out from afar, and was jerkily rubbing them together. If Reece had to guess, he'd say his friend was trying to start a fire.

"No…" Eldritch hissed. The Kreft began to threateningly swell, its white limbs flailing like angry serpents. "No!"

Reece wrung everything he had left inside of him so one last drop of adrenaline hit his nerves and sent them up in flames. He bolted upright.

"Hayden!" he screamed raggedly over the banister. "Hayden—do it! Do it *now!*"

Behind him, Eldritch roared wordlessly—a sound like thunder, rumbling deep in Reece's chest. Reece spun, and despite himself, gaped. Eldritch was taller than two men stacked one on top of the other, and he was still shooting up like a weed, gathering himself to charge, to put a stop to Hayden's efforts…to put a stop to Hayden. For a second, Reece hesitated. And then he figured…Eldritch wasn't getting any smaller.

With a breaking shout, he leaped at Eldritch and groped for some kind of handhold amidst the coiling tendrils of white. He immediately found a solid core to the mass, and he felt the groove of muscles, and a thick skin like rubber, but skin all the same. He hadn't noticed during his pummeling, but he should have guessed as much from when The Kreft had first rocketed him up here…the light and the mist weren't Eldritch's body, not anymore than Reece's fingernails or hair were his. *This* was Eldritch's body.

Reece sensed rather than saw an arm coming forth from the mist. Something like what he imagined a hand with no fingers might feel like wrapped itself around his right bicep; a second later, a second alien hand gripped his left. He tried to pull away, writhing. This time when The Kreft laughed, it sounded like the entire planet should be crumbling apart, the laughter was so loud, so deep. The fingerless hands tugged Reece's arms in opposite directions so that his feet bounced like they were attached to a clothesline that had been pulled taut.

He began to lose consciousness.

He was here again. Watching while his friends fought for him, waiting for one of them to die because there was nothing he could do. Full of knowledge, full of facts…useless. Hayden's hands trembled on the lantern, and he cursed down at the flint, the wick, the oil, and the damp burstpowder taken from Gideon's single bullet. Useless.

Reece's echoing scream made his stomach whither up, and he jerked his face toward the ceiling, glaring through his cracked lenses. The brilliance of The Kreft, grown to the size of a small house, gobbled up Reece, hid him from sight. But the screams said enough.

Nivy was fighting Liem. She had saved him. Dived in and drawn Liem to herself. Hayden had heard him break two of her fingers with a kick—heard the *snap*, not Nivy. She hadn't made a sound. Which made it that much worse.

Again, Reece screamed, and it propelled Hayden to his feet. He had to do something—anything! The burstpowder had failed, but he couldn't just sit there, wishing it to catch fire. He would help Reece…climb every last stair to the observation deck on his sprained ankle if that's what it took!

A voice surprised him—Nivy's. "*Hayden!*"

Hayden instinctively turned and grunted as a sideways boot thumped into his gut, bending him backwards. He fell sliding on the marble. Liem, holding a lightning cap weapon just like a real Vee, towered over him with an insane grin. Clucking his tongue, he lowered the gun, and as Hayden wriggled on his back, trying to get away, fired.

Electric jitters raced from Hayden's good ankle up to the middle of his thigh, and his leg went as dead as a tree stump. At least it didn't hurt, Hayden thought absurdly. His pain tolerance was a joke. He could never take what Reece or even what Nivy, crawling toward him, dragging legs as dead as his own, had taken. He wasn't like them. He shouldn't have ever pretended he was.

"Liem! Enough!" Nivy growled. She rolled, dodging the blue electric fizz Liem shot casually her way, but came up from the dodge with difficulty.

As Hayden continued sliding himself back toward the Stream, his elbow slipped on something. He gazed down at it blankly. Reece's jacket, flight wings still attached, curled, disheveled, around his arm. Without knowing what for, he picked it up and squeezed it to his chest. If he thought seeing something of his brother's would pull Liem up short, even for a second, he was wrong.

With Liem approaching, his face bent on killing, Nivy crawling after him with her teeth grit and her eyes watering, and Reece shouting something, the strength in his voice fading—Hayden felt a small bulge in the pocket of the jacket. His hand slipped into the silk-lined, inside pocket. His fingers rolled something small and smooth out into his palm. It glinted in the half-light, a marble, dark blue and white swirled, like a miniscule planet trapped between his thumb and forefinger. He looked at Nivy. She looked at him.

Shouting with all his might, Hayden picked the marble up over his head and then threw it to the ground.

The dark swelled at the edges of Reece's vision, blurred everything he saw—which wasn't much. Just white, flowing light. It was the quietness that let him know the end was coming, the eerie, muffled silence. He couldn't feel much, but he wasn't unaware of his body, either. It was like going to that place between sleeping and waking, where even lifting a hand felt like an ordeal when he'd rather just sleep.

What was that…an earthquake? That's what it felt like. Maybe he really *was* dreaming. Which was strange, because that meant he was alive, and if that was the case, then what was with all the white?

Abruptly, he was falling—just far enough to lose his breath when he landed on his back on the trembling floor. His eyelids felt chained shut, but he wrenched them apart with a groan. There was a film of dust on the smooth wood under his splayed hands, and more of it spiraled in the air, drifting…sparkling…

He bolted upright as all the rest came back to him—his father, the masquerade, Eldritch, The Streams—and at the same time, clamped his bloody hands over his ears. The noise was deafening. Like the braying horn of a locomotive combined with the screech of a windstorm and the squeal of a hundred rusted hinges.

The noise was coming from the opaque cloud looming over the observation deck—Eldritch. Reece shuddered and tried to crawl backward without the use of his hands. For a second, he'd seen something like a face in the white mass, seen two hollows for eyes and a nose and an open mouth too elongated to seem human, undetailed and smooth, as though they were pressing out against an elastic membrane.

That was when Reece knew the fight was over, and not just because he felt like someone had enthusiastically beaten him with a mallet. That scream was inhuman, but he knew the sound of defeat when he heard it—two parts hate, one part despair.

He stared through a gap in the banister where the wooden rails had been blown to sawdust by Eldritch and down at the ballroom in horror. He barely registered the small piles of fire sitting here and there on rubble-turned-kindling, or the big black tarry spot on the marble floor, or the lingering smell of burstpowder, like sulfur. Nivy and Hayden. Where were Nivy and Hayden? Where was Liem?

Almost as an afterthought, he noticed the flicker of color and movement that had been tracing lines back and forth across the scene. As he honed in on it with some effort, he felt a hysterical laugh rising in his chest. Whatever else Hayden had done, he'd had done this much right. There was fire in the Streams, and it was racing the path to Eldritch like a spark running the fuse to a pile of explosives. The ball of fire zipped through a Stream a few paces beneath the balcony ledge, and Reece squinted against the bright orange heat, sweat instantly beading on his face.

A whole of ten seconds had passed, but each one suddenly felt like a loss. That fire was coming here. *Here.* He gaped over his shoulder and up at the gas pipes and the open-bottomed balloon carrying the body of the sickly *Jester.* He wasn't a chemist—he'd barely passed his chemistry class with a .3, for crying out loud—but he didn't have to be to know that coal gas was highly flammable. In another thirty seconds, he'd be charcoal.

As Reecee rolled onto his stomach and awkwardly pushed up onto his knees, the piercing death scream cut off, the white seething mass twitched, and Reece knew The Kreft's eyes were on him, and that they wanted him to see him dead. Almost but not quite as much as they wanted to live.

There was a pause of indecision, and then The Kreft bolted over the banister, a smear of light diving into the ballroom. Reece's brain sputtered in surprise before forcing the rest of him into blind action; he tripped more than jumped off the balcony and into the fresh Stream left by The Kreft.

It was like landing in a somehow solid steam, warm, moist, clammy, breezy. He jerked as the momentum of his fall redirected into a slanted downward glide and held his stomach as it tightened at the sight of nothing but a thin vapor keeping him from a body-shattering fall to the ground. One of his legs dangled out of the Stream, and he was sure that any second, gravity might decide this was more than he should get away with and yank the rest of him out as well. But he couldn't readjust—he couldn't move at all. The Stream felt like steam, but it held him in place like concrete. He must have used up all of his panic. He was stuck—he couldn't fall, but he couldn't pull himself to safety either—and all he really felt was exasperated, as if the worst joke in the world had backfired on him.

He was coming up fast now on Eldritch, who at the end of the Stream (or the beginning of it), had come to a stop over a cowering body spread prostrate on the floor, and was bellowing something at it, his voice like a gust of winter wind.

Liem's voice screeched back as he leaned up from kneeling in reverence, "You promised! You promised I would be king! You—"

He yelped like a kicked dog, and Reece felt an unexpected welling of pity for him as Eldritch shrieked wordlessly and struck him again and again, because he knew what Eldritch much want—Liem's body. Safety from death. Why hadn't he just taken Reece's?

The Stream-borne fire reached the observation deck, the pipes of coal gas, and the balloon. There was a flash, a roar that swallowed even Eldritch's screams—a tug on Reece's exposed leg, wrenching him from the Stream—a warm body enclosing him in safe arms—

The darkness was hedging in on Reece's vision again, but he saw enough. The explosion could've competed with the sun for brightness, heat, and violence; it tore at the whole ship, but the balloon caught the real brunt of the inferno, and burned from the inside-out. Before, the fire trapped in The Streams had moved like a spark meandering down a fuse…now it sped like a bullet of roiling, blistering flames, tearing through the final Stream, racing the track to Eldritch until at last, with a whoosh of wind and a crack like thunder, blinding fire collided with and overtook brilliant white. The mass that was Eldritch and the small shape that was Liem disappeared in a storm of brightest color, hottest heat, and deepest sound.

Reece was being hefted over someone's shoulder, carried at a run. He didn't know by who. He didn't know where they were going, or if they'd get there before the ship plummeted planetside. He heard screams and shouts and *The Jester* drawing shuddering breaths and felt lost in the chaos.

He shut his eyes, and time must have passed, because when he opened them, he was lying on his back on the dark bridge of the heliocraft, looking up into the duke's face. Reece knew it because his grip on reality was less than stable at the moment, but for a second, even though the spasming of *The Jester* and the fluttering in his stomach told him the ship was definitely crashing—he thought everything might be alright after all.

"Lie still," the duke ordered calmly, his face smooth but his eyes grim.

That sounded appealing, but Reece's body and brain seemed stuck on different frequencies. He unwillingly sat up and glared about. Sophie, Hugh, and Abigail were strapped into the crew seats against the back wall, and all three were staring at him like he'd sprouted wings from his ears. Or like he'd just come off the bad end of a battle with a Kreft and had a few new deformities to show for it.

As Reece grimaced and glanced toward the flightpanel, Gideon, who was still at the yoke, growled, "Get him buckled! All'a you, get buckled!"

That "all'a you" was meant for Po and the duke. Po's boots, the only thing sticking out from under the flightpanel, kicked. Gid grabbed her by the belt and dragged her one-handed out across the floor.

Po pushed her half-unwound braid back from her oil-stained face. "I can—"

"There ain't nothin' you can do now!" Gideon shouted over the various warning alarms sounding from the panel. "Now *sit*, before I bleedin' make you!"

"What's happening?" Reece slurred, letting the duke half lead, half heave him to the crew seats, where he collapsed numbly next to Hugh. He patted his side absently. A wad of fabric had been bound against his cut.

"I would have thought it'd be obvious," the duke answered flatly as his hands glanced across Reece's seat and expertly buckled him into place. "There's no saving the ship, now. We're crashing. The best we can hope for is a smooth landing."

"Bleeding bogrosh," Abigail whispered fervently.

His arms tight around the sniffling Sophie, Hugh leaned forward and asked with fearful eyes, "Reece...where's Hayden?"

Hayden. Maybe Reece did have a little panic left in his system, after all.

He wasn't quick enough to mask his emotion. Hugh's throat and jaw went taut, and he nodded once and then put his face into his daughter's hair, almost as if bracing himself, not against the impending crash, but something else, something worse. Reece clenched his bloodied fists and felt his pulse hammering hard. Much worse.

The pressure back behind his naval told him they were gaining speed, while the view out the canopy window showed they were losing too much altitude too fast. Gid was trying to steer the ship down in a spiral to coast out their momentum, and he was doing a good job, but the ship just wouldn't—or rather couldn't—cooperate with what his hands were trying to make it do.

Suddenly, the ship heaved hard to starboard in a jolt that made Reece rise up against his safety harness and then crash back into his seat with a grunt. Steam gushed out of the flightpanel; a new bell of warning started sounding with all the rest, a shrill, woeful peal. Gid spat a Pantedan oath and reached to pull the emergency temperature-control lever just as the ship pitched to port. His head snapped forward and struck the flightpanel with a muffled but solid *kkrrch* that Reece related to a dropped melon splitting open on the ground. He slumped over sideways in his seat and didn't move again.

"Gideon!" Reece screamed, hands jumbling with his harness. "Gideon!"

The Jester careened wildly to the left without hands to hold her yoke, and Reece and the others thrashed to the right, pasted against their seats by the centrifugal forces at work. Reece felt like his insides were being flattened against his backbone, turned to jelly, and he could feel a similar pressure against his face, kneading his cheeks.

Po, glued to the copilot's chair, reached with a scream for the secondary yoke and steadied it with effort. As soon as the invisible fist of gravity stopped grinding Reece back into his chair, he snapped free of his restraints and fell toward the flightpanel and Gideon.

"Blast it all, boy!" the duke's growl, and then a sequence of clicks, followed him despite Abigail's cry of, "Thaddy!"

Gideon looked bad. Paler than usual beneath the glaze of blood coating his face. With a gasp of effort, Reece tried pulling him from the captain's chair and onto the floor with his good arm and only made an inch or so of impact.

And then the duke was there, firmly pushing him aside, stooping, and hoisting the limp Gideon up and over one of his broad shoulders.

"Well?" he snapped when Reece stood there staring like a numpty. He glared meaningfully at Gideon's vacated seat before shuffling toward the back wall, where Hugh had unbuckled and was standing, prepared to help. Like Hayden would be, if he were here.

Hayden...

"Cap'n!" Po squeaked.

Reece spun down into the captain's seat without another thought. As soon as his palms closed over the smooth golden handles of the yoke, Po let go of the co-pilot's yoke and sank back into her seat, rubbing her wrists. Reece grit his teeth. The yoke strained against him, vibrating as if it might take flight all on its own, and each vibration bit into his bad shoulder like a hungry nightcat.

He made a quick assessment of his surroundings. He'd only flown a heliocraft two or three times, not counting simulations, but they were all the same. Standard applicators and levelers, Class-A Synthetic Gravity Inducers...

The balloon was gone, but *The Jester* still had her rear propellers and her tiller, and if the rest of the ship hung in there long enough, those might be enough to ease her into what captains called a Skid-Down. A sliding landing, rather than a sudden, potentially deadly stop. All Reece needed was the right landing surface, and for that, he had an idea.

"Po, what's the engine got left in her?"

"Not much." Her voice rattled with the ship. "The Quadrant 7's hardy, but the explosion sucked up all her coal gas. She's runnin' on fumes."

Reece's shaking fingers curled around the yoke, sweating. He felt hot, but knew from being able to see his breath cloud before his face that he shouldn't. Like *The Jester*...he was on his last leg.

"Shut her down," he barked, his voice cracking.

Po's eyes widened. "What?"

"The Quadrant...shut her down. But be ready to bring the propellers back on to full on my mark. We need to save every bit of juice the engine has left for that one burst. Can you divert any more power to the Quadrant from nonessential systems? Any lighting that's left, thermal generators, sonic muters—"

"—divergence compensators, coolant trappers." Po's little hands sped across the golden flightpanel with easy know-how. Reece felt a dip in his stomach when the propellers went offline. "Done."

The airship sank down and down, still reeling and spasming even with Reece's hands clutching the yoke in a death grip, until the weedy tops of the tallest oaks at Emathia began skimming the bottom of the canopy window. They were close, now. The mansion zoomed by in a smear of bright lights far on their left. The motor vehicle stables. The gardens. The forest.

The lake.

"*Now!*" Reece cried, bracing himself against his seat.

Po smashed both of her hands down on a bar above her lap, and *The Jester* jetted forward in a gush of energy, her noise tilting up toward the sky.

Shouting, Reece slammed the yoke forward. Moaning like a great, airborne whale, the heliocraft unwillingly tipped back down again, so that the patchy white ground rolled by beneath them, leading them toward Emathia's lake.

With *The Jester* slanting ever closer to the ground, still shooting forward at nauseating speeds, Reece began to lose his fight against himself. His eyelids were drooping, his shoulders were slumping, his head was nodding. It felt like his body was caving in on him. He wanted to run away from it, and yet he *needed* it, needed his arms and his hands to hold on to the yoke, needed his eyes to judge the distance to the water, which was close now, close enough to reflect the dark mass of the airship's shadow, rippling and wrinkling...

His struggle felt totally internal, but Po must have seen something of it on his face.

"Hold on, Reece!" she screamed, and put both her hands on one side of the yoke to help him hold it. "Hold on!"

Reece screamed through his teeth with her and thought he might rip apart from doing what she said, and holding on too tight. The darkness was coming back. It felt thicker than before. Unforgiving.

"Hold on!"

The nose of the ship plunged into the lake in an explosion of ice and water, and Reece fell spinning into the darkness.

XV

Welcome Home, Son

Laughter. It cut through Reece's thick dreams and came muffled to his ears. His eyes were closed. He fitfully rolled his head to the side. Something crackled beneath him—scratchy, papery bed sheets.

With effort, he opened his eyes and stared blearily at the nightstand beside his bed. It held an assortment of personal effects— his pocket watch, flight wings, and leather riding gloves, all of which looked like Reece felt...worse for wear. He'd never in all his life been so sore. His skin felt stretched tight across his aching muscles. And he felt *tired*. Rested, but tired.

He was in a hospital chamber, but that he gathered from his uncomfortable bed and mortifying ensemble. Everything beyond his bed and nightstand was hidden by the white curtain penning him in, and all he could make of the chamber was that it had smooth wooden floors and a domed ceiling painted with fluffy, friendly clouds. He had no memory of being brought in. The last thing he remembered was...

His head suddenly pounded. The onslaught of memories was less than pleasant; most of them were too vivid, and the rest were only made more nightmarish by the things he remembered fuzzily. Like staring down at that smooth, grey lake, losing consciousness...like hearing Eldritch's death scream...like not knowing if his friends were alive or not...

Reece lifted his head as he heard more laughter, and scooted till his back curled against his headboard, bringing him upright. One of his arms was in a sling, which reminded him...his collarbone. He tentatively touched the bump on his shoulder and was pleased when it barely smarted.

Clearing his throat, he called hoarsely, "Hello?"

The laughter cut off abruptly. Quick footsteps thumped against the hardwood floor, and then someone ripped back his curtain, flooding his little pen with clean white light.

"Reece! You're awake!" Po exclaimed, beaming. For the first time since Reece had met her, she was wearing normal clothes—sort of. She still had on a mechanic's jumpsuit, but beneath an oversized grey sweater and a red scarf. "Gideon, he's awake!"

Gideon appeared beside her with a bandage wrapped around his forehead, and grinned. "Knew he wasn't gonna die."

"Die?" Reece choked. "Really? Was it that bad?"

Po and Gideon swapped a look and nodded. Reece wonderingly started to lift his blanket and inspect his side before Po said, "It wasn't that. Well, not *just* that. It was mostly the serum."

"What?"

"The Vee's serum," Gideon said dryly. "It about killed you. *Should've* killed you, the doc said. Settled for puttin' you in a coma for four days instead."

Well, that explained why Eldritch hadn't taken Reece's body when he'd had the chance. He hadn't wanted to go down with the ship. Ha ha. "Four days!"

"Yeah. The doc said somethin' about a, uh…sim-bee-somethin' relationship…" Gideon uncertainly shrugged a shoulder and glanced at Po, who helped, "He supposes Vees are slowly brought up on the serum, till their bodies and it kind of have a—"

"Symbiotic," Gideon remembered.

"Yeah, a symbiotic relationship. You takin' it all at once should have been fatal. They pumped everythin' outta your stomach, and even then…" Po cringingly tucked a strand of hair behind her ear. "You had us worried, Cap'n."

Reece considered that for a minute, made aware of the hollow emptiness in his stomach by Po's words. It let out a mutinous grumble right on cue, and Po, smiling, stood up and left to fetch him a tray of food. Reece was glad for a minute alone with Gid—he had a lot to sort through, and Po's glowing smiles could be distracting.

"Hayden?" he asked, and then after a pause added, "Nivy?"

"Both fine. Aitch got pretty roughed up, but they let him outta here yesterday, so he must be on the mend."

Reclining in his pillows with a sigh of relief, Reece asked, "What *happened*? I thought we were scrap metal."

Gideon just looked at him blankly, then stood, wandered to the other side of the sparsely-furnished chamber, and returned with a wrinkled evening newspaper. He unfolded it and snapped it open so Reece could see the front page, decorated with, "Palatine Second Pilots Burning Heliocraft to Safety".

"There are more," Gideon said, handing over the paper with an unreadable look on his face. "All namin' you the hero'a Parliament. Not one person died in the crash, though the hospitals are still pretty well stocked. You landin' in the lake saved all our necks."

Reece gave a low whistle as he scanned the article, admittedly a little proud. The writer of the article rambled on and on not only about him "valiantly steering the dying *Jester* to a gentle touch-down", but about him saving the duke from an assassination plot hatched by persons yet unknown, though it was implied Eldritch was involved in the scandal. Most of the article was bogrosh—especially the bit that mentioned Reece was a handsome, strapping six foot two inches tall (he was only five foot eleven)—but that was likely for the better. The public wasn't ready for the truth about The Kreft.

"What about the duke and Abigail?"

Gid shrugged, staring at nothing. "They'll be alright."

Something about the way he said it made Reece cock his head and frown. Meeting his eyes, Gid sighed, "Liem's dead, Reece."

Reece's empty stomach twisted as he dropped his head into his pillows and glared up at the ceiling. Something indefinable broke off inside of him; he felt the jagged edge it left behind, unsmoothed, rough, and sharp. Liem, dead. It would have been easier to swallow if he could just picture Liem shaking hands with The Kreft, agreeing to help kill his own father…but all he could see was his stepbrother as a kid, grudgingly playing magnetic blocks with him. No matter where Liem had ended up, he had had the same humble beginnings as Reece, the same chance at different choices. There would be no more choices, now. His last had been his most important, and it had been costly.

Gideon slowly updated him on everything else, but Reece only half listened. Robert Gustley hadn't turned up on the airship, or anywhere else, and Parliament had put a steep reward on his head. That had been the duke's idea. Apparently Parliament was groveling to get back in his good graces, now that Eldritch's threats of blackmail and murder held no water. They had even heard his proposal regarding the disbanding of The Veritas.

"That's another thing," Gid said with a foreboding scowl, "the Vees have disappeared."

Reece bolted upright, gasped at the stitch in his side, and repeated as he massaged it, "Disappeared?"

"Yeah. Parliament sent ambassadors to them to talk about the duke's proposal…but The Tholos Stone or whatever they call it was abandoned. And the apothecary's gone. The bleedin' cowards, they're prolly halfway across Epimetheus by now."

"Probably," Reece repeated quietly. "Let's hope they didn't go looking for The Kreft."

They gave that a moment of solemn silence.

"Look," Gideon began after a time. He sat on a neighboring mattress that had been stripped of its bedclothes. The springs squeaked beneath his weight. "I know you haven't had much time to think on it, but I've gotta know."

Reece studied him curiously. "Know what?"

"What's next. The Kreft are still out there. Most'a the planet doesn't know about them, but Parliament, they're catchin' on to the duke's urgings. It's come out that Eldritch was the one who wanted to build our armies, but the armies are *still* bein' built. Only now, instead'a bein' used by The Kreft, they'll be used *against* them. There'll be a war. Just not the way The Kreft figured." Gideon hesitated, and then said in a gruffer voice, "I can't fight in the war, but dirt if I'm gonna be useless when it comes. With Panteda…not doin' anythin', even against a lost cause, was almost worse than the thing itself."

"What do you mean?"

Gideon grappled with his words for a moment, a fold of wrinkles deepening between his eyebrows. "Mordecai can tell you how it happened, but he can never tell you how it *was*. Waitin' on an airship, chosen to be sent to safety, me because I was a kid, him because he'd been wounded…and lookin' out the window, watchin' my whole world fail. I know there was nothin' I could've done, but I at least… I should've…"

"Gid, you said it yourself," Reece said carefully, "you couldn't have done anything."

"But I should have!" Gideon snapped. His face softened after a moment of stiffness, and his shoulders slumped, defeated. "I'll always feel like I should have."

Reece absently rubbed his bad shoulder and frowned at his friend. "Why are you telling me this now?" He weakly teased, "I'm not going to die, right? This isn't a deathbed confession?"

Gideon shrugged uncomfortably, still not meeting his eyes. His dark hair looked like he'd run his hands through it all night. "You ever wonder why I became friends with you and Aitch?"

"I was kind of hoping it was our winning personalities."

With a snort, Gideon replied, "It was seein' you save him, on Bus-ship Ten, when no one else gave a second look at the kid with the pail and the ugly bifocals." Squinting up at the cloud-patterned ceiling, he let out a heavy breath. "I've promised myself I'll never do nothin' again. If you go off to war—"

"I wouldn't count on that," Reece interrupted, and Gideon looked at him sharply. "I have a promise to keep, too. *The Aurelia* belongs to The Heron, Gid. I told Nivy I'd take her home, and I will."

For a moment, Gideon studied him fixedly, almost as if expecting Reece to take back what he'd said. Then the chamber door reopened, and Po entered with a hum, bearing a wide silver tray stacked with food enough for the three of them. She set it at the foot of Reece's bed, making the toffee-colored juice in the curvy glass pitcher jump and splash. Iced chocolate tea.

"It's lucky you woke up today," she chatted as she handed Reece a plate of fruit, bread, and cheese. "It's the first day since you were brought in the corridors aren't chalk full'a visitors."

Reece stacked the cheese on the still-steaming bread and packed it into his mouth. "Like who?" he asked, imagining the sorts of rabid fans the newspaper article would have brought. Hopefully they weren't admitted to see him in his scanty bed robe.

"Hayden's family, and your parents, for a little bit…though they've been pretty busy since the masquerade, you can imagine. Mordecai and Nivy keep tradin' shifts with Owon—"

Reece choked noisily on his bread, his eyebrows climbing up his forehead as he shot Gideon a wild look. Gideon flushed.

"Me and Aitch filled her in," he grumbled and accepted a plate of food from the smugly-smiling Po. "Seemed like we ought to, after everythin' she already knew from the masquerade. Besides. She's pushy."

"Anyways," Po went on, "they keep tradin' shifts so they can come see you, so Nivy should be here any minute now. All your tutors came through—even Agnes—and a lot'a people from The Owl, and even some from The Guild House! Oh, and your friend," she said casually, but watching his face intently. "What's her name? Scarlet?"

Reece nodded. "So where are they today?"

"Well," Po suddenly looked cautious, "the snows are keepin' most people at home with airship problems. Actually, if I'm not back to the shop soon, Gus and Tilden will likely tie my braid in a knot."

Twisting uncomfortably, Reece glanced out the oval window over the spare bed. Snow was piled high on the sill, and more was dropping outside, great, cottony tufts of it.

"And, um, today is…the funeral. Liem's, I mean."

Reece could have sworn he felt his stomach shriveling; his hunger went out like a snuffed candle. He decisively put his plate on his nightstand and used his free hands to rub his tired eyes. He hadn't been to many funerals—just his grandparents', and Scarlet's father's—and

the thought of attending his own stepbrother's when what seemed like
only hours had passed since he'd last seen him was so surreal it fogged
his mind.

"It ain't bein' made real public...and the duke, he didn't tell
anyone about what Liem did," Po said gently, chasing her fruit around
her plate with a fork.

Gideon, eying Reece, grunted, "Do you wanna go?"

Reece drew a breath that stretched the aches in his ribs. "Yes." He
kicked back his blankets and swung his legs over the side of the bed,
briefly distracted by how thin they looked. Then he remembered Po
could see them too, and he belatedly yanked a blanket over his lap,
holding it like a towel around his waist as he stood and wobbled. "I
should be there." He knees buckled, nearly giving out, and Gideon
caught him by the arm, slinging it around his shoulders like a yoke.

"I'll come with you. Make sure you don't steal the show by fallin'
over your own feet."

"You don't—" Reece started, and then thought the better of it.
"Thanks," he said instead, meaning it.

Gideon made a never mind noise and half dragged him toward the
chair in the corner that was piled with a few clean sets of clothes. "I'll
have to borrow a suit," he mumbled.

"It'll be too small."

"I'll slouch." Straightening up, Gideon pointedly jerked his chin,
and Reece glanced over his shoulder, wincing as his neck muscles
balked.

Nivy was leaning in the chamber doorway, as silent as ever, her
eyes holding him. He said nothing, just smiled tiredly in greeting, and
she smiled back, the smile of an ally.

The three of them went to the funeral alone, and stood
inconspicuously off to one side of the casket, on a small rise beneath a
bare-branched oak tree that hid them from most stares. All throughout
the ceremony, Reece felt as if he were dreaming awake. He didn't
move forward to scatter rose pedals on the closed amber coffin with
everyone else, didn't raise his hand in salute when it was lowered into
the hard, snowy ground. Something kept nudging him inside, telling
him to say goodbye, but he couldn't bring himself to do it. Those
nudges scraped the raw edges of whatever had broken off inside of him
when he'd heard Liem was dead, and the deep, internal stinging was all
he really felt.

The duke and Abigail stood nearest to the rectangular hole in the ground, Abigail in a black veil that draped to the ground and unfurled like a banner when the wind gusted. Reece couldn't see their faces, but more than once, he thought he felt the duke's eyes graze the shadow of the tree…and he felt warmer inside for it. Things were never going to be the same, but in some ways…that gave him hope.

He listened to the bland voice of the long-faced speaker and had to keep swallowing impatient sighs. A life of sacrifice, giving…"unwavering conviction". Lies meant to make the people in attendance feel better. He wondered if the duke and Abigail felt as badly as he did, hearing those lies. It was hard to imagine what that would feel like.

The funeral ended, and the crowds scattered, some people lining up to offer the Sheppards their condolences, others seeking the warmth of the mansion or wandering curiously in the direction of Emathia's flooded lake, where the battered *Jester* was still roped off, the last shreds of her ravaged balloon deflated over her like a blanket.

Reece tugged up the collar of his jacket to block cold wind and unwelcome glances alike. For a time, he stood there with his good hand on his collar and stared at Liem's grave without really seeing it. Slowly, feeling returned to him. Cold as it was, he still felt as if he were melting, and all his stiffness was leaking out around his feet. He shut his eyes and let out a breath that haloed around his head.

When he turned around, he had an audience.

Nivy and Gideon were there, sitting with their backs against the gnarled oak, but so were Hayden, Hugh, Sophie, Po, and Scarlet. He looked at them one at a time as the wind roughed up his hair. Hayden, wearing a long dark overcoat and hobbling on a pair of wooden crutches, smiled and nodded at him encouragingly.

"What are you doing here?" Reece asked.

The others exchanged uncertain looks.

Pushing his bifocals up the bridge of his nose with a finger, Hayden asked, "Where else would we be?"

Reece looked at Po, and she shrugged, stepped forward, unwound her red scarf from around her neck, and looped it instead around his. "This was more important than any old shop. Gus and Tilden…they'll understand."

"You didn't have to come. None of you did."

"That's kind of the point, Reece," Scarlet said patiently. She stood a little apart from the others, stealing surprisingly insecure glances at them when they weren't looking.

Not sure he understood, Reece absently reached up and scratched at the wool scarf. His friends' stares were expectant in a wary way, as if he was a geyser in a Freherian deadland liable to explode if they didn't tread just so.

"Thank you," he finally sighed, smiling an unintentionally-lopsided smile. "I'll be fine."

But if they managed one more knowing, seven-way look, he really *was* going to explode.

"Of course you will." Sophie stomped through the snow that nearly spilled over into her bluebird-egg-colored boots and hugged him. "It gets better, Reece," she whispered, and despite her smile, her voice caught. "The emptiness, I mean. I remember. From Mother."

"Does it?" he asked doubtfully.

"It does," she promised. "It fills back up, if you let it."

As if directly connected to the pressure of her arms around his middle, a lump bobbed into his throat. It didn't feel like he'd refill. It felt like a leak had sprung inside of him that would slowly tap him dry.

Clearing his throat, Reece patted the top of Sophie's head and resignedly pushed her out to arm's length.

"You should go inside," he said, sweeping his eyes over the rest of his friends so they'd know they were included in that almost-order too. "I didn't know this, but apparently, it's customary to serve profane amounts of food at funerals. You should see it all. Clam chowder, stuffed shells, hot lemon pudding…" When they just stood there, their faces collectively sympathetic, he exasperatedly tossed up his unslinged arm and groaned, "Just go, alright? I'm fine."

They obeyed, if grudgingly, starting with Sophie. Hugh, Scarlet, and Po each had a hug and a quick, warm word for him, and Po even came back for seconds before she hurried after the others with a face as red as her scarf. Nivy was the last to go, with an extra penetrating glance in his direction and a nod he took to say, "When you're ready." Right.

Surprisingly, he *did* feel better by the end of the little procession. He was a long way from jumping around and dancing, but he really was fine. Just focused. And cold, now that the feeling had come back into his extremities. It was nearing on dusk, and even though it had stopped snowing, there was enough wind to make him think longingly after the hearth in his mansion bedroom and the hot soup the guests inside were no doubt tucking into. Maybe there'd be some left. A gallon or so would suffice.

Gideon's hand clapping his shoulder buckled his knees, and he jumped.

"Hey," Gid said, almost cheerful, "we've got somethin' for you."

"Huh?"

"What, you think a funeral alone would be enough to get Aitch outta bed? He's been makin' such a bleedin' fuss about his foot, you'd think—"

"I came for the funeral!" Hayden exclaimed indignantly before glancing at Reece and earnestly insisting, "I came for the funeral."

"What are you talking about?" Reece tiredly laughed.

Hayden juggled his crutches for a second, propping one against the oak tree while balancing on the other and digging inside his patched jacket. "I hope this is alright," he began, sounding nervous, "they wanted to make it a ceremony, but I thought—what?" he demanded of Gideon, who had coughed noisily.

Gid lowered his voice as if Reece wasn't a mere two feet away from him. "Maybe I should do it."

"I thought we agreed I would."

"Yeah, because you bullied me into it."

"*I* bullied *you*? You—" Sighing, Hayden hung his head in surrender and held out in a fist whatever it was they were arguing over. "Go ahead."

Reece watched, confused and amused, as Gideon discreetly took the thing from Hayden and straightened up as if to make a presentation. He went so far as to clear his throat and open his mouth before hesitating and frowning down at his big, cupped hands.

"Yes, Gideon?" Hayden asked in a longsuffering voice.

Gid growlingly thrust his hand back at Hayden. "You've ruined it. It's awkward, now."

This time, Reece intercepted the pass-off, grabbing at the flash of silver and pulling it to himself before either of them was the wiser. His face went slack with shock as he realized what he was holding.

"Is this some kind of joke?" he asked, voice deadpan. He turned the silver badge over as gingerly as if he were handling the tiny wings of a real owl. These weren't a captain's first feathers…these were flight wings, *real* flight wings.

Chuckling, Hayden reassured him, "No, they're real. It seems Eldritch really *was* behind you being failed. The judges were quick to revoke their ruling once they realized he was…gone. And if they hadn't done it, The Guild House would have."

Reece continued to stare with open mouth and glazed eyes. He was still stuck on the fact he was even *holding* a pair of captain's wings, never mind that they were actually his.

"Er," Hayden continued uncertainly, looking for help from Gideon, who shrugged, "they wanted to present it to you in the hospital…bring in members of Parliament—"

"No," Reece finally managed, sounding hoarse. "This is better. This is much better."

With clumsy fingers, he tried pinning the wings to his jacket above his slinged arm, feeling weirdly nervous, as if there was a chance the wings might not fit. Hayden helpfully took the wings and fixed them on in silence. Then he backed away, and he and Gideon just stared at Reece, waiting for Reece didn't know what.

He had expected to feel different, but not like this. Dainty though the wings were, the left side of his jacket felt distinctly heavier of a sudden. They weighed on him to the point he thought he must be standing lopsided. He sighed heavily and rubbed a hand through his hair.

As he resituated his crutches, Hayden asked, "What's wrong, Reece? The wings—"

"It's not the wings. And it's not any of this." Reece gestured limply at the site of the funeral. For something to do with his hands— though he could conceivably keep scratching his head for all eternity, what with everything he had to think about—he crouched and picked an acorn out of its small crater in the snow, examining it, but at the same time, seeing through it. "It's just that I feel…I don't know…like we've lost."

Hayden blinked. "Lost?" he repeated at the same time Gideon grumbled, "Losin' looks strangely like winnin'.'"

Reece stood. "I feel like it's just us who care. All the rest of the world goes on—all the rest of the Epimetheus—and it's just us, here." He wound back his arm and launched the acorn out of sight, wishing it would take all his bleeding troubles with it. His exhaustion seemed to have opened a kind of shambling floodgate inside of him. "I feel off, inside. I did everything I meant to, but it's just not enough. And I think I know why. I think it's because I know what I'm supposed to do, only I don't know how to do it. I have to fight The Kreft," he said in answer to his friends' blank looks. "I can't *not*, now that I know what I know. But how can I do that? How can one person do that?"

"One person?" Gideon said wryly, scratching his cheek.

"Me."

For a monosyllable, it came out awfully harsh, but Gid just raised his eyebrows, unimpressed. And Hayden was actually smiling, if in an sympathetic way that made Reece grind his teeth. They just didn't get it. Maybe if he tallied how many times they'd nearly died and put the parchment right up to their noses…no, probably not even then.

Still smiling kindly, Hayden put a hand on Reece's shoulder. "It's okay to ask for help sometimes, Reece."

Reece blinked. That was almost word-for-word what Hugh had said…right before he'd gotten kidnapped. The irony would have had him in stitches if it didn't sting as much as a slap in the face. His most helpful assets—his friends—were also his biggest liabilities. Because if anything happened to them…especially on his watch…it'd leave the kind of mark on him that never rubbed off. He'd gotten a taste of that on *The Jester*.

But…wasn't that the point? Hayden—what a shock—was right. Flight wings or no flight wings, he wasn't much of a captain without a crew he could trust…a crew he would fight for. It was time to come to terms with what that meant.

They'd been silent for quite a while, Reece realized in surprise as he squinted around. The white sky had darkened to a cloudy slate. Warm golden light from the mansion's windows made patchwork on the snow, and the oil lamps across the grounds had been lit, but the bluish dark was too heavy to be lifted much.

Reece tipped his head toward the house. "Hungry?" he asked his friends. His stomach tried to answer by giving an enthusiastic growl.

"To be honest," Hayden began as he gazed at the mansion windows, rippling with the silhouettes of mingling guests, "I *do* have a hankering for food that hasn't been deep fried in burnthroat or impaled on a stick."

With a wolfish grin, Gideon nudged Reece and muttered, "Guess it's a required taste."

"Think you mean *ac*quired, Gid."

Gideon shrugged, undaunted, and as he started for the mansion, rearranged his holster so that his revolver was situated front and center, for all the Easterner guests to see. Maybe this evening would end on a high note after all—Gid could clear a buffet line almost as fast as he could draw his gun.

As they trudged through the snow, a weird peace stole over Reece. He really shouldn't even be alive right now, so he wasn't going to take even this bitterly cold night that he had a feeling would be another long one for granted. Besides….the food smelled awfully good.

This wasn't the end. He knew the truth about Liem, Eldritch was gone, the duke was safe, but it wasn't the end. It was just a new beginning. It felt oddly like starting over.

"Reece, you know…about what you said…"

Reece glanced at Hayden, eyebrows raised. His friend's bespectacled face, washed in the orange tones of the mansion's cast light, looked sheepish.

"I was thinking…even if it is *just us*…" Hayden smiled feebly. "Well, I'd think that was quite enough for The Kreft to be getting along with."

At that, Reece couldn't help but smile.

"Dirt straight."

DON'T MISS THE NEXT ADDITION TO THE ARCHIVES:

VOLUME TWO
AIRSHIP AURELIA

Coming soon

The Aurelian Archives Vol. II:
Airship Aurelia

Chapter One
The Unwilling Veterans of the Emathia Tea Party

It was winter.

The Estate at Emathia, home to the Grand Duke of the planet Honora, sat alone on a country lane a short automobile drive outside the planet's capital. The estate's rolling grounds were covered in several inches of wet, sticky snow, and the brick-laid drive leading up to the mansion had great heaps of the stuff piled on its edges, heaps that leaned against the trunks of the tall oak trees flanking the drive. Though bright against the colorless landscape, the green and yellow carriage trundling down the drive, its horses' hooves clopping in slush, faded into the background as it squeaked to a stop before Duke Thaddeus Sheppard's mansion.

The mansion was a flinch-worthy teal, roofed with red and white shingles laid in patterns of swirls. Icicles clung precariously to the edges of the three balconies looking out over the grounds while smoke drifted smoothly out of the mansion's almost sinister-looking, too-tall chimneys. Someone who hadn't seen inside the mansion might actually think the colors and the icicles and the cheerful chimney smoke quite quaint.

Scarlet Ashdown had never considered Emathia quaint. Not even as a little girl, all those times her mother had brought her to the estate for tea meetings and recitals before the duchess. She had been awed—cowed, really—by the enormity of it. Frightened by what even then she understood as the strange, double-faced nature of nobility. One might be quaint and pretty on the outside, but on the inside, there had to be composure, order, steadiness. No compromise.

The inside of the mansion was dark and handsome, meant to leave visitors with a feeling of smallness. A chandelier of red and black stained glass provided the entrance hall with an atmospheric glow, but most of the real lighting came by way of the gaping hearth beyond the duchess's grand piano. The mansion was eerily quiet; sitting in the tearoom off the entrance hall, Scarlet could hear both the crackling of the fire and the ticking of icy snow sticking to the tearoom window.

Despite the silence, the mansion was not empty. There were, in fact, seven people in the tearoom alone. Looking over the rim of her teacup as she sipped, Scarlet studied her company with a practiced eye. Her own mother sat by her elbow, her tea untouched. Mother's hands tended to shake, and she would never draw attention to herself by rattling her cup in its saucer—that wasn't her way. She'd rather blend into the walls and listen. A job not easily done, when you were the kind of beautiful that made men sit up and pay attention. Scarlet had inherited her mother's deep golden hair, almond-shaped hazel eyes, and svelte figure, but when Rowena Ashdown was around, she felt faded and bland.

Lucious Tobin, a big boy with a ruddy complexion and receding yellow hair, was sitting on a dark green sofa between his much smaller parents, who were reading different copies of the same book, neither acknowledging the other. Scarlet called Lucious a boy, but at twenty, he was actually a few months her elder. Noticing her glance, Lucious leaned up out of his slouch and grinned. Scarlet's eyes continued to pass over him. No matter his age, Lucious really was still just a boy. Most men were.

The tearoom had its own fireplace, one with a large sculpted mantle that curled down like bull horns. A deep-chested man stood before it, his back to his company, his hands clasped behind him as he studied the black and white photographs hung over the mantle.

"Where is he?" he asked without turning. Duke Thaddeus Sheppard had a voice like dark chocolate, smooth and deep and rich.

"I told him noon," the duchess, Abigail, said. She sat in a high-backed leather chair by the tearoom's bay window, her sleek gold dress catching the sheen of the firelight. The dress was the latest in fashion, tight at the hips, flaring at the knees, complete with a high-waisted jacket and black silk gloves. Scarlet's dress was cut similarly, but it was a conservative blue.

"You should have told him eleven," the duke rumbled, sounding amused despite himself. "That way he would have been on time."

Abigail sniffed disdainfully. The duchess could put disdain into any small sound, any gesture, any look. But then, she was a very disdainful person.

An ominous roar that began in the distance and gradually grew loud enough to rumble the floors beneath Scarlet's ankle-high boots warned them that he had arrived. With a snort, the duke turned to face the mantle again, shaking his mostly-bare head. The roar died out, footsteps stamped clumsily up the mansion's front stairs, and the front door banged open.

A moment later, Reece Sheppard, heir to Honora's dukeship and Scarlet's friend for going on nine years, skidded into the tearoom, leaving streaks of melting snow on the polished wood floors.

"Sorry," Reece said loudly, breathless. His brown hair was windblown and messy, parted by a pair of riding goggles that he seemed to have forgotten about, and though he'd obviously tried to dress for the occasion, wearing a half-decent suit...he'd missed a button on his jacket, and done up the rest crookedly to compensate for it.

Scarlet inwardly sighed, wanting very badly to put her face in her hand. After all the notice his recent heroics had earned him, he was still Reece, through and through. She supposed she was glad for that.

"Sit," the duke instructed calmly.

Reece looked around, panting, and unsurprisingly picked the empty chair beside Mrs. Tobin rather than the one by his thunder-faced mother. The Tobins had both put away their books in favor of studying him with the same expression of bland curiosity they had worn while reading.

"Sorry," Reece repeated, addressing the room at large. "I didn't mean to keep you waiting." His dark brown eyes twinkled at Scarlet's flat stare, and she rolled her eyes at him.

"Didn't you?" Abigail said hotly. "It's nearly one o'clock, Reece Benjamin."

"That late already?"

Abigail simply glared at him till he felt the top of his head, discovered his goggles, and tugged them off with a sheepish smile.

"Abigail," the duke said, "go and tell the servants that we're ready to move into the banquet hall for lunch." Turning to fully face the room—impressive in his dark military suit—the duke leveled Reece with a wry stare. "Finally."

Today was a revisiting of old days, when Abigail had held banquets in the hopes of sophisticating her unruly son. Lucious and Scarlet were two of the banquets' veterans—both children of politicians, both destined for Parliament. Scarlet was due to finish her education at the prestigious Aurelian Academy in a matter of weeks and, right on schedule, begin her tenure as Junior Ambassador overseeing relations with the people of Zenovia. Lucious had already begun his work as an intern at The Guild House.

Reece, still so much like the boy who had snuck out of his mother's banquets in favor of running unchecked and barefoot through the countryside, was going to be an airship captain. He had never retaken the career aptitude test he had failed some four months ago, but, questionable circumstances notwithstanding, he had saved the lives of every important member of Parliament by steering their crashing heliocraft to safety. Scarlet included.

As Scarlet drifted behind her mother and the Tobins, Reece fell back to join her, redoing the buttons on his jacket.

"Almost like old times, isn't it?"

"Yes," Scarlet said, arching an eyebrow. "Except you have your shoes on, and you aren't hiding your Westerner comrades under the table."

"They don't fit anymore."

Smirking, Scarlet turned into the candlelit banquet hall, where a large round table was already laid with sparking crystal dishes. Despite the early hour, the light falling in through the tall windows lining the hall was blue and gloomy. Scarlet wasn't much anticipating the return carriage drive to Caldonia.

"Horrid weather, what?" Lucious commented, tucking a napkin into the front of his dress shirt. "All that ice...but say, Reece, you came here on a bimotor, didn't you? I thought I recognized all that dreadful rumbling."

Nodding as he pulled out a chair for Scarlet—he remembered at least that much from the old days—Reece glanced out the window and grimaced. "The bim does alright in the ice. It's the Dryad I'm worried about. Dryads don't do well in this kind of weather—the ice gets into their compressors, and then they produce too much steam."

"Well, I won't pretend to know how that all works." Lucious lifted his goblet to shoulder height and held it there till a servant in white bustled over, looking a little harried, to fill it. "But, you know, I find bimotors simply fascinating. Sort of rugged, aren't they? A real return to man's roots."

"Be quiet and drink your wine, Lucious," Mr. Tobin grumbled. He was a cantankerous old man—respected greatly in The Guild House, avoided everywhere else. "You sound like a buffoon."

"Hush, darling," Mrs. Tobin tut-tutted, glancing embarrassedly at the duke and Abigail, who were joining them at the table. "This isn't The Guild House."

"For which I am shamelessly grateful," the duke spoke up, smiling as he sat. Duke Sheppard had seemed almost a different man, these last few weeks. Still hard, still stately, still intimidating—but he smiled more, and when Reece was around, the man could be almost...impish.

Something had changed between the father and son. Scarlet had witnessed their relationship in its prime, before Reece had started at The Aurelian Academy and had still silently humored his parents' vision for his future. Even then, it had felt...strained. Reece and the duke had even gone through a two year stint when they had not spoken at all. That stint had been miraculously broken by the events of a month ago. Events that Scarlet still didn't fully understand.

The first course of lunch arrived, but she just idly tossed her salad with her fork, watching and listening.

"So, young Mr. Sheppard," Mr. Tobin said, pausing to wash down his salad with a generous gulp of wine. "You've gotten your wings. When do you expect assignment?"

Reece twiddled his fork. He wasn't eating, either. "I can't officially take a crew of my own until I finish out school. So it'll be a few more weeks, at least, until I hear from the Regulatory Air Assignment Patrol."

Lucious made a fascinated noise through a mouthful of food and raised a hand as if to hold his place in the order of conversation. "You know, Reece, The Patrol work out of The Guild House. I could stop by their offices and see if I couldn't find out what's coming to you. A little favor for an old friend."

"Thanks, Lu," Reece said with a crooked smile. "But don't trouble yourself. I'm qualified to fly in The Streams now, so that's likely where I'll be headed."

"The Streams, eh?" Mr. Tobin squinted at Reece. "I thought it wasn't till a captain's second promotion that he qualified for The Streams."

When Reece merely shrugged and continuing raking through his salad, Mr. Tobin turned to the duke, who had been silently working away at his lunch. This seemed to be the chance Mr. Tobin had been waiting for.

"Your boy must have really outdone himself at that masquerade. I wasn't there, myself, but I have the Missus's firsthand account. And the wireless reports have been talking of little else for the last month. I've even seen his face on the evening papers."

"How utterly disconcerting," Reece whispered so only Scarlet could hear. She shot him a look.

"Yes," Lucious spoke up quickly, "it was just dreadful, but you know, rather exciting."

"Pah, you don't know what you're talking about. You were as drunk as a bleeding Westerner," Mr. Tobin snapped at his son, who flushed. Tobin nodded his head apologetically to the duke and Abigail and loaded another forkful of salad before continuing. "An assassination plot...hatched by the headmaster of The Aurelian Academy himself! Can't imagine you knew it was coming, Thaddeus, but you have to admit, it was a mighty bit of luck that landed Reece of all people with the chance to stop Eldritch's Vee before it got a shot off on you."

"Very lucky," the duke agreed, nodding. His dark eyes and stern expression betrayed nothing, but in Scarlet's studies, even that meant something.

Scarlet carefully eyed Reece, who had suddenly honed in on his neglected salad and was focusing all his attention on his bowl. Scarlet had been there that night; she had spoken with Reece and learned that he had come to the masquerade to protect the duke from said assassination. That, frustratingly, was all she really knew for sure. Oh, she had guesses, the same guesses as Mr. Tobin's evening papers. Headmaster Charles Eldritch, whom she had previously ascertained was the real power behind most of The Guild House's decisions, had turned out to be what Parliament classified as a N.H.A.; a Non-Human Alien, one capable of taking human hosts. Where he had come from, or whom, was being kept closely guarded from the Honoran public.

Scarlet and the newspapers all suspected that Reece was in on the secret, but he thus far hadn't been very forthcoming with either. Which was altogether unsurprising.

Mr. Tobin didn't seem pacified by the duke's answer. He fidgeted in his chair with a grimace, glancing sideways at his wife, who urged him on with a little nod. "But there was a second assassin, wasn't there? A gold-masked fellow, all the rumors name him."

"There was." The lines around the duke's eyes deepened as he frowned at a point over Mr. Tobin's head, seemingly lost in thought. Try as she might, Scarlet couldn't comprehend his expression; it seemed strangely…sad. And why had Abigail's face gone so pale?

After a pause, Reece cleared his throat and spoke while watching his father out of the corner of his eye. "There was a second assassin, and he did wear a gold mask. But he was killed in the explosion."

With a cough that barely passed for a laugh, Mr. Tobin picked up his goblet and tipped it at Reece as if offering a toast, all the while staring beadily at him. "Well, you're probably something of a hero at The Owl, I imagine. Unmasked an imposter, saved the duke and Parliament…killed a Vee, too, and I imagine that's no small feat."

Frowning slightly, Reece said, "Actually, I just pushed him off a balcony."

Nobody said anything for a long moment.

Finally, Abigail, whose eyes looked rather red, snapped, "Well, are we ready for the second course or are we going to keep yapping our appetites away?"

The second course—fruit salad garnished with mint leaves—stretched impossibly longer than the first, with the Tobins always returning to the night of the masquerade, ferreting for gossip. The duke took it all with that dark grace of his, but Abigail's disdainful sniffs kept growing more and more pronounced.

"Blasted shame about Liem, by the way," Mr. Tobin said as he cleaned the bottom of his fruit dish, affecting an appropriately mournful expression.

"Terrible, just terrible," Mrs. Tobin echoed. "But the funeral was lovely."

The duke nodded grimly, and Abigail drank deeply from her goblet. There was definitely something there, Scarlet decided. She'd already had her suspicions, of course. Liem pronounced dead the same night as the horrific heliocraft crash? It was too great a coincidence to be left alone, and this settled it in her mind. For whatever reason, Liem had been on The Jester. She had mentioned her theory to Reece before, but all he gave was shrugs and curt, monosyllabic answers. She hadn't pushed the subject.

"I wonder," Mrs. Tobin said in a conspiratory voice, "if Headmaster Eldritch had something to do with Liem's abduction?"

Scarlet's keen eye picked up on the short glance that passed between Reece and his father.

"I'd say that's likely," the duke said, and Mrs. Tobin swelled with pride.

Sweet nut and honey bread and lamb stew came and was then replaced by apple pie and tea, and the conversation dragged, but still Scarlet listened, mentally filing valuable little tidbits—such as Reece and the duke's shared glance, and Abigail's red eyes and heavy drinking—away for later. It was boring, tedious work, but necessary.

"...can't blame a man for wondering, of course," Mr. Tobin droned on. "But us in the Economics Department, we don't hear much of these things. The army is still being raised, then?"

Scarlet tipped her head in interest, swilling her tea gently. That particular nugget of information was one she had mined months ago and shared with Reece. Parliament had enacted the involuntary draft to raise the numbers of Honora's ground and air forces—undoubtedly for war. What war, however, remained yet another mystery. Reece, along with his friend Hubert, had actually been drafted before his father had belatedly exempted them in accordance with The Duke's Rite of Imbuement, but if he knew any more about who his enemies would have been than Scarlet, he'd kept the knowledge to himself.

"Yes, Theodore," the duke answered, sounding impatient at last. "The army is still being raised. Surely you are not that cut off in the D.E. offices. Several of your co-workers' sons were drafted, after all."

Waving his goblet, Mr. Tobin bumbled, "Had to hear it from the mouth of the horse, as it were. No one seems to know what it's being raised for, you see."

"I would have thought that'd be obvious. Charles Eldritch's extensive infiltration of Honora begs us to be prepared. I doubt it will be the last time aliens make a bid for our planet."

"Is that what the creature was doing, then? Making a bid for our planet?"

"Oh, for pity's sake!" Startling them all, Abigail slapped a palm to the tabletop and glowered around at her company. "Can we speak of nothing else? I've been too busy to see daylight this past month because of that wretched night. Scarlet."

Scarlet looked up expectantly, wiping her face of her look of concentration.

"How are your twin sisters? Are they liking The Academy?"

Scarlet inwardly grimaced and outwardly smiled—a skill she had honed with years of practice. "Well, they certainly like it...but I think they'd do better if there were fewer boys at The Academy to distract them." Fewer boys meaning no boys. Kitty and Darcy could make a career out of chasing boys with no intention of chasing them back, and they'd excel at it, the silly things.

"Hmph," Abigail snorted, clicking her fingers for a servant to clear away the empty dessert dishes."I'll have to keep my eyes on them. If I can't marry Reece off to you, that leaves me at least two other Ashdowns to pick from."

Once, this comment would have made Scarlet squirm inside, would have made her work to hide a blush. Now it just made her smile, as if sharing in a joke. Composure was everything.

"Abigail," the duke chided, chuckling with Mr. and Mrs. Tobin as Lucious frowned to himself. He had looked a little too interested in Scarlet's mention of her younger sisters' fancies; she made a mental note to keep him clear of family picnics.

"What? I'm being perfectly serious, Thaddy. If we don't marry your son before he heads off to The Streams, we'll die without any grandchildren."

"Please forgive my wife, Mrs. Ashdown," the duke bowed his head to Scarlet's mother, who had barely said two words since the lunch had began, though hardly for lack of thought."Of course," Mrs. Ashdown said lightly, smiling. "Either girl would be delighted at the thought of an arranged marriage to our young new captain."

"There, you see?" Tossing her ashy brown hair and leaning back in her seat, Abigail said to Reece, "Well? Does my hopeless son have anything to say on the matter, or can I expect our family name to stop here?"

Reece, who had been staring into his apple pie with glazed eyes, started and lifted his head. He looked from his mother to Mrs.

Ashdown, and then turned to face the duke, wearing an unfathomable expression. "I'd like to make sure the Dryad is seen to before the storm gets any worse."

"Go," the duke said before Abigail could put words to the anger coloring her face. "For goodness' sake, just go. Before your mother starts performing the nuptials."

Coming to The Archives soon

About the Author

Courtney Grace Powers has been cramming notebooks full of stories since she was six years old and determined to see her short stories about flying unicorns and vampire princes adapted to the big screen. Although she has since decided to leave the unicorns and vampires on the shelf, science-fiction and fantasy stories have retained a special place in her heart, along with theatre, chai tea, bomber jackets, and adventuring.

To learn more about The Aurelian Archives, visit http://www.aurelianarchives.com and http://www.facebook.com/TheAurelianArchives.